PIGSVILLE

GUERNICA WORLD EDITIONS 52

PIGSVILLE

Mark Fishman

GUERNICA
World
EDITIONS

TORONTO—CHICAGO—BUFFALO—LANCASTER (U.K.)
2022

Guernica Editions Founder: Antonio D'Alfonso

Michael Mirolla, general editor
Interior design: Jill Ronsley, suneditwrite.com
Cover design: Allen Jomoc Jr.

Guernica Editions Inc.
287 Templemead Drive, Hamilton (ON), Canada L8W 2W4
2250 Military Road, Tonawanda, N.Y. 14150-6000 U.S.A.
www.guernicaeditions.com

Distributors:
Independent Publishers Group (IPG)
600 North Pulaski Road, Chicago IL 60624
University of Toronto Press Distribution (UTP)
5201 Dufferin Street, Toronto (ON), Canada M3H 5T8
Gazelle Book Services, White Cross Mills
High Town, Lancaster LA1 4XS U.K.

First edition.
Printed in Canada.

Legal Deposit—Third Quarter
Library of Congress Catalog Card Number: 2021951239
Library and Archives Canada Cataloguing in Publication
Title: Pigsville / Mark Fishman.
Names: Fishman, Mark, 1954- author.
Series: Guernica world editions ; 52.
Description: First edition. | Series statement: Guernica world editions ; 52
Identifiers: Canadiana (print) 20210380497 | Canadiana (ebook)
20210380519 | ISBN 9781771837279 (softcover) | ISBN 9781771837316 (EPUB)
Classification: LCC PS3606.I835 P54 2022 | DDC 813/.6—dc23

First is first, and second is nobody.
—Philip Yordan, *The Big Combo*

1

W ALT HARGROVE SHUT THE door behind him, leaving the rest of the organization known as El Manojo still seated around the table playing cards at the back of El Perro Llorón, a bar and restaurant in Pigsville, a valley settlement also known as Happy Valley or Little Hollywood. It was an area of ten square blocks that got its name because of a couple of hundred pigs kept by a man called Freis on his farm on the west bank of the river around 1890.

Hargrove hadn't lost much tonight, sitting in on a card game with them, but he felt the liquor and wasn't used to drinking more than a couple of drinks stronger than bottled beer, and he knew that tonight all he'd get out of it was a bad headache and no relaxation so he'd decided to go home and put something in his stomach and go to sleep.

It wasn't raining anymore.

Eduardo "Vince" Negron looked up, saying, "Bye, Walt," but Hargrove was gone and the door closed behind him. Then he looked at his cards.

Jake Bielinski and Joe Whiten folded, the others kept on playing. Bielinski turned toward Whiten.

"I read something in the papers," he said.

"What's that?"

"A thirteen-year-old punk from the South Side was arrested for aggravated battery yesterday near Washington Park on the 1200 block of West Pittsburgh around three o'clock."

"Yeah? I heard it from a guy."

"One of the victims was a twenty-three-year-old kid from the neighborhood, driving home past the park when two punks from a gang threw a brick through his windshield."

Bielinski picked up his drink, looked at Whiten over the rim of the glass, drank from it.

"The kid got out to face them when another kid came up on a bicycle and said he'd help him fight the punks that were throwing bricks," he said, putting his glass down.

"Shut up, will you?" Negron said. "I can't concentrate when you two sissies are gossiping."

"No, listen to this, Vince," Bielinski said.

"It's true. I heard it from a guy," Whiten said, pulling at a cigarette he'd bummed off Al Joslyn.

"So, one of the punks, the thirteen-year-old charged with the crime, quickly ducked into a nearby alley and came back right away with a loaded handgun, fired two shots at his first victim, hitting him in the hip, and a third at the kid who'd been on the bike, hitting him in the calf."

"Fucking stupid, that's what I call it," Joslyn said.

"The police got wind of it and sent a description of the shooter over the radio and around five o'clock the thirteen-year-old punk got picked up and copped to the whole thing."

"Jesus! A fucking thirteen-year-old," Whiten said.

"I thought you already heard it from a guy?" Negron said.

"Yeah. A guy told me about it. You're right, Vince."

Ray Graham folded, saying, "Blow it out your—"

"All right, you guys, calm down," Paul Madley said, interrupting him.

"What've you got?" Negron asked him.

"A flush. You?"

"A pair."

"That's right," Graham said. "A small pair."

"Keep your mouth shut, Graham." Madley gathered the cards, shuffled them, started dealing, then looked at Bielinski. "I've got one for you, Jake."

"Okay, let's have it."

"A guy was in his car when another guy ran up to him with a handgun at his side. Instead of waiting for the mugger to force him to give up whatever it was he wanted from him, the victim jumped out of the driver's seat and pointed his lighter at him instead of an actual gun and shouted, 'What the fuck you doing?'"

"Did he shoot him?" Whiten asked.

"Shut up, Joe." Madley looked at Bielinski. "The mugger fell for the lighter-as-gun routine, an amateur, begged the guy not to kill him, then ran away and took off in a Chevy."

"That's rich," Graham said, lighting a cigarette. "Where'd it happen?"

"West Fulton, around four in the morning."

"For once a guy uses his brains," Negron said, without lifting his eyes from the cards in his hand.

"Lake City's a big city, and a big city's got big crime—that's what it is," Whiten said, chewing on a toothpick.

"That isn't big crime, that's an embarrassment," Negron said. "I don't want to play anymore. Pour me a drink, will you, Ray?"

Negron put his cigarette out in the full ashtray, got up and went to the toilet.

"Investment for the future—that's what it's all about," Graham said, tipping the bottle to fill Negron's glass. "If anybody's going to get dividends out this kind of work it's going to be us and not the kind of punks who don't think, and if they do think it's about how they're going to spend what they stole off somebody on something that's expensive and shines, without considering maybe they ought to put a little something away so one day they can retire. The problem is there isn't going to be any future and no retirement for anybody if it keeps on going like it's going now. They're a bad example, and they're pathetically disorganized."

"Philosophy," Madley said, getting up to put the cards away. He turned to look at Graham. "They're just plain stupid."

"It's more than that, Paul. I built a theory around what I been observing, and I've been seeing it every day—so open your eyes," Graham said.

"Shut your theory," Madley said.

"Take it easy," Bielinski said.

"I'm in," Joslyn said. "Let's have a theory."

"Ray, you're beautiful," Madley said, grinning. "A really talented guy. When Vince comes back, let's go to the toilet together, you know, like a couple of—"

"How long since you've been to a dentist, Paul?" Graham interrupted, making a fist.

"I want to hear the theory," Whiten said.

"Shut up, Joe—I'm talking to Paul," Graham said.

"Take it easy, Ray," Bielinski said again.

"Yeah, let's hear your theory," Joslyn said.

"So, they're the next generation of professionals," Graham said. "They're coming up, like ball players out of school or the minor league or something, but these punks, they're trying to make it on their own, and if they go on acting like that when they come up they're coming up to nowhere—'cause they got no organization, no smarts, no respect for nobody."

"Like you, for example, got respect for somebody?" Madley said.

"Like I said, there isn't going to be any future if it keeps on going like its going now."

Negron came back from the toilet rubbing his hands together. He sat down, picked up his drink.

"Ray's got a point," he said. "Guys working on their own think they're going somewhere when they're really going nowhere on account of it ain't just about one guy sticking up some poor fuck in a car for fifty bucks who defends himself with a cigarette lighter, which makes it greed and stupidity without plans or any idea what they're doing—they're punks and what makes them punks is they don't have an organization like El Manojo. It's the group that counts, individuals don't count for nothing."

"Anything," Whiten said.

"Okay, *anything*."

"Builds strong bodies twelve ways," Whiten, said.

"What does?" Joslyn said.

"Wonder Bread—and El Manojo," Whiten said.

Negron finished his drink, put his hands flat on the table. "I'm serious," he said. "And if you don't believe me you can quit and see what happens to you. Nobody's going to pay attention to one guy working on his own."

"That's a fact," Whiten chimed in. "Got a cigarette?"

"What do you know about it?" Graham said.

"Take it easy, Ray, will you?" Whiten got up from the table, turned to Bielinski, saying, "What's eating him?"

"Nothing's eating me, Joe."

Graham left the table and pulled his raincoat off the rack next to the window that showed a light rain falling in the street.

Bielinski got up and joined Whiten at the bar, standing far away from the others. He liked Whiten and knew that Graham was picking on him because of all the people that tried to get over with Lily Segura, Ray Graham tried the hardest and wasn't getting anywhere with her and never would get anywhere with a smart girl like that who wanted nothing to do with a loser like Graham.

If anyone was getting anywhere with her it was probably Walt Hargrove, not Joe Whiten, and Hargrove hadn't done it on purpose and didn't care or even realize that he'd got anyplace with the Mexican girl, he had someone else on his mind, but didn't know her name, and it was because Hargrove wasn't anybody in Graham's book that Ray Graham took it out on Joe Whiten.

Joe ordered a scotch on the rocks.

"I've had my fill of Graham," he said.

"Sure you have," Bielinski said. "I'll have a beer, Chucho."

Graham passed them on the way out, saying, "Good night." He wasn't going to wait for Lily to come to El Perro Llorón to see her mother.

"So long, Ray," Bielinski said.

Joe Whiten ignored Graham.

The bartender set their drinks in front of them.

"Thanks, Chucho," Bielinski said.

Whiten nodded, raised his glass.

"Here's hoping I'll have no more to do with Graham than Lily Segura."

"Don't be like that, Joe."

"Why not be like that? The guy's a nuisance."

"He'll get over it."

"Maybe. But it's hell waiting until he does."

2

BIELINSKI WALKED PART OF the way with Madley, who wasn't drunk but had had more to drink than he was used to so there was some weaving as they went along side by side, and his legs had barely kept him upright when the fresh air hit him just outside El Perro Llorón, he almost went down on one knee, but Bielinski held him up just as Whiten came out and patted him on the back, wishing them good luck and good night. It was two-fifteen. Al Joslyn was still inside with Negron.

At West Florida and 2nd Street Bielinski told Madley he'd have to make a go of it on his own, he was tired and there wasn't a bus running so he'd have to walk it, he didn't want to walk it, and there was no question of a cab and he had no choice but to let his feet do the walking, so good night, Paul, and see you tomorrow. But Madley grabbed his sleeve and held him there.

"What is it?" Bielinski said.

"When Graham wants it badly enough, he always manages to get it."

It was quiet for some moments while Bielinski took it in, realizing that Madley wasn't even a little looped if he said what he'd just said, so Bielinski lit a cigarette and offered one to Madley.

They smoked, then Madley went on, "I figure it's because he can't get some girl into bed. Whoever it is, she's no more interested in Whiten than she is in you or me. So what's he got against Joe?"

"I can't say, and I don't know."

"He's going to crack, then blow a fuse, and when that happens it amounts to an art but it's the kind of art that makes everybody

sick who sees it and threatens the safety and well-being of whoever's unlucky enough to be around—and I don't want to be there
when he goes off the handle."

"Flies," Bielinski nodded his head. "And that's one too many."

"Right, *flies*," Madley said.

A car turned the corner of West Florida and 1st and it was
creeping along in their direction.

"There's nothing we can do about it but stay out of his way,"
Bielinski said. "He's a first-rate performer when it comes to losing
his head—"

"There's a cab, I've still got twenty-five, I'll buy you a ride."
Madley stuck out his arm, waved the taxi to the curb. "Get in, Jake,
it's on the house."

3

THERE WASN'T A LOT of light in the street once Hargrove left the block with El Perro Llorón in it, the streetlights along the way having been wrecked by the impact of cars driven by drunk drivers who'd crashed into them or the bulbs weren't replaced after they'd burned out, so he walked in a straight line in darkness most of the time the five blocks south on Third past empty wine bottles and shards of glass and a couple of wet pages from the *Journal*. When a light did burn above him a shadow got thrown out in front of him but for the most part it was a kind of blindman's buff as he approached West Walker. The street was damp. He turned left, passed under a streetlight, climbed the first set of cement stairs to the front door of the house where he rented an apartment.

Hargrove slipped off his shoes without undoing the laces. The apartment consisted of two rooms, a bedroom and a living room with a sofa, an armchair, a television, a table and a couple of folding chairs. There was a small kitchen that had space enough for a narrow refrigerator, a combination stove and oven, a counter and cabinets. The bathroom had a large, old bathtub with claw feet and a pipe rigged to it with a flexible hose and a shower head and there was good water pressure and the water heater gave him plenty of hot water to make it a decent shower.

He went into the kitchen. He opened a can of tuna, cut a stalk of celery and a red bell pepper and made a tuna salad with mustard and mayonnaise and ate it and washed it down with a bottle of beer while sitting in front of the television. He fell asleep watching TV.

4

RAY GRAHAM HADN'T SLEPT well for the second night in a row because of Whiten and the lousy night playing cards and it showed in the grim expression on his face as he walked along the sidewalk in front of a hardware store, a department store, a couple of restaurants and a Jewish delicatessen, turned the corner and walked along Waterford Street toward the river. Before he got to the river he felt a knot tightening in his stomach reminding him that he hadn't had a thing to eat since breakfast and it was already going on two o'clock.

He turned back and went straight to the door of a restaurant that had booths along the big windows facing the street and a dozen tables scattered around in the middle of the room. It was nicer than a diner but served more or less the same kind of fried and heavy food which was what he wanted to take his mind off worrying about how he wasn't getting anywhere with Lily Segura.

He slid into an empty booth, a waitress told him it was reserved for two or more, and he gave her such a hard look that she just shook her head, handed him a menu and walked off. He stared out the window at Waterford Street, the passersby gliding past like they were on wheels.

When the waitress came around he was ready to order. He looked up from the menu and smiled at her because she wasn't bad looking and he felt sorry for the way he'd given her the shove with his eyes the first time she came around. He didn't like being told what he could and couldn't do.

"Ham and cheese omelet, potatoes, wheat toast burnt, a salad and coffee," he said, handing her the menu. He gave her another smile, saying, "Sorry about the lousy mood, guess I'm hungry."

"Don't worry about it, mister."

She came back with a cup and a pot of coffee and filled the cup.

The way she went off swinging her hips just a little told him she had something definite in mind. The other customers didn't pay attention to him or to the waitress, they just went on eating and talking and minding their own business. He liked sitting in a place where he was just another guy who'd come in to get a meal. They didn't know he couldn't get to first base with a Mexican girl he knew nothing about except that she was a student and her mother cooked enchiladas, fajitas and tacos in a joint where he spent a lot of his time.

The waitress put down his omelet and potatoes and toast, set the plate of salad beside it, gave him the eye and now it was outright flirting and no warning and it caught him off his guard and he fumbled with the knife and fork while looking up at her.

She said, "Don't get excited, mister. I'm just looking," and went away with her hips moving under her uniform.

He ate voraciously and the worrying that made him hungry fell away from him as the food settled in his stomach with the coffee chasing it. She came back to refill his cup but didn't look at him and didn't say anything. Graham looked out the window at the cars passing in the street. He looked around him at the other customers. A man sat down at the table nearest to him in the middle of the restaurant. He was carrying a flat, rectangular package wrapped in brown paper.

The man was dressed in overalls like a warehouse worker and when he unwrapped the package and slipped the contents out Graham saw from the corner of his eye that the contents were two new automobile license plates from the Department of Motor Vehicles with their state stickers and registration.

Ray Graham finished his salad, put the empty plate on top of the plate scraped clean of a ham-and-cheese omelet and potatoes with a few scattered toast crumbs and pushed it away, finished the coffee in his cup, looked for an ashtray but there wasn't an ashtray on the table, and when he looked to see if there was an ashtray on his neighbor's table there wasn't one there either and then he noticed the warehouse worker had got up and was walking away and toward the toilet.

The waitress came up and left the check, said there was no smoking in the restaurant and he could wait to have a cigarette outside and Graham nodded at her before she went away.

He leaned out of the booth toward the table with the brown paper wrapping and new license plates, picked up the plates and peeled off the state stickers and registration and stuck them to the fingertips of his left hand, slipped the damp check from beneath a glass of ice water he hadn't touched, got out of the booth, left a generous tip and went to the cashier to pay his check keeping his left hand out of sight.

5

HARGROVE PRESSED THE INTERCOM button. He was still half asleep so it took him a second to realize whose voice he was hearing when it was Lily Segura at the other end. He looked at his wristwatch. It said twelve-thirty. He didn't know what she was doing at his place at this time of night, but told her to come up, pressed the button to release the catch on the front door, and went to the bathroom to rinse his face with cold water.

She knocked at the door, he dried his face, let her in with the towel in his hand. She went across the living room straight to an armchair standing at an angle to the TV. She leaned forward, got out of her wet slicker.

He went back to the bathroom, put the dirty towel on the rack, picked up a clean, dry towel, went back to the living room, shut off the TV, gave her the towel, sat down on the sofa. She was short, slender, maybe five-two, weighing ninety-two, and nineteen years old, with smooth brown skin and long dark hair tied up in a pony-tail. She wore a pair of jeans, a shirt and a short sweater buttoned over it. Her worn leather boots weren't feminine-looking, but the toe was pointed and the size was small. Her hair was damp from the rain. She untied the ponytail and dried her hair.

She gave him a smile but it wasn't a natural smile, behind it there was worry and the worry made her look older than she was but not by much because she looked younger than nineteen. He reached for a cigarette, automatically offered her one although he knew she didn't smoke. He lit the cigarette, took a long pull and exhaled a cloud of smoke.

19

"I'm sorry, Walt, it's late."

"You all right?"

"Sure, I'm all right," she said. "You told me I could talk to you whenever I needed to talk to someone, and I've got to ask you something."

"Anything the matter?"

"Nothing's the matter—or there might be, I don't know. That's why I'm here. I want you to help me see it straight."

"You want a drink, Lily?"

"If you've got a Coke, I'd like a Coke."

"Sure."

Hargrove got up off the sofa and went to the kitchen and took a clean glass off the rack and put a couple of ice cubes in it, opened a can of Coca-Cola and poured it over ice. He opened a cold bottle of beer for himself, poured it in a glass.

When he came back to the living room Lily was sitting up straight in the armchair, staring at the windows that gave onto West Walker and the rain that fell quietly on the street. Streaks of fine rain cut diagonally through the downward glow of a streetlight. She turned away from the windows. He handed her the glass and sat down on the sofa again.

"So what's bothering you?"

She drank from the glass, swallowed hard. "It's Graham. Ray Graham. It's getting so I can't come into the restaurant to see my mother without him hanging around and creeping me out—and I don't like anybody creeping me out, especially him. He's a loser."

"There are two things about Ray Graham, and the first one is I don't like him, and the second, he's angry."

"I'm afraid of him, Walt."

"I never knew anyone like him where I come from."

"I grew up here, in Lake City, I've seen just about everything and still he gets on my nerves."

"What do you want me to do?"

"You know El Manojo, Vince Negron—talk to him. Tell him to make Graham go away."

He didn't answer. He lit another cigarette, watched the smoke curl up in front of his face. He was far away, thinking. Without sound she was begging him to say something. But all he did was sit there showing her his profile as he took slow, calm drags at the cigarette.

Oh, well, she thought, and shrugged inside herself. But the shrug didn't work and she almost shouted when she said, "Please, Walt. You've got to do something!"

Hargrove turned his head, left the grin he'd aimed at empty air behind him, then his eyes focused on Lily Segura and her oval face, dark skin and dark hair, smallish breasts and hardly any hips at all, her fragile slenderness, and he accepted it out of a sense of responsibility with the sentiment for someone who could've been a kid sister to him, he accepted that he was going to help her.

"Okay, I'll talk to Vince," he said, taking a swallow from his glass of beer.

And then he wanted to laugh, not loud raucous laughter, more on the quiet side, like he was trying to hold it back because it made him nervous to think about talking to Negron, but it didn't come out, it got stuck somewhere in his throat because what he thought was funny wasn't funny at all, it scared him thinking about what he was going to say to Vince Negron.

"I guess it's my fault," Lily said.

"What's your fault?"

"My problem with Graham, my problem with the bunch of them."

"What do you mean?"

"What I mean is that it's moments like this I understand clearly and completely that it's my fault. I go there to see my mother and I act like a kid who doesn't know any better and maybe I flirt with them without being able to help myself flirting because I act like an adolescent when it comes to men and so it's my fault."

"Your almost nineteen."

"What difference does it make? I flirt with you."

"Don't be ridiculous."

"Maybe if I'd grown up with my father."

"Maybe what?"

"I might not need that kind of attention from men."

"Now you're being something like way past nineteen. Finish your Coke and go home."

6

JOE WHITEN DROVE AROUND the block a third time looking for a place to park on upper Jackson Street. It was the middle of the afternoon and there were cars and buses and taxis, pedestrians and people window-shopping and children just out of school. There was as much of a chance of Whiten finding a parking place on upper Jackson as there was of finding a hundred-dollar bill in his wallet.

He gave up on upper Jackson and thought of the block-long, three-story parking garage at the corner of Jackson and Whitfield Terrace that was lower than lower Jackson and lower than the worst all-night spots on lower Jackson, and even though it wasn't the neighborhood he was looking for he knew he'd find a place there to put his car.

At night there were a lot of lights on lower Jackson Street, rich and garish and flooding the darkness with the all-night glow of restaurants and bars and cut-rate shops and throwing off-beat colors in the doorways, but way down there at the corner of Whitfield Terrace and Jackson Street the bulky shapes of cheap, two-story apartment houses in the gray afternoon light made him think of a prison block.

He put coins in the meter and left the parking garage heading toward upper Jackson. On the way he stopped in a grocery store, went down the aisles until he found what he was looking for and put two boxes of men's hair dye and two boxes of Bayer aspirin in the inside pockets of his coat.

Whiten looked around at the few customers moving through the aisles, in a hand mirror he saw the security man examining his face, he nodded at the girl behind the cash register and walked quickly through the front doors to the street.

Whiten stopped to look at his reflection in a shop window and in the overcast light from a cloudy sky he saw the gray hair at his temples and the crow's-feet and the expression on his face that resembled a sad clown without make-up. He went into a hotel bar for a Coke to wash down the pain pills. Graham was in such a foul mood lately that just thinking about him gave Whiten a headache.

He stood for an moment beyond the checkroom to let his eyes adjust to the soft lighting. There were seven low round tables in the room, a lucky number for the house, and five barstools at the bar. The burgundy leather armchairs at two round tables were occupied, two barstools had customers sitting on them. Whiten sat at the bar. The waiters and busboys in the dining room adjacent to the bar were straightening up after the lunch crowd.

He opened one of the two boxes of aspirin, broke the seal and shook a couple of them out into the palm of his hand. When the cold Coke washed them down his throat a smile broke over his grim face. And a few minutes later Ray Graham's rotten presence in Whiten's head got washed away with them.

7

RAY GRAHAM FINISHED SHAVING and scrubbed his face clean with a washcloth which gave his complexion a reddish glow when really his skin was pale from lack of sunlight as if he'd spent the last six months in prison. The early winter daylight drew all the color out of his face. He'd slept all day.

It was five o'clock. He put on a clean khaki cotton shirt, tucked it into his jeans, added a sleeveless blue sweater vest and a dark leather belt, a pair of laced-up brown leather work boots, slipped on a hip-length leather car coat, combed his hair without looking in the mirror, put on a baseball cap with a Midwestern team's logo and went out the door.

Darkness closed in on Lake City. The din of the square was audible as Graham neared it. There were car horns sounding from the one-way street to his right, and in the distance a siren wailed above other noises. Soon the crawlers would appear and throng the Square with its crummy dark bars and strip joints. Graham waited at the bus stop with a couple of kids that couldn't keep their hands off each other, kissing. He forced himself to look the other way.

But when he got off the bus and started walking the two blocks to El Perro Llorón, he still saw the kids with their hands moving all over each other, up and down the nice, round ass of the young girl wearing jeans so tight and low on her hips that he'd seen the string she was wearing for panties, her hands pulling at the empty belt loops at the back of the boy's jeans, shoving her fingers down there and rubbing and scratching him, and it gave his cock a jolt so he rubbed them out of his eyes with his hands.

It was early for Negron, Joslyn, Bielinski and Madley to be at El Perro Llorón so he didn't expect to see anyone but a few customers with Chucho standing behind the bar cleaning glasses and arranging things for the after-work crowd that would come rolling in any minute. He didn't think of Joe Whiten except to remind himself to ignore him when he saw him again because Whiten continually pissed him off.

He stood at the bar.

"How you doing, Chucho?"

"Fine, just fine, Mr. Graham."

"Give me a bottle of beer, will you?"

"Bottle of beer coming up."

"Make it cold."

"You got it, Mr. Graham."

"Seen the boys?" Graham lifted the bottle to his lips and drank.

"Too early. Just a couple that needs a pick-me-up."

Chucho jerked his head in the direction of a tall man wearing a torn overcoat standing at the other end of the bar lifting a shot glass and a woman about five feet three weighing around a hundred and eighty pounds standing next to him and turning a glass of tap beer in circles on the bar.

"When you got to have one, you got to have one," Graham said, reaching in his pocket for a cigarette.

Chucho lit it for him.

"That's right, Mr. Graham."

"What's the special tonight?"

"Luz is fixing a chili con carne, cooking it real slow. Wouldn't let me put a spoon in it—said it wasn't right unless it cooked all day long."

"She knows what she's doing. Got to stay out of that kitchen, Chucho."

They laughed. Out of the corner of his eye Graham saw one of the customers at the other end of the bar make a sign, he gave Chucho a nod, moved his chin toward the tall man and stocky woman, Chucho turned, looked at them, got the sign and went down there to refill the shot glass and the glass of beer on tap.

Graham thought of Lily, and of her mother cooking chili all day, and how Lily was going to college so one day she wouldn't have to work in a kitchen like her mother or be a cashier or clean houses and that her mother did what she had to do to give her daughter a life she'd never had when she lived in the Huasteca region of Veracruz, and that made him want Lily more than he wanted a bowl of chili even though the weather was right for something hot and then there were those kids with busy hands that got him thinking about fucking.

He took another pull from the beer bottle, heard the front door open and automatically swung around to take a look at who'd come in. It was Lily Segura, wearing tight jeans and a washed-out red sweatshirt with a hood, a short leather jacket and her haired tied back in a ponytail hauling a backpack full of books hanging down beside her from her right hand. It was so heavy she almost dragged it along the floor.

Graham looked away, he didn't want to catch her eye. He raised the bottle of beer to his lips until he emptied it. He listened to the sound of the heels of her cowboy boots as she went past him toward the kitchen, then heard the kitchen door swing open and shut. He called out to Chucho and ordered a shot of tequila, swallowed it, ordered another, threw it down his throat and asked for a second bottle of cold beer. The drinks poured a warmth deep into his chest and his face felt flushed. He smiled, breathed easily, looked around the room.

By nine-thirty Paul Madley, Joe Whiten, Jake Bielinski and Al Joslyn were sitting at the back table playing cards. Vince Negron wasn't expected until after ten. Graham spent a few minutes talking to them, ignoring Whiten, and then he'd gone back to stand at the bar. He had a heat on and wasn't paying attention to anybody but himself but he could still walk a straight line.

He wasn't entirely out of plumb because he heard Lily say good-bye to her mother after a meal in the kitchen and telling her that she'd be back around eleven to pick up her backpack. It kept Graham just on the sober side of the kind of drunk that would've put him to sleep.

He watched other customers come and go, a lot of them eating Luz's homemade tortilla chips and enchiladas and tacos and fajitas, drinking beer and tequila, and he'd eaten a huge bowl of chili a half hour ago that left his mouth burning from the jalapeños. He had another shot, then nursed an ice-cold beer.

Vince Negron still hadn't shown up when Lily came back in promptly at eleven out of the cold autumn night with a scarf tied around her neck over the hooded sweatshirt and short leather jacket and a pair of thin woolen gloves on her hands. Graham sat by himself at a small square table with just enough room for two people to sit down to dinner. He was staring at his hands and the empty shot glass and three small rings of spilled tequila it had left behind on the tabletop in front of him.

He turned his head when he felt the breeze against the back of his neck under the hair that was already turning gray. Lily came in and the door shut behind her and his eyes followed her small ass in a pair of jeans as she made her way into the kitchen.

Graham went to the bar with his empty shot glass and Chucho filled it with tequila and Graham shot it down his throat. The kitchen door swung open and Lily came out with her backpack, heading for the exit. Graham left a large bill on the bar and his baseball cap on an empty barstool; he almost stumbled chasing after her just to hold the door open as she went out into the cold night.

She turned when the door she'd swung open seemed to stay open all by itself, and said, "Oh, it's you, Ray. Thanks," and started out along the sidewalk with the longest strides her legs gave her.

Graham hung back for an instant, let the door shut behind him and stood aside lighting a cigarette. There was a light wind and he had to cup his hand around the flame so it wouldn't go out. When he'd put the lighter in his pocket and looked up, Lily was just a vague dark shape moving away between the dim glow of street-lights. He started after her.

8

JOE WHITEN WAS PLAYING cards with Madley, Bielinski and Joslyn, when he turned his head away from the game and saw a completely drunk Ray Graham leave El Perro Llorón right behind Lily Segura.

"Joseph, there's the flop. You going to make a play?" Bielinski said.

"He isn't paying attention," Madley said.

"Don't call me Joseph, my mother calls me Joseph," Whiten said.

"Now nobody's paying attention," Joslyn complained.

"She does?" Bielinski said.

"Yeah, she does. Where's Vince?"

"Vince is late," Madley said.

"I don't need you to tell me that." Whiten said.

"He hasn't arrived, so he isn't here," Joslyn said.

"That's all you need to know, Joseph," Madley said.

"Is this Hold 'em or do you think you're playing gin with your grandmother?" Joslyn said.

"I told you not to call me Joseph."

"Fine. No Joseph. Now make a play."

"No, I'm out," Whiten said.

"No, I'm out," Madley imitated him.

"At last, he's made a decision," Joslyn said.

Joe Whiten pushed his chair back and got up. He went to the coat rack, put on his jacket and hat and headed toward the door.

"Hey, where you going?" Bielinski called after him.

The door of El Perro Llorón slammed shut behind him.

9

IT DIDN'T TAKE WHITEN long to catch up with Graham because Ray Graham was drunk, so drunk he'd run into a garbage can and knocked the lid off it as he cut the corner short going after Lily Segura. Whiten was sober. He dodged into a doorway and watched Graham pick up the rocking lid of the garbage can and clumsily fit it onto the rim. Graham turned the corner, Whiten followed him. He looked down at the garbage can as he went past and saw a greasy brown paper bag sticking out of the top with a blackened banana peel hanging out of it.

The air was sharp with a steady wind and winter was right behind it. His eyes searched the dimly lit street for Graham and found him half a block away, and beyond Graham was the slender shape of Lily Segura with her backpack passing under the sodium-vapor spray of a streetlight.

She crossed in the middle of the street to the opposite sidewalk that bordered a long rectangle of grass more dried-out than green with trees planted evenly along the far side that might have been called a park but was too small for anything but city decoration. Graham crossed the street after her. Whiten was just behind him, but he stayed on the other side of the street.

Once Graham disappeared into the shadows of the park Whiten followed him. He turned his head as a car came up the street alongside the park and it slowed down and there were people in it making noise, laughing hard at something, and when he turned his head to look at where he'd last seen Graham he couldn't see a thing, it was too dark and there weren't any lights in the park, just the streetlights placed along the two streets that bordered it.

He was afraid he'd lost him. He knew that if he didn't get a glimpse of him before he got out of the park he might not catch up with him at all. The park was narrow, almost the width of two average streets, and more than the length of an entire city block. He was half-way through the park and still he didn't see a thing but the ground rose and fell in front of him and he tripped on clumps of cold, packed earth that had been dug up for some reason and he cursed the reason without knowing what it was.

Standing under a streetlight on the other side, just past the row of trees, he looked up and down the street and didn't see Graham or Lily, just a lone tabby sitting on the top step of four cement stairs coming up from the sidewalk to a house on Rio Street with no lights on in the house where reasonable people were fast asleep. He crossed Rio Street under the watchful gaze of the cat.

Melancholy rolled over him, and worry. The melancholy crushed him and the worry made it worse because it added a thickener to the melancholy and he couldn't climb out from under the weight of all that gloom. It was like he was seeing something that hadn't happened yet knowing it was very bad and he couldn't stop it from happening and it gave him a heavy dose of the blues.

He hadn't liked the look on Graham's face when he saw him leave El Perro Llorón. It wasn't because he didn't like Graham it was just that there was something fierce in the half-closed drunken eyes staring at Lily as she left the restaurant and bar hauling the backpack alongside her. He'd seen all that out of the corner of his eye. Whiten didn't miss anything, but now he'd lost Graham on account of being distracted by a bunch of joyriders, and it worried him.

Whiten heard a woman's voice shouting. It came from an alley off Townsend Street one block up and to the left. The alley was called Florist. He started running down Townsend following the echo of the shouting that bounced off the sleepy low-rent buildings with their closed-up shop fronts and small, dingy apartments occupying the upper floors.

The leather soles of his shoes made a loud noise on the surface of Townsend, and it was something he hadn't heard before, no matter how familiar. But it wasn't a familiar sound, after all. This was the first time he'd ever heard his footsteps with such urgency on this particular path at night in winter. Or anywhere, maybe.

Florist lay in front of him, silent and with no more light than what the two medium-watt bulbs gave out from fixtures attached one to each side in the middle of the alley, and it was the silence that ground Whiten to a halt, listening.

He started walking slowly forward down Florist. A scraping noise made him jump into a doorway. Another scraping noise and a woman's rasping voice that couldn't bring out a word but kept trying, or it was just a pair of lungs out of breath. He didn't like that part of it, a pair of tired lungs that gave out something on the order of a little sigh, and then a little gasp for air.

He peered around the edge of the doorway and down the alley and the two spotlights on Florist showed him Lily partially hidden behind a row of garbage cans staggering backward and leaning against the brick rear wall of a crummy bar with a reinforced metal door kept unlocked because the bar was a real fire hazard. The thickness of the door prevented all the noise from seeping out into the alley. The entrance to Mackey's Bar was on Rio Street. He wondered where Ray Graham was.

He stared hard at Florist looking for a sign of Graham and at last caught a glimpse of Lily's backpack, then a pair of laced-up brown leather work boots sticking out from a pair of jeans and his eyes followed the legs upward a short distance and saw the turned-under-and-sewn edge of a hip-length leather car coat. The rest of the inert body was behind two garbage cans. Whiten's eyelids lowered slightly. And a dim, lazy smile drifted across his lips.

What he didn't want now or ever was a run-in with the police and seeing that Lily was the worse for wear but on her feet he figured he'd turn around and go back to El Perro Llorón to play cards with the money in his pocket that would pay for another shot and a glass of beer.

10

NEGRON WAS MORE THAN a couple of hours late to meet El Manojo downstairs at El Perro Llorón and he blamed it on the girl who'd spent the afternoon and evening with him until five minutes ago. Five hours, and she'd sworn up and down that she was nineteen years old when he knew perfectly well that she wasn't any more than sixteen. It didn't matter to him what age she said she was but he wasn't going to get into trouble on account of a minor no matter what country she said she came from.

No one had seen them together, she'd gone straight to his room without bumping into anyone, the agency had given her the address and instructions. When she finally left his apartment she left with a pair of lightly bruised arms and a puffy lower lip because he'd held her down and bit her hard while they were fucking.

He got out of bed and went into the bathroom to take a shower. He looked at his face in the mirror, a tired expression looked back at him but he was too played out from fucking to worry about it. The shower woke him up, he got dressed, then took a shot from a bottle that stood on the dresser to iron out the wrinkles, then two more. He lay down again on the unmade bed, lit a cigarette, smoked it down while he stared at the ceiling, picked up the *Journal,* then fell asleep.

A loud knock at the door woke him up. He didn't know where he was at first because he'd been in a deep sleep after giving the paper a once-over. He'd been dreaming about a plate of steaming hot chicken enchiladas smothered in sauce and how he'd burned the roof of his mouth because he was so hungry he couldn't wait for the meal to cool down and that Luz told him there wasn't a cold drink left in the place and there wasn't anything he could do about it. She wasn't mad at him, she was just stating the facts as a responsible manager. He looked at the alarm clock on the bedside table and it said five-ten. He got up to answer the door.

Al Joslyn was standing there with a funny look on his face because he hadn't figured on Negron being there to answer the door. As far as he was concerned, Negron might've been out for the night which explained why he hadn't shown up for the usual game downstairs.

"Come in," Negron said, taking a step away from the door, sitting on the arm of an armchair. His long, stringy hair was messed up from sleep.

"I didn't want to bother you. It's late, but it's important."

"It's after five in the morning."

"Yeah, it's late."

"Somewhat."

"Like I said, I'm sorry."

"So, what is it, Al?"

11

LILY SEGURA BUTTONED THE top button of her jeans, straightened her clothes beneath the washed-out red sweatshirt, picked up her gloves, pushed her hair back under the hood and raised the fur-lined collar of her short leather jacket against the cold night air. Her cowboy boots were scuffed where she'd scraped them against the garbage cans and brick wall fighting off Ray Graham. Her face was damp with sweat despite the light winter wind that blew in off the lake.

She wiped her mouth more than once with her sweatshirt and still couldn't get the taste of the alcohol from Graham's mouth off her lips. What happened didn't amount to rape but attempted rape and it made her sick and before she knew it was happening she was bent over behind a garbage can spewing out most of what she'd eaten with her mother in the kitchen of El Perro Llorón until her stomach was so tied up in a knot that the hollow retching tore her up.

Lily's scarf lay on the ground next to her backpack and her eyes went past the backpack to a pair of feet wearing work boots that stuck out from under jeans covering two twisted legs and above them the torn hem of a hip-length car coat that belonged to Ray Graham.

She stared hard at Graham's body, saw his unconscious mouth take in a gulp of air that filled his lungs and heaved them up in his bulky chest beneath the car coat. She kicked him in the ribs with the pointed toe of her boot, kicked him twice, heaved the backpack over her shoulder and started down Florist, turned right and made the next corner and turned left on Rio where there was some traffic and streetlights and more than a lot of pedestrians moving on the sidewalk, and she kept on going away from where she'd left Graham on Florist.

The reinforced rear door of Mackey's Bar swung open and with it came noise from the customers and loud music from the jukebox, and a drunk man wearing a wool lumberjack-style shirt staggered out into the dimly lit alley unzipping his trousers. Graham came to when a splash of urine hit his face, and through a pair of watery eyes and a sore head he saw a man pissing against the brick wall on the other side of a garbage can.

He got to his feet without making a sound and took a wild swing at him but the drunk spun on his heels and his right hand, hard clenched, sent a roundhouse punch into the side of Graham's head high on the neck just behind the left ear that knocked Graham's against the wall and dropped him with a thud that the drunk heard rise up through the music and noisy conversation coming from the bar.

He shook his cock in his hand, zipped up his trousers nearly catching himself in the zipper without once looking down at the motionless body of the man he'd hit and the pool of blood that was coming out of the back of a smashed-in head, then staggered to the half-open metal door of Mackey's, going in and shutting it behind him. Ray Graham was dead.

12

LILY TOOK THE WIND from the river into her lungs and kept swallowing mouthfuls of it until she felt the oxygen reach her brain and her mind clear. She knew she was walking fast, she heard her hurried footsteps in the night, but she wasn't aware of her legs carrying her away from the river along the streets empty of traffic and taking her in the direction of El Perro Llorón. She didn't even hesitate in front of the restaurant and bar but went straight on past it, heading south on Third, and when she got to West Walker she turned left, passed under a streetlight and stopped in front of the cement stairs leading up to the house where Walt Hargrove lived. The backpack weighed a ton.

Hargrove, wearing a cardigan over a pair of jeans, stood at the half-open door waiting for her to climb the stairs and when he saw the look on her face and bleached-white skin and her weak legs he stepped out to help her into the apartment. He let go of her, turned around to lock the door behind them.

Lily stood there looking at him with a blank expression on her face, dropped the backpack to the floor, then fell into his arms and broke down, crying with her shoulders jumping as she sobbed and gasped, trying to catch her breath. Hargrove shivered with a chill that ran up his spine. He thought he understood what was wrong, but waited for her to tell him.

He helped her out of her leather jacket and coaxed her into the armchair, unbuttoned his sweater, took it off and covered her trembling shoulders hunched-up beneath the red sweatshirt. He stood above the small girl as she dried her tears, and she looked even smaller than she was. Hargrove felt pity for her, and he was plenty mad at the world for the suffering doled out to a kid like her, and then behind the last tears running down her cheeks he saw the menacing image of Ray Graham.

"What is it, Lily?"

"That fucking bastard!"

"Who?"

"You know who, Walt. It was Ray Graham. And I killed him," she said slowly, sniffling and holding back her tears.

"Hold on, Lily. Let me get you a drink."

Hargrove went into the kitchen and poured a thumb of whisky into a small glass out of a bottle kept for medicinal purposes, put water on to boil, then came back to Lily and handed her the whisky.

"I don't want it." She waved it away.

"Take it, please."

"He reeked of tequila and beer. I'll throw up if you bring it any closer."

"Hold your nose and drink it. Then you can tell me what happened."

She downed the glass of whisky, coughed and gave it back to him.

"Don't move, I'll be right back."

In the kitchen he put a teabag in a cup and poured boiling water over it and stirred in a spoonful of honey. He came back to the living room, handed her the tea, but she didn't move to take it.

Lily was wrapped in Hargrove's cardigan, tucked into the arm-chair with her legs folded under her and her eyes shut, exhausted. She'd pulled the hood of her sweatshirt over her head. Hargrove stood looking at her, then reached out with the cup of tea.

"Hey, come on. Pull yourself together."

Lily raised her head, opened her eyes, extended a slender arm, took the cup from Hargrove and put it down on the table.

"That's better. Now, what happened?"

Her teary eyes stared blankly at the windows that gave onto West Walker and since nothing came back to her from the street she was forced to look at Hargrove for a sign of life to tell her where she was and help her face up to what had happened.

"He jumped me, Walt. He tried to rape me and I fought him and he fell down and I killed him. Just like that, he's dead—and I murdered somebody. He was a snake and a slimeball, but I killed him."

Hargrove knelt in front of her, took hold of her hands, looked up into her soft black eyes. She looked away from him. He grabbed one of her cowboy boots and shook it, she turned, looking straight at him.

"When did it happen? Where?"

"I came straight to you. It happened just before the time it took me to get here from Rio Street. He's lying on Florist behind Mackey's."

"That's where you left him?"

"What did you expect me to do, drag him along Florist all the way over here so you can take a look at him?"

"That's not what I meant."

"I'm sorry, Walt."

"You've got nothing to be sorry about. It's me that ought to be apologizing because I couldn't do anything about it and now it's too late."

"Too late is right. Only he didn't get what he was after."

Hargrove stood up, paced the floor, ended up at the window and stood looking out at West Walker and a couple of cars that went past in a hurry.

"Let's go back there." He swung around, went toward Lily and walked right past her into the bedroom.

"Are you out of your mind?"

"That's not a question," he said from the other room. "There's no sane reason to do what I'm suggesting we do except that I want to see him for myself."

He came out a minute later wearing a V-necked sweater and getting into a black canvas jacket with a corduroy collar, saying, "Come on."

"And then?" She got up, reached down for the cup of tea, swallowed a couple of times until the soothing warmth traveled down into her chest.

"And then, I don't know. We'll have to see what happens. I'm more creative when I'm spontaneous."

Walking quickly north on Third away from West Walker, Hargrove and Lily passed through the downward spray of light that shot from the evenly spaced streetlights that weren't blinking or completely out of commission.

13

Vince Negron put Al Joslyn in the armchair, went to the closet and got himself into a bathrobe, then sat down on the end of the bed opposite Joslyn, lighting a cigarette. Joslyn was nervous, he didn't like interrupting Negron at five in the morning for anything but a cash delivery and there wasn't anything like cash in his hand.

"Okay, what's on your mind?" Negron pushed his longish hair back out of his face.

Joslyn fidgeted, reached into a pocket and drew out a crushed pack of cigarettes. He lit one, took a long haul on it and blew out a cloud of smoke.

"Graham got himself in a jackpot."

"So, what's new?"

"It's serious. Graham's loaded to the gills and he leaves the bar to go after Lily Segura and just like that Whiten gets up to tail him. Whiten catches up with them and by then all he sees is Graham out cold behind a couple of garbage cans in back of Mackey's, and Lily looking like she's been jumped by Graham. Lily's on her feet, so Whiten comes back to play cards, and gives us the lowdown. We play. Everybody goes home. I'm sleeping and I get a call a half hour ago from Bielinski, and he's got word from a friend at the cop shop that Graham's D.R.T. on Florist behind Mackey's, and now he's laid out."

"What the fuck!" Negron said. "Dead right there?"

Joslyn didn't say anything, he stuck the cigarette between his lips, rubbed his sweaty palms on his trousers.

"He won't do us any good now," Negron said. "What a lousy fuck-up!"

"That's cold, Vince."

"What do you want me to do? It's five in the morning."

"Nothing, I just thought you'd want to know."

Negron looked up at Joslyn who was staring off to the side as if Negron wasn't there. He had a pretty face except for a tiny razor-thin line that might have been a scar above his left eye. The surgeon had done a good job stitching it up and Joslyn had paid plenty for a dermatologist to work on it. Then there was the wavy dark hair and blue eyes and an average, narrow nose.

"Okay, handsome, so now I know. We'll have to deal with it later. I don't want any trouble. Not right now. Go home and go to bed."

Joslyn finished his cigarette and got up. His hands weren't sweating anymore. He put the butt out in an ashtray, went to the door, put his hand on the knob and turned around to face Negron before opening it. Negron stood up and put his cigarette out in the ashtray.

"It's half-past five in the morning and I want to get some sleep."

"Sorry, Vince. Good-night."

"Be here at ten-thirty."

"Ten-thirty."

"Good-night, Al."

The door shut softly behind Joslyn. Negron went over to the door and locked it, then got out of his bathrobe and into bed but didn't shut his eyes because he was busy staring at the ceiling with a blank look pasted on his face.

Then he frowned clinically and went through the information Joslyn had given him and when he'd added it up there wasn't much to go on except for the fact that Graham was always getting in a jam when he was drinking, and putting his hands on Lily Segura he really got himself into a good one with no way out and the jam was permanent. But there was just a little detail that didn't make sense and that detail was Lily herself, who didn't have the weight on her to handle a guy Graham's size even if he was falling-down drunk.

14

THE LAST THING HARGROVE wanted to see was a dead body, much less the dead body of someone he knew, so when Lily guided him to the intersection of Townsend and Florist and the exact spot on Florist where she'd left Graham knocked out next to a few garbage cans, he shut his eyes for an instant wanting the dead body to go away. It was still there when he opened his eyes.

Lily couldn't look at him, she just pointed at Graham and turned awkwardly toward Mackey's reinforced metal door. Hargrove looked around at Florist and the garbage strewn all over the place.

"Did you touch anything?" he asked.

"What do you mean touch anything? He knocked me around and I must've touched a lot of things trying to keep my balance."

"Were you wearing gloves?"

"Are you a cop or something? What's going on?"

"Were you wearing gloves?"

"No."

Hargrove stood over Graham's body and gave an empty kick at one of Graham's laced-up brown leather work boots. The brown boot rocked from a loose ankle.

"There's nothing we can do about it," he said.

"I could've told you that."

Hargrove shook his head, looked up and down the alley for a witness or bystander and didn't see a thing, took Lily by the hand and led her away in a hurry toward Townsend.

"Hey, slow down!"

"There isn't time to slow down," he said. "And be quiet!"

Hargrove got her to the corner and they kept on moving fast along Townsend until they got to Rio Street and then he had to jerk her arm to get her going again. Finally he saw the little park that was more like a stretch of dried-out grass coming out of the middle of nowhere; they cut through the park over the grass and at last he slowed down and they walked side by side down the sidewalk like a normal couple.

Lily took his arm. Hargrove turned to look at her as they passed under a sodium-vapor streetlight. He forced a smile, she couldn't return it, lowered her head, and then between streetlights when he couldn't see her face he thought he heard a sobbing sound from deep down in her chest.

"Listen, I'm going to take you over to your mother."

"I don't want to see her, Walt."

"You don't have a choice. You're going to tell her you're going on a little trip and won't be seeing her for a while and when she asks you why and for how long, you can't tell her anything. Got it?"

"Go where? I don't want to see anybody."

"Maybe she hasn't left work. They'll be closing up."

"I'm shut down myself. I can't look at her." She paused. "Let me stay at your place. It's late, she's already gone home." Then, as if she just understood what he'd said, "What are you talking about? Where am I supposed to go?"

"Got to hurry if we want to catch her," Hargrove said, ignoring her question and going as far away as he could from the sadness in her voice.

"Walt, please don't."

There wasn't enough strength in it to make it convincing, but she was played out and might've meant what she was saying. He gave her a smile, brushed her hair back with his hand. He was tired, and he shivered from the corpse and the cold night.

Standing in front of El Perro Llorón, a neon tube glowing behind the bar and a bright light creeping out under the kitchen door, Hargrove gave Lily a gently push toward the entrance. She leaned back against his hand, he had to hold her there as if she were a wooden post planted in loose soil that was about to fall over in slow motion.

"Try the door, she might still be in there."

"I can't," she whispered.

"Sure you can."

She turned around, facing him, and said slowly, "I'm asking you again, please let me stay at your place. I'll sleep on the sofa."

Now there was something desperate in her voice and Hargrove heard it, thought he'd better take it seriously, and nodded his head, saying, "Okay, come on."

The lights went out behind them as Walt Hargrove and Lily Segura walked toward West Walker and Third Street. Some of the streetlights weren't working, one burned hesitantly, flickering weakly. They climbed the cement stairs to the house where he rented an apartment.

15

AL JOSLYN WASHED HIS face and hands in hot water, buttoned up a pair of pajama trousers and got into bed. There wasn't a lot of time between now and ten-thirty, but he figured he'd try to sleep at least a couple of hours. But when he shut his eyes it was Graham's face that leapt up out of nowhere to keep him awake. He wondered if he felt pity for Graham's soul. He was sorry for what happened to him, but just as sorry as he would've been if Graham was a complete stranger because he knew that he'd been somebody with no sense of humor, a lot of violence and no humanity at all.

He turned to face the windows and the early morning light that came into the room past the edges of the drawn shades. He wondered where his ex-wife was and what she was doing and who she was doing it with, feeling lucky they didn't have kids and happy to have got rid of her after being married five years, but missing the warmth of a body lying next to him, and then he shut his eyes and went to sleep.

Joe Whiten was fast asleep dreaming the minute his head hit the pillow because he didn't have a worry in the world since he'd heard Graham was dead. The call came from Bielinski and he'd sat up in bed with the phone in his hand and his feet planted on the rug laid down over the three-by-fourteen-inch strips of wood that made up the floor in his bedroom.

It was hard to believe at first, Lily Segura didn't have the skill or weight to finish off a guy like Graham, so it must've been luck, and he poured a glass of water and drank it down before taking up the phone again to make Bielinski repeat it. Every now and then life really surprised him by a good turn when he knew for the most part that it was one drag after another with no rest. Whiten smiled when he put down the receiver, switched off the lamp next to the bed and drew the covers up to his chin.

Paul Madley told the girl lying next to him to shut up so he could hear what Bielinski was saying over the phone. He was high from sniffing cocaine all night. He got an earful of the Florist story, told Bielinski that okay it was enough all right he'd got it and didn't want to know the details because we get just one short life to live, and I'm living it, said goodnight, then slammed the phone down. The girl was facing away from him when he turned toward her.

Madley was thirty-eight years old, just under six feet tall and weighed one fifty-five, gray eyes and medium-length sandy blond hair combed back off his forehead. He looked at the back of the girl's head. She was ash-blond, in her early twenties, on the slim side and stood around five-four. Just now he couldn't remember her name, but he'd only met her a couple of hours ago when he'd left El Perro Llorón and gone to a pick-up joint two blocks away.

He reached around her shoulder with a snake tattoo on it, got hold of the lower part of her throat and pulled her close to him until he felt his cock between the cheeks of her ass. Contact with her warm body got his cock hard right away. The cocaine didn't bother his chances of getting a hard-on and he didn't bother with a condom this time. She didn't resist him.

Jake Bielinski couldn't sleep because even with his eyes shut he kept seeing what he'd been told was lying behind a couple of garbage cans on Florist near the reinforced metal door of Mackey's Bar and what he saw amounted to something like the grainy, still frame of a movie that showed Ray Graham with the back of his head caved in, a puddle of blackish blood flowing out from under it and a crumpled pack of cigarettes caught in a river of blood that ran all the way to Townsend Street.

Graham was a sort of monster whose presence in El Manojo Bielinski grew to accept over a period of more than five years. They worked together now and then, made money, exchanged a lot more than a few words of no importance, played cards and joked. That was as close as Bielinski let himself get to Ray Graham and as near as he wanted to get to a man he respected for the violence that poured out of him. It wasn't respect on the order of deep admiration, but the kind of respect that kept him a safe distance from a chronically angry and frustrated colleague.

Bielinski got out of bed and went to the kitchen to drink a glass of apple juice. The clock said four-thirty. He sat at the kitchen table with a glass in his hand, casting a shadow across the table that swept over the edge of a soft-cover book. He picked it up, leafed through the pages, looking at the pictures of a manga, *Ju-on 2*, by Takashi Shimizu, adapted by Meimu. He read manga when he ate breakfast.

He opened the front cover to the third page, read the first written words: "When someone dies in the grip of a powerful rage, a curse is born. That curse lingers in the place of death. Those who encounter it will be consumed by its fury … And the cycle continues as a new curse is born."

Bielinski shut the book, held it tightly in his hands. He thought of Graham, the frustration that moved under Graham's skin, and he wondered if it wasn't the same thing as the sort of rage that gave birth to a curse. Graham was dead from rage or a variant of it that blew up in his face with violence, so Bielinski figured a grudge like a curse, separated from the body itself, must be hanging in the air around the place where the body was found, waiting to infect an innocent passerby.

He cried, tears fell on the stiff paper cover of the book. He got up, went into the bathroom, wiped his eyes with a Kleenex, took a prescription bottle out of the medicine cabinet and broke a scored blue pill in half, swallowing it with a handful of water from the tap. He switched the light out and got back into bed.

16

W ALT HARGROVE, WEARING A starched white shirt and a tie with wide diagonal stripes, stood in an area displaying ventilator hoods, ovens, gas and electric grills, and a little further away blenders, juicers and other kinds of kitchen appliances; his face was reflected back at him from the glass door of a large microwave oven. From where he stood he could see the circles under his eyes.

The night with Lily had been a long one without much sleep because of the natural tension in the air on account of having a young woman staying overnight in his bed while he was stretched out on the sofa with a blanket drawn over him. There wasn't enough room in the apartment for him to get a good distance away from her, and he'd sworn he smelled the perfume she wore as strongly as if it were drifting up from a vaporizer on the floor next to him.

She'd got undressed in the bathroom but didn't have anything to sleep in so he gave her a T-shirt which, when she'd come into the living room to say goodnight, barely covered her small ass in a pair of panties made of black translucent material. His eyes focused on her bare knees slightly turned in as she stood like a doll in front of him. It was just an instant's sensation, but he felt the vibrating attraction of seeing her like this and not taking into account that he'd always thought of her like a little sister.

He wasn't different from any other man in a similar situation and he was content to fit in with the rest of the world, which meant he felt one thing but was going to do another. He squeezed his eyes shut, opened them and saw her looking at him, and her eyes were saying, I don't understand what's wrong with you but maybe you're

49

tired and I know I'm really worn out so let's get some sleep, okay? He gave her a harmless smile as his cock disagreed and it was like he'd just woken up standing in the middle of his own living room without knowing how he'd got there.

"Goodnight," he said.

"Goodnight, Walt, and thanks again."

Hargrove poured himself a medicinal whisky, drank it down in one gulp, got undressed and stood in his boxer shorts and T-shirt looking at his own living room as if for the first time. He paced the room, trying to figure out how he was going to get Lily out of town. He lay down on the sofa, pulled the blanket up under his chin. His eyes were fixed on Lily's leather jacket and red hooded sweatshirt on the chair across the room and her cowboy boots standing on the floor next to the chair, and those items of hers stared back at him after he'd switched off the light up until the moment he fell asleep.

The store manager came up behind him and he didn't notice it until he felt the woman's hand on his shoulder. Hargrove spun around and looked the woman in the eye, then lowered his head. He was so tired he didn't want to have any kind of conversation with her, or with anybody else. He wondered how long he'd been staring at the window of the microwave oven.

"What sort of problem is it, Walt?"

"I didn't sleep well."

"Something you want to talk about?"

"No, nothing like that. Sister spent the night. Up late, talking. Just tired."

"Take an early lunch. You sound like a telegram. Have a big lunch, and plenty of coffee."

"Okay, Mildred. Thanks."

The store manager was walking away, but before she got further than the convection ovens he hurried after her.

"Mildred, how do I go about getting an advance on my salary, or an outright loan?"

"Is that what's on your mind?"

"My sister's got to take a little trip for her health. Need to raise some money. Right away. Nothing serious, but she's got to have it."

"There goes the telegram again. Listen, Walt, come to my office before you leave today and we'll work something out. We don't have a union for this kind of work, it's strictly salary and insurance, but you're a reliable man, so it's the least I can do for you. I'll make a call."

"Right, Mildred. And thanks."

She patted him on the arm, smiled in a friendly sort of way, then swung around and headed back in the direction of her office to put in that phone call.

Hargrove went the other way, walking between rows of washers and dryers some of which were stacked one on top of the other until he got to a door marked Employees Only and he turned the knob and leaned into it and the heavy door swung open. There were lockers lined up along one wall, toilets and sinks were behind two separate doors that said, Men and Women, to the left and the right.

He opened his locker and put his coat on and wrapped a scarf around his neck. He went out of the back door reserved for employees and stood for a moment in the bright early winter sunlight looking at the half-filled parking lot.

A car pulled into the lot just as another car backed out of its spot and moved slowly toward the exit. Beyond the empty parking spot he saw big oaks, elms and sycamores scattered in the back-yards of dwellings along Orchard Street and the view he got from here gave the neighborhood the look of a small version of a suburban landscape. The houses themselves weren't in very good shape, they might be called structurally weak, but they were kept up as well as possible by the people living in them who took pride in where they lived.

There was a restaurant and bakery two blocks away on Vernon Avenue just off Orchard that he went to when he didn't bring his own lunch to work with him. His tired legs took him there, he found a seat at the counter, ordered a bowl of soup, a sandwich and coffee. There was a stack of newspapers at the end of the counter and he found a copy of the *Journal* and spread it out on the countertop next to him.

On the front page there was an article about the discovery of Ray Graham's body on Florist behind Mackey's Bar. The police didn't have much information except what the medical examiner told them about the cause and time of death. There were indications of violence, a large bruise was found just behind the victim's left ear, and there was a lot of alcohol in Graham's system, too, and they weren't ruling out the possibility that it was an accident, that he might've fallen down on account of being so drunk, smashing the back of his head in.

Hargrove folded the newspaper and left it on the vacant seat beside him when the soup and a couple of packets of crackers were placed in front of him. He swallowed a spoonful, added a pinch of salt and pepper, crumbled crackers into the soup, took a sip of coffee. When the sandwich came he was still hungry and quickly finished it and the coleslaw and potato chips piled next to it. Another cup of coffee, then he went back to work.

17

ILY SHOWERED, SCRUBBED HERSELF with extra attention between her legs to wash away the filthy idea that Graham could've been successful the night before if she hadn't found an exceptional strength to keep him away. She spent a long time letting the hot water wash over her face and neck with her eyes shut tight and her mouth open, taking mouthfuls of water and spraying them out against the shower wall between her compressed lips. She watched the imaginary grime from Graham's hands run off her with the water and circle the drain and disappear with the knowledge that Graham himself had already gone down the same path.

Hargrove was in the kitchen making coffee for the two of them. Once she'd dried her damp hair with a towel and got dressed, she brushed her teeth; she put on her socks, left the bathroom and found Hargrove in the living room sitting on the sofa with a cup of coffee in his hand. He moved to stand up.

"Don't get up, I'll get it," she said, heading straight for the kitchen to pour herself a cup of coffee.

As she sat down across from him she said, "I had to stay somewhere I didn't have to answer questions and I would've had to answer questions if I'd seen my mother. I was scared—it was written all over me, she would've seen it, and what's the point of making her miserable over something she can't do anything about?"

"You don't have to explain it to me, I know. And you're welcome here whenever—"

"Thanks, Walt, I know it. So what do you think I ought to do?"

"I slept on it, and what I came up with is I'm going to get some money—I don't know how or where—and I'll give it you so you can leave town until this blows over, which will take the time it takes—so don't ask. I'll be in touch and let you know."

"I thought about going to the police—"

"Forget about it, Lily."

"But I don't want to take your money and I don't want you mixed up in it."

"You'll take it because you're the only one I've got who's like family to me in Lake City—do it for my sake, okay?"

"But where will I go? And what about school—I've got classes to go to at the university."

"You can't go to classes if you're locked up, and as long as I'm around you aren't going to spend even a night in jail for something you probably didn't do. No matter what you think you've done—you don't really know if you killed him, and as far as I'm concerned, it doesn't matter."

Lily lowered her head, she held the cup in both hands, cradling it for the warmth and to have something for her hands to do or they'd reach out with her arms for Hargrove and hold him tight. She fought back a few tears.

"I don't know what to say," she said.

"Say you'll do what I tell you to do, that's good enough for me."

"Okay, Walt. And for right now?"

"Right now you go talk to your mother, say what you want but don't tell her too much, then pack your things and come back here. I'll see you later tonight."

"You going to work now?"

"Yeah, just lock up after yourself. I'll give you a spare key."

Lily stood up, finished her coffee, picked up her boots, sat in the chair and put them on, got up and stomped her feet firmly on the floor, reached for her sweatshirt and pulled it over her head; she picked up her leather jacket and looked at Hargrove, saying, "No, I'll leave with you."

They went down the cement steps together, Lily kissed him on the cheek, Hargrove put his hand on her shoulder, smiled and walked away, she turned right at the corner of Third.

When she got home, she gave a simple reply to her mother's question that appeared only as a frown on her mother's face, explaining that she'd stayed at a girlfriend's house, and she apologized for not calling to let her know where she'd been or when she'd be coming home. But when she told her she'd be going away for a while on a research program for school she said it in a deadpan tone using just a few words while she looked her mother straight in the eye. Her mother didn't ask her anything except how long she'd be gone. Lily told her it depended on how fast she did it and how much she got done. She went to her room, threw her backpack on the bed, then saw herself in the mirror.

A young woman looked back at her that wasn't the same woman she was used to seeing in her mirror, and she knew then that she'd left her girlish reactions to things in an alley called Florist just behind Mackey's Bar. The change didn't upset her, it was there and there wasn't anything she could do about it, she just stared at the new and still familiar face knowing that there wasn't any evidence on the surface for anyone else to see how she'd changed, but she felt the cold hand that gripped her heart. Stubbornly, she went on looking at herself, she wasn't even sure it was a human face until she saw a tear leak from the corner of her eye, roll down her cheek, and only then did she tell herself that a human being needed sleep and it was all right to get in bed and stay there until nightfall before she went back to Hargrove's apartment to spend the night.

18

THERE WASN'T A LOT Hargrove could do with the education he got at the state university, jobs were scarce in a big city like Lake City, and they didn't pay well even if you got one, so after looking for something to do for more than a month and living off what he'd saved, he was lucky enough to find a steady job and took it and worked as a salesman in an appliance store on the ground floor of a rundown building on a street a quarter mile away from old downtown with other commercial businesses in the nature of discounted household goods and a hardware store lined up one after the other and punctuated by a large supermarket and a discount office supply store as bookends at opposite ends of the street.

His education didn't stop when he finished university, it went on anyway, although it was a very different kind of education, and it included weekends and holidays and went on twenty-four hours a day and came under the heading of life in a big city.

Days and nights in Lake City slowly put a change into how he saw things, a filter like a curtain came away from his eyes and what he saw right in front of him made an impression and shook him out of the narrow world in which the average man and woman worked hard to make a living. It put him in touch with other kinds of people, the kinds of people he hadn't known before and wouldn't have met when he lived in a small town up north. They gave him other ideas on how to live and make a living.

Every weekday and one or two Saturdays a month when he finished a supplementary day of work at the appliance store, he got on a bus that took him to a stop near El Perro Llorón.

Hargrove lived a fifteen-minute walk from there. If he wasn't too worn out, he'd go straight to the bar for a Mexican beer. If he didn't have anything to fix for dinner at home, he ordered a plate of enchiladas and frijoles and treated himself to a second bottle of beer, all the while keeping one eye open for Lily Segura. She'd come in regularly to see her mother, Luz del Ángel de Segura, who ran the place with Chucho. Hargrove always kept an eye on Lily because she was like a little sister to him.

He first met Vince Negron at El Perro Llorón. Negron usually sat at a table in the back surrounded by a few men, and together they were known as El Manojo, and they talked and laughed and confided in each other about what they'd been doing and what they were going to do and at least half of what they said floated away like gas on a breeze because it was mostly talk for the sake of talk and the things they were really up to were things they weren't going to admit in public.

Hargrove heard plenty of it from across the room, and what he listened to and kept fresh in his mind was said in an unfamiliar language that described a violent way of life. There was a persistent rumor that Negron had a lot of money put away even if he looked like he didn't have more than what was in his pocket. Anyway, it was obvious that he was the boss.

Hargrove was interested in what they said in the same way he was interested in all the things he knew nothing about, but he didn't make a move to get closer to them, just listened to the raucous laughter and low whisperings coming his way from men who varied in number from three to five, not including Negron, depending on the time of year and according to whether or not one of them was in jail or out of town on so-called business.

The education he got from them didn't happen overnight; it took about a year before they got used to seeing him sit alone at a table and talk to Lily and lean against the bar gossiping with Chucho and go to the kitchen to thank Luz for the food she'd cooked for him, and then because he never stirred up any trouble and avoided getting in their way and didn't try to butt into the conversations he might've overheard, they added another six months at least before they invited him to join them one night and have a share in a bottle of tequila and whisky and gin that stood in the middle of the table where everyone could put their hands on them.

Introductions to El Manojo went around the table. The first was Ray Graham, then Jake Bielinski, Paul Madley, Joe Whiten and Al Joslyn. Hargrove shook hands all around. He smiled and nodded his head but didn't know what to say. He pulled out a chair and sat next to Vince Negron, who shoved the half-filled bottle of tequila toward him.

Hargrove didn't drink hard liquor, but poured himself a shot, knocked it back and smiled awkwardly. They returned his smile, then each looked at Negron as if they were expecting something, and Negron started in on Madley, giving him a hard time about a specific thing the others were obviously in on, needling him until the others started laughing and Madley was laughing just as hard as or harder than the rest of them. Hargrove saw that it was routine and kept his mouth shut.

Then it was time for Hargrove to say something so he told them a story about his family and their nonworking farm up north, the job he got at an appliance store in Lake City, and a woman who came regularly into that store with a paper sack filled with cash and bought whatever it was that came into her head to buy, spilling money over the counter; he poured himself another shot, nursed a bottle of beer, but spent most of his time listening to what they had to say without ever putting himself into what they were talking about because it wasn't his business, he was a stranger, someone way out of El Manojo. That was at the beginning, and it lasted for another six months.

The ideas he got from listening to them maybe two or three times a week for the first year didn't even stick in his head, and he didn't believe most of them because they made jokes out of what they were saying, and when he finally did believe them, the things he'd heard he didn't like or couldn't use because he couldn't relate to them, he was glued to a certain way of thinking and the job he had and the regular salary and he didn't have any experience in that kind of world, an irregular world that went by irregular rules.

But El Manojo gave him another point of view on the matter of money in an unequal world. He wasn't ready or willing to do the sorts of things they talked about doing when they confided in him on how they brought money into El Manojo. His routine gave him stability, he depended on it, but a goal was a goal and he kept that goal alive in the back of his mind because he wanted to come up with something on the order of an angle that would make him financially better off than he was now, working at the appliance store.

He went on listening to them because it didn't hurt to listen, and the only thing he'd figured out for sure was that if he ever tried to do as an amateur half of what they were used to doing as professionals he'd probably get himself into a lot of trouble, but if he tried, he might make a little extra cash if he was lucky, and no matter what he did he wouldn't hurt anybody while doing it.

19

WALT HARGROVE AND LILY Segura stood in a cemetery in the suburbs of Lake City on a hill planted with sturdy, barren oak trees overlooking the expressway; the winter felt like it had really begun, it was cold enough to wear an overcoat and scarf and there was a light rain and a ground mist weaved like a lazy ribbon through the legs of mourners, including the members of El Manojo, standing around the hole and the pile of earth as the coffin with Ray Graham in it was lowered into the ground.

The chill of light rain and mist driven by a wintry wind sent a shiver down Hargrove's spine. He looked down at the coffin, then up at the others, and the others were busy with their own kind of mourning, and for the members of El Manojo it wasn't really grief, just business, loose ends, but he knew that from Negron's point of view the loss of an essential member of an organization was the beginning of the end of the organization itself, El Manojo was flying on a single engine, and Vince Negron would ignore it.

Guilt was written all over Lily's face, and she seemed to be waiting for him to say something and he tried to say something but couldn't find the words. He choked back a couple of tears, more on account of Lily than Graham, then thought about how she'd got herself in the middle of a thing that was going to be hard to get out of. He took a deep breath, squeezed her hand. Everyone took a turn tossing a scoop of earth after the coffin.

20

THE FUNERAL WAS TAKING the time a funeral took when the corpse wasn't anyone special and there weren't a lot of people there, but a ceremony was a ceremony and the people that were attending it and the number of flowers and wreaths stacked up around the cold hole in the ground told anybody with their eyes open a lot more about the mourners who'd sent them, El Manojo in general, and in particular, Vince Negron, and that together they weren't going to settle for less than what they paid for, a show of solidarity, but Hargrove didn't give it much more thought, he aimed his mind at the events of last week.

He rooted around in the pile of pictures in his mind but there weren't enough details to build something out of it. All right, let's stop it right there, he told himself. You don't know any more about what happened than what Lily told you, and anyway, you don't want to know more than that—let's just say you're here out of respect for the dead, because of Lily, and out of fear that if you didn't show up El Manojo might plant you next to Ray Graham.

Hargrove and Lily left the cemetery together and it was just outside the gates at the bottom of the hill while they were waiting for the bus that he handed her a thick envelope containing enough cash to last her at least several weeks if she didn't spend it too fast on things that weren't necessities but let it out slowly like a long piece of rope on the essentials, including room and board. She took his arm and snuggled against him as the wind and damp cut through their clothes.

An hour later they were sitting in a coffee shop eating what was a late lunch for her that was going to be Hargrove's dinner because he was going to bed early after a long day that included cashing a check that amounted to a loan the store manager gave him in time to pick up Lily from the university to catch a bus and head straight for the funeral.

"Have you decided where you're going to go?" Hargrove said.

"I worked it out so that I'd spend a couple of weeks visiting a girlfriend at a school upstate where she lives in a dorm and doesn't share it with anybody right now since the girl she used to share it with dropped out. I leave sometime tomorrow."

"When you're settled in up there let me know that you're okay."

"I'll give you a call and I'll let you know. It'll take the time it takes to blow over, Walt, so we'll have to go on with our lives."

"Without worrying?"

"Without a moment's thought."

"You really are something like way past nineteen."

21

THE TALL CLOCK TOWER of the *Journal* building downtown was little more than a dark penciling on the gray sky. A stiff early autumn breeze whipped the flag on the Post Office Building and swayed the slender pole. It was going to rain.

George Sender was half a mile away from downtown Lake City in a part of Midtown where cream brick tenements and crazily leaning frame houses with worn crooked shades still down at three in the afternoon persisted in the windy gray daylight while more than fifty years of progress and changing times passed them by.

Renovation dominated the crumbling neighborhood of downtown Lake City, and apartment houses and condominiums and businesses sprang up regularly around the neglected, dismal buildings, and it was all brought on by real estate developers hungry for the wasted space and potential income, while the presence itself of new construction pointed a finger at the remaining run-down buildings and their residents, and told them there wasn't any future for them here.

There wasn't anybody else at the newsstand and cigar store, only a tired-looking brunette at the counter. Sender stepped up to buy a cigar. He smiled weakly at the woman, who didn't seem to see him because her bleary red eyes were busy staring past him at the burst of rain falling in the street. She was still young but worn-out from the kind of work that didn't change from one day to the next and gave monotony its bad reputation.

As if she'd read his mind, she said, "The hours are long, and my feet hurt."

"For everybody," Sender said, forcing a smile.

He bought a cigar, took off the band and slipped it on his little finger while he took his lighter out of his trousers pocket. He took his time lighting it, drawing tobacco in short puffs, exhaling smoke and staring at the brunette.

Sender himself was pretty tired and it wasn't going to let up until he quit the *Journal* and the rush that went with it. But that situation wouldn't come for a long time because he needed the money and the excitement that came between periods of routine, and those were things he couldn't and didn't want to live without.

"I guess we've all got to work," Sender said as if it had to be said. "And when we work hard our feet hurt."

The brunette shrugged, she seemed too tired to argue or resist the tedium, she just took things as they came, and Sender saw the whole picture by the way she looked at him, he didn't have to know any details.

It was her life and all the things she couldn't do with it that made him feel bad for her and anybody that lived like that and couldn't do anything about it. But at least she had a job to go to even if she didn't dream anymore about finding a lot of money blowing around loose in the street.

He slipped the cigar band off his finger, crumpled it and dropped it in the sand of the ashtray. He left her a couple of dollars. A man came up next to him and asked her for a pack of cigarettes.

"So long," he said, giving her a smile.

It was a heavy late autumn downpour raining big, cool drops, and he stood in front of the newsstand and cigar store under the awning listening to the sound they made striking the canvas. The street wasn't busy. He was going to get soaked. He pulled up the collar of his raincoat, started down the street, taking a look behind him now and then to see if a taxi was going his way.

22

CORAL RASMUSSEN GATHERED UP the few packages around her in front of the revolving door of a hotel restaurant on Crane Street where she'd treated herself to an expensive salad, dessert and coffee after a day of shopping. She stood on the sidewalk with the umbrella in one hand and the packages in the other and looked for a taxi but didn't see an empty one so she started on her way home in the rain but got so wet after walking one block despite the umbrella that she headed straight for the nearest entrance of a big apartment house with an awning to protect her from the downpour.

She put down the packages and folded the umbrella and stood watching the traffic on Crane heading downtown. A gust of wind blew her skirt up. Her slim legs were long and tanned like the rest of her because she spent a considerable amount of time in tanning salons when there wasn't any sun and already the Midwestern winter was on the horizon with a miserable cold wintry rain.

A car slowed in front of where she was standing as her skirt climbed again and she hurriedly pushed the billowing skirt down and made an effort to ignore the car that stopped and the passenger window rolling down and the face that appeared where the window streaked with rain had been. And then through the big cool drops she recognized the face that was looking at her as the face of Ramón López.

Coral waved, picked up the packages at her feet, ran without letting herself slip on the sidewalk toward the idling car and open passenger door, and when she got herself settled into the car and rolled up the window Ramón López gave her a broad grin and wink, leaned toward her and kissed her cheek.

"I've always said you've got a great pair of legs, and I mean it—where to?"

The car pulled away from the curb, the windshield wipers swept away the rain.

"What are you doing in Lake City, Ramón?"

"Vacation."

"From what?"

"Let's not talk about it."

"I didn't say anything."

"That's right.

"I'm really happy to see you."

"I bet you are—it's pouring."

"No—because it's been a long time, and you know and I know that I don't like it when I haven't seen you or heard from you in such a long time, Ramón."

"You're too kind," he said. "But we both know you're fed up with the screwed up way I deal with women. Don't worry, I'm not here for any reason that has anything to do with what interests me most. No reason at all, for that matter. Vacation. Like I told you."

"That's right." She imitated him.

"Still seeing George?"

"Yes—still seeing George."

"You going there now?"

"No, not now. You can take me home, Ramón."

"I've been waiting years to hear that."

"Now you've heard it."

23

DAYLIGHT WAS ALMOST GONE. George Sender switched on a couple of lamps. He didn't want to be hard on her but he thought he didn't have a choice.

"Scratch the surface and you'll come up with just about the same thing that's on the surface," Sender explained. "There isn't any depth to him. Not anymore. What you see is what you get."

He looked at her as if to put a line under what he'd said, then faced the window.

"You like him, and I like him, but that's the way it is," he said.

It didn't make her happy to hear it, she turned the glass of bourbon and ginger ale in her hand, looked at the glass like she didn't know where it came from. She gazed up at George Sender, standing with his back to her at the five story window with his head down, eyes fixed on the street below. He rubbed his hand up the short bristly hair at the back of his head. The flow of traffic on Prospect Avenue was light. The lake beyond it was blue-gray steel. The big Midwestern city looked clean, almost dull in the rainy evening light.

"What's wrong with that? It's López we're talking about," she said. "Why do we have to expect something more than what we get from somebody we know? It brings disappointment down a notch."

"I'll let you answer that for yourself," Sender said. "Let's just say he's had his time and now it's passed."

"But he was good at his job, wasn't he?"

"López was the best in his time, but he isn't a threat to anyone anymore. Nobody can maintain that level of commitment and enthusiasm forever. Don't forget, he's retired. He might as well be dead."

"That's going a bit far, isn't it?"

He turned around, put his drink down and went to the book-case to search for a book, and when he found it wedged between other large books of the same binding that looked like volumes of an encyclopedia, he carried it to the desk and started leafing through it.

Coral Rasmussen got up from where she'd sunk herself com-fortably in the soft cushions of the sofa and her legs brought her over to where Sender had his nose buried in the book, inspecting the pages he turned with the kind of concentration that gave her the impression he was looking through a microscope. He didn't hear her come up behind him.

She looked over his shoulder.

"What is it?" she asked.

Her breath on his neck gave him goose pimples.

"The letter *L*."

"Okay, but what about it?"

And then she knew what it was about, and at the same time told herself that she couldn't know, it didn't make sense, but that didn't get her far because she was kidding herself.

Then she *did* understand why Sender was looking at the en-cyclopedia and it made her even more uncomfortable, she didn't like it, it was something on the order of a nightmare even if the volume he was looking at wasn't the letter *N*—so what really scared her now was that Sender kept on digging into the subject named Ramón López, even when López didn't seem to have any connec-tion to the current subject, and this digging on Sender's part today or any other day made her think that maybe López *did* have some-thing to do with whatever it was that was going on in Lake City despite her conviction that it just wasn't possible.

She thought she'd shake it off if she tried hard enough because it couldn't have anything to do with Ramón López, since he was long gone and out of their lives and this afternoon when he gave her a ride home it was the first time she'd seen him in a couple of months. Maybe her imagination was playing tricks and she was letting anxiety get the best of her. But then the feeling that he *was* up to something in Lake City even though he wasn't living there pushed her in the ribs and prodded her and told her Sender might be right about López.

When Ramón López lived in Lake City, Coral and Sender and their friends used to drink with him, they went to restaurants together, went to the track, a ball game, a nightclub, staying out until early morning. So at first it was easy to look after him, López was the kind of man she liked to take care of, he showed his weaknesses when he wasn't on the job which wasn't what she'd expected of a cop, and the sense of humor, he was funny without making a fool of himself, a first-class human being, so when he got into a spot with a woman, because that's where he got himself into trouble, she did her best to get him out of it; they were friends and she liked helping her friends.

It was a pattern that went on for years and the pattern became a routine and then a full-scale habit, but everything changed when Jean Fleming dropped him and it really tore him up and she saw the lengths he'd take to make himself suffer and those lengths and that suffering finally wore her out; after that there were too many women, too many problems, it was more than she could take, and she couldn't keep up with him and was forced to tell him he'd have to learn to take care of himself.

In those days Ramón López worked for the Sheriff's Department. He had a degree in Criminal Justice, graduated from the School of Police Staff and Command and the Department of Justice's Death Investigation School and the Drug Enforcement Administration's Basic Narcotics and Dangerous Drugs Course and the FBI National Academy—it added up to the fact that he knew how to take care of himself. He worked hard and made the grade of captain, served a variety of assignments within the agency, including a Detective in the Criminal Investigations Division, and as the Supervisor of the Drug Enforcement Unit. When he retired he bought a house near a river in a town in the northern part of the state.

Now if he'd got himself into some kind of mess with a woman she wouldn't do anything for him. And if he was in the middle of investigating something more dangerous than a woman, there was nothing she could do for him and little he could do for himself because he wasn't a detective and didn't have the support of the Department anymore, he was teaching at a technical college and that was no kind of backup and he didn't have a private license or the right, according to how she felt about it, to do anything involving extracurricular danger that might get in the way of leading a quiet life in a small town.

Then she wondered why he'd risk doing what he was doing in Lake City. And right away she had an answer for that because she knew he couldn't sit still in a classroom for very long, it wasn't in his nature to live a settled life that didn't have some kind of edge to it, and it might have something to do with Jean Fleming, who was going out with Lloyd Frend.

She shook her head at what Sender was reading in the encyclopedia, and she shook her head at the possibility that Ramón López was trying to peel the skin off Vincent Negron or Lloyd Frend or both by investigating their businesses when he had no business doing it.

"*L*, for life after death," Sender said.

"What?"

Coral Rasmussen finished her drink.

"Life after death," he repeated.

"For Christ's sake leave him alone," she urged him.

Sender shut the book, crossed the room and sat slumped in the cushions of the sofa. Anyone else might have complained, might have told her she was dead between the ears because she didn't get what was right in front of her, but he was silent, staring straight ahead at nothing with the impatience he reserved for women he loved. He frowned at his own judgment of her because no matter what he was thinking the sum of what he really thought amounted to the fact that he respected her.

The silence made her scratch her head.

24

THE PHONE RANG. JEAN Fleming crossed the living room to answer it. It was Lloyd Frend. She sat down on the sofa, hiked her skirt up to make herself comfortable while she listened to him go on about what he'd heard Vince Negron was doing with the money he brought in through El Manojo. According to Frend, he'd turned into some kind of a businessman or something and among other things handed money over to a man who worked at an investment security house with an office in the Grant Building.

Jean looked around for a cigarette, found a pack of menthols and lit one, exhaling into the phone.

"What? Am I boring you?" Frend asked.

"No, of course not." She took another drag.

"So, I guess the little fuck is putting his money to work for him, as the investment boys say." He cleared his throat. "I'm just about fed up. He owes me plenty. Not cash, but respect. I set him up, and now he acts like there's never been anything but a hello, how-are-you between us and I'd like to crush his little fuck head."

"What am I supposed to do about it, Lloyd?"

"You're supposed to listen to me complain."

"I'm already doing that."

"Don't get smart with me."

"Why don't you put López on him?"

"What?"

"You heard me, Ramón López. All he's doing is teaching up north. You think he won't jump at the chance? You want to get at

Vince Negron, put López on him. Ramón's bored. I know it without even having to ask him."

Lloyd Frend sighed. He didn't answer her, but let his thoughts
come out of his mouth, his tone of voice relaxed. "It's not a bad idea,
after all. But how do you know he's bored?"

She didn't answer his question. "What are you going to do?"

"Nothing, you're going to do it."

"Now listen, Lloyd—"

"No, you listen. You aren't going to call him, you might get
all fouled up. You're going to send him a note, like that it's better.
Explain to him that you want to see him and tell him it's personal
and make it sound good with a lot of nice words that'll make him
feel comfortable and make him want to see you. Give me a couple
of days, then do it."

She was listening but she didn't hear him because there was
something getting in the way of the words and it was like a lot of
static without sound that made her want to shake her head at what
she felt was a demand on the order of an irritation, grains of sand
getting under her skin, making her itch and scratch herself until the
scratching made her skin bleed.

She got it under control and saw that it was just plain sadness
at the fact that Frend wanted her to go after another man; she was
disappointed, and she wasn't going to do it.

Jean jammed the cigarette out into the ashtray and it snapped
in half. She reached up and scratched an itch on her bare thigh then
pulled the hem of the skirt down over it. She didn't hang up on him.

"Are you listening to me?" Frend said. "Or are you playing with
yourself?"

"You're the one playing with yourself if you think I'm going to
get involved with him again."

"I'm not asking you, I'm telling you. Let me read it before you
send it. And you don't have to get involved with him—just get him
down here."

"And I thought you liked me a little."

"I like you a lot more than that and you know it."

"I just wanted to hear you say it."

25

CORAL RASMUSSEN HUNG UP her dress, it was slightly damp from the downpour that fell just as she was getting out of the taxi coming back from George Sender's apartment. She examined her shoes that were soaked, but her hair wasn't wet because she'd kept her jacket pulled over her head as she ran up the stairs to the entrance and the jacket had been like an umbrella.

She let the water run in the tub with the bath soap she'd put in it while she made a cup of chamomile tea in the kitchen. She was tired, looked forward to a hot bath and sleep. She took the cup with her to the bathroom, set it next to the sink, looked at herself in the mirror which was beginning to steam up.

She started brushing her blond hair. It fell straight and loose around her neck to her shoulders. The mirror was veiled over with steam because she'd shut the bathroom door behind her. She put the brush down, took a swallow of scalding tea, scowled at it, shut off the faucet, tied up her hair with an elastic band and got in the tub of soapy hot water.

Coral drifted in and out of sleep lying in the tub. Her legs were bent, turned sideways beneath the soap bubbles. She opened her eyes and looked dreamily at the bathroom door. She shut her eyes and George Sender came out of the sleepiness and hot water and soap and steam, he came out of a soft dream she wasn't yet having but was on the verge of starting up when she saw that it was Sender and seeing it was Sender snapped her back to reality, to where she was lying half-asleep in her bathtub.

Then she felt warmth in the lower part of her belly, and it went up to her chin and down to her stomach and twirled itself and kept twirling as the sensation got hotter and the heat took her away from all other thoughts and it opened her eyes and brought her to the front door of an appliance store on Walnut and Fifth and a salesman who'd given her a business card the day before yesterday. The name on the card said Walter Hargrove.

And the face that went with the card followed the card itself and came closer and grew in front of her eyes, the face kept expanding, not as a face but as a sensation in her belly, showing her the simple and ordinary happiness she wanted, the happiness she expected to find with a man like that, the clean and decent kind of happiness of being in love with an ordinary man and putting kids into the equation, and as the picture expanded the sensation became something complete and very big inside her, it was hard for her to concentrate on keeping her head above the bathwater.

While the temperature in her belly rose and twirled and Walt Hargrove's face came close and she caught a glimpse of his brown eyes, she got hold of something she hadn't known about herself or at least didn't want to admit, which was that the happiness she wanted wasn't what she'd been chasing after because the happiness she was used to having in Lake City was something on the order of having money and knowing important people and the package had to look important on the outside whether or not she herself really believed in it. What she really wanted was something else, and it was beginning to look like maybe George Sender wasn't part of it anymore.

26

JAKE BIELINSKI AND AL Joslyn had an office in a house at the corner of North Drake Avenue and West Huron Street near a hospital and a small park. Bielinski liked having a hospital nearby for good luck. One day, Al Joslyn left Bielinski in the office and rented a couple of apartments located in the 2600 block of West Haddon Avenue. They put an ad in the *Journal* seeking tenants for the apartments. Within twenty-four hours they received a number of calls on a separate phone line they'd set up from parties interested in renting the apartments on West Haddon, and they made appointments with these "renters" at intervals of one or two every couple of days spread over a period of two-and-a-half weeks.

Bielinski took a taxi to the intersection of West Thomas Street and Western Avenue, paid the driver and got out, turned around and walked back two blocks on West Thomas, turned right on Rockwell and left on West Haddon. He stopped to smoke a cigarette in front of one of the apartments they'd rented with Joslyn stationed upstairs and both of them waiting for one of their clients to arrive in order to extract rent and a security deposit in a scam they'd put together collecting money for apartments they didn't own. So far they'd got around six thousand dollars.

Joslyn drew the curtain aside and looked down into the street and saw Bielinski standing there with a cigarette between his lips, working it for a lot of smoke, getting the smoke out slowly at first, then steaming it out in a volley, rocking on his heels, looking at the neighborhood and the dry leaves scattered on the ground from the barren trees of fall. He liked Bielinski all right. They'd worked together on cons like this for more than a few years and brought some good money into El Manojo.

A compact car pulled up at the curb. A young man and woman got out, shook hands with Bielinski who'd thrown his cigarette into the gutter before the driver had shut off the engine. Bielinski led them up the steps to the front porch. Joslyn let the curtain fall back into place, straightened his tie and briskly rubbed his hands together.

27

NEGRON TOOK OFF HIS trousers and draped them over the back of a chair, pulled off his socks and threw them in a corner of the room, switched off the overhead light and went to the sink to wash his face. He shut off the light above the mirror, got into bed wearing his T-shirt and a pair of boxer shorts, drew the covers up with one hand and in the other held the evening newspaper, then started leafing through it as he leaned toward the glow of the lamp on the bedside table. Through the half-open windows he heard Mexican music coming from El Perro Llorón. Chucho and Luz were closing up the bar. He let the paper down on his lap, listening.

Eduardo "Vince" Negron rented a room two floors above El Perro Llorón directly from the owner of the building, a man named Lilybourne, who had investments in the neighborhood and rented El Perro Llorón to someone named Zamora, who never showed his face in the restaurant and bar and left the management of it to Chucho and Luz. The music was a *vals bajito* by Juan López. Negron raised the *Journal* and opened it to the sports page.

A cool damp breeze came through the windows with the sound of an occasional passing car. He couldn't concentrate on the sports page but tried anyway and went on staring at the words, pulling his eyes down the column but retaining nothing of what was written in it except the words *strike* and *outside*. He tossed the paper next to himself, swung his legs out of bed, reached for a cigarette and lit one.

His brain hopped around in circles trying to get away from the gnawing in the vicinity of his guts that went straight to his head.

He put out the cigarette, got out of bed and got dressed, poured himself a shot of tequila from a bottle on the dresser, drank it down and rinsed the glass and went out the door, locking it behind him. At the bottom of the staircase he looked around at the yellowed walls with the paint peeling off here and there and a bare bulb hanging from the ceiling far above him with nothing to cover it.

The door swung shut behind him. All the lights were off in the Mexican bar and restaurant except an advertisement for beer that glowed happily behind the bar with its electric waterfall flowing downward and the electric water feeding an electric river surrounded by an electric forest, and the river like the river nearby kept on moving toward destination unknown, a place no customer at El Perro Llorón ever saw.

Then Negron was walking away from the restaurant and bar and heading in a direction that really didn't matter to him because he was just in the mood to move, to get himself away from the feeling in his guts, while knowing all along that he was taking that feeling with him, it was inside him and there was no way to get rid of it unless he tore it out with his hands.

Then he started to wonder if he didn't actually like it because it was familiar and it took him away from the routine, and so he was telling himself he liked it there, go ahead, keep going deeper into it, that feeling was a feeling he'd had most of his life, and so he took that road in his guts without fighting it, it was something on the order of automatic pilot, and now that he was there, it was a very nice place, he really liked it.

Vince Negron looked up at the starry sky and didn't see many stars for the glow of the city at night but he loved the city at night and all the possibilities out there that his burning guts offered him. He left the corner of West Florida and Third Street far behind him. He wasn't going to take it out on just anybody, that was the best part of it, picking an anonymous sucker and making him pay for the source of the burning in his guts.

A taxi slowed down alongside him as he walked and when he turned his head he saw it was empty and the driver was looking him up and down and likely saying to himself that this pedestrian might want a ride in a taxi. Negron smiled, waved him to the curb.

Where lower Jackson met upper Jackson it was always busy, and so the driver let him off where streetlights and neon signs made crazy swirling patterns of color on the sidewalk and the roofs and hoods and windshields of cars parked the length of the street. He stood there without moving after the taxi pulled away from the curb and bathed in the blue neon from an arcade with coin-operated games. A couple of passersby jostled him but he didn't notice them because he really was in the sea of that blue neon and the smell of exhaust and noise of a busy city street filled his head and took his mind off the irritation in his stomach.

So bathing in a blue light, listening to noise and smelling everything and seeing out of the corner of his eye the blur of countless passersby, he thought of getting himself a woman instead of giving someone a beating to within an inch of their life because whether or not he really knew it, frustration was what gnawed in his guts and made him want to hurt somebody, and now that he'd decided that finding a woman was the right thing to do he started feeling more of a participant than an observer. It was a soothing thought, and now he felt friendly toward everyone.

If you can only keep it going like this, he told himself, keep it steady on a road heading toward something soft instead of something sharp and dangerous that for some guy might be his last experience in life because the sucker wouldn't know what hit him, there's a chance maybe you'll make it back to West Florida and Third tonight without having to call an ambulance for somebody or catching a case. He was dwelling on that idea when a hand fell gently on his shoulder.

"Couldn't sleep?"

He was startled, swung sharply around ready to lay into whoever it was taking him away from feeling friendly, but it was Walt Hargrove. Vince Negron looked up at him—he was more than a few inches taller than Negron—and smiled.

"Where'd you come from?" he asked.

"Had to get out of my place," Hargrove said. "There's a couple of kids living upstairs and they haven't stopped fucking and it's got so I can't think of anything else myself."

"What do you say we have ourselves a drink?"

"I could use one. I'm worn out from playing at those games—" He pointed at the arcade. "My eyes are killing me."

"Okay, Walt. Let's do it. Let's fall in love." Negron laughed at his own joke.

They walked side by side heading toward upper Jackson until Negron indicated a bar with a sweeping gesture of his arm and the palm of his hand out flat behaving like a cartoon maître d' showing Hargrove the way to his table. Hargrove crossed in front of him, bowed, then opened the door. Negron nodded as he went past Hargrove into the soft light of the entryway, holding a thick velvet curtain aside at the threshold until Hargrove joined him.

28

LLOYD FREND AND JEAN Fleming paid a visit to George Sender at his desk in the *Journal* building. It was three-thirty and Sender shut off his desk lamp, sending a shadow across the calendar and a photo; he looked up to find Frend standing there in a dark suit with a handkerchief sticking out of his pocket and a flower in the buttonhole of his jacket. Behind him, a woman wearing a tailored suit with a short skirt played with strands of her red hair.

He didn't want to look surprised but he couldn't help it because it was written all over his face, so he quickly got up to shake Frend's hand and introduce himself to the woman and get a conversation going that would bring the surprise down to just a casual encounter. Then he saw the big, white-gold ring on Frend's hand and just above it the scraped knuckles that made him wonder for a second about the other guy until experience told him he really didn't want to know anything about what Lloyd Frend was doing with his hands. It was unhealthy to ask questions when Frend didn't open the door himself.

"Do you have a minute, Sender?"

"What can I do for you?"

"Maybe just a few words?"

"I'm on my way out of the building."

"Going someplace?"

"Now look—"

"I'll buy you a cup of coffee downstairs," Frend said, turning away from him and taking Jean Fleming by the arm and walking toward the elevators.

When they got out of the elevator together they went straight to the plate-glass entrance of the *Journal* building and out the revolving doors into the fading afternoon light and damp lake air that hung out there with a palpable weight which Sender felt was crushing him down as it mixed in with the weight of fear anticipating the conversation he was going to have with Lloyd Frend in front of Jean Fleming, who, if nothing else, was a witness.

It was late enough in the afternoon for the sun, already covered by clouds, to play itself out just above the horizon and the sad gray light sent a further chill into George Sender. They walked to the corner and went into a coffee shop franchise.

Jean Fleming found an empty table away from the windows and threw herself into a chair that scraped against the polished floor. Frend sent George Sender over to keep her company. He sat next to her in a low, uncomfortable chair, looked at her legs, then his eyes went up and saw the roots of her medium-length hair and that it was really brown hair dyed red.

"How long have you known him?" she said, looking at Sender.

"Who?"

"Lloyd Frend."

"A long way back when he was pushing lawyers for judges and city aldermen for state politicians."

"And when was that?"

"Before your time, Ms. Fleming."

"Nice of you to say so, Mr. Sender."

Frend came to the table carrying a tray with three cups of coffee in cheap ceramic cups on cheap ceramic saucers, dragged a chair over from the next table and sat down. He tossed packets of sugar around that landed like playing cards in front of their saucers.

"Making friends?" he said.

"Passing the time, Lloyd," Jean said.

"Yeah, but what is it you want from me?" Sender stirred the sugar into his coffee, looked around for some milk.

"I'll get it," Jean said, sliding forward out of her chair, her skirt riding up.

"Nice looking woman, isn't she?" Frend said.

"You've always had good-looking women around you, Lloyd."

"How's Coral?"

"Fine, just fine. You didn't ask me out here for a family reunion because if you did—"

"George, I've got a favor to ask you."

Jean came back with a little pitcher of milk which she put down in front of Sender. He picked it up and poured some in his coffee, stirred it again.

"After coffee, we'll take a little walk while Jean goes shopping. It's Thursday. The department stores are open late." He smiled at Jean, then looked at Sender. " You're not going back to the office, are you?"

"It's your party." Sender swallowed a mouthful of coffee, frowned at the flavor, grinned at Frend.

29

THEY ORDERED TWO MORE drinks; they weren't at the same bar they'd started out in, it was the third bar they'd hit in an hour, and then Negron just left Hargrove standing there while he went to the toilet. Hargrove stared at his reflection in the mirror behind the bar, the face stared back but didn't seem to recognize him until he raised his eyebrows and the eyebrows in the mirror went up and Hargrove squinted at his reflection and saw himself. He'd been thirsty when he ran into Negron, and now he was drunk, which he put on Vince Negron's ability to drink without getting drunk and his own inability to have more than a couple of beers. It wasn't what he'd been looking for when he'd tossed and turned and couldn't sleep.

Walt Hargrove felt himself sliding downward and away from the bar and away from the loose grip he'd kept on it until now. He might've been a mile or two away from the bar on upper Jackson, he didn't remember which bar he was standing in, but it didn't matter where he was because he was concentrating on the fact that at the moment he was a mile away from catching the edge of the bar with his outstretched hand.

This is the sort of place where nobody is surprised or shocked when a paying customer folds up on the floor, he told himself, just as a pair of hands got hold of him under the arms, brought him back up and leaned him against the old scratched wood that might've been mahogany.

"Hey, Walt, where you going?" Negron said with his face right in front of Hargrove's face and giving him a big smile.

"Vince, it's bedtime."

"Not yet."

"It is."

"It isn't."

"I was just going to get a little sleep here on the floor."

"You can't do that."

"I've got to work tomorrow, Vince." Hargrove was clinging to the bar with one hand, lifting the glass the bartender had left in front of him with the other. It was a very heavy glass.

"Tomorrow's Saturday, Walt—you don't have to do anything but sleep."

"No, that's where you're wrong, Vince. It's open, and it's my turn. *You* can sleep."

Hargrove tilted his head back and with it the glass and he swallowed a mouthful, then coughed as he put the glass down on the bar. The coughing went on for a few seconds until he caught his breath, smiling stupidly, saying, "The appliance store's open all day Saturday, Vince, and I've got to be there from noon to five. Five hours. Count 'em." Hargrove stuck his hand out and spread four of his fingers.

"I'm not counting anything—" he reached into his trousers pocket and took out his wallet—"except maybe the money I've got left to pay for a woman. You want me to have a woman, don't you?"

"I want you to have whatever you want to have, Vince."

"Well that's what I want and you're not going to stop me."

"Who said anything about trying to stop you? It's bedtime, Vince, and I've got to go to sleep."

"You've been drinking."

"We've both been drinking."

"But you're drunk."

"Yes, and I'm tired."

"Then you've got to get some sleep, Walt. No kidding."

"You've been listening, Vince."

"Yeah, sure I have. Good-night."

30

EGRON TOLD WHITEN TO explain to Madley that even if he didn't like it he had to take Hargrove along with him on a couple of small jobs just to see how Hargrove handled himself. When Madley heard the news he shook his head and told Whiten that Negron was out of his mind but Whiten reminded him that Negron was the boss and he'd better do what he was told or there'd be plenty of trouble waiting for him when he got back to El Perro Llorón.

Madley laid it out for Hargrove to see and said there was no question of backing out because it's what Negron wanted like it or not and Hargrove agreed on condition that he was going along as an observer and didn't want to commit any kind of crime on his first day.

At ten minutes to three on a Wednesday afternoon Madley crossed West Adams with Hargrove and a fifteen-year-old named Dickerson in tow, who worked for Madley on small jobs because so far he hadn't been caught and even though he'd reached the age of criminal responsibility he probably wouldn't be prosecuted like an adult on any infraction as long as it didn't involve a weapon. Dickerson limped from a fall in a nasty ice-skating accident and it made him look more vulnerable than he really was. The sky was overcast with a light wind that blew in from the east but there wasn't any sign of rain.

"Want a free lunch?" Madley asked Dickerson.

"There isn't no such thing as a free lunch, Madley." The boy shuffled his feet waiting to see if Madley would slap him for answering him back like that.

Madley ignored it. "Yes, there is. See that guy? Just go over there and take his money. Then we'll get a free lunch because he'll be paying for it."

Hargrove kept himself away from them by a two-foot distance and the protection of the shadowy entrance to a high-rise apartment building.

"Okay, Madley. Whatever you say. I'm buying lunch," Dickerson said. He zipped up his leather jacket and pulled the hood of his sweatshirt over his head and put his hands in the pockets of his baggy jeans and sauntered awkwardly diagonally across the street.

Madley stepped back to join Hargrove in the entrance and they watched Dickerson mosey along the sidewalk on the opposite side of the street toward the big man standing alone in the vestibule of a building.

Dickerson kept moving his eyes from left to right scanning the street and sidewalk for any passersby that might interfere with his play and he was ready to flip out on the big man if it was necessary to get what he was after by scaring the shit out of him. He felt Madley's eyes burn into his back as he stood in front of the man in the vestibule.

"Give me your money," Dickerson said.

The man was looking with empty, tired eyes past him at the sidewalk and street and houses on the other side of the street and the gray sky hanging over all of it and not paying attention to what was going on in front of him until the moment the words the kid said registered in his head. He looked at Dickerson, his eyebrows went up.

"What?"

"Give me your money!"

"What?"

"Give me your money. You deaf?"

"I'm off duty now, you little fuck, but I'm going to arrest you anyway, not because you're dangerous or you scare me or I don't like that limp that makes you look so retarded but because you're so fucking stupid and unlucky that I can't help it and it's a pleasure—okay, you're under arrest."

Madley and Hargrove watched the big man hold Dickerson by the arm until responding officers came to take him to the First District for processing.

A week later Dickerson was hobbling alongside Madley on North Trumbell Avenue on a cold night with Hargrove a few steps behind them shaking his head at his growing fear of arrest and the prospect of wasting time with two guys that were beginning to look like a couple of amateurs. The plain disappointment he'd felt when Negron insisted that he go along again with Madley and Dickerson was written on his face. It was six forty-five, the sun had already set.

They turned left on West Iowa and when they got to the 2700 block, Madley spotted a woman in her thirties who looked like she'd just got off a Transit Authority bus on her way home from work walking alone down the street and Madley jabbed his elbow into Dickerson's ribs.

"You like music, don't you?" Madley asked Dickerson.

"Yeah."

"Go get yourself something we can listen to."

"Okay, Madley. The tunes are on me."

Dickerson scooted ahead of Madley and Madley dropped back falling into stride with Hargrove who was looking down at the cracked concrete sidewalk and didn't look up and kept on ignoring him.

The woman turned her head, noticed a boy in loose-fitting jeans, a sweatshirt and zipped-up leather jacket, and she picked up her pace and walked a lot faster than she'd been walking when she'd got off the bus, but the boy kept on walking haltingly a few feet behind her. She heard a voice say, "Wait on the porch," but didn't turn around to find out who said it. The boy approached her more rapidly, his footsteps came up fast, she stopped, spun on her heels, and he nearly collided with her.

"Give me your iPod, don't make me hurt you," Dickerson said.

She shook her head, then said, "No."

"You'll regret it."

"No."

"You will."

She saw people standing in a nearby alley and ran toward them.

"You bitch!" Dickerson shouted.

He doubled back and got to where Madley and Hargrove were waiting for him. Madley raised his open hand to give him a slap across the face but Hargrove stopped him. Madley didn't argue, he lowered his arm and let it hang loose at his side. Hargrove started back in the direction they'd come from without saying anything. The raw wind cut through his clothes to his skin.

"Don't say it, Madley," Dickerson said.

"I'll say whatever I want to say."

"Go ahead—if it makes you happy."

"That's the last time you're working with me," he told Dickerson. "I see your face again, I'll shove my fist through it."

31

THE ELONGATED PARK STRETCHED out north-south with Humboldt Street on one side and the north branch of a dried-up river on the other, and when Sender and Frend got there dusk had already gathered over the brown grass and trees, the swings and junglegym where two children wearing winter coats hung upside down with bent knees and arms waving at their mother who paced in front of them in the sand.

Lloyd Frend pointed at a park bench and they sat there beneath the overhanging branches of an elm tree. There was a wintry breeze pushing past them into the falling twilight. Sender took the band off a cigar, snipped the end of it with a pocket knife and lit it, exhaling a cloud of smoke.

"So, Lloyd, what's this all about?"

Frend looked at the darkening sky and felt alone with Sender sitting beside him not because he didn't like Sender or that Sender didn't amount to anyone special but because he was worried about the very thing he was going to ask Sender, and he felt down deep that what his intuition was telling him was really the truth, what he'd been thinking for a week already, and that he was going to have to make a far-reaching gesture to deal with it. There was going to be wreckage and he was afraid it would be wreckage that couldn't be repaired. He wouldn't get stuck in the middle of it, but he didn't want it to spread too far.

"What it amounts to is a suspicion and nothing more than that—but it's the kind of suspicion that won't go away unless a lot of information pushes it away into a column that says it's merely suspicion without basis in fact," Frend said.

"Columns I understand, but maybe you should just say what's on your mind." Sender stood up and moved in front of Frend and looked down at him.

Frend didn't look up at him. He said, "Sit down, George."

Sender shrugged his shoulders, sat down, stretched his legs out in front of him and took a long haul on the cigar.

"Let me tell it my own way," Frend said, lighting a cigarette.

"I'm listening."

"You know me well enough, George, to see my point of view even if you don't agree with it. I like to take care of things myself, keep my business to myself, and the guys that work for me, when they need to know something, I let them in on it up to a point. I don't like taking anyone down a notch, no violence in any way, shape or form—that's all in the past. I've got investments in real estate, a shopping center, trucking companies, investment houses—respectable businesses. I don't need trouble, and I don't want anyone looking into my affairs. Do you follow me?"

"I'm right behind you. The next thing the poor guy knows, he's a kidney donor. Like with the Chinese."

Lloyd Frend ignored it, saying, "Good, now stay there. I've got a problem, and I think you can help me with it. There won't be anything in it for you except that I'll remember you did it and that'll be like a promissory note and maybe one day you'll want to cash it in and I'll be there for you when you do."

"I'm still right behind you."

"Will you do it for me?"

"Depends on what the *it* is—what do you want me to do, Lloyd? I work for a newspaper, or maybe you forgot that?"

"I ran into a guy the other night who told me something I didn't want to hear. Maybe you know him, but that's not important."

"Okay."

"He paid me a visit while I was in a restaurant. He put a line of facts to me and I had to knock them down. I didn't think they were true. Jean was with me, she'll tell you about it if you don't believe me. But now I'm not so sure they're not true. Maybe I don't really want to believe it—it just came out that way. I wasn't looking for it."

"Kill the messenger. Where is he now?"

"Hell if I know—it doesn't matter, and he's all right, if that's what you mean?"

"I'm right behind you, but trailing off."

"Don't get funny with me, George. It has to do with Vince Negron."

"Are you sure you're not just talking jealousy?"

"Jealousy's got nothing to do with it. Jean might've fucked the guy a couple of times, but she sent him on his way. She's been with a lot of men and told me about every one of them—what's to be jealous about?"

"So, now we're straight on that. What next?"

"Don't go too far, George." Frend dropped the butt of his cigarette and crushed it with the sole of his soft leather boot. "How long have we known each other?"

"Twenty-five years, more or less. But since we got to the legal age, you've stayed on your side of the street and I've stayed on mine."

"And that's how it should be, but now I'm asking you for a favor and it isn't the kind of thing you'd have to worry about knowing which side of the street you're on. The word's been going around that Negron is trying to get into my business using a slick-haired guy I know who works in loans for real estate at the bank, a guy who doesn't know a binder from a laundry list. Check him out."

"Who?"

"Vince Negron, who do you think? Leave the lacquer-head at the bank to me."

"I'd rather leave it all to you."

"You don't owe me anything, I know that. I want your help because I trust you and you've got nothing to gain from it but a good story when it's over because I'll give you something to write about after I straighten out Vince Negron—if it's true." He lit another cigarette. "I'm playing a legitimate game using legitimate rules."

"Okay, but if I'm going to play along with you I've got to have more information. What's the name of the guy at the bank?"

"O'Dell, Doris O'Dell. Ex-soldier out of Iraq, working in the loan department."

"Doris?"

"Don't ask."

"And the bank?"

"Midwest Bank and Trust."

"Where can I get hold of Negron?"

Lloyd Frend reached into his jacket pocket and brought out a fountain pen and a business card and wrote Negron's phone number on the back of it, handed it to him. Sender put it in his wallet, puffed at his cigar and looked up at the end of twilight. The sky was dark, a quarter moon and clusters of stars hung far back in the depths of it, and a gust of wind made the overhanging branch of the elm tree tremble.

"Let's go see what Ms. Fleming spent my money on," Frend said, getting up and flicking his cigarette butt at the dry grass.

32

WHEN NEGRON GOT TO the corner of West Florida and Third the sun was out and he felt the weight of a hangover with a lot of alcohol taking up space in his blood, the street rolled a little in front of him, and his legs were unsteady due to the exhaustion of a long night of fucking a girl he'd met in a bar without knowing her name. He hadn't paid for her, just bought her plenty of drinks. He ignored El Perro Llorón, climbed the two flights of stairs, unlocked and opened his door and shut it quietly behind him.

He threw his jacket on the sofa and went directly to the medicine cabinet for a couple of aspirin. They scraped his throat as they went down even though he chased them with water. The bed was unmade just as he'd left it and he undressed and let his clothes fall and got into bed wearing his boxer shorts and a sleeveless T-shirt.

It wasn't the kind of sleep he'd wanted but it was sleep just the same and the alcohol and sex dragged him into it with a heavy hand. There wasn't much in the way of dreams either, he was too saturated for that, but by the middle of the day, when he'd slept for six hours, he began to see himself in a tropical landscape wearing a Hawaiian shirt and white trousers and white canvas shoes with the wind blowing around him as he faced the sea. He woke up because it was as close to paradise as he'd ever been and he wasn't sure he liked it but he felt the urgency to do something with the energy it gave him.

After two cups of coffee and a few slices of toast, Negron was under the shower, dried off, dressed and lacing up a pair of brown leather boots. He left the apartment with a hundred and forty dollars in his pocket. The early afternoon air was clear and cold, and wind sent stray sheets of newspaper along the sidewalk and swept through his hair.

He moved quickly away from West Florida heading north through the streets, went right on Wicker Street, up an alley, then turned right at the corner of the alley and St. Paul's Avenue, looked up and down at the cars on the street and the pedestrians walking on the sidewalk, wrapped a scarf around his head, covering most of his face and his longish, straight black hair and went into a sandwich shop.

The young man behind the counter looked up but didn't say anything because Negron had already jumped over the counter, pushed him out of the way, opened the register and helped himself to the cash in the drawer, jumped back over the counter and went out the door. There wasn't any point to it except that he wanted to know he could still rob a place and get away with it.

He walked hurriedly in a straight path down the alley to Wicker while tucking the scarf into his pocket, then slowly along Wicker to the first corner that allowed him to turn east going toward the lake. At Barry Street he turned left, and Barry was crowded and his path was blocked by various people chattering, or engaged in business transactions, edging along like snails in front of shop windows and looking at cut-rate supplies in the window of a large discount electrical supply store. He drifted through most of them in a determined manner staring at the obstacles in front of him.

A man left the electrical supply store without looking where he was going and collided with Negron who stepped backward and punched him in the face, deftly lifting his billfold just to see that he could do it before the man hit the ground. Negron kept walking without turning around to look at the crowd that gathered around the man laid out on the sidewalk.

He turned right off Barry onto Everett Street, went to a public phone and dialed a number, said, "O'Dell? Negron. Twenty minutes," then hung up, continuing along Everett until he got to North Riverwalk Way, emptied the billfold, dropped it into a garbage can and took the pedestrian bridge across the river.

33

B Y THREE-FIFTEEN RAMÓN LÓPEZ was in his car heading south with the intention of going to the East Side. He
swung the wheel around in a hard right turn and felt a pain
in his chest. He took an aspirin everyday, and a pill at night for high
cholesterol; a sharp pain in his chest and he cringed at fear. López
drove across the Young Street Bridge, eased up on the accelerator
and reached for a pack of cigarettes on the passenger seat. He lit
one and pulled hard at it, the smoke filled his lungs and the pain
went away. He switched on the radio.

There was a news program and when it'd passed from the national to the local news the announcer said a few words about a
local businessman, Lloyd Frend, who'd donated money for a couple
of kidney dialysis machines at University Hospital, then went on to
the weather, saying there was going to be cold with a lot of wind
and rain for the next few days. He pulled his car onto the gravel at
the side of the road, switched off the engine, gracefully managed his
cigarette and looked at the darkening sky.

A series of early winter storms were passing over the Midwest,
centered mostly in the region of the Great Lakes, and the weather
was so bad that the oldest inhabitants were saying they hadn't seen
anything like it in fifty years. A strong wind blew in from the lake.
The clouds seemed low enough to brush the upper stories of the
high-rises facing the lake and the office towers downtown. There
were a few nervous blasts of wind carrying big drops of rain, López
felt one of the gusts give the car a shove.

He tossed the cigarette butt out the window, switched on the ignition and put the windshield wipers in motion, stared at the waving blades as they wiped the glass clean.

He pulled the car onto the road and headed farther south. He hadn't been in the city for a couple of months. He felt an occasional dull thud that was a lack of a heartbeat in the life he led up north, and that dullness bothered him until he found a way out of it, and the only way he got out of it was to get involved with a woman or go into the city for a few days.

López parked in the lot at the back of a small restaurant at one end of a long series of businesses that included a shoe store, a fruit and vegetable market, a pharmacy, a luggage store, a movie theater that was closed down waiting for renovation. He walked around the back of the restaurant and went into the front entrance that faced Linwood Avenue.

He waved at the cashier, said hello to a waitress who told him he shouldn't stay away for so long and wanted to know how everything was going with his teaching job up north; he sat in an empty booth with room for four in a restaurant that wasn't busy because it was already late afternoon.

Ramón López ate a lettuce-and-tomato salad with five black olives and a few carrot shavings thrown on top and everything covered in Thousand Island dressing, a grilled cheese sandwich with potato chips and two extra pickles, a slice of hot freshly-made cherry pie; he drank three cups of coffee. It was almost five-thirty when he left the restaurant and got into his car and drove out of the parking lot heading east toward the lake.

He got to where Prospect Avenue intersected Lafayette Place, but Prospect was a one-way street going in the wrong direction for him, so he swung the car around the block and parked on Lafayette, a block away from where he was going, and then walked around the corner to where George Sender lived on the fifth floor of an apartment building.

He pressed the button on the intercom and Sender buzzed him in and he got in the elevator and rode it up with the hope that Sender would put him on to something good because he didn't want the option of the distraction of another woman when he'd been doing well enough without one until now, when now meant just the last six months.

George Sender stood at the open door waiting for him with a stretch of plush Persian rug behind him that made López think sadly of his unpolished wooden floor at home. They shook hands warmly and when the door was shut behind them and Sender was leading him down the hallway into the living room with a view of Prospect and the darkening sky and dull lake beyond it, López felt completely out of place and thought he'd made a mistake coming to the city when he'd been safe and sound at home, until it came to him that he'd known George Sender a long time and that he was as close to a good friend besides Coral Rasmussen as anyone got these days.

"Sit down, I'll fix you a drink."

"Thanks, I'll have a whisky with a splash of water."

"How long has it been?"

"A couple of months, George—not more."

"Do any fishing at the end of summer? I hear the lake's full of them and they're okay to eat, which says a lot these days. Don't eat this fish one week, don't eat that one the next. You know this country's the biggest polluter in the world?"

"Who doesn't know it? Maybe the Chinese, George."

"Pretty soon they'll be running things, Ramón." Sender handed him a drink, sat down in a chair opposite him and crossed his legs. "They've got a lot to teach us. A reporter on the financial page told me that the Asian Development Bank revised its economic growth forecast for China for 2006—upward from 9.5 percent to 10.4 percent. The Bank also projected full-year growth for 2007 at 9.5 percent."

"Yeah, I read that somewhere."

"With China's fixed-asset investments—investments in long-term tangible property that isn't expected to be converted into cash for at least a year—and foreign trade rising dramatically, the nation's gross domestic product grew by 10.9 percent in the first half of this year, building on the 9.9 percent growth in 2005."

"That's a lot of facts and figures, George. But you've always had a head for numbers."

"Maybe I do, but we were talking about it at lunch today."

"I figure the only reason the Chinese have any standing in the world is because they know how to take advantage of old stuff—at least that's what Wang Shuo says."

"You've been reading. Anyway, don't read the newspapers. All they'll give you is indigestion."

"What I know is that this country is afraid of losing a swell monopoly on the world to the Chinese. Big China is a bigger threat than Hong Kong."

"If it isn't the Chinese, it's the Indians. We might as well be talking about India," Sender said, smiling. "Anyway, what's there to be afraid of? We've had a long run and we've made a mess of things. Maybe it's their turn."

López stared past Sender at the skyline. "Growth rates," he said quietly to himself. "George, I'm slipping so far that pretty soon the word will go out that *my* growth forecast is being revised downward, and fast. I've got to have something to do, George. I'm going crazy doing nothing, teaching in that jerkwater town."

López leaned forward, set his glass down on the low table and put his head in his hands.

"I thought that's what you wanted."

"So did I—and I do, but not all the time."

Sender got up, went to the window and looked down at Prospect Avenue in twilight.

"Well, I might have something for you," he said.

He turned away from the window and walked slowly back to the chair opposite López, sat down, watched him until he raised his head from his hands and his teary eyes looked at Sender, who'd been waiting for López to say what was really on his mind.

"First, I've got to ask you if you have any news?"

"She's no good for you, Ramón. You know that. She's been with Lloyd Frend for almost a year."

"Don't you think I know that? How is she?"

"I saw her day before yesterday with Frend. They came to the *Journal,* and I went with Frend for a walk in the park. She looked fine, Ramón, a little older—we're all a little older but not wiser, aren't we?"

"You know how it is?"

"She's the first one that dumped you when you've spent your life doing the dumping yourself. Of course, I understand. It's not like it hasn't happened to me, although a little bit the other way around."

López smiled, wiped his wet eyes with a sleeve, reached for his drink, finished it and got up to pour himself another.

"You don't mind?"

"Help yourself."

"So, what is it you've got for me, George?" He walked back to the chair and sat down.

"Frend asked me to do a little checking up on somebody. He took me to the park and we sat down and smoked and he asked me to do him a favor."

"What kind of favor?"

"And I don't want to do it myself. I'm not cut out for it."

"Who is it and what does he want to know?"

"Negron, Vince Negron."

"No."

"What do you mean, no?"

López took a sip from his glass of whisky and water. He swallowed and both of them heard him swallow like someone had turned up the volume just to make a point of how he felt about having anything to do with Vince Negron. López lit a cigarette, pulled hard at it.

"Look, George, you and I both know that whatever Negron is up to is none of our business and that he's more dangerous now than he was when I was working for the Department, not because he's more violent but because he's lasted this long which makes him legitimate, more respectable—politicians, ugly buildings and whores get respectable if they last long enough, to quote a man—and it gives him power, and he's got plenty of good connections. What Frend wants to know he can find out for himself. You'd be better off telling him that than getting yourself mixed up in something you know nothing about except from the outside. Columnists. I wouldn't touch it."

"I thought you said you're going crazy doing nothing but teaching?"

"I said it, but I'm not suicidal."

"You're exaggerating."

"I'm not, and I'll prove it to you."

"You don't have to prove anything to me. I respect your opinion, and you've got a lot of experience—I know you're right. Vince Negron looks like he's got nothing, but I know he's got plenty of money, and that little club of his, and El Manojo—those guys hanging around are there just to remind him of the good old days. He's after the big time."

"Now, tell me about it," López said, smiling.

34

N EGRON MADE THE DATE for the third installment when he
met Doris O'Dell on the afternoon he'd robbed the sandwich shop just for fun, and the next day during O'Dell's
lunch break he left a bundle in a briefcase with O'Dell in a parking
lot a block away from Midwest Bank and Trust. He had him on the
phone from the bank and O'Dell said it was set but wanted to know
where he'd got his hands on the cash. Negron told him to mind his
own business which included their deal but didn't have anything
to do with knowing where the money came from because it was
his job to put that money where Lloyd Frend invested his, join the
money up and make a bigger bundle out of it.

"Tell me something, O'Dell. Do you ask Frend where he gets
his money?"

"No, of course I don't."

"Then wise up, do your job. That's all I'm asking you. You get
your cut, don't you?"

"Yes, yes I do."

"You want me to let Frend know what we're doing? It'd hurt me
but it'd be a lot worse for you."

"No, Vince."

"All right. Goodbye."

When he hung up he told himself that O'Dell was a risk and too
curious and he'd dump him and the whole scheme once he made out
on the setup. He laughed at the way he was elbowing in on a thing
that belonged exclusively to Lloyd Frend. Frend would kill him if he
found out, and the possibility of it put him in a really good mood.

35

ORAL RASMUSSEN PARKED HER car a half block away from the appliance store on Orchard Street where Walt Hargrove was working the afternoon shift until eight o'clock. She didn't know what she was going to say to him; she walked straight up to the front door, opened it, and heard the sound of it closing behind her while she looked at the appliances lined up in rows beginning with the kitchen beneath green signs that hung from the ceiling, and washers and dryers under blue signs at the back of the showroom, and microwaves and small and large ovens displayed along the walls under washed-out red signs. She closed her fists, felt the nervous dampness of her palms, wiped them on the fabric of her coat.

She lifted a moist palm to her face, rubbing trembling fingers across her trembling mouth, but it really wasn't a case of nerves, it was thinking about the man that Walter Hargrove seemed to be that threw a heavy pounding into her heart making it pump faster than usual and starting something hot going between her legs that was like a tiny current of electricity.

Then Walt Hargrove came out of the backroom where he'd been drinking a cup of percolated coffee and eating a sandwich. He'd washed his face and hands knowing it was time to get out on the floor. Hargrove squinted under the awful glow of florescent light and then saw the long legs of the attractive blond he'd given his card to the last time she was in the store. She was leaning over the top of a washing machine with her left hand flat against the side.

As he came closer, he saw her long fingers and painted red fingernails. Seeing her posed like that made him think of the women he'd seen as a boy modeling clothes in mail-order catalogues his mother got when they lived in a town in the north-western part of another state. Hargrove smiled, watched the woman; ordinarily he would've gone straight up to a customer, but he felt intimidated by her, and so he let a few seconds pass, looking her up and down, before he moved in.

Coral felt him standing nearby, she straightened up and turned her head and looked right into his eyes which immediately looked down at the floor, and a voice in her head said that this was the one and she was sure now if she wasn't sure before. But the same voice went on to ask her what she planned to do about George Sender; she tried to shake it off, but it told her he was good to her and filled her social life with the interesting people of Lake City she'd always wanted to know, even though that social life added up to nothing. The voice stopped there because Walt Hargrove's voice interrupted it, taking its place, asking her if there was something he could show her in the way of a machine to wash her clothes.

When the words came out of his mouth he felt ridiculous because there wasn't any substance behind them except maybe that he wanted to talk to her and what better way to start a conversation in an appliance store than to talk about washing machines. He felt like a fool. This wasn't what he'd hoped he'd say or how he'd seen it work when he'd talked himself into believing a woman like this might really be attracted to a man like him.

Then he went even further by asking himself how a man on his salary could do anything for a woman like that, but he told the question to go away and that he'd look at it later when there was a reason to look at it, and not before.

Coral said, "I'm not really looking for a washing machine," and her eyes told him something else, and it was more on the order of telling him to give it all he had because she was ready to listen to anything he had to say if he'd just give it a try because both you and I know that this has nothing to do with anything that's for sale in this store. "Maybe a microwave?"

That was how she played it at first so he'd feel more at ease and she could listen to his voice which carried a little of the northern Midwestern accent he hadn't left behind him. So she followed him down the aisle and to the right to the wall displaying more than a half-dozen microwave ovens beneath the washed-out red signs that listed the make and specifications, but she wasn't thinking about the machines, she was anticipating hearing his deep, soothing voice.

Hargrove smelled the scent she wore even though she was walking behind him, and he saw her taking long strides with long legs even though he really couldn't see her but she was indelibly printed on his mind and the appliances that surrounded him had disappeared the minute she came into the store, leaving only the image of the blond woman and the sound of her heels clattering in his ears.

Once they got to the display of microwave ovens Hargrove stood still without a word to say and calmly folded his arms in front of him because he knew as well as she knew that there was nothing here to talk about except the vague connection between them that was more electricity than anything factual or real, and the tension in the air was just about who was going to start in first on the subject unless, because of the weight of it all, he just gave a pitch for a microwave that she wasn't going to buy.

Walt Hargrove decided on the latter program and opened his mouth to give the pitch and pointed with his thick index finger at a product he really thought would make all the difference in the world to a kitchen like hers because it was the latest model with everything going for it that a combination microwave and grill and oven could have when she quickly stuck out her hand and touched the top of his hand and he pulled his arm back and let it fall to his side defeated before he'd got a word out.

Hargrove left work through the back exit reserved for employees and stood under the glow of a wall-mounted spotlight that lit the doorway and a corner of the parking lot, and he looked at his watch which told him it was eight-twenty. He'd agreed to meet her in a bar at nine. The bar was just around the corner. A co-worker named Roy Cline came out through the door and said good-night.

Hargrove gave him a pleasant tap on the shoulder, watched him get into his car and drive away; he took out a pack of cigarettes, lit one and blew out the smoke, then did his best not to think about Coral, but it didn't get him anywhere because there was nothing else on his mind.

The place was called Damske's and the customers were two deep at the bar, people who'd just got off work in the neighborhood jammed together like they were in a subway rush, all talking and laughing and spilling their drinks.

Hargrove looked around the room, he didn't see Coral and he couldn't imagine her in a place like this because according to him she wasn't the type, but he recognized a couple who owned a florist shop down the street and the manager of a bank branch and a guy from a real estate office and figured that if they were drinking here it was just possible she wouldn't stand him up.

He wasn't going to have a drink unless she came in to join him so he kept away from the bar and smoked, watching the crowd and nodding hello if someone recognized him. He looked at his watch, it was almost nine. When he looked up she came in. He felt like he'd taken a breath of fresh air.

There were a few booths along the wall opposite the bar and a couple got up and it was vacant and Hargrove led her there without saying anything which went along with what seemed to him like the dead silence from the customers in Damske's, as if they were all thinking the same thought he had which was that she was something special. They sat opposite each other.

When the waitress came to the table, they gave her their order; Hargrove a beer, Coral a vodka on the rocks with a twist, and they sat looking at each other, a soft and gentle stare that went both ways and didn't expect anything in return, and then the waitress brought their drinks and they reached at the same time for them, Hargrove to pour his bottle of cold beer into a glass, Coral to take a sip of vodka.

The cold beer loosened his throat and he relaxed, saying, "I thought you weren't going to come."

"Why did you think that?"

"This isn't the sort of place—"

"Yes, it is. I like it here. With you."

"I know, that's how I feel, too." He picked up his glass of beer and swallowed a mouthful.

"Say it."

"That I couldn't be happier because I'm with you."

"That's right. That says it for both of us." She took another sip of vodka.

"I don't even know how it happened," he said, looking at the tabletop. "I never thought—"

"You don't have to know."

He looked up at her, saying, "What's the point of figuring it out?"

"It's something that goes both ways, and when a thing like this goes both ways it's special and now that we've established that it's special, it's fixed and we've got it, so there's only the being in it that counts."

And the conversation went on like that for a few minutes until they realized that they were saying nothing more than what's been said for a thousand years by a couple of people in love and that the words didn't amount to much then and didn't amount to much today because they weren't saying more than clichés and asking questions that didn't have answers and it was obvious in the stupid, giddy feeling that went with those non-words that from now on they could leave the words alone, just drop them off at the side of the road and continue on their way with only the feelings they had for each other to keep them going.

"Are you hungry?"

"Yes, I am now."

"Let's get out of here," he said, leaving money on the tabletop, getting up out of the booth, looking at her legs as she turned and slid out of her side, right in front of him.

36

A s he typed the last words for the day Sender told himself that he ought to sit properly in front of the machine because his shoulders were killing him. He leaned back and rocked a little in the chair, shaking an ankle to stir the blood that wasn't moving in his foot. He wasn't meant to be writing anything that had something to do with Vince Negron, it wasn't good for his health and the Metro editor wouldn't like it, but he couldn't ignore what Frend had told him and he'd put López on to it and Sender himself had dug up a little background on his own; the rush of the checking up on Negron was more powerful than worrying about self-preservation.

But that's as far as it had got, it was just the beginning of another investigative piece for the *Journal,* if they accepted it, and in no way was it finished. Then there was Ray Graham's death. There were professionals who wrote about death for the newspapers, he'd done a little of that himself when he was nineteen, and so he'd left the end of Graham to them. But Sender had followed the marks along the way and when they were connected they led him to a man seen frequently in the company of Vince Negron. The man's name was Walt Hargrove, but there was nothing to put him in the picture of Graham's death.

Sender wrote most of his columns from home and sent them to the *Journal* by courier because he couldn't stomach going in to the office more often than he had to and he'd been on the staff for so long that he didn't count the years, which gave him the luxury of doing pretty much what he wanted to do as long as he sent his work in on time.

He showed up a couple of times a week just to make an appearance and satisfy the Metro editor and let the others know he was a special case. The *Journal* mirrored life as it's lived from day to day—at least that was the general intention. News had *some* value, even slanted or butchered news, and Sender's column spread that news in the form of a daily feature in the op-ed section like it was gossip although it was far from gossip and closer to the truth.

He had a good salary, plenty of respect and some pull with city officials, and whether the content of his column was political or social wasn't the point, readers wanted it both ways, and every now and then he proposed four half-page columns worth of straight-forward investigation, and it was how he wrote that made the readers pay attention to him. They knew that he wasn't afraid of anybody, but as far as the paper was concerned he stayed clear of men like Lloyd Frend and Vince Negron.

Sender got up from behind his desk and went to the window and looked out at the lake and down at Prospect Avenue. The street was bright with late sunshine, and there was a thin vague winter afternoon haze over everything. In the distance he saw the same yellowish haze. It made a nice picture, but it was pollution that did it and it stretched out of the city into the nearest suburbs.

Standing at the window looking down at the street he began to think. It was a cold day, he'd switched the radiator on low and didn't feel the pollution in his lungs or the inland air that collided with the moisture coming off the lake, just the warm, dryness that floated out from the wall-mounted radiator near his desk and tickled his throat.

Five stories separated him from the world below, but really they didn't separate him from anything because there was the telephone, television, radio, and newspaper, a hundred new things to buy each month if there was money to spend and he felt like going out to buy them, high unemployment and a war 6,412 miles away, and the sum total of it kept everyone moving and fearful and alive and plugged in so that they didn't miss a thing, while most of them didn't care if the rest of the world was going to hell just as long as they lived their lives with or without a struggle, without sticking their nose into anyone else's business, and having something to keep them busy or distracted while the whole world went to hell in a hurry.

He was caught up in that net and his life was mixed up with the lives of hundreds of others in the city whether he liked it or not, men and women just like himself, but he wasn't comfortable seeing himself as just another moving speck with hundreds of others, it was impossible to come to terms with anything on such a large scale so he brushed it off like dust.

He leaned forward, bracing himself against the sill. One thing he didn't have to worry about was coming home to yelling kids, complaining wives, bills, when all day long he'd had nothing but hardship. That routine went on day after day, month after month, year after year, and it wasn't what he called living even though most people lived that way and had no way out because the choice wasn't really a choice it was more on the order of biological and necessary for the continuation of the human race. He was lucky because he just wasn't cut out for it.

George Sender had an ex-wife living somewhere west of the Mississippi, a sister who lived with her family two hundred and fifty-nine miles away; then there was Lloyd Frend, Ramón López and a half-dozen other less intimate friends. He shook his head, rubbed his unshaven face.

He gave most of his energy to writing for the *Journal,* and what was left came under the heading of research in the guise of a social life by making the rounds in restaurants and bars and clubs and concerts, seeing people and places to dig up ideas for his column. And he slept with Coral Rasmussen four nights a week.

City officials gave him plenty of passes for political, social and sporting events, and he made good use of them, taking Coral out with him to meet the people she wanted to meet, and it gave him the social standing of a man with a beautiful woman on his arm. Maybe he didn't love her, but he'd got used to having her around, and if he was honest about it she meant more to him than he figured she meant, and he knew it could grow into something important.

Sender walked back to his desk. The view from the window hadn't told him anything he didn't already know.

He stared at one of the photos on his desk of a lake with no horizon line because the sky met the lake's surface in a seamless wash of greenish-gray.

There was definitely something going on that he couldn't figure out like that bit saying there were more things on heaven and earth. He wanted to get a line on what the *it* was or anything like it with an edge that would stimulate him so the words would flow out of his fingers to fill up a minimum of a full page for the weekend edition.

Whatever it was going to be he was determined this time that it would make headlines unless he wasn't right about what his guts were telling him and Frend was jerking him around and then it would land him on the street in front of the *Journal* building with his walking papers and a tough guy like Negron looking to cave his head in.

He reached into the humidor on his desk and retrieved a cigar, snipped the end of it and removed the band. He took his time letting the flame of his lighter lick around the end of the cigar as he drew slowly and steadily on it and exhaled a blue cloud of smoke.

37

"You won't be able to keep it up because you'll never get used to what he doesn't have," Sender said. He wasn't bitter but matter-of-fact. "It won't last."

Coral rubbed her reddish eyes. "He doesn't have the money you have, and he doesn't know the people you know—that's what you mean, isn't it?"

"Yeah, that's what I mean, Coral."

She drank from a cup of hot tea.

"I've got to find out," she said imploringly. "What if he's the one, George, and I never give it a chance, and then I've really messed up my life?" she said, a tear falling out of the corner of her eye that she wiped away with a Kleenex.

"Why is it you're always telling me things I don't really want to know?"

"I trust you, George."

"I wish you wouldn't—not that far. I want to be doing more with you, not less."

"We've known each other a long time. It counts for something, doesn't it?"

"Of course it does, it's just that I don't know what to do with what you're telling me. You know how much I like you."

"You're listening, aren't you?"

"Yes."

"Then you're doing something."

"Don't be sentimental," he said. "Maybe you love him, maybe you don't. I'm not saying you're better off with me, but if you stay with him there are going to be big changes in your life—for example, you're going to have to get a job. With the money he's earning it'll never be enough, and I'm sorry but I can't picture you living in a two-room apartment on West Walker and Third, and then on the salary of a guy that works in a—"

"An appliance store."

"Appliance store, really."

"I'm trying to tell you the best way I know how to tell you that when I think about it, I've got no choice, I'll hate myself if I don't give it chance. It'll be just one more thing I haven't done for myself."

"You're always digging up something from the past. Don't start in on it again. You'll make yourself sick."

"Never mind that," she said. "Every word we said to each other meant something more than the meaning of the words themselves. What we were saying wasn't anything special, it was more on the order of music that came out instead of words, and it crawled around us and slipped down and slowly made its way back again, and when it reached into us and played around in there it went all the way down, then came up, kept slipping and climbing and going down and coming up until finally we were drunk on it—but they were just words we were saying. The dull words that told us what we didn't have to say but what we know."

"That's very romantic." Sender wasn't being sarcastic. "I almost envy you."

"And when we didn't say anything it was like we were talking a mile a minute but it was our eyes not our mouths and it felt very good."

"Now I *am* jealous. It's a feeling we don't get very often, isn't it?"

She nodded, finished her cup of tea.

"Can I have a drink now?"

"Bourbon?"

"Yes, George, please."

He poured her a small bourbon and ginger ale and gave it to her and sat down again.

"Then the whole time we're having dinner—the whole time there was that music without sound again, and it carried me, and I know it carried him, too, and there wasn't even a question about whether or not I ought to be going along with it because it was taking me on a very pleasant trip, and I wanted to be there more than anywhere else. Whatever it was we felt—because it wasn't about what we were saying—we wanted that feeling to always stay and then we'd have all we wanted."

"He told you that?"

"He didn't have to tell me."

"Okay, spare me the details. A man can take only so much."

Sender calmly got up, poured himself a drink, sat down again opposite Coral and swallowed a mouthful of bourbon and water, felt the heat of it inside him, and he smiled.

"Maybe I could fall in love with you, but I'm not in love with you, and if that makes any difference—use it to get away from me. No hard feelings."

Tears really came to her eyes now since he was making it easy on her and she knew he was doing it on purpose because he didn't want her to feel any worse than she felt already, and for an instant she was more confused, this kindness and sensitivity confused her, and she told herself it'd be a lot easier if he'd shout and throw her out but that wasn't the way George Sender did things, and the voice was telling her again that she really wished he wouldn't do this, wouldn't be so understanding, then it concluded with a question, What if you're wrong about Walt Hargrove?

Coral told the voice to shut up, and then her head was quiet and she finished her bourbon and ginger ale, got up off the sofa. Her eyes were burning. She went into the bathroom, ran cold water, cupped her hands and splashed her face, then patted her skin dry with a fluffy towel. She kept her face in the towel, breathed the smell of scented detergent, her eyes were shut.

"What are you going to do?"

It was Sender standing in the doorway, watching her. She folded the towel and hung it on the rack, turned around. His arms were folded across his chest. She couldn't read any expression on his face, it was blank, and she reached up and put the palm of her hand against his cheek and kept it there until he put his hand over her hand and the warmth passed between them and he smiled.

"I'm going home and get a good night's sleep."

"I'll call you a cab."

38

JEAN FLEMING WAS ON her knees dressed in an expensive short skirt and jacket and blouse blindfolded in front of Lloyd Frend wearing a tailored suit, with Frend's cock in her mouth nearly choking her. There was someone else in the room, a guest, who came in after Jean was blindfolded, that hadn't been introduced to her, and she was aware only that it was someone sitting nearby in a chair that creaked when the occupant leaned forward for a better view or backward to relax a bit.

She made an effort that really didn't require any effort at all because she liked what she was doing, noisily, sloppily sucking his cock which involved a lot of saliva and drooling and choking, making a big deal out of the performance for Frend's sake and her sake and the benefit of the unknown guest, which was the whole point of the agreement she'd had with Frend to stimulate both of them with a viewer of their own in tribute to the films they watched together.

It was almost seven-thirty and when she'd finish the blowjob and he'd come in her mouth and she'd let some of it run down her chin for the guest's satisfaction, the guest would leave them on their own to fuck, and after they were finished with making love they'd still have plenty of time for dinner at a Japanese restaurant twenty-five minutes from Frend's country house. As she licked his balls tasting her own saliva she thought of the pleasant sweetness of hot saké running down her throat.

With her eyes covered she heard only the sounds she made in conjunction with the soft moaning that came from deep within

Frend's throat and chest, and when she paused for dramatic purposes and to catch her breath there was the distinct rustling of
the leafy branches of a couple of elms in the front yard that came
through the partially open window combined with the creaking of
the forward-moving chair.

The moment arrived when Frend could no longer hold back and
he came in short spurts sending splashes of thick, whitish sperm on
her tongue and face to the accompaniment of the creaking chair
and a palpable sense of the guest's excitement.

"Okay, you can go," Frend said with a weak but content voice.

Jean listened to the quiet footsteps, a pause at the door, the door
open and shut. She removed her blindfold as she licked her lips but
left some of his come on her chin. Frend was leaning back against
the cushions of the sofa, his eyes shut.

She reached over to the silver cigarette case on the low table,
opened it and took out two cigarettes. She lit them both, rolled the
filter of one in the sperm on her chin and gave it to Frend, stood
up, crossed the living room to shut the half-open window, then she
sat down in a chair. Frend put the cigarette to his lips, pulled on it,
tasted his come, and smiled.

"I felt a chill," she explained, but right away saw he wasn't listening. She smoked in silence, felt the come on her chin as it dried.

They finished their cigarettes, she got up to put hers out and
he leaned toward the ashtray on the low table to do the same thing
and they almost bumped heads, looked up into each other's eyes,
smiled and kissed. Frend wet his finger and wiped the dried sperm
from under her lower lip, she led him by the hand to the bedroom.

Lying under Frend with her arms around his shoulders, Jean
drew herself up a little closer to him, her voice close to a whisper.
"If you've heard the talk, you already know."

Frend stiffened automatically. He said quietly, "I haven't heard
any talk."

"According to talk, it's one of your bunch that killed Ray
Graham," she said.

39

WHEN CORAL GOT HOME from Sender's apartment she was too worn out to call Hargrove although she'd said she would and instead she ran a bath and spent forty-five minutes soaking in it and nearly falling asleep. She was tucked in bed five minutes after she got out of the bath and did her best to keep her eyes open reading a few pages of the *Journal*. The paper told her nothing because it wasn't the paper that interested her it was the lifted burden of having told Sender she was through with the romance that kept her from paying attention to the print, but she held onto the paper anyway, like it was telling her something when it was really just keeping her arms up and making her eyes tired and the thoughts in her head swim. She fell asleep with the beside lamp on.

Walt Hargrove paced his room, bumped into the sofa, rubbed his thigh where he'd collided with the sofa but kept on moving until he was standing in front of the armchair, then spun around to look at the screen of the television flashing images without sound, crossed the living room to switch it off, changed his mind, ran into the table and at last let himself sit down in a folding chair. It was after one o'clock in the morning.

Now he leaned forward and put his elbows on his knees and his head in his hands and asked himself who he thought he was kidding, and the answer came back that he wasn't trying to kid anybody because he knew for sure that she wouldn't give up all the connections and important people and expensive nights out that went with George Sender just because she thought she was in love with him. And he let out a sigh, waited a moment, looked off to one side, getting his thoughts all lined up in order.

Hargrove got up and went to the phone, picked it up and pressed the button to listen for a dial tone to make sure it was working and the usual working sound came from the receiver so he put it back on the stand. He bent down and pinched the wire that ran from the phone to where it was plugged into the wall and gave it a little tug to make sure it was connected and hadn't come loose, and it hadn't come loose and he was really frustrated wondering why he hadn't heard from Coral so he straightened up too fast and felt a twinge in a muscle in his lower back. A grimace came out of it, and he groaned, then shook his head.

He told himself to go to bed but what he really wanted to do was to run down the stairs and out of the building and walk over to West Cherry Street near the park to talk to Coral and find out what had happened when she saw George Sender.

He couldn't bring himself to do it. He didn't want to show her that part of his personality because he knew he'd be filed as just another weak male that she'd never be interested in since she'd already had a taste of a successful man with a column in the *Journal* who knew practically everybody worth knowing in the city, and that weakness and lack of self-assurance was the last thing he ever wanted to put in front of her. He tried to distract himself by thinking about Lily and how she was and what she was doing upstate with her girlfriend. It didn't work.

Hargrove got undressed and stood in front of the bathroom mirror in a pair of boxer shorts, and he shaved and brushed his teeth before climbing into bed and pulling the covers up over his chin, squeezing his eyes shut. That didn't get him anywhere so he switched on the light and hauled the loose pages of yesterday's *Journal* out from under the bed and started to read. He skipped over Sender's column.

He was sure he was listed minus zero with Coral, that was it, there was no other reason she hadn't called him, he was strictly useless when it came to a woman like her or she would've picked up the phone to tell him it was all right, that she was through with Sender, that she loved him, that it was okay with Sender, but Sender must've reeled her back in and she hadn't put up a fight. That's the way it was.

And it wasn't the first time he thought he'd rated the minus zero. It was like that with the other kids in high school and university when he was working part-time and they didn't do anything but play ball or hang around girls in the afternoon when school was out, and that was when he'd felt it, that state of things telling him he was nobody but a faded man long before he was twenty.

An echo of it had come back to him when he met Vince Negron, a criminal type but successful, and Hargrove had got the minus zero going against himself because he wasn't even in a crook's league, the difference being that he really didn't want to have a rating like that or to be anything like Negron. The appliance store didn't mean more to him than a regular salary, but it was a job and it kept him going.

It was either minus zero or he worked himself so hard all of the time in high school, university, the service station, the warehouse and the appliance store that he shoved the weight to the opposite end of the spectrum and it swung him upward into the list of potential maybes that believed in themselves and stored up hope and goals and a picture of a rosy future that hadn't yet come true. So he spent a sleepless night tossing and turning, high and low, and never finding the right position in which to fall asleep because it wasn't his body but his head that kept him awake.

Coral woke up late and refreshed from her night's sleep. She sat at the kitchen table drinking black coffee and reading the morning paper. It was the usual thing in the paper, the political pork that newly elected chairmen of the House and Senate appropriations subcommittees, the cardinals, raked in for their states was no different than the money per capita in earmarks—pet projects lawmakers put into major spending bills—that the other side had going for it when they were in office.

Her eyes shifted to a double column on the right, reading an article that told her that the insurgency which looks like civil war in Iraq was now self-sustaining financially, raising $70 million to $200 million a year from kidnapping, corrupt charities, counterfeiting and oil smuggling. Another page, and a small, quarter-column saying that in a closely watched retail measure known as same-store sales Wal-Mart's November sales fell 0.1 percent at its stores in the United States open for at least a year.

In the Metro section, an article explained how a twenty-three-year-old man was killed leaving his bachelor party at a strip club, with two others seriously wounded. They left the club around four in the morning, got into their car, collided with an unmarked police minivan, reversed, nearly hitting an undercover officer, shot forward striking the minivan again, and a spray of bullets from police riddled their car. Forty-five shell casings were numbered by investigators on the street.

The news gave her a headache and she tossed the *Journal* on the empty chair beside her, finished her coffee, rinsed the cup and went into the bathroom. After she'd showered and dressed and put on her makeup she thought of Hargrove. She really hadn't forgotten him, she was just feeling the freedom of having straightened out the business with Sender. Her head was clear. She picked up the phone.

Walt Hargrove was pale, deflated. His hand holding the cup of coffee trembled visibly and some of the coffee spilled onto the newspaper spread out in front of him. A cigarette burned in a green ashtray. He picked up the cigarette and dragged at it. The early wintry sun shone brightly and it was a miserable morning after a night without sleep.

The phone rang, he jumped and hit his knee against a table leg as he got up; he went to answer it and as he lifted the receiver he already knew who it was. When he'd let her say hello and weighed the sound of her voice as she'd said it and decided that he liked what he heard he told her to hang up, he'd be right over.

He hailed a taxi, and twenty minutes later he was standing at the entrance of the apartment building with his finger pressing the bell next to her name. His coat collar was turned up against the chill in the air, he looked up at the sky, and as she buzzed him in he told himself it was a fine morning.

40

S ENDER WENT EARLY TO the office. The Metro editor called the
night before telling him to come in around ten and there was
an urgent tone in back of the words that for once in his life
made Sender follow the editor's instructions. He got out of the elevator, went past the rooms like glass boxes or fish tanks that had
the usual inhabitants floating around in them and knocked at the
editor's door, went in without waiting for a reply. Outside this glass
box almost all the desks were occupied.

The Metro Section editor's name was Griffith Evans and he
was sitting in a swivel chair behind his desk in front of a stack of
competing newspapers. He was chunky, in his middle fifties. There
was some white in the dark hair cut close to his temples and his face
was without lines and had a ruddy complexion. He didn't look up
right away, Sender had to clear his throat to make Evans' head jerk
up just to notice him.

"Sit down, George."

Sender sat down in one of the two chairs that faced the desk.
Evans rolled his chair back, looked past Sender at the fish in their
tanks, then down at the pile of newspapers, edged up to the desk
and, leaning forward, reached for a humidor to his right.

"Have a cigar," he said, opening it and turning it toward Sender,
who reached out and plucked a cigar from the box. "Smoke it later,
you'll want it later after I've finished talking to you."

"What's up, Griff?"

"Nothing you haven't heard about or seen before—a murder."

"Ray Graham?"

"Yeah, and no. And before you tell me it's old news and just one more dead man, I want you to hear me out. It's not Graham, but what guys like him, who are part of an organization, big or small, are doing in this city. I know you don't do that sort of thing anymore—you've got a column and it's easy street unless you can't find a ready subject, which doesn't happen to you or you wouldn't have been given the column in the first place. I know you know Vince Negron and company, and we both know Graham was one of them until he landed on his back with his head cracked open on Florist—so see what you can dig up on El Manojo. The law-abiding individual has rights in this city and those rights include safe passage on the city streets, day or night, without interference from scum like them—one down, more than a thousand to go."

Sender crossed one leg over the other.

"Who cares if Graham got himself killed?"

"Exactly nobody. It's just an opportunity to drag them into the spotlight. If somebody murdered Graham it was more than likely justified. If it was self-defense, more power to the guy. I don't give a fuck. I *do* give a fuck about vigilantism or acts of violence. I want the punks to know it's how they'll end up if they keep on playing at big-time gangster or small-time hood. When guys like Negron get away with the things they get away with the average man or woman doesn't take an easy profit. Those crooks ought to use Lloyd Frend as a role model. He was their type a long time ago, and now he's legitimate."

Sender avoided the subject of Lloyd Frend. "Why don't you write it up, Griff—you're busting with ideas and enthusiasm," he said.

"Doesn't it make any difference to you?"

"It makes a difference only if writing it makes a difference. And I'm not so sure it would—like I'm not so sure fucking with Negron and El Manojo is such a good idea."

"All I want to do is take the starch out of them, that's it."

"When I get a lead, I'll do what I can."

"Fine."

"Just as long as they don't tear me in little pieces and toss them in the river."

"The paper will back you up."

"That's encouraging." He laughed without anything behind it.

Griff Evans swung his chair around to look out the window, tilted it back. "How are you and Coral getting on?"

"Split up—finished because she fell in love with a guy that works in an appliance store."

"No kidding!" He was sincere without trying. "I never thought she'd do that. I'm sorry, George."

"I'm sorry, too. I'm not as sorry as I thought I'd be, but I miss her—I didn't figure on that. I wasn't far enough in it for her, and now that I'm not in it at all and it hasn't changed the way I live my life, I miss her. I guess I liked having her around, and that makes one step forward for the two of us."

"Philosophical, aren't you? I'd take it seriously if I were you. If you really want to talk about it, call me at home. What time is it?"

"Twenty after ten."

"Get going, George," Evans said quietly, matter-of-factly.

41

HARD WINTER LAY IN the corridor waiting to make an entrance when Doris O'Dell got out of bed feeling a distinct chill in the air; he put on a bathrobe, went into the kitchenette to make coffee and toast and read the morning paper. There was a handwritten note propped against an open cereal box on the small Formica tabletop reminding him of his appointment with Vince Negron at six that evening.

O'Dell was thirty-six, had a stocky frame, wide shoulders, a paunch, his legs were very thick and muscular. His skin was pale, and he had greasy, salt-and-pepper hair, blue eyes with creases like cracks at the outside corners, and a nose that had been broken more than once. The broken nose gave the absent-minded, almost cruel expression a lift that told anyone paying close attention to him that he was a man who'd made more than a few mistakes and plenty of enemies and would keep on making them and never admit it. His face was saying it right now while his eyes were glued to the front page of the newspaper and his hand raised the steaming cup of coffee to his lips.

But his face was an asset as far as he was concerned, he thought it gave him authority as long as no one really looked beneath the surface, and added to the smooth way he talked to customers at Midwest Bank and Trust that wanted to invest their savings in some plan they thought might bring a point or two of interest when all they'd end up getting looked more like a decimal fraction of that point on account of the way the federal government played the average citizen. The total came to getting away with murder. And when he didn't scare them off, the sum of the broken nose, absent-minded expression and smooth talk also meant that he was a pretty good salesman.

By seven o'clock that night there wasn't enough left of that face to show any sign of life much less an absentminded expression and he was too worn out from the severe beating he'd got to think of anything except whether or not he was going to live or be killed by Negron. He shivered beneath his overcoat and was thinking he might go into shock from a loss of blood.

O'Dell had a mind for numbers and some of those numbers were rolling out in front of him on a strip like a ticker tape as he lay in the shrubbery several feet from the road. The numbers represented the sum of money he'd skimmed from Negron's earnings which, whenever he had the chance, he'd put in a drawer of a disused dresser in the basement of his parents' house where they'd never think to look for anything. The ticker tape broke off with a strong whiff of the lake which must've been nearby because the smell of it swamped his head along with the throbbing pain that made him dizzy.

Negron looked down at the crumpled form of O'Dell, who couldn't lift his head off the ground, pushed his hair back with his hand, turned around and walked slowly to the car parked a few feet away. He opened the trunk and a light came on and the light showed him an undersized spare tire, an empty gasoline can and an empty space big enough for a man, and he was thinking that it had all gone so fast he didn't remember anything but the solid smack of the punches and a little vibration that went up his leg when a kick struck something solid like bone.

The setup with O'Dell to cut in on Lloyd Frend's profits had produced a decent amount of cash for two months, but O'Dell himself was a problem and just hearing his voice got on Negron's nerves because O'Dell was a pain in the ass. He was nosey, and Negron didn't trust him to keep his mouth shut if Frend put any pressure on him. Negron didn't trust anyone except his own mother and she'd been dead for almost nine years.

Killing O'Dell was the only way to get rid of the worries he had every time money changed hands between them, and it would fuck things up for Frend when he cut off a pipeline for a significant amount of cash. Negron bent over the body and lifted it from under the arms.

The physical effort of carrying a man who couldn't offer help moving himself was more than Negron figured on since he'd thought he was in pretty good shape, but O'Dell's body was stocky, compact but with a fat belly, and the deadweight strained muscles in Negron's lower back that would take a couple of sessions with a chiropractor to straighten out.

Once the body was in the trunk, a gurgling sound, a gasp and a prolonged expiration preceded the dull thud of slamming the trunk shut. He got in behind the wheel, cut across the road making a U-turn and put the headlights on when he got past the broken wooden fence to the dirt road heading into the forest going toward the lake.

42

THE WATER LAPPING AT the edge of the lake formed tiny pools between large and small rocks strewn along the shoreline and when the pools stagnated a thin film of scum formed over the surface until something came along to stir them up.

There weren't many animals that came to drink at the edge of the lake in early winter, though there was an explosion in the deer population the last couple of years that became a nuisance to residents who lived near the wooded areas of the suburbs. When the body of a man was found tipped headfirst with his heels in the air in a stagnant pool at the water's edge, the scummy water had already reformed and settled around the head, while strands of hair floated beneath the surface like sea grass.

What was left of the face hadn't been in the water a long time, he'd been dead about twenty-four hours. There were bruises all over the exposed parts of the body with a remarkable bruise on his forehead where it had struck the larger of the three rocks that formed the circumference of this particular stagnant pool. It wasn't cold enough yet for the water to freeze. A couple of kids found him while they were looking for a place to smoke grass at the lakeside.

When the scene investigators of the Criminal Investigations Division were finished photographing and examining the position of the body and looking for and gathering whatever evidence they could find until a more thorough search could be made in full daylight, two detectives raised the lifeless face out of the water, turned the head gently to look at him, more photographs and flashes of light, and then Doris O'Dell's spirit climbed out of the bluish-gray skin of his stocky body, unfolded itself because it was as fragile as a piece of parchment paper like all souls, stood upright next to the photographer, and gazed up with empty eyes through the wet strands of hair at the wavering branches of an elm tree as if he'd never seen an elm before.

The two investigators gently let go of the man's head, wiped their gloved hands on trouser legs, felt a chill and stood up.

"Okay, you can take him away," the Detective-Sergeant said, turning his back on the body bag and the rest of them, heading for the car.

Ramón López, keeping out of sight of the police, stood off to one side leaning against a tree looking at the body being zipped into a bag. He'd been waiting for a sign that Negron had made a move, but he didn't expect anything like this; when he got a call with the information from a friend at the local police station, he followed it up and now that he was looking at a corpse at edge of the lake he was sure Vince Negron's name was written on it.

He backed away from the scene and moved his feet like a cat past the broken branches, through shrubbery, over damp ground, in shadows without making a sound to draw attention from the investigators putting yellow police tape around the spot where the body was found. A few minutes later he was in his car backing out of where he'd parked it onto a dirt road that took him away from the lakeside.

This isn't one for the question mark boys, he thought. There's nothing about the body that tells you Negron did it, but you don't have to be told it's Negron, nobody has to say it, because a twist in your gut and the way the body's banged up and the fact that it's a guy who worked on the side for Lloyd Frend at Midwest Bank and Trust says if it isn't Negron it's nobody, so you know it can't be nobody which puts it in big letters right before your eyes and the letters say it's Vince's handiwork or it wouldn't be the body of Doris O'Dell tipped headfirst in the lake.

A mile and a half away from the protected forestland bordering the lakeside, López headed south and west toward downtown. It was almost eight and his stomach was grumbling because he hadn't eaten anything since lunch so he could wait until after he'd had something to eat to give Sender a call from the restaurant parking lot.

Sitting alone in a burgundy Naugahyde booth to the left of the main wall facing the full dining room at the center of the restaurant, López finished his steak, baked potato and asparagus tips, downed the rest of his glass of wine, waved at a passing waiter who started to clear the table, and told the waiter he was ready for the mixed green salad with Danish Blue dressing.

Beyond the large picture windows the sky was cloudless, wintry and lit by a canted half-moon. There was a garden that became a neatly mowed lawn rolling downhill in the moonlight behind the restaurant that López watched as he waited for his coffee. A pair of incandescent eyes looked back at him, maybe a pair of raccoon eyes, then they were switched off like light bulbs as the animal turned away, lumbering downhill toward a couple of bare trees.

The richly brewed coffee went down hot and scalded his throat but it was soothing when the warmth hit his stomach. He finished the cup of coffee and had another but still felt sleepy from the protein of a thick steak shuttling through his veins.

Now he didn't want to talk to Sender, he didn't like having to be accountable to anybody except when he was working for the Department, but Sender gave him the standard rate, and the money and staying in the game after stagnating in a small town meant a lot to him. He kept thinking of Jean Fleming and wanted to talk to her, but that wasn't going to happen, and then the idea of being home in bed was tempting, but since he'd agreed to keep an eye on things for Sender for ten days it wasn't a question of should he stay or should he go. Sender had put him up in a hotel on the East Side.

After he'd paid the check, he stood in front of the restaurant and lit a cigarette. The air was fresh and cold and he stared up at the moon and starry sky, trying to spot them through the bright glow of the city's lights.

López started walking. By the time he got to the car he'd decided to forget Sender for now and instead put the focus on Coral. He got behind the wheel and started the engine. He had to talk to Coral about the empty nights and wasted years and the whole drama of his life up until now because that's what he was feeling, it was a never-ending discomfort like a dull pain that crawled around in his belly ever since the day Jean Fleming left him.

He wanted the feminine angle on the subject of women, he didn't have the slightest idea what women were thinking, and when he guessed, he guessed wrong. It wasn't being accountable to George Sender that bothered him right now, nothing like that bothered him, so it was something else, and when he honestly added it up it came to the fact that he was still in love with Jean Fleming.

He dragged at the cigarette, inhaling very deeply and letting the smoke come out slowly. The cash he got from Sender meant a lot to him because it told him he was being paid to do a job he did well. He turned a corner and headed toward a quiet street, pulled the car over to the curb and switched off the engine. He called Sender from a public phone. Sender picked it up after three rings.

"What have you got?"

"Don't rush me," López said.

"Okay, I'm not rushing you. Why'd you call if don't have anything to say?"

"The police found a guy turned upside down in the water. Actually, it was a couple of kids that found him. I think it's Negron who did it."

"I already heard it—about the guy. We already printed it."

"I know you did. But I know something you don't know."

"What's that?"

"The guy was Doris O'Dell."

"You sure?"

"I saw his face—and you can't mistake the rest of him. It was O'Dell, all right." He tossed the cigarette out the window. "I hear the damnedest things coming out of my mouth."

"Why'd you say that?"

"I've seen enough dead bodies it doesn't mean anything to me anymore."

"Oh well, that's too bad."

"Yeah, it's too bad—and it makes me sick."

"So, Negron got what he wanted, but he's covering his tracks."

"That's what it looks like, he got what he wanted, but I can't give you more. Not yet. And I don't go along with the idea that he's covering his tracks because the scene looked so bad—there are tire marks and footprints all around where they found the body, and some of them are going to be his."

"So, what do you think?"

"He doesn't want to get caught, if that's what you mean."

"It comes down to money. It always has with him, and you know and I know it always will for most of us."

"Okay, we both know it, so does everybody else. There's no future without it. When we grow up we all get the same idea and we learn to respect it. How old are you, anyway?"

"Cut the sarcasm, Ramón—what's money?"

"It's a necessity, among other things," López said.

"Yes, but not if you can't spend it. If Negron's left himself in the wide open what good will money do him if he's in jail?"

"Don't be naïve, George. Nobody stays in jail forever. Not anymore. And not somebody like him."

"Money means no worries. No worries means you've got the freedom and a future to think up more ways to make money."

"It's money, yes, but it's also about position—and position is better, much better. Riding high, and everybody patting your little head and kissing your ass and all the grateful people you do favors for so they can return them. Just think of it. For the rest, I don't know what's going on."

"He wants to be Lloyd Frend."

"That's what it adds up to. But isn't that what you figured from the start?"

"I'm just doing a favor for a friend."

"Yeah, that's his name."

"Thanks, Ramón."

"Bye, George."

López switched on the ignition, gunned the engine and pulled the car off the curb onto the road. The headlights showed him the way to the entrance of the expressway about a mile ahead. He took the Van Buren exit, headed for the park, then turned right on West Cherry Street. He found a parking place between a beat-up van and a compact Japanese car. He turned off the engine.

He leaned forward, looked up through the windshield at the lively face of the building where Coral Rasmussen lived; whether or not the curtains or blinds were drawn almost every window had a light burning in it that streamed out of the panes of glass onto the dark surface of night. He lit another cigarette, smoked it for a minute, got out of the car, then dialed her number from a public phone. The line was busy.

43

APPARENTLY BY POLICE REQUEST, the first news report of the crime made the headlines. For the next two days, it was front page news, then half a page, and finally it was relegated to page four. You had to look for it after that because the few lines the press gave it were buried in no man's land. George Sender had nothing to do with any of the reports on Doris O'Dell, his column avoided the subject even though he got the green light from Griff Evans and toyed with the idea and wrote a couple of opinion pieces that he never sent in to the *Journal*.

Most of the angles were covered in other papers, but Sender had a few of his own with the reports that came in from Ramón López that he wasn't ready or willing to reveal to anyone. When he finished breakfast he shaved and showered and got dressed, then decided not to go in to work but do a little checking up by himself on Negron.

A flat, dark gray sky looked like a forecast of snow but it wasn't cold enough for more than a really cold downpour of rain. He wrapped a cashmere scarf around his neck before he put on a waterproof overcoat, went out the door and down the five flights of stairs instead of taking the elevator to stimulate the flow of blood in his veins because the flowing blood gave him courage to do a thing he didn't have a lot of courage to do. He hailed a taxi at the corner.

He wasn't sure if it was the right thing to go where he was going, but he told the driver to take a right, and as the taxi rounded the corner going away from the lake and the driver looked in the rearview mirror at him, he told the driver, "West Florida and Third Street."

Vince Negron folded the newspaper, yawned, finished his coffee, got up from the little table and went to the mirror to comb his hair. He put on his coat and reached for the doorknob, and the phone rang; he let go of the doorknob and walked back to the nightstand and lifted the receiver. It was Lilybourne, the man who owned his apartment and El Perro Llorón and the whole building along with a run-down empty apartment house across the street.

"Yes?"

"I'm in my car, about a block away. Can I stop by?"

"I was just going out. Is it important?"

"I'll be there in three minutes."

"Right, see you then."

He put the phone down without slamming it but felt like throwing the thing across the room because he was asking himself what that money-grubbing crook wanted with him when he'd had nothing to do with Lilybourne except to pay the rent which he did in installments of six months at a time in advance to the slumlord since the day he took the one-room apartment.

He paced back and forth in front of the door muttering under his breath. I've got about as much time for him as I've got for an afternoon swim at the Y with the chief of police, fuck shit, and I've got to make time for him, fuck shit, because he owns the goddamned building—I can't play hooky, I can't put the freeze on him, and I can't kill him.

Negron wasn't going to let him into his room so he left the apartment and headed down the two flights of stairs and at the bottom of the staircase he went past the yellowed walls with the paint peeling off and a bare bulb hanging from the ceiling without giving anything a second glance.

He was standing tapping his foot on the landing above the steps that went down to the sidewalk with the front door shut behind him when the car pulled up at the curb. Lilybourne wasn't alone. It was too early for El Perro Llorón to be open for business. Negron wanted a drink.

Lilybourne was smoking a cigarette. He took a few drags, put it out, then got out of the car walking purposefully and when the door swung open Negron got a better look at the passenger, a young girl who couldn't have been more than sixteen years old with soft blond hair cascading over her shoulders. She wore a tight flower-patterned dress and from the way she was sprawled in the passenger seat the hem was more than halfway up her thighs.

She leaned toward the open door and called out to Lilybourne, "Got a smoke, Daddy?"

"Sure thing, kid." Lilybourne tossed the pack of cigarettes in through the open door, it landed against her and she caught it by crossing her arms in front of her chest.

"Is that your kid?" Negron said, while Lilybourne stood looking up at him from the bottom of the stairs.

"I don't have any kids, Vince. I can call you Vince, can't I?"

Lilybourne was in his early fifties but there wasn't any gray in his hair. He stood about five-eight, weighed around one-eighty. One leg was shorter than the other but the difference was compensated for by a wedge and an extra slice of heel on his shoe. Lilybourne sometimes gave the impression of a man on the verge of tipping over if he wasn't leaning against something to keep himself vertical.

"Let's go inside," Lilybourne said.

"No, let's walk. Your girlfriend can wait in the car."

Lilybourne rolled himself back to the car and leaned in toward the girl. Negron couldn't hear what he was saying to her but when Lilybourne faced about and came toward him grinning, Negron saw the girl put a sulky pout on her lips as she switched the ignition to start the music, reached for the door handle on the driver's side and slammed the car door shut. She rolled her window down, music blasted out of it.

"Jesus," Negron said.

"Yeah, let's go. We've got twenty minutes before she'll lose her concentration."

They walked away from El Perro Llorón, kept on going until they got to the intersection of Third Street and Quincy Avenue, turned right on Quincy and headed for a large empty parking lot where the only resident was a rusted-out wreck of a car standing on cinder blocks with a smashed-in windshield, ripped-out seats and a torn-up dashboard. Lilybourne lit a cigarette, offered one to Negron, who lit his own with a Zippo.

Lilybourne leaned against the wreck where the metal hadn't rusted through the body. Negron looked around the parking lot bathed in a sunny golden winter light, then his eyes came to Lilybourne.

"So, what's so important we have to talk here where your girl-friend can't hear us? You going to tell me that you love me?"

"I'll love you when you're ready to say what I want to hear."

"I'm too old for you."

"Cut the crap."

"Which is what, exactly?"

"Are you ready to talk about it."

"Give me more than a hint."

"Doris O'Dell. How's that for a hint?"

"He's dead. I read it in the *Journal*."

"You knew him."

It wasn't a question, Negron looked him straight in the face, and the way Lilybourne, leaning on the rusted-out car, looked back at him without blinking an eye made Negron smile nervously.

"I don't know anything about him."

"I knew him, but you didn't know that. He made investments for me. And he talked a lot about the kind of people he did business with. You're one of them."

"Maybe I was, maybe I wasn't."

"Okay, what do you know about the setup?"

"Life expectancy at birth in the United States in 1901 was forty-nine years. Seventy-seven point seven in 2005."

"And the average life span of the Russian male is now just fifty-eight. Here, in America, it's what we've got now—cash, women, property—and whatever we can put away for ourselves, for the long, drawn-out end of our lives."

"Investment."

"That's right."

"Plenty smart. You're always thinking about what's around the corner, aren't you?"

"You're a pretty smart guy, yourself."

"It doesn't concern you."

"It concerns both of us."

"Well, what am I supposed to do?"

"Invest in our future."

"I can't tell you anything you don't already know." Negron dropped his cigarette and stepped on it.

"Mistake number one. Stop playing games with me, Vince."

"Yeah, that's what they all say. O'Dell stopped playing games, or maybe he played too many of them—look what happened to him. He isn't going to make any investments for anybody anymore."

"What are we going to do about it?"

"'We'?"

"Yeah, you and me."

"For Christ's sake."

"It's more than just pulling the oars together. It's sort of like pumping the money-making machinery."

"What's the angle?"

"Consolidate our funds."

"Give me another cigarette."

"What do you say?"

44

CORAL LISTENED TO THE phone ring on the other end of the line, she let it go on for almost a minute before hanging up the receiver convinced Hargrove was fast asleep after a long, hard shift taking inventory in the appliance store. She sat down on the edge of her bed, folded her hands in her lap, looked at them. Her head snapped up, there was someone at the door.

She went to the window, raised the blinds and looked down at the street. She didn't recognize any of the cars parked on West Cherry except the beat-up van and a compact car that belonged to a couple of her neighbors. She pressed the intercom button, heard someone exhaling cigarette smoke in front of the speaker, then she said, "Who's there?"

A familiar voice said, "Ramón."

He sat in an armchair opposite her in the living room with the lights on and the blinds drawn as if they had something to hide from someone looking in, but there wasn't anyone looking in and if there had been someone looking in they knew they wouldn't be interested in what they were saying or doing. No action, just talk. City nightbirds might have been singing but they couldn't hear them, it was late and they were fast asleep. López looked her up and down. It seemed as if he hadn't seen her in a year.

She smiled at him, let him get a good look at her face without make-up and her messed-up hair. She didn't feel a bit self-conscious that she wasn't wearing anything but a T-shirt and panties since she was wrapped up to her neck in a terry cloth bathrobe.

She'd known López for such a long time that nothing like that mattered to her, he was just twisted up inside and confused and it was written all over him that what he really wanted was to talk about Jean Fleming.

"So, with a gun at your back?" she said.

"Okay, the hell with the gun," López said. "There's more important items on this list. Like maybe she's got feelings left over for me, for one thing—and then, will she dump Frend or won't she dump him? If she's willing to dump him will it be on account of me? And then what am I going to do about it? Maybe I want her because she's with somebody else. Those are the kinds of questions that are making my head spin. And it's the answers that I want to know."

"It's between Frend and her, isn't it?"

"And that's how it should be. I don't want to drag her away from him, I don't want to drag anybody away from anyone if they don't want to be dragged."

"I don't see her much if I can help it—I don't like her. And when I did see her I was with George, and I'm not seeing George anymore, but when I did see her she was with him, with Lloyd, they were together, Lloyd and Jean, and for all I know they're happy. Stop torturing yourself."

"I don't understand anything." All of a sudden he knew what it was, knew what he had to say next, then he heard himself saying it: "It's a suffering arrangement, that's what it is—you see what I mean?"

"Yes, Ramón, I see what you mean. I want to help you, really, but I'm not going to tell you what you want to hear just to hear myself say it."

"What I really want is to crash through, to break down whatever it is that's standing like a wall between her and me, but it's a very high and solid wall and there's no climbing over it, and I can't figure out what's holding it together—it's called Lloyd Frend, I guess, and even you can't give me a glimpse of what's on the other side." He took a deep breath. "You got anything to drink?"

"A glass of wine?"

"You kidding me?"

"Yes, I'm kidding you."

Coral got up, tightened the belt around the terry cloth robe and went to the kitchen. She came back with a glass of straight whisky, handed it to him. López turned the glass in his hand before taking a drink.

"You have any beer? I'll need a beer chaser."

She got up again, came back with a bottle of beer and a glass. She sat down, raised her leg and planted her foot in front of her on the cushion. She picked at a toenail, pulling at a corner of it. She stretched her leg out in front of her, turned her ankle inspecting the foot, then straightened the bathrobe when she'd put her foot back on the floor.

"A great pair of legs," López said, taking a sip of whisky, then a swallow of beer. "But then I already told you."

"So, what're you going to do about Jean Fleming?"

"What should I do?"

"Talk to her. See her and talk to her face to face—that's what I think you should do."

"You think I should tell her what I'm thinking?"

"I'm not telling you I know what you ought to say. Ask her questions. When she answers them listen to what she's saying, but really listen, then you'll know more about what she's feeling than if you lose control and jump out of your skin and spill everything before she's had a chance to trust you again."

"Trust me?"

"That's right, trust."

"And what do you think I'll hear?"

"You're still in love with her so you've got it bad, Ramón. When somebody's got it as bad as you've got it the best way to handle the situation is just to listen to her, let her do the talking and tell you what's on her mind. Don't push her. It never works if you push her, take my word for it. And when it's over, when you've got the picture, it might not be what you want to look at but it'll be the truth, as far as she's concerned and as far as there's any truth in what she's got to say, or anyone else for that matter."

"The future's what we make of the past, is that it?"

"That sounds right."

45

HARGROVE WENT TO WORK, worked a lot of hours, saw Coral when he had the time and he found it as often as he could even if he was ready to drop from exhaustion because Coral was what got him going and it was love with no time to waste. He got another call from Lily asking him if anything had come out of the investigation of Ray Graham's death. He reassured her by saying that nothing involving one Lily Segura had come to the surface but reminded her that she hadn't been away from Lake City for very long.

His attraction to El Manojo's business practices fell below the line of curiosity and straight into the garbage can and with that fall the desire to make money in their world of tricks, manipulation and violence didn't look good to him anymore.

So Hargrove took any extra shift they gave him to make money to take Coral out and buy her things and pay for his own rent and living expenses. The extra hours weren't enough, but he kept after them and she understood and didn't ask him for more than he gave her, and he didn't feel one bit guilty about it because he was drowned in the sensation of being in love and for the time being that was enough to keep his spirits high.

The winter started to weigh down on Lake City and the sky was always gray and laden with clouds that threatened snow but didn't make good on their threats, the river was half frozen, the wind tore into the city off the lake, keeping the city's population bundled up and shivering but curious about the direction the climate would take for those who had a memory long enough to remember the days of heavy winter weather that seemed gone forever with the melting of the polar icecaps.

El Manojo moved out of El Perro Llorón after Vince Negron parted with some of his savings to rent space in a renovated build-ing with a clean, sandblasted front on Meyering Boulevard at Seventeenth Street opposite the Meyering Building in a block of mostly disused industrial structures being transformed into ware-houses and shops and studio apartments near a narrow part of the river, and they put a sign up over the inner door of frosted glass that said, *Seventeenth Street Social Club*.

Hargrove visited the social club on the odd Wednesday after-noons when he didn't work a full day shift even if he wanted to and Coral was working at the library at the local extension of the city university and he had a little time to spare for a drink with Negron and whoever out of the regular members of El Manojo was hanging around the club.

Hargrove took two buses, one going away from the east-facing lake, the other, south a few blocks, and luckily he'd caught one bus right after climbing down from the other. He'd eaten a sandwich and a piece of chocolate cake and had drunk a glass of milk at the counter of a diner near the appliance store and now he wasn't hungry but his throat was dry when he got to the glass entry to the building on Meyering and Seventeenth. It was two twenty-five.

The outer door was open, he let himself in. There were two doors in the empty foyer one not very far away from the other. He knocked at the frosted glass door on the right with the name of the club on it and when there was no answer he turned the knob, gave the door a gentle shove and it swung open. The anteroom was new, but the sparse furniture was more on the order of secondhand furniture.

A beat-up old wooden table with a task lamp on it and a pad of blue-lined yellow paper next to the lamp with a pencil lying across the blank paper was the only sign that someone had been in the room in the last twenty-four hours, and there was nobody sitting in the worn leather chair behind the table. There were no windows

in this room. A curtain in front of the cloak-room off to the right
wasn't drawn and Hargrove saw winter coats hanging from wire
hangers on a polished metal pole and a pair of fur-lined, rubber
boots on a rack beneath them.

Hargrove took a few steps to the right toward a door that wasn't
completely shut and heard a couple of low voices, then quiet laughter. He looked at his watch, which said two-thirty. He cleared his
throat, went to the door, knocked lightly with his knuckles. Then
he remembered his overcoat, slipped it off his shoulders, hung it up
with the others behind the curtain, then answered the voice saying,
"Who's there?" with his own: "It's Walt."

Jake Bielinski sat with Joe Whiten at a Lifetime thirty-sev-
en-inch, square almond folding card table with a round bronze
hammer-tone frame that was pushed up against another card table
with empty chairs tucked under them beneath a large, matte-white
Oriel Pendant lamp hanging from the ceiling by a long white cord.
Windows with blinds drawn over them faced the alleyway parallel to and between Seventeenth and Eighteenth that intersected
Meyering Boulevard.

Greasy paper bags were strewn over the tabletop, paper wrap-
pers smeared with mayonnaise, loose bits of tomato and lettuce
leaves from what remained of their lunch, a half-eaten bag of potato chips, donuts laid out on a Styrofoam tray, two ceramic cups of
steaming coffee with the name of a Chinese restaurant printed on
them in red ink, and a thermos. There was a cigarette smoking itself
in an ashtray. A makeshift bar on wheels was set up in a corner of
the room next to a long, worn leather sofa.

"How's it been, Walt?" Bielinski said. "Take a chair, have a cup."

"Walt," Whiten said, half standing to shake his hand.

Bielinski got up, went past the sofa to a cupboard and came
back with an empty cup that had a picture on it of a Sichuan pepper
with one eye shut wearing a crooked smile.

Hargrove turned the cup in his hand, looked it over, then
unscrewed the thermos and poured himself half a cup of coffee.
Whiten handed him a half pint and he poured bourbon into the

steaming coffee. He was used to drinking now, and it was cold outside and a chill had gone through him on the way over to the club
which justified a drink before five o'clock.

"Negron been in today?" Hargrove asked just to pass the time.

"Yeah, this morning," Whiten said.

"Haven't seen him in a couple of days."

"He's been working, Walt," Bielinski said, lifting his cup to finish his coffee and bourbon.

"Who hasn't," Whiten added.

"You're telling me," Hargrove said, holding the cup between his
hands, warming them.

"Want a donut? Got 'em fresh on the way over here," Whiten
said, smiling.

"Thanks." Hargrove reached across the tabletop, picked a chocolate glazed cake donut, bit into it, then leaned back in his chair.
He finished the donut, started on the coffee that wasn't so hot it
would burn him.

A noise came from the foyer just on the other side of the frosted
glass doors that was loud enough to carry all the way through the
building back to the room where Hargrove sat with Whiten and
Bielinski. Whiten jumped up from the table, spilling coffee from
his cup, the sugar donut fell from Bielinski's hand onto the table
scattering sugar granules over the newspaper he was reading.

"What's that?" Whiten said.

"How do I know? But I heard it and it don't sound good."

"Doesn't."

"What?"

"Doesn't sound good."

"You're right, it doesn't sound good, let's go," Bielinski said, hurrying away from the table toward the door that opened into the
anteroom.

Before he got to the door it swung wide open framing Vince
Negron with blood streaming out of a deep cut above the hairline
on his forehead and out of a loose flap of sliced skin over his cheek-
bone and running from his smashed nose down his chin, messing

up the front of his pressed white shirt and sport jacket under the unbuttoned black wool overcoat he wore in winter. He raised the scarf in his right hand to wipe the blood away from his mouth, then brought it up to the wound on his head somewhere above the swollen left eye.

"Here's your hat, what's your hurry?" Negron said, winking at them with his good eye. "That's what I told the fuckers after I kicked the shit out of them."

He came into the room, the others didn't move, he threw his coat on the sofa, dropped the scarf and headed toward the bathroom and slammed the door.

"You all right, Vince?" Whiten shouted, coming toward the bathroom.

"Fucking hell!" Negron complained, looking at himself in the mirror, then searching the medicine cabinet for Betadine, povidone-iodine ten percent, an iodine complex with a polymer, and then for something more than a box of Band-Aids to bandage his face.

Hargrove came up behind Whiten at the bathroom door, calling out to Negron, "You need anything, Vince? You want a doctor?"

"López," Negron muttered from the other side of the door. "That dumb, fucking Mexican, Ramón López."

They answered in the same voice: "Who?"

"López hired some guys to jump me right in front of the club. He's got big balls to do a thing like that."

"What makes you think it's López?" Bielinski said, more to himself than to Negron. "Maybe it's Frend."

"They were greasers."

"Call me a yid," Bielinski said, "but you could be wrong."

"Cut the name calling, that ain't the point," Negron said, at last opening the bathroom door.

"Isn't," Whiten said.

"What?"

"That *isn't* the point. What's up with you two?"

"That's what I said, now shut up."

46

HARGROVE SAT ON THE worn sofa and looked at his hands. There hadn't been much to put his finger on, but he remembered what Coral had said when she talked about her old friendship with Ramón López which gave him enough to figure she might know something about what happened to Negron and if she didn't know anything now she could find it out later. Then he realized what he was doing thinking he'd ask Coral for information about Negron from López and how it would bring her into something he didn't want her involved in at any cost.

It sounded funny to him that Negron cursed out López as a Mexican since Negron himself might be a Mexican, or maybe he was from Nicaragua at the time Anastasio Somoza Debayle resigned on July 17, 1979 and fled to Miami and the Sandinista five-member junta entered the Nicaraguan capital on July 20 and assumed power. The Sandinistas scared a lot of criminals out of the country and maybe he'd been one of those between the fall of one government and the rise of another to catch a plane or head north to the US by whatever means possible.

When Negron came out of the bathroom he was bandaged up with fresh blood seeping through layers of gauze and Band-Aids that crisscrossed his forehead, cheek, the corner of an eye and two pieces of adhesive tape making an *X* that covered the bridge of his nose. He had pieces of toilet paper twisted up and stuck in his nostrils. He walked like he'd been hit in the kidneys. His stringy, long hair was wet.

Hargrove got up, Whiten and Bielinski made him lie down on the sofa, and they got ice cubes out of the freezer and wrapped a towel around them and put the towel gently on his forehead, covering his eyes. Hargrove stood by watching nervously. Negron wasn't too pissed off to make a couple of jokes.

Hargrove counted the fingers of his hands, wondered why he never wore a ring, then stared out the window at nighttime Lake City while riding the bus home after he'd left the Seventeenth Street Social Club when Negron fell asleep on the sofa with Whiten and Bielinski looking after him.

He got off the bus, headed toward the corner of West Florida and Third Street with the idea that he'd look in at El Perro Llorón to get some news about Lily. There was a low, rumbling sound that came from behind him with a vibration that crawled up his legs from the sidewalk and he turned and saw that a big truck of the sort that carried broken-up concrete slabs with twisted, rust-rotten reinforcement rods left over after a demolition job was coming his way at a good clip. What it was doing here at this time of night he didn't know.

The truck ran down the middle of the street ignoring the dividing line and before Hargrove understood that it was aiming at him, the truck veered and he jumped over a hedge just in time to avoid being hit by it, landing uncomfortably on his side, bruising his ribs on the hard ground next to a thorny leafless bush in a small garden. The truck swerved off the sidewalk and onto the street, took a right turn at Third and Winston, then disappeared.

Hargrove stood up and brushed himself off and felt the trembling in his arms and legs and the pronounced beating of his heart that was going to burst through his chest. He immediately put the truck together with the muscle they put on Negron in front of the social club and came up with a dose of fear and the certainty now that anyone who had anything to do with El Manojo was going to find himself in the middle of trouble meant to scare them off, and the proof of it lay in the fact that while he had virtually nothing to do with El Manojo, he'd almost been knocked flat.

47

AL JOSLYN SWITCHED OFF the flashlight and gave Whiten a shove toward the piece of wood he'd removed from covering a hole in the back porch of a bar shut for the night. Whiten picked up the wood and set it aside and wormed his way into the opening, it was a tight fit, but he was slim enough to make his way through the duct leading to the bar, holding a small pencil sketch crumpled in his hand of what he'd find once he got inside. Joslyn backed up and crouched behind a few tall shrubs to watch the street and sidewalk, and from where he was he saw Whiten's legs as they disappeared into the hole.

The bar had been closed for hours and the only light came from a small out-of-date electric sign behind the bar advertising a brand of beer whose wet-glowing allusion made him thirsty. Whiten wore gloves, so when he opened the refrigerator behind the bar and took out a cold bottle of beer and opened it he didn't leave any fingerprints. He drank from the bottle as he looked for the backroom and safe drawn on the crumpled piece of paper Joslyn had given him.

In the safe, which was left open by whoever had closed the bar, he found a thousand dollars in cash, and he stuffed the bills in his coat pocket before finishing the beer. He looked around at the dingy office which had an old-style adding machine on the corner of the desk, an old-fashioned desk lamp, a wire waste basket next to the desk, a recent photo on the wall above the safe of a half-naked girl kneeling on the seat of a Harley-Davidson, two metal file cabinets against the opposite wall.

Whiten took another look around as he climbed back through the space into the duct on his way out with the money in his pocket and an empty bottle of beer in his right hand. He didn't get rid of the bottle until he and Joslyn were two blocks away on Cortland, when he dropped it in a garbage can standing alone on the sidewalk.

Jake Bielinski, who didn't work with Paul Madley very often because they were close friends in El Manojo and Negron didn't encourage close friends to work together very often, was checking the time in order to synchronize his watch with Madley's. It was three-fifteen a.m. A sharp cold wind blew across the empty parking lot into their faces.

Madley held the wire cutters in his hand, climbed the ladder, turning his face out of the wind, reached up to cut the alarm wires after having carefully removed the metal cover and dropped it down into Bielinski's hands. It was an unsophisticated alarm system that didn't need much attention to disable it. A prowl car came around the corner and its headlights swept the parking lot making both Bielinski and Madley turn their head directly back into the wind. Their eyes watered from the icy cold that burned them.

The prowl car went along the street passing the parking lot without slowing down. The burglars sighed but didn't hear each other make a sound. Out of service, the colored wires dangled from their posts like catgut. Madley grinned, and his gray eyes smiled at Bielinski, who guided him safely off the last rungs of the ladder. A gust of wind blew Madley's sandy blond hair into his face. He didn't wear a hat in winter.

Once they'd broken into the bar they went straight to where the safe was and began working on it. They peeled the bottom off the safe to get at the cash inside. It was almost too easy and they didn't feel they'd done anything but walk into a bank and make a withdrawal so they left the wire cutter next to the metal cover outside like a calling card far below the dangling wires of the crippled alarm.

Bielinski adjusted the scarf under the collar of his overcoat, Madley rubbed his hands together briskly to keep them warm. He didn't wear gloves in winter other than the double pair of surgical gloves he wore while he was working. They decided to do one more job just for the sake of doing it. On the way to Damen Avenue, Bielinski used a pay phone to let Joslyn know where they were going. It would take them forty-five minutes by car to get there because they were going to stop for coffee and donuts. Joslyn told him that he and Whiten would meet them at the corner of Hamilton and Greenleaf, and they'd do the job together.

Al Joslyn and Joe Whiten got there first. They waited in the car with the heat blasting because there was more wind outside now that they weren't so far from the lake, and when Joslyn challenged him on the point, Whiten just shook his head. Madley and Bielinski arrived, Madley pulling his car over to the curb on Greenleaf just behind Joslyn's car, then he switched off the engine. He carried the half-empty bag of donuts and Bielinski held two cups of coffee in his hands as they came up to Joslyn's car and the window rolled down and Whiten gratefully took the hot, doubled paper cups from Bielinski's hands.

They got in the backseat of Joslyn's car and Madley handed the bag of donuts over to Whiten in the front seat. An all-night jazz station played on the radio at low volume as the two in the front seat ate donuts and drank black coffee. No one said a word. Joslyn didn't complain that there wasn't any sugar in his coffee. Madley smoked, Bielinski checked his fingernails using a penlight. When they finished, Joslyn lit up, Whiten asked him for a cigarette, Joslyn grumbled but gave him one, and when Whiten had it going the combined smoke of three cigarettes completely filled the warm interior of the car.

They got out of the car at the same time, taking care not to draw attention to themselves at this hour by slamming the doors shut. Their destination wasn't far away, two of them were carrying tools in their pockets, Joslyn had a medium-length crowbar up his sleeve just in case they needed it.

A restaurant and bar called The Tavern House stood at the corner with a parking lot next to it and two-story houses along both sides of the street with streetlights spaced evenly along the sidewalk under a clear late-night sky. There were no lights in any of the windows of the houses in view. The four men walked under that sky with moist breath hitting the cold air and making a puff of iciness out of it as they walked almost solemnly on Damen toward The Tavern House.

The places they'd hit that night had been scouted in advance and The Tavern House was no different. They went around to the back and the employees' entrance and easily broke the latch of the screen door, then started on the lock of the wooden door that would let them into the kitchen.

According to the diagram Negron had drawn for them the safe was in the back of a clothes closet in the manager's office. There were two woolen winter coats on hangars in the closet and a pair of worn rubber boots with a band of Velcro that tightened the upper part of the boot around the leg. Whiten was pissing in the toilet, Joslyn shoved aside the two winter coats, Madley was looking through the industrial-sized refrigerator in the kitchen, Bielinski stood behind Joslyn holding a flashlight on the safe at the back of the closet.

There was a loud sigh that came from Whiten as he zipped up his trousers while heading toward the manager's office. Joslyn and Bielinski turned their head to look at him as soon as he came into the room. Madley was right behind Whiten with a small bottle of drinking water in his hand. Joslyn grunted, trying to keep himself balanced while crouching in front of the safe. Bielinski moved closer, standing just behind Joslyn with the flashlight beam passing over Joslyn's shoulder. Whiten stamped his feet which felt numb. Joslyn turned his head to look at him and frown. Madley drank the entire bottle of water in one gulp. Bielinski concentrated on the safe lit by the unwavering flashlight beam.

A car door slammed shut in the parking lot and the noise echoed in the vacant air of the winter night. The three men froze where they stood while Joslyn teetered back and forth, trying not to fall over from his crouching position in front of the safe. They all held their breath. The safe wasn't open.

They heard footsteps climb the stairs to the front door of The Tavern House which then creaked open and slammed shut. A door in the adjacent supply room opened and something like a bucket and mop were dragged out of it and down the short hallway and the bucket turned over and rolled across the dining room floor. There was a muffled curse, then footsteps came closer to the manager's office and Joslyn stood up and the four men moved away from the safe in the closet.

Bielinski stood point in front of the others with the flashlight directed at the doorway. Whiten came up alongside him, pulled a bigger flashlight out of his overcoat pocket and aimed it where Bielinski trained the beam of his light. A tall, bony old man with an exhausted face came into the blinding beams and the four members of El Manojo put the sound of the bucket and mop together with the time of night and came up with the fact that this was the night-shift cleaner making late rounds under the agreement of an almost fraudulent contract he'd signed with his employers.

The flashlights ruined what little vision was left to the old man's cataractous eyes, he couldn't see much of what was in front of him but ghostly human shapes and before he could put his closed fists up to rub the light from his eyes the shapes moved quickly away and faded toward the rear exit as Bielinski and Whiten crept backward keeping the rays on the old man's face as Joslyn and Madley preceded them out the back door. The bright aureoles surrounding the shafts of light receded before the old man's eyes like distant stars. The last thing the cleaner heard was the screen door slam shut.

48

EL PERRO LLORÓN WAS busy, a lot of customers were having their supper and half a dozen were at the bar drinking theirs while eating tortilla chips with salsa which was the standard setup at the bar. Hargrove stood at the bar between two white-collar working men with loosened neckties who'd obviously been in there a long time because they were looking down at the bar and running their index fingers through the wet circles their glasses left in front of them, their eyes focused so hard on what they were doing that Hargrove figured they'd burn holes in the wood.

He was plenty scared by the truck that almost knocked him down, he knew that a whisky might settle his nerves but wouldn't solve a thing when thirty minutes later the overall effect of that near miss came home to him, so he ordered a bottle of draught beer and lit a cigarette and moved to the far end of the bar as far away from the two drunks as he could get while still having a little space to himself.

Now there wasn't even an inclination toward getting any closer to El Manojo and what they were up to so he could earn extra money to improve the way he lived by half and buy things for Coral. He was sure of it. You can take the man out of the farm but you can't take the farm out of the man, he told himself. But the words made him choke. His eyes were open, the truck had done its job, and they'd stay open so that the only thing he let himself think about now was his future with Coral because there wasn't anything as big as investing in the future when it amounted to a future with love.

All the things he felt but didn't say came to the surface when he was with Coral. He told her about his life in a small town up north, and what he saw as the big truth of it until now, and she quickly understood not only the thoughts and emotions of Walt Hargrove, but his actions out of sight, past and present, and whatever fatigue he'd felt since he came to Lake City to work hard for an average salary and make a life for himself where he didn't have any real experience in how to make a life in a big city. He told her things he'd never told anyone else.

He finished his beer, looked at the dining room, saw an empty table and told himself the only thing he could do right now was to get some food in his stomach, then when the kitchen rush was over and he could talk to Luz he'd find out what she knew about Lily. He didn't know why he wanted to see her except that maybe he wanted to know that she was all right. He took a long time over the meal, there wasn't a hurry, and he even valued now the process of chewing his food more than he had before a truck almost flattened him.

Hargrove smoked with the second cup of coffee, staring at nothing but a thin crust of ice cobwebbed in a corner of the window facing Third Street. The streetlight outside clearly defined it against the pane of glass for him and he wondered if it took a lot of work in the same way a spider took a lot of care making a web. Screwy thoughts kept shooting through his mind, the balance up there was seriously damaged.

Chucho straightened up behind the bar, Blanca the Skeleton wiped down the empty tables, putting chairs on tabletops even though she was so skinny she didn't weigh enough to lift more than a menu, picking up whatever the customers had let fall to the floor, and when she bent over her skirt went up but there was nothing much to see but skin and bones. Snow flurries fell softly to the street. He was calm and the falling snowflakes made him thoughtful and a bit sleepy. He wished he was lying in bed with Coral.

He got up with the cigarette between his lips, went past the bar, nodded solemnly at Chucho's handsome face, sending special sympathy at a man who worked hard at his job for a minimum wage; he walked to the kitchen and pushed open the door.

What struck him first was the light, it was always the thing he noticed before anything else when he came into the kitchen of El Perro Llorón because it was awful, it was bright, and it made everything stand out looking more sick than alive, there was just too much of it, a room didn't need that much light unless maybe it was a room where doctors performed surgery or dentists pulled teeth, but he told himself maybe with cooking it called for the same thing and since the food she fixed was so good there was no point asking questions, the answers didn't matter, and then he knew he was still just plain nuts on account of the goddamned truck.

Luz del Ángel de Segura was shaking out an apron, Jorge, a fat twenty-year-old dishwasher, was scrubbing plates, rinsing them, cleaning glasses, holding them under clean water in a sink until there wasn't any dish soap on them, and he looked up from his work to give Hargrove a smile.

Luz had her back to him while she arranged bottles of spices and cooking oil and counted fresh jalapeño peppers in a bowl and surveyed drying red peppers hung by a thread behind the stove and closed a jar of black olives and looked down at the colorful pattern on the front of her dress to see there weren't any stains on it, and she turned around to find Hargrove near the wooden surface where she prepped the fresh vegetables.

"Hello, Luz."

"Hello, Walter." She wiped her hands on a towel, smiled at him, but it was a forced smile, then shook his hand.

"Walt," he said.

"Yes, Walt."

"How are you? How's Lily?"

"Everything's okay, Walt. Like always, working—and business is good, so everything's okay—and then Lily and I, we've got our health. And you, Walt, how you feeling?—you know, good health is an important thing. Maybe the only thing. With good health we can make a good living."

"I feel fine."

"How was your supper?"

"Delicious. Like always. Thank you."

"How's the job?"

"Things are fine, Luz."

This wasn't getting him anywhere, he didn't understand why she always began their conversations saying nothing and being so polite saying it, but it was a ritual and he respected rituals so he didn't try to cut it short.

"How is Lily?" he said again, as if he hadn't heard from Lily and didn't know where she was.

"Lily? Yes, she's a good girl. Studying, working hard."

"I haven't seen her lately. I was wondering—"

"You know how it is, Walt. She went off on some study program with a girlfriend—research, that's what she told me."

"Yes, I know how it is." He gave her a sincere smile. "She could be my own kid."

"Thank you, Walt."

Chucho stuck his head in, excused himself, then said, "Almost done."

"Wait for Blanca, walk with her until she gets home—she could break in half if the wind's blowing—then you go home, too. Jorge will close up with me. And Mr. Hargrove's here."

The kitchen door swung shut.

Hargrove smiled at Luz, gave her a kiss on the cheek, turned around because he was ready to leave, but she held him by the sleeve of his coat.

"As time goes on, Walt, you're going to need help," she said.

Luz looked Hargrove over carefully, head to foot, her eyes still the same intuitive brown eyes, and her voice sharp even though it was a whisper, respectful, not worrying, but about to give advice.

"What are you talking about?"

He waited for what she was going to say, urging her with a look in his eyes, begging her to hurry up and tell me what you've got to say if it's so important because there's something else I've got to do right now, even if it doesn't look like I've got anything to do with the rest of my life.

"I saw Negron come home the other night bent over and all beat up with bandages on his face and I know it was a sign for me to tell you—because you're part of El Manojo and the social club whether you like it or not—that if you don't watch your step, Walt, you're going to get in trouble."

It came out in one breath like something she'd been holding in for a long time and Hargrove hadn't known that anything like it was in her and he didn't move but stabbed his eyes at her because what she said scared him, both her knowledge and intuition and his lack of it, and because the possibility of danger frightened him.

"Let me finish in here, then we'll talk, okay?" she said, and she was busy putting the sharp knives away in a drawer that slid out from under the prep table.

"Okay," Hargrove said.

He turned around, went out through the kitchen door into the bar where he watched Chucho finish his job, retrieve his coat from the coat rack, put a hat on his head and wrap a scarf around his neck.

"Goodnight, Chucho."

"Goodnight, Mr. Hargrove."

"Walt."

"Yes, goodnight, Walt."

Hargrove took a chair off a table, flipped it right side up in his hands and set it down gently, then sat there staring at nothing and then at the room itself, waiting for Luz to finish her work in the kitchen.

The walls of the restaurant were festive, decorated with paintings and old photographs and the walls themselves expressed a rich, dark green indifference that was strangely comforting. There were two beautiful hand-stitched sombreros hanging from invisible hooks that gave him a picture of a bright blue sky with a palm-tree-lined sandy beach on the Gulf of Mexico in the Torrid Zone where there was nothing to do but sleep and dream and soak in the rays of the sun.

Hargrove was still lying on that sandy beach when Luz came into the dining room wearing a cardigan sweater over a pair of black jeans. He took down a chair for her, she sat on it.

She looked at what he'd been looking at, the sombreros, and she must've seen the same thing, the thing that went beyond the sombreros and out into fantasyland. Luz leaned forward, put her elbows on her knees, saying, "It's a haven, that place, isn't it? It's oblivious to what happens here, or outside El Perro Llorón, it's a faithful place where a kid can dream, worry and make plans while she's growing up."

"Lily?"

"Lily."

"Maybe you had somewhere like it," she said, sitting up and folding her arms across her chest. "Maybe you had somewhere far away where it was safe to dream and worry and make plans, Walt. No matter what circumstances we're born in we can always make plans for the future, even if they aren't realistic plans, because that's our right—maybe the only right we've got because most of us aren't born with any more than what God gave us stark naked with our weak flesh and a mind that's half-awake most of the time—they're our dreams, they belong to us, and we're the ones that decide to smash them up, crumple them and throw them away if we want to. Only, we don't have to do it, we don't have to throw everything away, there's some part of those dreams worth their weight in gold—and we don't have to go sniffing around stray dogs looking for them."

"I guess you know me pretty well, Luz." Hargrove leaned back in his chair, balancing himself on its on two back legs. "That's what I've been doing, and now I'm fed up with it—you're the only one besides Coral I've been able to talk to about what's really on my mind. I want to leave the dogs behind and move on—the dogs you're talking about, they're El Manojo. Maybe I don't have any-thing to do with what they're doing, maybe they're just a bunch of guys acting like jerks, and maybe for me it's only an amusement ride, a break from work, a few beers and nickel conversations, but I don't want anything they've got to offer and I don't want to keep

wasting my time with grinning idiots trying to cash in on somebody else's money. Okay, I admit it might've looked good at the
beginning, when I just got here, but now I've met a woman and
I'm in love and I'm going to pick up where I left off—like you said,
those dreams or whatever you want to call them—and keep on going and don't stop, and I'll go wherever they take me."

"That's a fine speech, Walt, with really fine words and good
intentions behind them. Now all you've got to do is make good
with those words and live like you're supposed to live in the first
place—before it's too late."

"It isn't too late, Luz."

"You don't have to tell me, Walt. I'm just handing out free advice.
It's up to you what you do with it. You don't owe me explanations.
And it's none of my business, really, except I had to say what I said
because I know you're a good man."

"Okay, so that's settled," Hargrove said. "And you're not so bad
yourself." He got up and kissed her cheek.

49

GEORGE SENDER GOT OUT of the elevator in the *Journal* building but didn't go straight to his office. Ramón López told him to hang around in front of the bank of elevators until he got there. The elevator at the far right opened its doors and López stepped out looking up and down the corridor for anybody besides Sender because he figured that he was being followed since Negron got himself beat up. It was either the link between himself and Jean, or it was Negron wise to the fact that he was in Lake City that put him on a list.

Sender waited at one of the windows for López to make his way across the corridor to him. López looked nervous with dark circles under his eyes like he hadn't slept in a day or two, and his clothes beneath a heavy winter coat were wrinkled. His hands were jammed into the pockets of his overcoat.

"You look terrible," Sender said, smiling.

"You don't look so good yourself, George, with that stupid grin on your face."

"I'm just happy to see you."

"Okay, I love you, too. Now listen. Negron got jumped in front of the social club and he took a beating and now he's sore."

"I don't blame him."

"Yeah, but he thinks I had something to do with it."

"Did you?"

"No."

"But you're still hanging on to memories of Jean Fleming—and if I know it, he knows it, because word spreads in the circles you're moving in—and if you're going to take her away from Frend you're going to have to get rid of him, and earn big money, and lots of it."

"You think I'm trying to get into bed with Jean again?"

"I don't know what I think, Ramón, but I can see how he might think it."

"That's crazy."

"It may be crazy, but Vince Negron doesn't think with his head. Remember, he killed O'Dell."

"You don't have to remind me—and that says O'Dell was skimming off profits, or he had something or knew something that could put Negron in a tight spot with Lloyd Frend."

"I told you on the phone that it makes sense. I'm not ready to put it in the *Journal,* not yet, but when I do it'll have to be tied up neat and tight so he can't wriggle out of it. That's my favor for Frend."

"Frend," López repeated.

"That's right, Frend."

López went on with what was burning him up, saying, "Now, I'm doing some work for you, out of friendship, *and* I need the cash. I don't ask you any questions and I don't want to know more than I have to know. I report what I see and what I hear. Either he makes me, or somebody working for him makes me—I'll get spotted sooner or later and it makes no difference by who—but what does matter in a big way is that right now he thinks I hired muscle to put on the pressure for money, for Jean, or I'm trying to finagle my way into his business, and he doesn't like it—"

"Okay, slow down," Sender said.

"Somebody's tailing me." He pulled on the lobe of his left ear. "What was it you said about Frend?"

"Did I say something?"

"Maybe Frend got somebody to put the screws on Negron. Beat him up."

"He wouldn't do that, and if he did, or if he was even thinking about it, he'd tell me. He's got everything to lose by keeping it to himself."

"You think he tells you everything?"

"When it come to this, yes. He's got legitimate businesses, and he's a businessman, he can't afford the publicity—if it ever got out, he'd be ruined."

"Then you're saying it might've been him?"

"No, I'm not saying that. We've got to look at what's going on closer to home—with El Manojo, or just outside of it. Look into it."

"I don't know where to begin."

It started snowing on the other side of the large windowpanes and Sender stared out between snowflakes at the gray city. From there the city looked almost empty and a bit sad, and the struggle with the weather seemed to dominate every other kind of struggle.

He reached into an inside jacket pocket and took out a leather cigar case and he put a cigar in his mouth. He didn't light it, he couldn't smoke in the corridors of the *Journal* building, a rule that didn't make any sense. The snow was falling softly past the windows. The corridor was hot, a lot warmer than it was a minute ago.

Sender wiped his forehead with a handkerchief, saw López was trembling a little—shaken up. The continued silence palled on Sender.

"Lloyd Frend is on the level," Sender said.

"Like a spiral staircase is on the level."

"I mean it, Ramón, he isn't going to do anything that would jeopardize his standing in the public eye."

"He'd put a stick in it if it helped him get ahead."

"You'll just have to take my word for it."

López sketched a table in his mind, put this new development on the table and studied it. There was something in it that suggested it was the right thing to do, even suggested some sort of profit, but the outlines of that profit weren't very clear at the moment.

"Okay, then let's look at El Manojo and its environs," he said, smiling.

"That's what I've been trying to tell you," Sender said. "But you've got to be careful. We'll find out what we want to know. And Frend stays out of it, okay?"

López turned to go away, take the elevator down to the street and pick up where he'd left off with Negron, but with the intention now of widening the circle of inquiry and observation, then he turned again to face Sender, but this time he sent him a quizzical look.

"I talked to Coral about Jean Fleming."

"Did you?" Sender indicated López ought to come closer.

"I think I have it fairly well put together," López said. "I have a deep feeling for Jean, always have had it, and I'm thinking of spending the rest of my life with her."

"That's interesting. Does she know it? What did she say? And Coral?"

"That it wouldn't work, not with a woman like her who wanted money, who'd do anything to get it and keep it."

"Coral said that?"

"Not in so many words, George—that's how I see it—but she did say I've got to listen to what Jean's got to say, give her a chance to explain who she is, and then I've got to accept it whether or not I like what I hear."

"Let's analyze your situation. Let's take the ingredients one by one and see if we can build a sensible conclusion from them," Sender said.

"All right, go ahead."

"Jean Fleming isn't stupid, she won't fall easily for whatever you're thinking you might try on her, you've got to work very hard if you're going to get her, she's beautiful and she's smart, she's got sex written all over her, I know, I've seen her out with Frend, and I wouldn't mind having her—well, that's not the point, the point is she'll see right through you, she may even turn out be a problem if you rub her the wrong way, so you've got to watch out, about Frend, I mean—then, maybe she's just too smart for you."

López frowned. "That's just one ingredient, but it's kind of you to say it. I guess I'll handle it my own way," he said.

"I want to be kind. I want to see that you do the things you really want to do, and have the things that will make you happy.

But it's a hornet's nest, you know that, don't you? Do you really want her?"

"I'll wear protective clothing."

"You don't have to answer me. Just answer yourself—honestly."

"Yeah. Thanks, George."

Outside, the storm grew worse. Snow swirled against the windows; there was a howling wind, a cold darkness in the air. The corridor lights seemed to dim. George Sender put the unlit cigar in his shirt pocket, shook Ramón López by the hand, walked with him to the bank of elevators, not having anything more to say now that he'd said what he felt about Jean Fleming.

50

LILY SEGURA CARRIED HER backpack over her shoulder and it almost dragged her down because of the weight of books in it. She hurried along the street paying close attention that her cowboy boots didn't slip on the slippery ice that had formed in the dips and cracks of the rocking cement slabs of sidewalk.

Hargrove was surprised to see her standing there across the street from him, waiting for the light to change. He didn't know she was back in Lake City, and he wasn't really sure she'd ever left. She was heading in the direction of the university.

"Lily!" he shouted.

She turned her head, waved at him, then crossed the street. When she got to his side of the street, Hargrove reached out, got his hands on her shoulders and pulled her toward him without using any force since she was doing most of the moving on her own. He tried to send a worried look but it came out as a smile because he was happy to see her.

"Where have you been? What are you doing here?—the two questions I'm asking."

"So now you're my father," she said, kissing his cheek and smiling up at him.

She put her head against his chest, he gave her shoulders a squeeze, then gently pushed her away.

"So quit kidding me, Lily. I just want to know what happened to you. No news since when you called to ask me if everything was all right—and then nothing. Let me take this," he said, helping her with the backpack. "Give your mother a break, will you?"

"What do mean?"

"Call her."

"I talked to her last night."

"So did I, but it was after you did. She didn't seem to get much out of it."

"Out of what?"

"What you had to say." He made a face as he felt the weight of the backpack. "You weren't gone long if you were gone at all. Where are you staying? You think it's safe to be back—"

"I never left. I've been staying with a friend—from university."

"Not wandering the streets at night in the cold." It gave Hargrove a lift to say it because he wasn't being too serious but was sure he'd made a point. "Who's the friend? It isn't the girl you said was living in a dorm upstate because you haven't been upstate."

"No, a boy."

"I figured that."

"From the physics department. I couldn't tell you, Walt. I thought you'd make a scene and drag me out of there."

"Well now, that's very interesting."

"I didn't know I'd do it when I left your place with the money you gave me, and I can't say it felt right, but then everything happened so fast I just went ahead with it because it seemed like a good idea at the time. He asked me so I said yes. I didn't tell him anything."

"Physics?"

"That's what he's studying. Mechanics, heat, light—and other radiation. Don't ask me what it's about."

"I wasn't going to, but it fits."

"What—that I don't understand it?"

"No, that he's your boyfriend."

Lily blushed, her face glowed and her eyes were bright as she pushed the hood of her sweatshirt off her head.

"Ah, very funny. Heat, light—I get it. You *do* like me, don't you?"

"What are you doing now?"

She looked down at her boots. "Lecture at four o'clock: Teaching in Urban and Diverse Communities." She looked up at him.

"Let's walk."

They walked carefully on the icy sidewalk.

"Listen, Walt, I'm going away for a while. I saved the money you gave me, all of it—I promise, I haven't spent a cent, so I'm going to use it. The boy, he's got a grant to work at a lab for a month downstate. I'm going with him, taking a month off."

"Upstate, downstate. We'll talk about it over a cup of coffee."

"Okay. Two blocks south, right turn on Webster Avenue, end of the block. Diner at the corner."

"Tables?"

"And chairs."

Hargrove lifted her backpack, made a face again at the dangling weight of it, took her arm with his free hand; they headed slowly south on the icy sidewalk toward Webster, no slipping, just walking west to the coffee shop on Webster a block away from the four o'clock lecture.

The diner wasn't a franchise. Hargrove recalled the sort of place he used to drink chocolate or cherry sodas and phosphates when he was a kid living up north, and the memory was good and it rushed against him. But it was nothing like this place on Webster Avenue.

Hargrove ordered a Coke with a slice of lemon, the waitress, a good-looking woman around thirty, poured a cup of percolated coffee for Lily, and five minutes later they were sharing a plate of French fries. It was three-fifteen.

The smell of fried food swam out of the kitchen through the opening in the wall between the kitchen area and the counter, climbed to the ceiling, drifted invisibly down the walls and across the countertop, covered sink, cutting board, salt-and-pepper shakers, catsup and mustard bottles, seats on single pedestals, tables and chairs, collided with the plate-glass window looking onto Webster, the glass front door, and on impact with the window and door it slid down to the linoleum floor and hung around there waiting for a customer to come in.

There weren't any ashtrays, there wasn't any smoke. There were students, and they sat in groups, three at a table, backpacks bulging

with books and notebooks, and the backpacks got in the way when
anyone got up to move around; there were large portfolios pinched
safely between dry winter boots, open textbooks, and pale faces
stared at them without any sign of life, elbows and arms and hands
occupying whatever free space there was between steaming cups of
coffee.

Hargrove set down his glass, looked at Lily with a gleam in his
eyes, and when she let the ardor of it sink in it made a grin break
on her face that gave him confidence to say what was on his mind.

"I've got something I want to say."

"Go ahead, say it."

He took a deep breath, and when he exhaled a stream of words
came out. "The short and the long of it's like this: I'm sleeping with
a woman I met in the store, she wasn't looking for appliances, she
was looking for me, and I guess I must've been looking for her, too,
without knowing I was looking for anything or anybody let alone a
woman. Well, it started something that won't stop. Now I'm thinking about the two of us, and a future—that's right—and I'd be lying
if I said I wasn't worried about it, about what I've got to do to keep
her, which is no small thing, because it takes more than ambition,
it takes something solid, something you can put in the bank. I used
to think El Manojo was the answer, that I'd make plenty of money
with them, but now I don't buy it. Not at all. The idea's gone sour."

"Everybody knows El Manojo's no good for anything but trouble. You're well out of it, Walt."

Hargrove nodded, picked up his Coke and finished it. He made
an *X* in the catsup with a cold French fry, then dropped it on the
plate. Lily watched him but didn't say anything. She didn't know
if he was through talking, if he'd said everything he had to say on
the subject of the woman he'd met, and she wondered why he was
telling her this at all and that was as far as she got with wondering
because he started up again.

"Her name's Coral. She was seeing a guy who works for the
Journal, and she left him, I guess she left him for me, I can't believe
it, he's got everything, money, important friends, connections, and I

don't have much. Maybe this is all exposition, but I just want to talk and you're a good listener. You don't mind, do you?"

Lily shook her head no, Hargrove smiled. He waved the waitress over to the table, ordered another Coke for himself, and the waitress refilled Lily's empty cup. Outside, the sky was dark, the wind was blowing but there were no snowflakes in the air and no snow on the ground.

"So, you're going to go away for a month?"

"That's right. More or less."

"We're young—okay, I'm a lot older than you are, but I know we're young, you and I, and that I'm not too smart, and I also know we're only going to live once, so you might as well do it, and these years we're living now, these are our best years—if only we realize it and remember it and keep it that way. We can't do anything to wreck it. You and your boyfriend, and me and Coral."

"Walt, this boyfriend, he's just a boy from school. Okay, I sleep with him, I really like him, but—"

"No, don't say it. Maybe this kid doesn't mean as much as somebody else will someday, but sooner or later there'll be someone who does mean more than the others, and when it happens, and it's big—it crashes into you—listen to it and trust it. Maybe it's this boy, maybe it isn't, but pay attention to what you're saying to yourself when it happens, listen to it because it really might be love, don't let your brain take over, and if it is love don't waste a lot of time trying to figure it out."

"It's like you're way out there in the cosmos, Walt, and it's a fine cosmos, with no other inhabitants but you and the woman you love—the two of you floating around out there. You can talk about yourself, but don't talk about me."

"Maybe I *am* floating around out there. Didn't you ever feel so definite about something that you knew as sure as you were alive that nothing could make you change your mind? Absolutely nothing."

"I haven't grown up that much, not yet."

"You will, and it'll happen before you know what's hit you. Well, I've got my mind made up—no, that's not the way to put it. It's got nothing to do with making up my mind." It was like he was talking to himself.

He drank from his glass of Coke, smiled at her, and she put her hand on his arm. He took another deep breath, leaned forward.

"Okay, this is how I figure it. Parts of love are like bits of dreams, and all those little dreams add up and they amount to something that counts for less than what we do with them—but they're a necessity, those dreams. And when they're thrown together with the rest of what we call life, that's reality—and real love. And then what we've really got is solid ground, and that's what I feel like I'm standing on when I'm with Coral."

"That's very pretty, Walt. But there's no solid ground that has permanence." Lily picked up the coffee cup, but didn't drink from it. "Solid ground gives way—you or I, we could disappear tomorrow. And so could she. Maybe it takes a long time, maybe not, but sooner or later it gives way and something else takes its place, and that's our solid ground until the next thing comes along to shake it up."

"'You keep out of my dream,'" he said, then burst out laughing. "'It ain't no nightmare.'"

She laughed, saying, "I've read that, too," then took a couple of swallows of coffee, looked at her watch, got up from the table and reached down to haul her backpack up from the floor. "I've got to go, Walt, I'm going to be late." She leaned forward and kissed him on the cheek. "Just take care of yourself. And give me a call to let me know how things are going—you won't see me until I'm back in town."

"'Love is all a matter of timing—it's no good meeting the right person too soon or too late.'"

"I've heard that, too."

Walt Hargrove ordered a cup of coffee, drank the coffee slowly while looking out the window at the night-lit winter, waiting for the waitress to bring him his check, and the coffee felt good going down, burning his lips and his throat, because it warmed him and gave him the right body temperature and maybe it was close to the scalding he felt when it came to Coral Rasmussen.

Lost in the hollow time of sleeplessness, Ramón López shifted his position behind the wheel of his car, waiting for Hargrove to leave the diner. It felt like he hadn't slept in three days when in reality it was only a single night that had gone by without shutting his eyes. He looked at the digital clock in the dashboard and it told him it was almost five in the evening. And I could be in bed right now and asleep in five minutes and stay that way for twelve hours, he told himself. He rubbed the fatigue from his eyes, lit another cigarette, blew smoke out through the window opened an inch.

Hargrove went on drinking his coffee. His waitress stood at another table, wiping it down after the customers had gone. When he noticed he was staring at her, he turned his head away and gave the room a once-over until he caught sight of waitress number two, no more than twenty-one years old, who was looking at her fingernails while at the end of a counter where clean glasses and plates were stacked and standing in rows. The diner was almost empty.

López left his car parked on Webster Avenue, crossed in the middle of the street through moderate traffic, threw the cigarette into the gutter before he got to the sidewalk, saw it spark as it hit the edge of the gutter before it went out, swung the diner door open, spotted Hargrove sitting at a table hunched over a cup of coffee.

He went to the chair opposite Hargrove and without a word or introduction sat down as if Hargrove had been expecting him, but Hargrove didn't look up, just held the cup in his hands, staring at nothing, then lifted his eyes from nowhere and focused them on Ramón López.

"Who are you?"

"I might be a friend, if you'll let me," López said.

The waitress came up with a damp towel in her hand. "Can I get you something?" She used her free hand to shove her auburn hair out of her face.

"What do you have in mind?" López winked at her. "Get me a cup of coffee, will you?"

She'd started out as a waitress at the age of nineteen, and because she'd worked regular shifts for a lot of years and many of them at night she'd heard a thousand customers say the same thing a thousand times, it didn't bother her, she didn't pretend she didn't like it, depending on who it came from, so she just nodded and smiled and went for the coffee pot, thinking of the night two days ago when she'd taken a guy home after her shift and fucked him until he couldn't stand up without having to lean against a piece of furniture. A grin spread across her pretty face.

She poured coffee into the cup she'd set in front of the man with naturally brown skin, lines around the eyes and a handsome face for somebody his age which she figured must've been past forty and more like fifty. The two men didn't look at her as she walked away from the table because they were busy talking.

"So what I'm trying to say without telling you more than you've got to know or that I want to tell you is that I think you can help me get closer to what's going on with Vince Negron and El Manojo," López explained, leaning forward with his elbows on the table, his hands folded under his chin.

"You've got the wrong guy."

"I don't think so. I've been doing some checking up, and I figure you're the right guy," López said. "If you'll cooperate."

"Don't count on it."

"There's money in it for you.

"I can't do it."

"You mean you won't."

"That's right."

"Stubborn, aren't you?"

"No, smart. There's nothing in it for me but trouble or for anybody else who'd be dumb enough to stick their nose into Negron's business—more than broken bones, maybe a permanently damaged face, maybe worse."

Hargrove looked for the waitress, waved her to the table, got up, handed her a few bills along with the check. "Keep the change," he said, then looking at López, "Coffee's on me."

López watched Hargrove leave the diner, walk past the windows with his collar up, a scarf wrapped around his neck; his hands were buried in the pockets of his winter overcoat. López looked at his watch. George Sender expected a call from him by seven o'clock. It was five-ten.

Hargrove waited for the bus at the corner of Webster and Magnolia, shifted from one leg to the other and stamped his feet as gusts of wind picking up speed shot down the length of the avenue through black trees standing naked at evenly spaced intervals near the sidewalk and made razor cuts in his face and burned his eyes with cold.

A man arrived to wait at the bus stop and Hargrove turned his head but didn't get a look at his face through the tears the biting wind put in his eyes; there wasn't any light nearby to illuminate anything and Hargrove couldn't be bothered with the effort to look him over; he was freezing. The bus pulled up a few minutes later, the brakes hissed and sighed and the chassis tipped downward to the right as he climbed aboard with the other man just behind him.

He took a seat, the bus jerked forward on Webster, and then Hargrove felt a hand gently grip his upper arm forcing him to turn around and since the heat in the bus dried the tears in his eyes he saw Al Joslyn sitting behind him. Joslyn got up and stood next to Hargrove, who looked up at him and felt something like a heavily muscled dwarf standing on his shoulder with a raised hammer that went along with the look in Joslyn's eyes and wouldn't have been there otherwise and it was a definite threat because there was something in the fact that here was Joslyn, the member of El Manojo closest to Vince Negron.

"What a coincidence. Sure is cold, isn't it?"

"Freezing. What are you doing here?" Hargrove didn't want his voice to sound nervous, but his throat was dry and the words came out like he had laryngitis.

"I came to see you."

"To see me?"

"That's right."

"How did you know I'd be here?"

"I've been following you, Walt."

"Following me, why?"

"Vince asked me to," he said.

It didn't seem like he was telling the truth. Hargrove didn't say anything.

"How's that for a good reason?"

The bus made a sharp turn at a corner, Joslyn leaned with it and his overcoat swung out brushing against Hargrove's left arm and Hargrove felt something heavy in the overcoat pocket bump against him and then the coat swung away from Hargrove as Joslyn straightened up and the bus completed the turn.

Hargrove stood up in front of Joslyn, they faced each other and moved toward each other and Hargrove said, "Why would Vince want you to follow me?"

"Big city, isn't it, Walt?"

"Not big enough, I guess."

"That's right. Not big enough to put anything over on Vince Negron—without him finding out about it."

"I don't follow you."

"You will. Let's get off here."

"What for?"

The bus slowed to a stop, the brakes hissed and sighed, Joslyn took hold of Hargrove's coat sleeve and pulled him along as he climbed down out of the bus into the icy winter night where thick snowflakes descended gently in a steady, uninterrupted, vertical fall past high regular windows in a row of houses in front of them.

51

GRIFFITH EVANS WIPED THE soles of his rubber boots on the mat in front of Sender's front door waiting for Sender to open it and let him in out of the hallway. Sender opened the door, stood aside and Evans took off his camel-hair coat and handed it to him as he looked around for a place to leave his boots. Evans sat down in a chair near the door to take them off, Sender put them behind the door in the warm kitchen to dry.

The headache that had chased Evans all day was gone now. The fresh air had taken care of it and he was grateful for that after having spent the entire day at his desk surrounded by newspapers, slips of paper with notes scribbled on them, red-penciled pages, and a small television chattering away at him while noise from clamoring journalists burned holes in his head with no break in sight; he'd even sent his secretary out to get him a sandwich because of the workload he'd been carrying for twenty-four hours.

Evans threw himself into the welcoming arms of an over-stuffed armchair, ignoring Sender who poured him a scotch on the rocks; Evans exhaled what he had in his lungs, breathed in deeply, rubbed his ruddy face with big hands and something clicked in his mind and all at once he knew where he was and what he was going to say.

Evans turned the glass in his hand using a mild movement of his wrist, the scotch and ice rolled around making a tinkling sound, Sender settled himself against the cushions of the sofa with a short, neat bourbon.

"You look tired, Griff."

"That's an understatement. I'm fucking exhausted, if you want to know the truth. So, give me the lineup. Who's playing what position. Start from the top. But for the sake of keeping our sources anonymous it better be a very small team you've put together."

"How long have I been doing this kind of thing?"

"I know, I know—just give me the details, George."

"There isn't any team. I'm on top, and whatever I know goes straight to you. I won't write anything down until you've heard it first. Ramón López, he's doing all the legwork. He reports directly to me. He's got a guy on the fringe of El Manojo, his name is Walt Hargrove. Maybe I shouldn't say he's got him. Nobody's got anybody unless they're on the payroll. He just made contact, and Hargrove's thinking it over, but I won't bet that he's going to do it. Too risky—and Hargrove's got sense."

"Where does that leave us if this man Hargrove doesn't join the club?"

"It leaves us with Frend. Listen, this is going to take more time than I figured. Lloyd Frend can do anything and everything if he wants to—but it'll be under wraps and it will take time. He's got to keep a blind between the business that's made him a success and the successful business he's got today. Confidentiality is the rule with him, he's got more than a front to look after."

"The way he's worked the last ten years they aren't fronts anymore. He ought to run for mayor," Evans said, quietly laughing.

A healthy, warm color flushed their faces as they drank.

"When will you find out about Hargrove?"

"López gave him a couple of days to think it over."

"In the meantime, write twelve hundred words on O'Dell as an employee, from the angle that banks only look out for themselves, and how he was just like the bank that employed him except he gave first-rate services to crooks—don't spread it on thick, just thin enough to make it stick. Ask questions on behalf of the readers, questions they've been asking themselves about institutions in general—banks, sub-prime mortgages, and savings and loans, in particular. Talk about family farms, and large-scale, industrialized, vertically integrated food production—you know, agribusiness, and Archer Daniels Midland and Cargill, with revenues of $62.9 billion in 2004—corporate farming versus family farms, because it's the family farm that's been taking it up the ass for a while now."

"Is that all? And in twelve hundred words?"

"Don't be sarcastic, George."

"I'm worn out, too, Griff."

"You've got a steady job, don't you?"

"Don't be funny. You want another drink?"

"No, I've got to get some sleep."

He got up and found his coat and put himself into it and went to the kitchen and sat down in a straight back chair and pulled his rubber boots over his polished, leather-soled shoes.

"Good-night, George," he said, then he turned the doorknob and let himself out.

Sender took a cigar out of the humidor, snipped the end of it, sat down against the cushions of the sofa and slowly put the flame under the end as he turned it round and round. He smoked, looked at the *Journal*, read an article about an African despot who claimed he could walk a tightrope like a professional circus performer with his eyes blindfolded while filling out daily reports on his ministers. He laughed, folded the paper and tossed it on the coffee table.

Sender thought about people and wondered why they weren't content to be just one thing, a dictator ought to be a dictator and say so, not a dictator who thinks he's also a fucking circus performer, just do one thing well, it's enough even if you're a tyrant—no, everybody nowadays wants to be two things, big skills, variety, not counting day-job living. The civilized world's getting too civilized for me.

He exhaled a cloud of blue smoke, watched it float in front of him, grumbling to himself, and as his eyes stayed with the smoke floating away up toward the ceiling his thoughts went with it to a series of nights he'd spent with Coral and how they'd made love for hours, they were stuck together not just because it was hot and humid and the middle of August but because nothing could separate them, but now it gave him a sick feeling because he'd known then that there was no guarantee she'd love him forever.

Something of a drastic nature had happened, even if it was less significant now, the thing had already been accomplished, it was over and everything had changed. Why it had happened to him Sender couldn't say, so he yawned, he was tired, and when he was tired he was obsessed with things he couldn't do anything about; he set the cigar down in an ashtray. He didn't want to write what Griff Evans told him to write, he wanted to go to sleep. And then he realized what he wanted was to see Coral again.

He finished writing what satisfied him on the topic of O'Dell and current banking practices in general in more than twelve hundred words and figured it represented what Evans wanted to read; he looked at the clock that said it was almost three in the morning and switched off the light and started taking his clothes off as he walked to the bedroom to get into bed and go to sleep, but once he was tucked under the covers his mind pulled him up into unwanted consciousness, his brain wasn't as tired as he was physically, and part of his mind started up again on the subject of Coral and the ache he felt now that was located below his heart and stomach and was centered between his legs.

At five-fifteen he was sitting at the kitchen table staring at his hands and waiting for the morning edition of the *Journal* to arrive at his front door so he'd have something to do besides listening to himself harping on about the fact that he was alone and at his age he wasn't going to find another woman who'd be interested in him the way Coral had been interested in him, and that before he knew it he'd be dead and buried without having loved anyone ever again. There wasn't any music accompanying him as he went down that road of misery but he distinctly heard the ticking clock on the wall.

After breakfast the acute lack of a good night's sleep accompanied by acid thoughts began to take their toll and his eyes shut involuntarily while he was washing the dishes. He spent a long time under a hot shower and had another cup of strong coffee to put the finishing touches on giving his body one jolt after another. He read through his copy before calling the courier who'd hand it to Evans at the *Journal*, lit a cigar, paced in front of the large windows overlooking the heavy morning traffic on Prospect Avenue and the frozen edge of the lake.

He looked at the lake and was looking as far across it as he could when he realized he wasn't going to call Coral Rasmussen. What was done was done. Sender congratulated Sender. He'd got over the difficult period of shuttling between the real and the imagined. He sat at his desk, stared blankly at two photographs by Weegee, hanging on the wall opposite, *Simply Add Boiling Water*, 1937 and *Sonata in G-Strings*, c.1950, when the phone rang.

52

THE CONVERSATION HARGROVE HAD with Al Joslyn wasn't the sort of talk Hargrove wanted to have twice in his life. He lay half in a pool of filthy water surrounded by dirty brown slush with his left shoulder propped against a brick wall in the exact position Joslyn left him after beating him up in an alley not far from where the bus had let them off.

Blood ran from a corner of his mouth and the source of it was his torn gums above a cracked molar. He felt dampness and a chill on his forehead where he'd scrapped it against the wall. His head throbbed from blows Joslyn had given him, his kidney ached dully from the punches he'd got when Joslyn shoved his face against the brick wall and started in on it to finish him. He bent forward and spit into the dark alley, wiped his mouth with the sleeve of his coat, saw his breath shoot out of his mouth in shallow puffs of frosty air.

Through the buzzing in his head he kept hearing Joslyn's voice warning him off any further contact with Ramón López. Whatever strength he had left he used to edge his way up the wall to a standing position, but his knees buckled and he slipped back down into the dirty pool of water and stayed there swaybacked on all fours with his palms flat on the uneven surface of the alley, his neck stretched forward and his head bent down like a dog.

Lloyd Frend told Jean Fleming she'd better hurry up because if she didn't they'd be late for supper and then for the theater and since they were guests of the mayor of Lake City, he'd have her killed and her body thrown into the river if she wasn't ready in five minutes. Within those five minutes he received a call from George Sender telling him that things with Vince Negron had got murky to the point of being dangerous.

When they left the townhouse in the city ten minutes later and got into the back seat of his chauffeur-driven Lincoln, Lloyd Frend was in a very bad mood and it wasn't just because they were late for supper. He didn't look at Jean's lazy, oval face, reddish hair or long legs that were shown off in a cobalt-blue dress with a slit that went almost all the way up to her hip. Her fur coat lay open across the front of her dress and the close-fitting fabric pressed tight against her small breasts. Her nipples were hard from the cold.

He didn't look at her and he didn't say a word because he was busy thinking about what Sender had told him over the phone. Frend sat wrapped in his black cashmere overcoat wearing dinner clothes with a bow tie Jean had tied for him at the collar of a white dress shirt. It was freezing outside but he rolled the window down to feel the sharp wind on his face.

Frend brought a clenched fist to his open mouth, trying to detour the shout that was climbing up his throat. The shout got past the knuckles pressed hard against his teeth, and it wasn't a shout that came out but a low groan with enough force behind it despite the presence of the fist to sound like an animal in pain. Jean turned her head to look at him.

"Lloyd, what is it?"

He rolled the window up, adjusted the scarf around his neck, kept looking straight ahead at the road coming toward them and passing beneath the car under the heavy wheels of the Lincoln that stabbed dully at the night and cut through layers of snow and slush sending watery and brittle tufts of snow and splinters of ice at the curb. He built a smile and tried to hold it as he turned toward Jean who still had her face close enough to his own face to feel her breath on his skin.

"Nothing, nothing at all. It's business, and I've told you a thousand times that whatever's got to do with business hasn't got anything to do with you and you wouldn't want to know and you'd be sorry if you *did* know what it was all about."

"You don't need to be so practical about it."

"You don't think so, do you? Well, we live in a practical world, Jean. And it's necessary that we protect ourselves if we wish to be secure."

"Secure against what?"

"Certain situations." He rolled down the window again. "Look, I provide you with whatever you want, and you've got to take it just like that because you've got what you want, so do I, and its on account of the fact that I'm careful—and generous. And above all, I must insist on guarantees."

"What kind of guarantees?"

"There are various forms. Some are on paper, but that doesn't concern us, some are in the shape of trust, between partners in business and friends, enforced by durable relationships, commitment, and then there are those in the matters of life and love, which exist with many of the same rules of play as the rest of them. Our guarantees are under the heading of the latter—life and love."

"That's not very romantic."

"You want to be with me. You agree fully that we're suited for each other. Well then, it's only reasonable that we have guarantees, and security."

"Don't put it that way."

"That's the only way it can be put."

The chauffeur pulled up to a stop light in heavy traffic. Sharp gusts of wind shoved the Lincoln which rocked slightly on its chassis. Then there was a loud thud and the sound of cracking glass behind them as the rear window was shattered by the faultless impact of something heavy swung hard and fast which didn't send a single splinter into the car itself.

Lloyd Frend turned around in time to see a baseball bat in the hands of a man with a ski mask over his face rise up above the rear window, crash down again, the crunch of glass buckling but not breaking loose, and he ducked his head, instinctively pulled Jean toward him and down into his lap, heard her fingernails tear into the leather upholstery, then felt them grip his arm like claws going up inside the sleeve of his coat just before he shouted at the driver to get the hell out of the intersection.

Lloyd Frend and Jean Fleming were treated in the emergency room of the same hospital where Frend had donated money for a kidney dialysis machine. There wasn't much to be done except patch up a long and fairly deep cut on Frend's arm where Jean had scratched him with her fingernails, and examine a bruise on Jean's forehead from lurching forward and striking it on the armrest. The impact had raised a lump the size of a golf ball. The chauffeur waited in the damaged Lincoln with the engine running at the emergency entrance of University Hospital.

What the emergency room doctor couldn't do anything about was the anger welling up in Frend which raised his blood pressure and made him grit his teeth forming a twisted smile on a generous mouth.

Frend asked himself whether there was anything he could do about it. There was nothing he could do alone. Not this time, not at his age and in the position he'd made for himself in Lake City. And violence was something he had to stay away from. That part of the solution would be up to somebody else. If he were going to accomplish anything at all he'd have to play it behind a curtain, quietly collect the facts and add up the facts and do his planning in whispers, and he was going to need help, another hand, someone who could fill in the blanks. And there were considerable blanks, there were question marks that couldn't be answered by what he knew.

Obviously, there was a leak of sorts in his own organization, his comings and goings were known by someone close to him, an adversary within the ranks of the men and women who worked for him in one of the branches of legitimate business he'd built up over a period of years.

He looked at the wash of Betadine painted the length of the scratch on his arm, the torn shirt and dinner jacket carefully draped over the back of a chair, and then at the doctor covering the raw groove in his arm, bandaging the mark Jean made when she'd got so scared by the baseball bat striking the rear window that she'd torn into his arm with her fingernails and wouldn't let go in a desperate effort to save herself from the torrent of blows meant to destroy her along with him. Jean held an icepack against the bump on her forehead.

On the way back to the townhouse they didn't say anything, Frend stared out the window, Jean had pressed herself against him, with her legs curled up beneath her not paying attention to the way it exposed her thighs with goose flesh marking the smooth skin of her legs.

The chauffeur let them off at the building's entrance and then took the Lincoln around the corner and down the ramp into the parking garage. Frend stood for a moment inside the lobby with Jean leaning into him, bracing herself against him, pulling the warmth of him into her. While they rode the elevator he looked at her standing with her back against the banister in front of the mirrored elevator wall, she looked tired and he smiled at her. The smile grew and became a grin, as if he was amused at something.

Hargrove, with a damp towel over his head, tried to stand still but shifted uncomfortably as Coral applied another cold compress to the bruise on the skin where Al Joslyn had repeatedly punched him in the kidney. She was afraid he was bleeding internally. He threw the damp towel into the sink, moaned, started to turn around when Coral told him to stop squirming and stand still she wasn't finished and if he didn't listen to her he'd die right there on the spot and she'd leave him to it.

Hargrove laughed because he loved her and when she talked to him like that it made his cock hard but the muscles that tensed and jerked on account of the laugh brought a dull aching pain with it and threw a frown across his face that looked disapprovingly back at him from the mirror above the sink.

He leaned forward, opened his mouth and examined the cracked molar in the reflection, prodding the tooth with his index finger.

"Fuck Al Joslyn! I don't have the money for a dentist," he said, with his finger in his mouth.

"Insurance," Coral said. "You've got insurance."

"I don't think it's covered."

"Read the policy, Walt. If it isn't covered, then you can get pissed off."

Hargrove took his finger out of his mouth, kept looking at himself in the mirror, felt the presence of her love larger than life and slowly the frown became a smile while his tongue played over the sharp edge of the broken tooth.

He straightened up and began to turn around, Coral had him by the waist with one hand, a finger hooked in a belt loop at the waistband of his loosened trousers, and she let him turn. She was crouched before him with the compress in the other hand and when he was completely turned around and leaning with his back against the sink looking down at her she looked up at him with tears in her eyes.

"Okay, turn off the waterworks—I'll live."

"I know you'll live, you dumb motherfucker." She tried to make it sound harsh but it came out like an admission of love.

He bent down, kissed her on the mouth. "Ouch, shit, fuck, piss—that hurts!"

"What hurts?"

"My head, mouth, kidney, and my self-respect. I didn't get in more than a single punch."

He stood up straight and gently put the palm of his hand flat against the bruise on his lower back.

"You'll have to get out of these filthy clothes—go take a shower, Walt."

With the back of her hand she wiped away the tears, and with urgent need for more she dropped the compress on the bathroom floor and unbuttoned his trousers. He shut his eyes, he didn't make a move to help her.

He was the victim of Joslyn's violence and it stimulated him now with Coral's fingers playing at the waistband of his boxer shorts, bringing them down slowly, brushing the lower part of his belly, holding his cock and stroking it and making it really hard to the point where he thought the taut skin wouldn't be able to keep the swelling blood vessels from bursting through the barrier of skin before she had time to put it in her mouth.

Her tongue curled along the underside of it and licked the length and bit the tip and the bite made him want more and she gave him more because she loved him, and so her mouth and throat took his cock in deeper and out it came again, and with his eyes open he saw the saliva covering his cock and dripping from her chin and her mouth was a warm receptacle waiting for the conclusion of this exaggerated desire that was the only positive thing to come out of the beating Al Joslyn had given him. She swallowed every drop of what he spilled in her mouth, he kissed her warmly on the lips, tasting his come.

53

GEORGE SENDER DIDN'T EXPECT to hear Coral's voice on the other end of the line when he put the receiver to his ear but when he did hear her voice it flowed over him like the hot water of a bath and the sensation gave him permission to shut his eyes for an instant.

"I know it's not the right thing asking you to help me with a problem concerning Walt Hargrove since I left you for him and it wasn't very long ago and you'd be more than justified in having a resentment a mile long just hearing me mention his name, but I really don't know who to talk to about a problem involving the sort of people I know you're familiar with and among whom you've got any number of contacts that might sort it out if you asked them— you being a newspaperman, who's covered all sorts of stories, fishy incidents, crimes."

She doesn't even breathe when she's wound up, he told himself, conscious of his own breathing, not asking himself why he felt the sort of excitement he was feeling hearing her voice because somewhere down deep he knew the answer was that he wasn't through with Coral Rasmussen.

"Wake up. You know who you're talking to, don't you—it's me," he said.

"Of course I know who I'm talking to, George. I've got to talk, and I've got to tell you and make you see because I want it to be as clear to you as it is to me. My mind is very clear now. I wish you could take a look at my brain right now and see what's taking place in there."

"I don't want to see what's taking place in there, Coral. I can hear it."

"Will you listen—just listen to me?"

"Okay, why don't you come over here? We can talk here and it'll be a lot easier than explaining something over the phone when it sounds like what you've got to tell me is as urgent and complicated as all that."

"Before it's too late, George. Walt just went to work, or what's left of him just went out the door to go to work."

"I'll be here, waiting for you."

"A half hour?"

"Yes, a half hour."

"Goodbye, George."

Sender didn't hang up right away, he just sat with the phone in his hand breathing hard and wishing he wasn't breathing at all and then he held his breath until he gasped for air. He got up, went to look out the windows again at the lake and the grayish-white morning sky, yawned.

Vince Negron was just getting out of bed when a knock at the door made him turn quickly around to answer it. His face wasn't covered with bandages but there was a cut on his forehead and a couple of bruises and a Band-Aid over the bridge of his nose and a black eye and he stared out of the good right eye at Ramón López standing in the doorway.

"I didn't have anything to do with it, Negron."

"You going to stand there looking like a sheep or have you got the balls to come in here and talk to me."

"I'm not coming in, I just wanted you to know I didn't have anything to do with whoever it was that jumped you the other day—and beat the shit out of you. Clear?"

"As crystal, pal."

"You believe me?"

"Why shouldn't I?"

"You don't sound convinced."

"Maybe I am, maybe I'm not—what's it to you?"

"I like things to be on the up-and-up and I don't like taking credit for something I didn't do. If I'd wanted to give you a personal message I'd have done it myself." López cracked the knuckles on his right hand, sent Negron an unpleasant smile.

"So, that's settled, is it?"

"As far as I'm concerned—we're done here."

"Watch your step going down those stairs on your way out."

Negron slammed the door shut in López's face.

Lloyd Frend woke up after a fitful night's sleep with Jean snuggled up against him beneath the goose-down bedcover. The gray morning shone through the long, narrow windows and threw widening swaths of cold gray light across the parquet floor toward the foot of the bed.

He didn't want to get out of bed today, he felt the fragile condition of his body and the jangled nerves and the worry in his mind dominate the usual desire to get himself going as soon as he'd had a cup of coffee. Everything seemed to be fire without visible flame as he faced the fact that he hadn't faced an attack of violence head-on like the aggression last night in more than a decade and wasn't sure he still knew how to handle it. He looked at Jean, who made whimpering sounds in her sleep. He got up, stood beside the bed, wearing his pajama trousers.

He was still looking at her when she rolled over, opened her eyes, and focused them first on the room and the gray light behind him, and then aimed them at his face, taking in the tender expression he held there for her.

Her eyes started talking and he made himself concentrate so he'd know what it was they were saying and what he heard was something on the order of you've got to protect me from what happened last night, and all the threatening things like it, and you've got to promise me, because there's an uncanny comfort I've got when I know you're willing to and capable of protecting me, and since I know you love me I know you'll do it, and then I'll love you even more for keeping me from harm.

Frend listened to what her eyes told him, went to her and took her in his arms, held her gently yet possessively, which is what he thought she wanted him to do. Jean pushed herself against him and they were both calm and clear-minded and felt they'd protect each other as long as they were together, and they knew that this moment was like an eternity of comfort and peace.

Bielinski put his arm around Joslyn's shoulders as they walked into the drugstore laughing. While the door was open the cold winter wind followed them inside. Whiten and Madley were waiting a half block away in an old four-door Pontiac, with the engine switched off, that Joe Whiten had stolen earlier in the morning.

Joslyn went up to the pharmacist and asked for a box of condoms and Bielinski was busy looking at the selection of toothbrushes. The pharmacist went around the counter and showed Joslyn to the display of condoms on a lower shelf where an array of water-soluble lubricants were lined up next to them. It was a small family-owned drugstore on a side street just off South Jefferson. The pharmacist in training who worked there part time hadn't shown up yet.

Joslyn stuck a long barreled revolver into the pharmacist's ribs when the pharmacist bent down to show him the brands he carried and told him to stand up slowly and get the Schedule II drugs, in particular the prescription opiates, out of all the locked drawers in the drugstore and fill a plastic bag with them. Bielinski stood in front of the entrance looking out at the street. The pharmacist went behind the counter directly to a low metal cabinet with Joslyn right behind him.

When the pharmacist unlocked two drawers, opened them and reached in with both hands to gather the boxes of Schedule II drugs, Joslyn struck him twice on the back of the head with the butt of his gun and knocked him out. The pharmacist's glasses fell off his face when he hit the floor. Joslyn kicked them away. He got two medium-sized paper bags from under the counter and went back to the open drawers and filled the bags with opiates until they couldn't hold any more than what was in them without bursting. He stepped intentionally on the pair of glasses, cracking the lenses, as he went to the drugstore entrance and gave Bielinski one of the two paper bags to carry. The winter wind blew into the drugstore as the door swung open and shut.

Sender let Coral in and took her fur-lined coat and hat and hung them in the closet and led her to the living room and sat her down in an armchair. He went on automatic pilot to the kitchen and on automatic pilot he poured two cups of strong coffee, milk and sugar in one of them, and like the moving mechanical device in imitation of a human being that he was at this moment, he marched right back into the living room and handed her a cup of sweetened coffee with milk.

Coral was crying. She was very involved in the emotion of it and so she didn't say anything when she took the cup from his hands and held it in front of her nose letting the steam and comforting odor of coffee drift upward into her nostrils which flared as tears streamed down her cheeks. Sender knew from experience that she couldn't hold out much longer before the necessity of putting it in words took hold and she'd tell him what was going on. He left the living room and came back with a box of Kleenex.

She set the coffee cup down, blew her nose with a couple of tissues, then said, "He got beat up in an alley last night by some hoodlum connected to a guy named Vince Negron—and I'd be surprised if you didn't know him or at least heard of him since you know everybody in Lake City."

"Why do you think it's got anything to do with Vince Negron?"

"Walt told me he knew the guy who knocked him down and beat him up and that the guy works with Negron as part of an enterprise called El Manojo that meets at the Seventeenth Street Social Club."

"What's your Walter Hargrove got to do with El Manojo?"

"Nothing. He used to play cards with them once in a while until they left El Perro Llorón for Meyering Boulevard at Seventeenth Street."

"Is he in bad shape?"

"I wouldn't call it good shape, George, but he's walking and talking and so pissed off that I'm afraid he'll get into even more trouble. I'm asking you—begging you for the sake of what we meant to each other—to help me keep him out of danger."

"I'll see what I can do—leave it to me."

"I can't drink this," she said, indicating the coffee. "It's burning a hole in my stomach and my stomach's empty and it's already on fire."

"I'll make you breakfast."

54

VINCE NEGRON WAS DRESSED and ready to go out but decided instead to have a drink at El Perro Llorón to chase the chill of the winter night out of his body. He'd slept well for the first time in several days and was feeling optimistic and wanted a woman, but the poorly sealed windows in his room interrupted that train of thought and let enough cold air in to remind him of the inhospitable weather waiting for him outside. He peeked through the curtains at wind-blown flakes of snow falling diagonally to the street.

In a taxi on the way to the Seventeenth Street Social Club he felt the warmth in his veins of two shots of good tequila that followed a cold beer accompanying a hot meal of one of Luz del Ángel de Segura's specialties from Veracruz which started with smoke-dried jalapeños, *chipotles,* stuffed with wild mushrooms, and from the Totonaca region, soapy black beans with chayotes, tomatoes, and jalapeños, thickened with ground pumpkins seeds, *frijoles en achulchut,* and then a plate of chicken mole with guajillos. He was bursting with food and nodding off in the taxi as they turned past a narrow part of the frozen river at the corner of Meyering Boulevard and Seventeenth Street when he saw a Pontiac parked halfway on the sidewalk in front of the Meyering Building and told the driver to pull over.

He paid the driver, pulled the collar of his overcoat up and put his palm down flat on the hood of the Pontiac. It was still warm. He looked up and down the deserted street, felt the key ring in his coat pocket. He kicked at the snowdrift shoveled out of the street and up against the curb sending feathery ice crystals into the air, then crossed the street.

It wasn't the first time he'd seen them high, but it was going from bad to worse each time they ripped off a pharmacy and he'd told them before in no uncertain words that he wouldn't stand for any behavior that jeopardized the growth and prosperity of El Manojo, but these particular Schedule II drugs meant more to them than anything he had to say.

If he thought he'd been on the nod in the taxi after a couple of shots of tequila, it was nothing compared to Madley who sat daydreaming with his eyes shut in the worn leather chair at the table in the anteroom in front of scribbled nonsense he called poetry on the pad of blue-lined yellow paper, Joslyn stretched out on the makeshift bed in a corner of the back room on wheels staring through sunglasses at the Oriel Pendant lamp hanging from the ceiling by a long white cord, and Bielinski seated on the long leather sofa with a cigarette burnt down to the filter between two fingers of the same hand that held a ceramic cup half filled with bourbon. One of the folding card tables leaned against the wall opposite the windows facing the alleyway between Seventeenth and Eighteenth.

Negron didn't say anything, turned around, went back into the anteroom and hung his coat in the cloak-room. Madley looked up from his poem, couldn't shape any words, then a rasping deep sound came out of his mouth and he was saying something with the low, gravelly voice narcotics always gave him.

"Where you been, Vince? We've been expecting you."

"What's that?"

"What's what?"

"I can't really understand what you're saying—your voice sounds funny."

"Funny? How?"

"Not laughing funny, Paul. Peculiar."

Madley knew he was in trouble as soon as he heard Negron use his first name, something Negron did only when he was going to shout at him and berate him for some blunder he'd made which breached the code of El Manojo.

"You goddamned fucking idiot! You motherfucker! Your brain's turning to mush. You, and the rest of them. Where's Whiten?"

"Gone out. Went on an errand."

Negron made a fist and showed it to Madley.

"You see this?" he said.

"You don't have to wave that around in front of me."

"There's something else I want you to see. And you better see it clear. I don't want any arguments from you. Just follow instructions. Don't think for yourself. You aren't capable of thinking for yourself. Understand?"

"Listen, Vince—"

"Don't *listen Vince* me. How do you expect to get anywhere if you keep shoveling pills down your throat? And you aren't some motherfucking poet scratching faggot words on a goddamned piece of paper. Where do you think your money's coming from? For Christ's sake! Focus your mind on one thing, and one thing only—what I've got to say to you is all you've got to worry about."

"Jesus, Vince."

"Okay, now go out and get the latest edition, Madley—and bring it back to me in one piece."

"All right, Vince."

Madley dropped the pen on the table, got up and went to the cloak-room, put his coat on, wrapped a scarf around his neck, pulled a watch cap down over his head and went out the door into the foyer without looking back. The street door that opened onto Meyering Boulevard slammed shut.

Bielinski and Joslyn heard Negron shouting at Madley and got themselves organized by the time Negron walked in. They stood apart but with the same posture and an innocent expression on their faces. Their pupils were the size of the head of a pin.

Bielinski's hands were clasped behind his back, Joslyn straightened his tie.

"You'd think that a couple of guys your age wouldn't waste their time fucking around with drugs," Negron said, walking to the sofa, sitting down and crossing his legs. "I'm beginning to wonder whether or not we ought to continue our business relationship. You got that? Under the circumstances, it's a relevant question."

Joslyn picked up a pack of cigarettes lying on the single card table standing under the ceiling lamp, shook a cigarette out of it and put it in his mouth. He didn't light it. He was looking off to one side, and it was like he was studying a purely technical problem.

"You think you've got things going the way you want them, don't you, Vince?"

"I don't see why I shouldn't be satisfied—I'm running this organization the way it ought to be run. And while it might look like you're partners, in reality, you're not—and you never were. Does that come as a surprise to you?"

"I'm not so sure you are running things the way they ought to be run around here. Isn't that right, Jake?"

"Al, I don't think it's the time—"

"Shut up, Jake. I think it's as good a time as any."

Negron uncrossed his legs, sat up straight, then leaned forward with his feet planted on the floor. "What is this?"

"I did you a big favor, Vince."

"Did I ever say you didn't?"

"I made sure that hayseed Hargrove didn't play into the hand Ramón López dealt him. Whatever he knows about us, he won't let slip now. In the short run it would've cost you plenty, to say nothing about the long run—but there isn't nobody can see that far into the future, not from where we're standing. The unpredictable nature of a fink, Vince. You know it better than anyone else."

"I'll ignore the drift of that remark, Al. But if you're about to make a proposal, get on with it. I don't have all night. There are women out there waiting to get laid."

"You've got all the time we're going to give you, Vince."

"What's this about?"

"A wrench in the works for you, I guess."

"I'm not going to agree to anything you try to shove down my throat, if that's your idea of a suggestion. You ought to know me better than to think otherwise."

"You're so sure of yourself, aren't you?"

"Why not? A straightforward business proposition is all I'm going to listen to. Maybe those pills are making your head into mush just like the mush that's Madley's brain."

Negron turned to look at Bielinski, who didn't blink but shrugged his shoulders just a little as if to say that he wasn't one hundred percent behind Al Joslyn. Not yet. Maybe it was a matter of timing and he didn't go along with the play Joslyn was making right now but would back him all the way some other time. Negron read them like books; he sat back into the worn cushions of the sofa, crossed his legs. Joslyn's eyes were fixed on Negron.

"Well?" Negron said. "I'm listening."

Joslyn lit the cigarette, tossed the match into the ashtray, drew a chair up to the card table, swung it around facing the wrong way and sat down. He braced his arms on the backrest, his legs on either side of the chair. He sent Negron a smile with a cloud of cigarette smoke behind it.

They heard the street door slam shut, then the frosted glass of the common door that led to the anteroom opened and closed; the door to the back room was partially open and Madley opened it wider and came in with a newspaper in his hand; the fresh cold night air followed him. Bielinski's and Joslyn's pinned eyes looked at him, Negron kept his eyes on Joslyn and the only move he made was to extend his right arm behind him, his hand outstretched, waiting for Madley to put the late edition paper in it.

"Thanks, Madley."

"Had to drive down to the all-night joint to get it," he said. "Nobody's out, it's freezing."

Madley went back into the anteroom and hung up his coat and scarf, threw the watch cap on a shelf above them. When he returned to the room they weren't saying a word but the air was so thick with tension he thought he'd choke on it.

"What is this?" Madley said.

"Joslyn's going to tell me something important. Sit down."

"First I got to fix myself a cup of hot soup. My balls are frozen, Vince."

"Take your time, Madley. We got all the time in the world, isn't that right, Al?"

Madley turned to Joslyn. "Got any Senokot?"

"Take it easy with these, Paul, you're eating 'em like candy." Joslyn tossed him a box.

"Yeah, take it easy, Paul," Negron said.

"What is this?" Madley said again.

Negron snapped the late edition open to the second page, ignoring Joslyn and Bielinski. Madley put water on to boil, opened a cabinet, took a packet of instant curry-flavored noodle soup and a bowl and set them down on the countertop.

Bielinski went to where Joslyn was sitting and whispered in his ear. Joslyn got up and followed Bielinski out into the anteroom.

"Two to one they're cutting you out of whatever they've got in mind, Madley."

He was too busy pouring the dried noodles into boiling water to pay attention to what Negron was saying, then he looked at his wristwatch, started counting off the two minutes necessary to cook the noodles, turned around and said, "Say, what is this, Vince? Who's cutting me out of what?"

Without lowering the newspaper he said, "Eat your soup, wait 'til your balls thaw out, then I'll tell you about it."

55

RAMÓN LÓPEZ FELT THE thing growing inside him, it was a compulsive need to prove a point, to prove to himself that he was something more than a meaningless item on a long list of names that included every man Jean ever slept with and got rid of and didn't think twice about now that she was done with them. It gave him the idea to ask Lloyd Frend a question or two, to hear from the horse's mouth the exact nature of what the future had in store for him and Jean Fleming.

He got it into his head and it stayed there and it played over and over like a song until he knew the only way to make it stop playing and give him an answer would be to drive out of the city into the suburbs and talk face to face with Frend. And then he came up with a bonus that said it would put him in a better position to negotiate with Jean when she saw he wasn't afraid of Frend, he was capable of being a man no matter what kind of life she thought he lived up north, with the final outcome and advantage of it the ultimate defeat of Lloyd Frend, like any other rival.

What he didn't figure on was the possibility that at the very moment he was making up his mind to go out there to talk to Frend, Jean was fucking him with her clothes on in his small house outside Lake City, and that he might end up making a fool of himself in front of her.

The drive took a lot longer on account of the condition of the roads in bad weather. He parked on the street in front of the house. He didn't want to give the impression he was snooping around, but there was no other way to look at it when they heard him knock an empty flower pot off a ledge outside and came out through the front door and found him scooping up cold black dirt with his hands under the full moon, looking embarrassed as he put handfuls of it back into the overturned pot.

His hands were freezing cold out there without gloves, and the watch cap on his head made him look ridiculous because he'd pulled it down over his eyebrows just above his eyes. They stood watching him. There weren't any questions, no one said anything, he just got up from his crouching position and followed them inside.

López knocked the snow from his boots, bent down to take them off when Frend said, "Don't bother, López. You aren't staying."

Jean stood behind Frend wearing a short, black cocktail dress, her narrowed eyes measuring Ramón López who squinted up at her. She decided right away that whatever he was doing here he wasn't up to the task, he was out of his depth and didn't stand a chance with a man like Frend even if he had a TAC squad behind him. López straightened up and looked Frend in the eyes.

"I've got something to say and when I've said it I'll leave and that's as far as it'll go, I swear."

"That's sales talk."

"Maybe it is. Maybe I want to buy time. I didn't come here to make trouble for anyone—least of all for myself. But I've got to have a little time to put it together, to give you the picture and let you know where I stand."

"More sales talk. I can see exactly where you stand. You're in my house where you weren't invited. Okay, why *are* you here?"

"Can I come in?"

"You are in."

"I mean can I come in and sit down and say what I've got to say? It's not as if I want to do this, not really, because what's happening goes way beyond choice and comes out of necessity, it's upstairs management telling me I've got to do it, or else—and the manager is always right. I wish it could be handled some other way, but it can't. I've got to do it this way in order to keep my head above water. Haven't I got a right to keep myself from going under?"

"Not on my time. But if you've got to do it, you've got to do it. Take off your galoshes—you better make it fast before my patience goes out the window and what's left of you goes after it into a snowdrift. And keep Jean out of it."

López was leaning against the door frame, pulling off his boots, and he looked up at Frend, saying, "That I can't do. I'm here on account of her."

Frend turned his head, gazed quizzically at Jean who took a backward step. ´

"What's this with on account of you?" Frend asked her. "Don't tell me you've been talking to him?"

Jean shook her head, but before she could answer him, López said, "She's got nothing to do with my being here."

"You dizzy or something?" Jean said to López over Frend's shoulder.

"Not dizzy. I've got to lay it out in front of him."

"Lay what out?" Jean said.

"Now wait a minute," Frend said. "First you say it's on account of her, now you're telling me she's got nothing to do with it. You better make up your mind, López, before I break your nose."

"What I've got to say to you has everything to do with her and she's got nothing to do with it."

Frend didn't answer. He moved in very close to López, and although he wasn't aiming his fist at anything in particular, he kept his arm extended, his hand clenched in readiness.

56

THERE WAS A LONG quiet. They stood there examining one another like they were goldfish in the same bowl. It was almost two am. López diffused the tension by asking for something to drink, Jean went to the kitchen and poured him a glass of water from the tap, handed it to him and looked at Frend for a signal, which she got in the form of a slight jerk of his head in the direction of the adjacent bedroom. She went out, left them where they stood.

"If you've come here to tell me some fairy tale you've dreamed up about a rosy future with Jean, you can forget it, put on your galoshes, and get the hell out. If it's business, I'm listening."

"Can we sit down?"

López followed Frend into the living room, sat on the sofa, and Frend sat opposite him in an armchair. López drank from the glass of water.

"I'm still listening," Frend said impatiently.

"George Sender, on your behalf, asked me to look into what Vince Negron's been up to. He said you wanted something you could use to put him out of business, or limit the damage he's caused by involving himself in some investment scheme you copyrighted or was copyrighted by someone who works for you."

"I don't put my signature to anything that might pop up and bite me. But if there's anything to what you're saying, and I don't say there is any truth to it, what's it got to do with Jean Fleming?"

"What I've got to say has everything to do with her, but it'll only be clear when I'm through with the introduction I'm going to make in my own time—my own way of telling it."

"I don't have all night, López. Get to the point."

"Negron got mixed up with O'Dell, and when O'Dell got curious, he killed him."

"I know. Sender told me what you told him after they found O'Dell in the lake."

"What you don't know is that some of the guys working for Negron are in the process of double-crossing him."

"That's very interesting. As far as I'm concerned he can go down the drain any way it's meant to be as long as it's quick. Jean and I nearly got our heads broken by a couple of guys who smashed up my car—"

"What?" López sat up straight on the sofa, clenched his fists.

"Thanks for your concern."

"I'm not worried about you."

"No kidding."

"How do you figure it's Negron?"

"Don't take it so serious."

"Jean got hurt?"

"We won't go into that," Frend said. "It's just a waste of time."

"Not to me." López's eyes were wide, staring uncomprehendingly at the floor. And then he frowned and said, "What are you going to do?"

"Negron was behind it. If I can prove he was, with your help, then I'm going to get him, and I'd prefer to use legal means to shut him down permanently unless he's unlucky enough to have some kind of accident."

"That motherfucker!" López was breathing hard, his face was red as a beet.

"You look like you could use a drink."

Frend got up, went to the bar, poured a whisky over ice and gave it to López.

When he looked up he saw Jean standing in the doorway, leaning against the jamb. Frend waved her into the living room, took a bottle of gin, poured one and a half ounces into a shaker, added half a lemon, a half ounce of kümmel, a half ounce of green crème de menthe, four dashes of orange bitters, shook it with ice and strained it into a glass. They'd been going at it at an even clip since five.

She took the glass and walked unsteadily across the room to the sofa, sat down an arm's length away from López. Her short, black dress climbed her legs. López stared at them. She sipped her drink.

Jean turned toward López, her lustrous red hair flowed thickly and fell across her shoulders, she sent a smile in his direction, but her eyes weren't focused on anything.

Frend sat down in the armchair holding a whisky and ice. He looked at Jean's legs, saw López giving them the eye and didn't like it, but thought better of mentioning it because he didn't want to push López away just when he'd hooked him. He didn't catch the smile Jean threw at López.

"I don't talk business in front of anyone, not even Jean, but what I've got to say won't change anything for any of us right now. It's all out in the open—between friends and business partners," Frend said. "Follow up on what I told you. Can you do that, López? Dig up something solid on Negron "

"Solid dick, Lloyd." Jean slurred her words.

"You've had too much," Frend said. "Keep quiet."

"It's funny."

"It isn't funny."

Embarrassed, López said, "I don't know what to say."

"Keep it that way—she doesn't even know you're there." Frend took a sip of whisky.

"Who's there?" she said.

They ignored her.

"Did you hear what I said?" Frend said. "I want something solid on him, and I want it as soon as you can get it. From now on, you work directly with me—leave Sender out of it."

"You're taking a risk, aren't you? In your position, and no go-between."

"Whether or not I'm taking a risk—which, if I am taking a risk isn't going to be a risk because I'm taking it—is none of your business."

"I don't follow you, Lloyd," she said.

"I wasn't talking to you. Go make yourself a cup of coffee."

"I don't want a cup of coffee."

"Make one anyway."

López finished his drink, stood up, saying, "I'll be going."

Jean got up, put her glass down, said, "Who wants coffee?"

"Sit down, I'm not finished."

Both Jean and López sat down.

"Not you, him," Frend said.

Jean got up, straightened her skirt, left the living room for the kitchen with her hips swaying. López's eyes followed her and it was all desire and wanting and pleading and what Frend saw written on his face couldn't have been anything but love. He didn't like that any more than he liked López sizing up her legs, but he wanted López on his side; he cleared his throat. He tightened his lips, the same tightness showed in his eyes. Then they heard cabinets opening and closing, the clattering of dishes. His face relaxed.

"I don't get it," López said.

"Get what?"

"That look just now."

"Drop it."

"What's it got to do with me?"

"The way your eyes are carving her up like she's a bird and you haven't eaten in weeks, and you're in love—I don't like it. It puts you on the useless list and I don't want you there until you've finished the work you've got to do for me. I want you one hundred percent useful and if you're that fucked up over her what's the good of having you on the job if you can't operate? Is that clear?"

"I'll do what you want me to do and you've got nothing to worry about—and my private life's got nothing to do with it—but you have to do something for me in return."

"I'll pay you plenty."

"That's not what I'm talking about."

"What are you talking about?"

He raised his head, his chin pointed toward the kitchen. Frend sat up straight. "Jean? Are you out of your mind?"

"Never been further from it. I'm playing with more marbles now than I've played with in years."

"Just get me results."

"I'll get results."

"Not with her—with Negron."

Jean came in carrying a tray with a pot of coffee and three cups. She set the tray down, crouched, poured out three cups of coffee.

She shivered. "It's cold in here." She didn't sound drunk. "Sugar?" she said, looking at López.

"You forgot?" he said.

"No, I didn't—"

Frend raised his voice, "That's enough."

She put two lumps in the coffee.

"Is that okay?" she said.

López leaned forward, saying, "We've got to talk sooner or later—you know how I feel, don't you?" It didn't slip out, he let it out.

"I don't want to talk to you. Not now, not ever. I've got nothing to say that you'll want to hear. It's all over."

"Leave her out of this," Frend said.

Jean stood up, handed Frend and López a cup of coffee in a saucer with a spoon. Frend took it, glared at her. She didn't get it. She gave Frend a sideways look. She saw the look on his face. She said, "What are you telling me?"

He didn't answer, he pointed a finger at López, then he said, "I don't want to hear another word from you."

"I got a right to say what I want to say to whoever I want to say it, when I want to say it."

"Not in my house. Not in front of her. You're a guest here—but not for long. Finish your coffee, get out, and get to work."

Frend put the cup and saucer down, stood up, reached into his trousers pocket, retrieved a money clip, peeled off a couple hundred dollars and threw them down in front of López, who picked them up, folded them and put them in his shirt pocket.

"Now will you shut up?"

"I came here in good faith—"

"Faith's got nothing to do with it. You came here with one thing in mind and that one thing is really two things that amount to the same thing, pissing me off by getting money out of me, then putting the make on Jean. You're a selfish prick. Do what I ask you to do and you'll get more money, okay, but you'll never get your hands on her."

López got up from the sofa, moved a couple of feet toward Frend with a peculiar look in his eyes, a flickering of reckless intent mixed with something sad that made it a purely crazy expression, and it was Frend who swung first, a quick right that connected just under López's left ear. López went down, dropped to the plush carpet next to the sofa.

57

JEAN FLEMING SENT LLOYD Frend a smile that was sooth-ing-warm and soft and human and he didn't know why but right now he really wanted something human to wash over him. He pulled the white gold ring off his right ring finger and slipped it back on and made it turn round and round above the bruised knuckle that had connected where he'd aimed just below Ramón López's left ear. López lay groaning on his side curled up on the plush carpet next to the sofa. A spray of light from the standing lamp lit his shifting legs.

Frend didn't move. He looked at Jean's lazy, oval face and red-dish hair and smiled dimly, somewhat dazedly as if he didn't realize what he'd just done and instead thought that López had fallen down or that he himself was in the middle of a dream because he'd resorted to violence and it wasn't like him. Then he looked down at López and saw the man trying to get up, groaning, and he grinned wryly at himself because he knew it wasn't any use for López to make an effort teetering like that on the brink of consciousness.

Jean picked up a heavy ashtray from the coffee table and raised it above López's head. She was drunk and didn't know what she was doing and the hazy concentration that went along with it made her stand there like a statue threatening to finish off Ramón López.

"Don't do it," Frend said. "Not now. Not ever."

"We can't just leave him."

"Of course we can. I'll take care of him. But you're not going to do it."

"What do you mean I can't do it? You took it this far and we might as well take it the rest of the way because if we don't he'll come back here and get us."

"Maybe yes, maybe no," Frend said, taking the ashtray out of her hand and putting it on the coffee table. "But killing him isn't the way to straighten it out."

"Okay, maybe not, but I don't owe him anything because there's nothing between us and there's never been anything between us. Not really."

"No, of course." Frend said it without conviction.

López didn't make a sound. He was knocked out and breathing evenly. Frend went around him, switched on another standing lamp, then crossed the living room to the armchair with a small antique lamp on the table beside it, sat down and lit a cigarette.

"What time is it?" Frend asked.

She looked at her wristwatch.

"Early. Four-forty."

Light from a fading full moon splashing the snow-covered lawn seeped into the room through the curtains drawn over the windows of the small house he kept in the suburbs outside of town, it was a sort of sullen, gray light that showed them the familiar walls, the carpeted floor, the furniture, and Ramón López lying unconscious next to the sofa. Jean bent down to switch off the lamp next to Frend.

"Leave it," he said. "I can't take natural light with him lying there."

Jean perched herself on the arm of the chair. The hem of her dress went high up, she cupped her hands and put them between her legs just above the knees and felt the stickiness where he'd come on them. He looked at the fine pale hairs on her thighs, went on smoking. She slipped a hand from between her legs and put it on his head, then leaned against his shoulder.

They sat there together without saying anything, Frend smoking until he'd smoked the cigarette down to the filter and Jean with her eyes shut but not sleeping. He reached out and crushed the butt in the ashtray.

She raised her head, looked at him.

"We've got to make a decision," she said.

"Yeah, I know we've got to make a decision, but I don't know what to say about which way to take it."

"We've got to get him out of here, Lloyd."

"This shouldn't have happened. Not ever. It was going along just fine until he stuck his face in it."

"Things don't happen the way we figure them. You didn't want it this way, neither did I, but you can't blame yourself," she said. "No one forced him to come here. He got what he asked for."

"It's going to be a problem when he wakes up."

"He doesn't have to wake up."

"I told you that isn't what we're going to do."

"What *are* we going to do?"

"I'll have to make a phone call. Where's his car?"

She got up, went to the window, drew the curtains aside to look at the suburban street covered by a blanket of snow. The leafless branches of trees in the front yard reached out above a car parked in front of Frend's house at dawn and the evergreen trees were weighed down by heavy sheets of damp snow. She stared at them. Jean Fleming sighed, the snow's unspoiled fairness contrasted sharply with the tension in Lloyd Frend's house.

"The car's parked out front," she said.

58

JOE WHITEN SHUT THE street door behind him, opened the frosted glass door and went into the anteroom, saw Bielinski and Joslyn huddled in a corner talking in whispers. They ignored him. He took off his coat, hat and galoshes and put them in the makeshift cloak-room. When he walked into the backroom with a package under his arm, he saw Negron reading a paper while Madley, holding a bowl of instant noodle soup in his hands, tipped it back in front of his face to drink the last drops.

Without looking up from the paper, Negron said, "Where have you been?"

Whiten went directly to the sofa and stood in front of Negron, who quickly folded the paper and set it down next to him. He looked closely at Whiten, examining the pupils of his eyes, which appeared normal, and he patted the sofa cushion, told Whiten to sit down.

"They still in there?" he said, indicating the next room with a jerk of his head.

"Yes, Vince. What's this all about?"

"You don't take that shit they're swallowing, do you? Those pills are poison, Joe. I always figured you had more sense than the rest of them. Am I right? Tell me I'm right, Joe, and we'll go from there. But only if it's true. I don't want to hear any lies coming out of your mouth because if I do—and I'll know it—they'll be the last words you'll ever say."

"You can trust me, Vince. I don't take anything but aspirin."

"You ever go fishing, Joe?"

"What's fishing got to do with it?" Madley chimed in from a drug cloud across the room.

"Shut up, Madley. I'm talking to Joe."

"Ever bring in a big one, like a channel bass, more than thirty pounds of fish, in a fight that went twenty minutes?"

"No, Vince. I never went fishing except one time with my old man and we sat at the edge of a pond and it was really hot and humid and we got eaten alive by mosquitoes and a bull frog jumped into my lap. No fish."

"That's fine, Joe. Well, if you're up for it, we're going to set the bait and catch a couple of fish. And together they weigh something on the order of three hundred and ninety pounds."

"There isn't no two fish out there that weighs anything near that much, Vince," Madley said, looking for the pad of paper he'd left on the desk in the other room.

"Shut up, Madley. Get your pen and paper and play Hart Crane somewhere else."

"What's that, Vince?"

"A fucking card game. Now, fuck off. Say, 'Goodbye!' and throw yourself overboard."

"But Vince, I don't know that game."

"I said get out of here, Paul, before I crack you in the mouth."

He left the room with a bad-tempered look on his face. Bielinski and Joslyn weren't in the anteroom, there was no sign of them except for the half-open frosted glass door they didn't close properly when they went out. He went over and shut it, then sat down at the desk in front of the pad of blue-lined yellow paper.

59

BIELINSKI AND JOSLYN WALKED to the corner of Meyering Boulevard and Seventeenth Street and then kept going another half block, bundled up against the chill wind that came in off the river. They stood huddled together talking, the wind blew most of their words into the night sky. Every now and then a car went past with its snow tires crunching on the salted street and chased by clouds of exhaust visible in the cold air. Two winos wearing worn-out jackets with fake fur-lined hoods staggered around the two men, heading toward a warehouse a block away with other helpless or homeless figures standing around a fire burning in an empty oil drum.

"He won't find the guys we hired to rough him up," Joslyn said, reassuringly. "They're from out of town."

"He's too smart, Al. We can't discount anything that has something to do with Vince."

"Not too smart for what we've got planned."

"I'm not saying that, just that we've got to be careful."

Joslyn had his arms folded and was stamping his feet on the ground. The cold wind bit through his gloves. "I can think and act as fast as he can and that'll get us where we want to go. Are you fading, or what?"

"No, Al. I'm right alongside you."

"I'm starting to think maybe you got doubts."

"It's just those pills are fucking up my head."

"Quit taking them."

"I got to take them now. Otherwise, I'm sick. And I'm consti-
pated. When was the last time you took a shit?"

"I don't think that's any of your business. Quit worrying because worrying is what's making you sick. And if you can't shit, take
a laxative."

"You got any on you?"

Joslyn went through his coat pockets until he found a few
Senokot tablets, gave them to Bielinski.

"The job we did on Frend's car," Joslyn went on, "it set them up
against each other—he figures it was Vince who did it—and if the
hostility cools down, we give it a goose. And if Frend doesn't finish
him, I'll put Vince upside down in the lake myself."

"These pills taste bad, Al."

"You're not supposed to chew them, you jerk."

"All right, Al, all right."

"Now, listen to what I've got to say."

60

WHITEN CAME OUT THE street doorway bundled up against the freezing night, slogging through a low wall of shoveled snow packed and curled up along the edge of the sidewalk by city machines that kept the roads clear in winter. He headed toward Bielinski and Joslyn huddled together under a streetlight half a block away. His legs were tired but he'd got an earful from Negron and what he'd heard inspired him.

Joslyn was digging in his coat pockets for something and gave whatever he'd found to Bielinski, who quickly popped it into his mouth and made an unpleasant face as soon as he started chewing, a face Whiten saw thanks to a good pair of eyes.

Avoiding the slippery patches of ice, Whiten moved in a curving path going slightly uphill and then the street flattened and the street was really covered in ice. He stopped. Still, they didn't notice him. Their voices were whispers and the gusts of wind blew in a direction that sent the whispers away from him, Whiten couldn't hear a thing; they looked like a pair of conspirators, confirming what Negron had told him.

Their heads were together as Whiten got near enough to tap Bielinski on the shoulder, Bielinski almost jumped out of his skin, and when he took his hand away, two heads went up at the same time, with a look of surprise pasted on both of them at Whiten's medium-sized shadow. He was just outside the spray of light.

"Christ, shit, you almost gave me a heart attack," Bielinski said.

Joslyn wasn't surprised, he was pissed off at Whiten who was always creeping around like a cat. Whiten put an embarrassed grin on his face that didn't bear any resemblance to real embarrassment, a technique he'd used so many times that the other members of El Manojo didn't see it anymore.

"What do you want, Whiten?" Joslyn said. "You some kind of spy?"

"Vince told me to see where you'd got to," he said, lying. "He said that when I found you I should tell you to take the night off. So, take the night off, you don't have to go back to the club—do whatever you want, he'll see you tomorrow."

"Don't you ever get fed up with being messenger boy?" Joslyn said.

"Maybe I do, maybe I don't. It's none of your business, Al."

"Snooping around like a spy *is* my business if you're snooping around me."

"All right, Al," Bielinski said, putting his hand on Joslyn's arm.

"Don't 'All right, Al' me, Jake." He pushed the grasping hand off his arm.

"Don't take it out on Jake," Whiten said.

"I'll take it out on whoever I want to take it out on, including you, you shit-for-brains little spy." Joslyn had his gloved fist clenched behind his back.

"There's no need to insult me, Al—"

The punch was an uppercut and it came out of nowhere and landed just below Whiten's chin and sent him reeling backward until he was sailing on ice, his legs flying out from under him, his legs shooting straight out, and he was almost parallel to the ground before landing with a thud, flat on his back.

Bielinski got out of the way and stood almost knee-deep in a snow-filled culvert watching the two of them go at it like a couple of animals. It lasted long enough for several thin streams of blood to stain the pure white snow, looking like they'd been squirted out of a turkey baster, and in one place warm blood crept down into dirty ice and firmly packed snow and spread outward just under the surface making a network of tiny broken blood vessels.

By the end of the tussle, their efforts exhausted along with their bodies, Joslyn and Whiten helped each other up out of the snow and shook hands. It'd gone exactly as Negron had told Whiten it would go if he followed his instructions to the letter. Using handfuls of snow to clean bloodied nose and mouth, Joslyn breathlessly confided his plans to Joe Whiten. Bielinski stood behind Whiten in case he fell backward because Whiten's legs kept going out from under him, he was in worse shape than Joslyn when it came to a fight.

61

GEORGE SENDER PAID THE woman for the cigars he picked out from a box she'd set in front of him at his regular news-stand in midtown Lake City. He removed the band from one of the cigars, put the cigar in his mouth, lit it. Sender turned, gave the brunette a smile, waved a hand, and started down the street looking for a taxi.

Two days ago Ramón López told him he'd met with Lloyd Frend, that he wasn't going to report to him anymore, it was just between López and Frend, and López skipped the part where he woke up in his car, five miles from where he'd parked it in front of Frend's house, with a bruised jaw, reeking of alcohol that had been poured down his throat and spilled down his shirtfront, the empty pint at his feet near the accelerator pedal.

A taxi pulled over. He gave the driver Hargrove's address at West Walker and Third. He promised Coral he'd look in on Hargrove on his day off, she'd spent more than ten minutes pleading with him to do it, and even though the idea left a sour taste in his mouth, he told himself it was Coral and not some stranger, and then he wondered if there wasn't something wrong that he didn't remember what she really meant to him until this very minute. At last he'd promised her, it amounted to a promise he was going to keep.

He got out of the taxi at the corner of West Walker and Third and waited until the taxi pulled away from the curb before lighting his cigar again; he smoked, looking confidently up and down the street, then started walking.

Half a block away, he stopped in front of the two-story house where Hargrove lived and he thought of Coral and the good times they'd had together, and then the picture switched to a picture of the play she must've made for Hargrove, the victory she enjoyed with him, that he'd lost Coral to another man, and then he tried to sum it up but got nowhere because it wasn't about the address or building or apartment, the answer to the question was to meet Walt Hargrove in person.

It was an innocent way of measuring a kind of rival, but his stomach dropped down to his feet, and his feet took a couple of steps away from the house. His self-confidence was slipping away. He really didn't want to know Hargrove since it would put a spotlight on the qualities he himself didn't have. He shook it off, crossed the sidewalk, climbed the first set of cement stairs up to the street doorway, rang the bell.

Hargrove buzzed him in, Sender climbed the stairs to Hargrove's rooms in the run-down house, making an effort to watch his footsteps on the creaky staircase. He stood in front of the door and waited for Hargrove to open it, rubbed his free hand upward against short bristly hair at the back of his head. Cigar smoke filled the hallway. Hargrove let him in.

"You don't mind if I smoke this thing in here?" Sender said, taking off his overcoat.

"No, I like it."

Hargrove took his coat, hung it on a hook behind the door. He threw himself down in the armchair in the living room, stretched his legs out, stared at the television screen that showed a couple of guys arguing in front of the county court house; the sofa was empty, and Sender sat on it, crossed his legs, leaned forward to knock a long ash off the end of his cigar into an ashtray.

He looked around the room. There was a table and a couple of folding chairs, a couple of pictures hung on the walls, a worn-out carpet; a deck of cards on the tabletop, a plate with half a stick of butter and an empty plate with bread crumbs, a jar of pickles, a can of Coke and a half-filled glass of Coke laid out in front of one of the folding chairs. Hargrove didn't pay attention to him.

"Have you got anything to drink?" Sender said.

Hargrove snapped out of his daydream, sat up straight, pushing his hand through hair. "Sorry, yes. Will a beer do?"

"Thank you."

"I guess Coral told you what happened to me. I guess I'm just worn out." He got up from the armchair, went to the kitchen. "I haven't had a day off until now, not since the night I got beat up by that clown who works for Negron," he said from the kitchen.

He came back with a bottle of cold beer and a glass and set them down in front Sender.

"Thank you. Which clown might that be?'"

"A guy named Al Joslyn."

"I don't know him, personally. A friend of mine, Ramón López—you met him at the coffee shop on Webster—he knows him, he knows everybody who's got anything to do with Vince Negron. And he saw Joslyn follow you that night."

Sender poured beer slowly into the glass, but didn't drink it. Hargrove sat down.

"And he didn't do anything about it," he said.

"It wasn't his job to do anything more than keep an eye on you."

"What people know or don't know about the life and times of Vince Negron doesn't interest me. What I want to know is what can I do about what happened to me. Coral said there's nothing that goes on here without you hearing about it, that you know Negron, and that you'll know how far I can take it with him. What I want from you is I want your advice—everything else being secondary, you know, about Coral and you and me."

Sender cleared his throat. "Everything else being secondary, as you put it, I'd say keep away from him. Keep away from all of them if you want to go on living and not end up in the lake with your lungs filled with water and your head caved in. That's my advice."

Hargrove raised the glass of Coke to his lips and finished it. Sender set his cigar down, took a sip of beer.

"That doesn't surprise me," Hargrove said. "What you're saying isn't news, and I figured you say what you had to say to protect me because of Coral. Now, let's forget about Coral for a minute. Let's look at the picture from another angle. Maybe I'm a hick from up north, maybe I'm not. I've learned a few things since then. And maybe that's not enough—what I've learned. And what I *haven't* learned definitely outweighs the other side. I'll give you that much, and more. I'm probably way out on a limb when I say that something's got to be done about it. I can't face Coral, I can't look at myself in the mirror without seeing what Joslyn did to me, and knowing all I got out of it was bruises on my face and a fucked-up tooth from a good beating, which isn't much of a payoff but what I deserve because I didn't have the guts to do anything about it."

Hargrove raised the glass again without seeing it was empty, made a frown and put it down in front of him.

"So you've got to get more out of it than being alive? That's plenty, isn't it?"

"It's a lesson, you're right. Okay, I got a lesson and I just want to return the favor."

"Let me tell you what I know, and what López told me about your friend Al Joslyn."

62

"I'VE BEEN DOING RESEARCH, and some thinking," Joslyn confided in Whiten. "That research and thinking told me Walt Hargrove's got a line to Frend through George Sender, by way of the ex-girlfriend, Coral Rasmussen."

"I don't follow you," Whiten said, holding a paper napkin stained with blood to his bloodied nose. "What's Sender got to do with it? He writes for the *Journal,* doesn't he?"

The waitress came up to the table.

"Want another refill?"

"Yes, fill 'em up," Bielinski answered for them. "Where's that order of pie? You said five minutes ten minutes ago."

"It's still cooling down in the kitchen. Can't slice it right away. It'll be right out."

"On its own?"

"Out in a couple of minutes."

"Now it's already a couple of minutes."

She poured three cups of coffee, left the table with her nose in the air and Bielinski's eyes followed her swaying hips.

"I beat up Hargrove saying it was on orders from Negron figuring Hargrove would tell his girlfriend who'd tell Sender about it, and Sender would tell Frend. And as a favor, Frend's going to do something for Sender on behalf of Hargrove's girlfriend who Sender's still stuck on—unless, of course, I'm talking out of the side of my head."

"Through your hat, Al," Bielinski said.

"Shut up, Jake. I'm explaining something to Joe."

"Since when are you and Joe such great friends?"

"Since he knocked me down a couple of times. You were there, remember? Now shut up, will you?"

"Okay, Al."

"And if I figure right, Frend's going to make trouble for Negron. Now, if Negron's got problems from Frend, and there's trouble from the other side, and he doesn't know where it's coming from when it's coming from us, he's going to go under, it's too much pressure, he's got to get out of the business or out of town—or get killed. Then it's me, I'm going to be the big chief."

"You've got to do what you've got to do, Al. That's it, isn't it? And that's how it's always been, you always do what you don't want to do, but you're compelled to do it—a kind of call of nature," Whiten said, putting the blood-stained napkin down on the yellow Naugahyde seat.

"Funny, but that's not far from the truth."

"You're under a lot of pressure, I can see that—anyone can see it. If you didn't have Jake here, you'd have nobody but yourself to do what you've got to do. And because it's a kind of duty, there's no choice, and when someone like you is supposed to do something, he does it. No hesitation. Am I right? Well, now you've got *me*, too. I'll be your friend."

Joslyn went for it; he believed what he was hearing from Joe Whiten because he wanted to believe it and it was useful to him and it really touched him, he knew it wasn't from the first of April, it was genuine, and now he was one man stronger than he'd been five minutes ago.

"Negron's forced my hand, he's making a mess out of an organized organization, and he's greedy—he's gone into Frend's territory without a complimentary ticket saying come on in the water's fine, he just did it because he wanted to or maybe he had to—I don't know and I don't care. I do know as far as financial problems go he doesn't have any. I don't get it, it's not for me to get, but it's greed and that's the way it is, so on account of that, sooner or later, everything's going to come crashing down on us when we don't deserve it, Frend won't stand for any interference, and I've got to knock Vince out of the number one slot of El Manojo before it happens."

The waitress brought a warm piece of cherry pie on a plate, set it down in front of Bielinski, who didn't wait a second before he grabbed a fork, started cutting into it, put a forkful in his mouth, sighed.

"You happy now?" Joslyn said.

"Most happy," Bielinski said with his mouth full. "And you?"

"What's that supposed to mean?"

He finished swallowing, then said, "Because Joe's with us, not against us. Guys like us are just like any other race. There's good ones and there's the ones that aren't any good, and then there's the tricksters. You satisfied?"

"Not until Negron is out of the way—one way or the other."

63

"Now that I know what you know about Joslyn, I'd rather leave him alone," Hargrove said, leaning back into the cushions of the sofa.

"It's better for you that someone on the outside handles your immediate problems," Sender suggested.

And Sender told himself that if he went ahead and helped Hargrove, he'd get Coral back, but the voice in his head was matter-of-fact when it said, If you really want her back, because I'm not so sure you do, you're fine just as you are, and anyway, suppose that help you're so generously offering doesn't work out and he gets himself killed, your shoulder will be right there for her to cry on, you'll wait and see what happens, let time pass and the world revolve a few dozen times, and when her mind is clear and the odometer turned back to zero, you'll be there, so when it comes down to it, with all your good intentions, you're some kind of scheming selfish rat, because you don't even know if you want her, all you know is you don't want anyone else to have her.

Sender involuntarily raised a hand to shoo away the thoughts buzzing around him like a fly.

"I don't think they're immediate," Hargrove said. "And I can't swear Negron had anything to do with it. All I got is Joslyn's word, which isn't worth the breath he used giving it. But I can't say letting somebody else teach Joslyn a lesson when I'd rather do it myself makes me feel any better about it. I still want something more than bruises out of the beating I took from him."

"I can't promise you anything."

"You going to put it in the *Journal*?"

"It's not for the *Journal*, Walt."

"Then what are you talking about?"

"I don't know, not yet. But I promised Coral I'd help you, and I'm telling you now that I always keep my promises."

64

FREND KEPT HIS HAND in a bowl of icy water until it felt so numb he couldn't stand it, he pulled it out and wrapped it in a towel. Jean was asleep upstairs, he was standing in the kitchen near the sink, López was unconscious on the floor in the living room.

"Goddamn you," he said to nobody in particular.

He was waiting for his chauffeur, Billy Gorman, who'd had the night off and was up to who knows what until Frend called him and told him to come to the house; he expected Gorman any minute. Gorman would take López's car with López in the trunk, and Frend would follow them.

It wasn't going to be a matter of finishing off López, he wanted him alive and willing to help him unravel the business of Negron's incursion into his territory, and the danger it posed to the way he'd lived his life for years and how he was now considered a legitimate businessman who spent plenty on behalf of public good while investing his earnings for private gain. It added up to getting López off his property, and far enough away from it to give López time to pull himself together so he wouldn't come back to finish what he'd started, which would amount to the same thing as committing suicide. Frend would have somebody kill him.

The bell at the back door in the kitchen gave two short rings; it was Gorman. Frend swung around, switched on the rear yard light, moved the curtain away from the upper part of the door and looked out at Billy Gorman's face. He'd worked for Frend for almost twenty years, he was fifty-eight, tall, and his full head of hair was almost all gray.

"I'm sorry to ruin your night, Billy."

"That's all right. It's almost morning, Mr. Frend."

"I need you to drive a car."

"Sounds like you've got yourself a problem, and that's what I'm here for—to help you if I can. You pay me a good salary, you've treated me well every day I've worked for you, so what've I got to complain about? Nothing. What do you want me to do, Mr. Frend? What we do for others is the same as doing something for ourselves—it's all capital for tomorrow."

"Either a good harvest or a red one, isn't it?"

"That's about it, Mr. Frend."

"Not everybody sees it the way you do, Billy."

"Not everybody has to—now, what can I do for you?"

65

JEAN FLEMING GOT UP and out of her own bed, looked for cigarettes and found a pack of menthols, sat down on the edge of
the bed and lit one. The taste of it made her sick, her stomach
was out of commission; she put the cigarette out in the ashtray. Her
hair was messed up from a deep sleep with her head buried in the
pillows, her face had a few creases in it. The light wasn't midday
light, the late afternoon was almost night; she got up and went to
the window and stood there looking out at the city.

In the bathroom, she splashed cold water on her face. Her head
throbbed and her thoughts were fuzzy from the drinks she'd had on
a bender with Frend. The cold water forced her eyes open wide; she
dried her face.

When she came back to the bedroom she sat on a low chair
in front of a mirror and looked at herself thinking she ought to
try hard and remember what had happened to López the other
night because it was important to her, he'd been lying on the floor
of Frend's house after Frend hit him and she had an ashtray in her
hand but she wasn't smoking. And there was the faint memory of
wanting to smash his head in. She saw the face of the alarm clock
reflected in the mirror, it said four-fifteen.

She'd gone out with a lot of men, but Ramón López was one
of them who'd meant something to her. She'd slept with him and
it was something she enjoyed and it had been pretty good and all
in all she liked him well enough, but she'd called it quits after six
months because she'd wanted a man with more going on than being an ex-cop with a pension and a part-time job and no desire to

make life bigger; she wanted a man who planned for the future, and Lloyd Frend was that man.

When she asked herself why López had shown up like that at Frend's place, she didn't have an answer because very little about López seemed to make sense to her anymore except that maybe he was jealous and jealousy was always as good a reason as any for a man to show up at another man's house when a woman was involved.

She really didn't think he was working for Lloyd Frend, but he'd said he had something to sell Frend, or tell him, she couldn't remember which it was, except that he'd said it was business, it had nothing to do with her, she should shut her head, and then he went on about something else and that was a blank like most of it. She was sure that whatever it was he was up to it was a pretext for checking up on her. Maybe she really wanted him to be jealous. She told herself it wasn't important, she didn't have to bother thinking about it, and then what happened and what was said came back to her.

66

López woke up on the back seat of his own car with the glow of moonlight falling through the damp windshield into the driver's seat and just skimming over the top of it and flowing in to spread out across the armrest and settle on the edge of the seat where he'd been curled up. His head hurt, his eyes were watering, he had a couple of bruised ribs, there was a lump the size of a golf ball on his jaw just below his left ear. Daylight wasn't more than an hour away.

Even though he was wearing his winter coat he shivered with cold on account of having been unconscious in the car without heat for a very long but indefinite amount of time as far as he could figure after looking at the clock on the dashboard.

He didn't remember anything at first, then saw Frend's fist coming at him quick as lightning and a blur of objects going by as he fell down in Frend's living room. He couldn't remember what might have caused his ribs to hurt so much. He reached in under his coat, rubbed the place where it really ached while the pain went on radiating outward in every direction.

López didn't bother getting out of the car to get into the front seat, he just climbed clumsily over the seat and settled in behind the wheel using his fingers to find the keys in the ignition without bending his neck because moving that part of his body sent a jolt of stabbing pain running from his neck down the length of his spine.

He switched on the engine and soon the heat came pouring out of the vents and the moisture that had formed on the windows began to evaporate. He lit a cigarette waiting for the temperature to climb.

When the car moved forward away from the curb he realized he didn't know where he was except that it wasn't Lake City but way out in the suburbs near an unfinished housing development and what he could make out of the neighborhood told him it was nowhere near where he'd parked his car in front of Lloyd Frend's house.

He rolled the window down and tossed the cigarette out. Two or three blocks ahead of him was a set of stop lights and the faint red glow drew him onward through the winter night. There wasn't a soul on the street. A car came toward him and his eyes blinked as the headlights shot into them. A mile later, the neighborhood changed, and he went past one residence after another each with the same small front yard and driveway leading up to a modest two-story house.

At another set of stop lights he pulled the car up at the intersection of a very wide smooth black street swept of snow, spotted with thin patches of ice, and he stared out through the windshield at the dimly lit parking lot of a strip mall. A few snowy cars were parked near the lighted entrance of a supermarket where employees on the nightshift were stocking shelves.

The green light sent the car out into the intersection, making a turn onto the wide street heading west, and in that first block there was a sign telling him the freeway entrance was up ahead and not far away and if he kept on going he'd find out where he was thanks to the signs indicating the entrance for the freeway going north and south. Just before taking the ramp a sign told him what he wanted to know, and with fatigue in his head and throbbing from his bruised jaw and heavy limbs, his foot numb with cold and bad circulation, he pressed down on the accelerator pushing the car north, knowing that he was on his way home.

It was on the freeway that his mind started to wander, he drove using a sort of built-in automatic pilot, and the wandering wasn't drifting because it was fueled by anger that kept him alert, anger at himself at first, but when that wasn't enough to keep him going it was anger directed at Frend on account of what Jean Fleming witnessed in Frend's house.

Then his anger made a big play. It was the word he'd given Frend that he'd go on looking into Negron's business, and his promise to put an obstruction, a kind of bottleneck into the flow of that business that went streaming out of the car along with the exhaust, sent by sheer force of anger, until that draining promise trailed behind him and it meant nothing and resembled only expired energy and fuel spent by the engine of the car that was taking him home.

López lit another cigarette, feeling more like himself now than he'd felt in days, and he switched off the heat and opened the window to breathe the invigorating winter air, conscious that he'd made a decision to throw a wrench into the works of the unholy trinity that was Negron and El Manojo and Frend.

He didn't question that decision until he'd parked the car a couple of blocks away from the midtown hotel where he was staying, and when the question came it was more on the order of feeling something twisting around his insides, squeezing them, getting something started in there. He knew what it was, it had happened before.

The knot in his stomach told him that if he threw the wrench into their lives, he might be throwing the wrench into his own life, too, and then he'd lose Jean forever or he'd lose the possibility of Jean coming back to him, and it was just that possibility of her coming back that kept him going.

The elevator took him up to his room and by the time he got the door unlocked and shut it behind him he had the pains running deep and raking his intestines and he went straight to the toilet, dropping his winter coat to the floor just outside the bathroom door.

There was yesterday's *Journal* draped over the edge of the bathtub, and as he sat there dripping with sweat like he had a fever he reached for it and tried to take his mind off the cramp he felt in his guts by looking through the Metro section and finding a piece by

George Sender and concentrating on the words without getting the meaning of them because the pain took him way out beyond the contents of the column.

Forty-five minutes later after he'd flushed the toilet half a dozen times, he was rinsing his face with cold water and patting his face dry with a soft towel and trying to figure an angle on how to use Sender to stir things up with Frend.

He sat in an upholstered armchair at the round Formica table near the window smoking a cigarette, switched off the lamp and stared out at the streets and gray dwellings and few lights burning in office windows, the wintry dullness of the lake too far away to see and the hotel not tall enough for a view of the lake's choppy surface reflecting the dawn.

He stared so hard at the window that he couldn't see beyond it, he saw the sparse furniture behind him reflected in the glass. He wasn't lonely, but he had nothing to do and no place to go. He put the cigarette out, shut his eyes and started to drift. It was always a problem, where to go and what to do. He envied people whose lives were based on routine, who lived by definite need and order, they seemed to know every minute of every day what they were going to do from the moment they got up at seven and went to work until they got home at six.

A big stretch of nothing spread out in front of him, he was falling asleep. He opened his eyes, his gaze penetrated the glass again. Unhurried fat snowflakes fell in front of the hotel windows. He decided to go out for something to eat rather than stay in the room with nothing to do but watch TV.

López shared the elevator with a tall middle-aged man and a young girl not more than five feet in a short skirt that could've been his daughter except for how she was dressed and the way he held her by the waist with her back against his belly, rocking her to the left and right, making an obscene gesture out of it. López shut his eyes until they reached the lobby. He let them out of the elevator first so he could watch the backs of her white thighs that would freeze the minute she left the hotel for the street.

A garbage truck traveled sluggishly on East Harrison over melting patches of ice on the salted road. López shivered when a sharp gust of wind off the lake shot through his clothes. He headed west looking for somewhere to get something to eat without having to pay more than he could afford. The falling snow tickled his face, the snowflakes fell like feathers in the air.

He walked as far as he had to walk in the gentle snowfall until he got to an old-fashioned diner with a long counter and round stools and six booths with miniature jukeboxes that didn't work and windows facing a street at the most southern point of what amounted to a wedge of city streets known as Greektown.

A familiar greasy smell that wasn't bad but not pleasant, just the smell of grilled and fried food, poured out of the poorly ventilated kitchen. He sat on a stool away from the few customers in the place with nowhere else to go, who were expert at making a cup of coffee last as long as the snow fell. He didn't want breakfast, he ordered meatloaf with mashed potatoes and peas, and a Fanta orange.

The food wasn't bad or good it just filled him up and that was what he'd come for, so he didn't have to sit and think and not find answers to questions that were too difficult for him to answer on an empty stomach. He knew that much about himself and more. He lit a cigarette. The more of it was that he'd better find a way to fix his image with Jean if he wanted to get anywhere with her because as it stood she'd have nothing but a low opinion of him since he'd let Frend knock him down and lay him out on the floor.

The more he thought about her the more a jumble of images resembling a pixelated face got in the way and that mosaic became a clear picture and it was Jean's face and she was standing over him with an ashtray in her hand. Her face got a lot bigger and the ashtray was really a heavy threatening object looming over him and he knew then that it wasn't a hallucination or bad dream but something genuine and fatal hanging there and it had jumped out of his subconscious where a lot of things were stored up just to spring on him, and the danger was as real as it had been at the right time and the worry greater than the danger.

López had no idea what it meant, it made him sit motionless for a moment, facing the short-order cook and grill, seeing the future in terms of something bleak and grim. He had to be sure he really wanted her because maybe she harbored some kind of crazy desire to kill him, and he found it strange, unlikely after the length of time gone by since they were sleeping together, that she'd want him out of the way, or hated him so much to hit him with an ashtray, and so he shook it off, got rid of that possibility that was so large he just couldn't believe it was true. It didn't fit in with his plan to win her back.

He couldn't rely on himself to make the right decisions since those decisions and the plans they affected seemed to change every hour and this was just the first day since he'd decided to wreak havoc in lives that according to his way of seeing things amounted to nothing, or less than that.

He went back to his room at the hotel, slept well as silent snow kept falling on city roofs and streets and parked cars, and in the early evening, the snow muffled footsteps and softened the rolling of tires in traffic and absorbed the racket while the heavy curtain in front of the window was drawn against the gray light.

López got up, made coffee in his room, it wasn't strong enough and it didn't taste very good but it sent a warm, mildly caffeinated charge down his throat and it helped him wake up sufficiently to open the door and take up the evening edition of the newspaper that came with the price of the room.

He stared at the front page as he sat on the toilet, opened it to the page where there were dozens of brief summaries of news items. The phone rang. He got off the toilet to answer it. It was George Sender.

67

CORAL JOINED HARGROVE AT the counter. He gave cash to the saleswoman, and the saleswoman in return handed him a wrapped package and he started out of the department store. Coral wasn't paying attention to what he'd been doing, she'd spent her time moving through the sale items on the floor pulling at sleeves and taking skirts and tops from the racks to hold them out in front of her, examining them under the fluorescent light.

Now she trailed after him, stopped to look at a simple black dress from the fall season hanging among other dresses included in what was left over in the sale, then hurried to him through the Saturday crowd where she was caught up in the jostle and buffeted from side to side, eventually taking hold of his arm.

They walked along the parking lot to the car she'd borrowed for the weekend. The sky looked like an endless field of dark ice. Leaning against the passenger door in the freezing afternoon, he took her in his arms, kissed her long and hard on the mouth, then removed the package from the bag and handed it to her. She quickly unwrapped it, tearing the paper from the box.

Coral reached under and around his goose down coat, grasping his waist, and he felt her familiar breath against his face. She was excited because he'd bought her an expensive gift, her favorite perfume, an item she pointed out when they'd gone past the counter. She held him there and pushed her face into his neck and breathed the smell of him.

The Chevrolet pulled into traffic with Coral behind the wheel and Hargrove fidgeting with the radio not looking at the street and the cars that went past them, not looking through the rear window or any window at all because if he had been looking he'd have seen that it was Joe Whiten in the car in the lane next to them, then behind them as they took the ramp down and merged with traffic on the freeway. There was plenty of traffic because it was a weekend, and if he'd seen Whiten he would've asked himself whether or not it was a coincidence, Lake City had a population of between one and two million, but the real question about what Whiten was doing there in the first place would have mixed in with unspecific curiosity.

He sat with his head thrown back and his eyes shut listening to the whoosh of tires on the freeway and the music from the radio and nothing more than that came to his mind until twenty-five minutes later when they pulled off the freeway and parked in front of a coffee shop and Whiten glided up into the empty space next to theirs. Hargrove got out of the Chevrolet, looked at him, but really wasn't surprised or glad to see him.

68

IT WAS THE FIRST time Joe Whiten got an eyeful of Hargrove's girlfriend and she was something to see walking on a long pair of shapely legs that poked out of a fur coat, and his eyes traveled upward and then he saw the head of blond hair on a Scandinavian face while a pair of gloved hands removed a hat that kept her head warm in winter. She pulled the hat back down over her ears and there was the nice shape of her face with the quiet line of brow and nose and chin, and the semi-delicate line of her jaw, and the way she moved her arms and legs told him she'd come from money or had got used to it and probably had enough money today to keep her looking as good as she looked to him right now.

He didn't ask himself why she'd gone for a guy like Walt Hargrove because he liked Hargrove and knew from experience the qualities he didn't have that Hargrove had and he couldn't count them on one hand because there were enough of those qualities to make Hargrove a really decent human being when they combined with the average faults that made him human.

Whiten was standing in the parking lot between the open door of his car and the car itself with his arms across the roof watching them as they got into a Chevy and started the engine. He swung down and into his car and slammed the door shut and turned the ignition and the heat came on and it felt like a dry wind on his face. They left the parking lot and he followed them, keeping two cars between them until they got on the freeway.

He kept near enough so he wouldn't lose them, and once he pulled up right alongside the Chevy to get a look inside but quickly slowed down and dropped back and into the same lane and stayed there without crowding them until he got off the freeway at the same exit, following just behind the Chevy. He took the empty space next to their car in the parking lot of a coffee shop.

Whiten saw right away that Hargrove wasn't surprised or happy with the spontaneous meeting in a parking lot of a coffee shop, standing there with his girlfriend without knowing what Whiten wanted other than maybe to continue the beating he'd got from Joslyn, but throwing the girl into it this time, so Hargrove started backing up slowly and reached for her arm and took the keys out of her hand.

"Don't get yourself worked up over nothing, Walt. I just came to talk to you. I've got something to say you'll want to hear," Whiten said, cautiously advancing a step.

Hargrove couldn't form a reply. He had his mind on the location and the position of the protagonists, computing time and measuring the distance between himself and Coral and the Chevrolet, and that it was more than likely Joe Whiten could get to them before they got to the car, and then the overall fight he'd have to make against this general threat from El Manojo.

Coral didn't move, her breath came quickly and it looked like vapor from a steam engine. Hargrove moved alongside her, navigated her to a position behind him.

He said, "All this trouble. And all this risk."

"There's no trouble, no risk. Why don't we just go inside and talk about it."

"She's got nothing to do with it, Joe. Let her go."

"I didn't say she has anything to do with whatever you think I'm here to talk about," Whiten said calmly. "There's nothing to be afraid of, Walt. For Christ's sake."

"You're a roach," Hargrove said. "I can't trust any of you. You're all roaches and somebody ought to put a foot down hard and crush you and break your backs."

All along Hargrove had been moving slowly toward the Chevrolet, edging in that direction a step at a time, with Coral behind him, even if he didn't believe they'd get to the car and open the door and climb in before Whiten was on top of them.

"Take it easy, Walt, you're upsetting your friend. Just look at her—"

"Don't tell me what to do!" he shouted, turning his head anyway to make sure Coral was all right.

Whiten took advantage of the split second he had to leap at Hargrove and take him by the arm and gently hold him there because he didn't want a fight and didn't want to scare him, but he knew if he was going to help Hargrove it had to be like this at first, until he calmed down and got the whole picture out of what he was going to tell him. Then Coral started smacking Whiten on the side of the head. He swung his arm blindly and struck her with his open hand.

There was something gentle in the grip Hargrove felt on his arm so he didn't react violently until Whiten's wild swinging arm almost knocked Coral off her feet. Seeing her stagger backward set his temper on fire and he lunged at Whiten tearing free of the gentle grip and giving Whiten a shove that made him slip on a patch of ice. Instinct rather than care made him reach out to catch Whiten before he fell and he steadied himself holding on to Whiten, using Whiten's weight as a counterbalance to his own and that total weight kept them both on their feet.

They stood there looking at each other, the three of them a little confused at what had happened, and then a laugh, low and hidden just beneath the surface of Whiten's face climbed out and became a full-fledged hearty laugh that spread to Walt Hargrove and Coral Rasmussen until they were all three reeling with laughter.

"That breaks the ice," Whiten said. "No pun intended."

"Coral, this is Joe. Joe, say your sorry."

"I'm sorry. I'm really sorry. Did I hurt you?"

"I'll get over it," Coral said.

"Let's go in, let's get something to eat," Hargrove suggested.

"That's what I been trying to tell you, Walt."

"Well, I heard you. Now *I'm* saying it, so it's all right."

He took Coral's arm and they went into the coffee shop with
Whiten trailing behind them. Hargrove wanted a meal and a couple of hours sleep. The meal was practically in front of him as he
picked an empty booth with a window looking out at the parking
lot, but the sleep would have to wait until later in the day.

The booth was an oasis, he pressed himself against the
Naugahyde seatback beside Coral waiting for calm while his jangled nerves sent electric pulses through his body, reminding him of
the fear he'd felt. Fear and stimulation and animal survival. And it
made him very tired. His eyes wanted to close and he had to work
hard to keep them from closing.

"You sleepy or something?" Whiten asked, taking a menu from
the waitress, then looking up at her: "Bring us three regular Cokes,
will you?"

"You fucked me up big time by showing up here—I thought I
was in for more of what Joslyn gave me."

"Not from me, Walt. Not ever."

"So, Walt, you *do* know people who don't want to kill you,"
Coral said.

It wasn't meant to be hurtful, she'd been scared by the panic
in Hargrove that passed directly into her when he'd seen Whiten,
and so Hargrove took that into account when he said seriously, "Joe
Whiten's all right. We can trust him."

The waitress brought three bottles of Coke and ice-filled glasses
and set them down in front of them. Hargrove, who wasn't paying
attention when Whiten ordered them said, "What's this? Coral,
you want a Coke? He ordered Coke."

"Diet Coke with Lime."

"Make that a Diet Coke with Lime. I'll have a beer, please.
Miller Lite."

"What do I do with these?" the waitress asked.

"Leave them," Whiten said.

"You going to order?"

"I just did," Hargrove said politely.

"From the menu."

"When you come back with my beer."

The waitress left. Whiten finished a full glass of Coke, then leaned forward across the tabletop.

"The situation is as follows: Joslyn's turning the organization upside down with Bielinski's help and what that amounts to is an attempt at a takeover—like big business only smaller. He's lifting what he can from Negron by pitting a guy named Frend against him, and Frend's big, important. He's way out beyond Negron's league which looks like a bunch of teenagers. In the clouds looking down at Vince, that's Lloyd Frend. God. But Negron's been scraping pieces off Frend's pocket money. None of the big stuff, not yet—and anyway, I don't think Negron's up to it. But it's going to get hot pretty soon and when it does a lot of people we know are going to get burned. You're part of the equation, Walt. Like it or not, you're part of the equation. That's why Joslyn beat you up."

"I wouldn't say that's impossible, but—"

"What?" Whiten interrupted him, but he hadn't noticed the waitress coming toward them with a Miller Lite and a glass. "Oh, yeah. It isn't impossible, no."

They didn't want the waitress to hear anything she didn't have to hear. She poured beer into the glass.

"You ready to order?" she asked.

Coral spoke up first, saying, "I'll have blueberry pancakes."

"Make mine a hamburger, medium-rare, no onions, and an order of fries," Hargrove said.

"Cheese?"

"No cheese."

"What kind of pie do you have?" Whiten said.

"Apple, cherry, lemon meringue—"

"Fresh?"

"Nothing's fresh."

"I accept that."

"Well, then?"

"Apple. No ice cream." Whiten had a satisfied look on his face.

Outside the sky was still dark and it looked like it was going to snow. When Hargrove looked out the window the others turned their heads to see what he was looking at and while it was just a reasonable view of an average winter afternoon it came at them like a menacing black cloud fused with the sad and hopeless feeling in their hearts.

"It's not as bad as all that," Whiten said, examining the look their faces.

"You don't have to tell me more than you've said to know that there's big trouble heading this way," Hargrove said, putting his arm around Coral.

"This is horrible," she said.

"Horrible is one way of putting it," Hargrove said.

"I'm not afraid for me, I'm afraid for you."

"I can take care of myself." It was bold but unconvincing.

"Please, Walt, don't talk like that."

"Like what?"

"Like you're going to take them on all by yourself? They're professionals," she said.

"Amateurs."

"Okay, amateurs."

"I wouldn't say that," Whiten chimed in.

"It's not just me, Coral. You're in it, too, because what they know about me includes the fact that I'm in love with you and what I got myself into I got you into—we're both in a situation. We don't have much to say and no choice but to pack our bags and leave town, skip and skip fast. Am I right, Joe?"

"You're right, but—"

"Circumstances," Coral said.

"Not circumstances, reality," Hargrove said. "And we can't stay around just to find out. It's you and me, and they know it's you and me or Whiten wouldn't be here telling us what he's got to say because he wants to help."

"It can't be as bad as that," she said flatly.

"It'll be worse."

"I've got a friend who runs the Gilbert Hotel on Dock Street near the gym, and she'll look after you if I tell her to look after you," Whiten tried reassuring them.

The waitress brought the food to the table and set the plates in front of each of them, saying, "Anything else?"

"No, nothing else," Whiten said.

"Suddenly, I'm not hungry," Coral said.

Whiten picked up his fork and cut into the slice of apple pie.

69

NEGRON DIDN'T KNOW THAT Whiten warned Hargrove off El Manojo, and Hargrove in or out meant nothing to Negron at this point since Hargrove wasn't a full-fledged member of the club, but Al Joslyn and Jake Bielinski worried Negron in a big way.

Whiten came into the Seventeenth Street Social Club with an easygoing stride, his hat in his hands, his overcoat buttoned up and a scarf wrapped around the lower part of his face, frozen to the bone. He hung up his coat and hat, kept the scarf around his neck. Bielinski and Joslyn hadn't been around since the night before last and they hadn't shown up according to schedule today at five. Madley called in sick because he'd shoveled in too many laxatives for more than two days and couldn't get off the toilet. It was now twenty after five.

They sat on the leather sofa, Negron smoking and Whiten watching him and waiting for words that didn't come until at last Negron jammed the cigarette out in the ashtray and started pacing the room until he came to a halt in front of Whiten. Whiten looked up at him.

"I've got to start with Joslyn, but I haven't figured what the first move's going to be. It'll have to wait. I could pay somebody to kill him, when guys aren't loyal anymore there isn't any point in maintaining loyalty with them—I don't have to tell you that, Joe. They sink so low they go straight into the minus and once they're in the minus they don't climb back out. Well, I'd rather kill him myself, but I know I can't afford to do it, too much risk—and I'm not even sure I want him dead, not yet."

"I can use some coffee."

"I fixed some a half hour ago, it's over in the thermos by the sink."

Whiten got up, poured himself a cup and began sipping the coffee. "Then what are you going to do?" He sat down on the sofa.

"Where's Walt Hargrove?"

"I haven't seen him for more than a week," Whiten said, lying.

"I want you to find him, tell him I've got to talk to him and convince him it's in his interest to talk to me. Get him to arrange an appointment for me with Ramón López. I know he met with López last week at a diner. At least Joslyn told me that much. Said he happened to be passing by and saw him through the window sitting at a table talking to López."

"And then what?"

"That's my business, Joe."

"You don't trust me—after what you told me the other night?"

"It isn't trust that's at issue here—the less other people know what I'm going to do the more unlikely it is they'll let something slip."

"I don't know, Vince. What good is López to you? And why get Hargrove mixed up in it? He knows less than nothing about what goes on here, and it's sure better that way unless you plan on bringing him in as a member."

"That's exactly why I want Hargrove involved. He doesn't know what I'm really doing and he isn't going to learn anything more than he already knows—which, like you said, is less than nothing. A neutral contact to get in touch with López, that's it. I'll take it from there."

"You're dreaming if you think he's neutral—if what Joslyn said is true and he was talking to López in the diner, then he's out of the inner circle, period."

"I don't give a fuck if they were talking or what they were talking about because there's nothing they could say that would pose a problem to me. I don't have anything against him, not yet."

"And how's that going to help you with Joslyn and Bielinski?"

"Did I say it has anything to do with them? Quit asking so many questions."

"Okay, I'll skip that and move on to the next subject which is something you aren't going to like since I know you well enough to warn myself this isn't a thing Vince is going to want to talk about, but anyway, I looked at it and I told myself I've got to talk about it—and that subject, while I'm moving around it and not right away putting a finger on it is the subject of money."

"Go on." Negron sat down in a straight chair, planted his feet solidly on the floor, rocked the chair back on two legs.

"The way it's been going I've been spending pretty heavily on this and that—you know how it is—and what I've got left isn't enough for anything like what I really got to have in order to live a life I'm used to living until the next job or until you decide to quit the revenge angle or quit waiting in the wings to knock Frend off the top. You've got to start working on something that'll put more than change in the pockets of El Manojo. I'm not pointing fingers, no way am I doing that—especially at you, Vince. Up until now you've been like a big brother to everybody concerned, but this obsession with Frend and sorting out Joslyn and Bielinski has got you by the nose and pulled you away from what's made you the boss—being smart and doing business."

Negron sent the chair down hard on all four legs and got up and started pacing the room again without noticing the expression on Whiten's face that would've told him Whiten was afraid of what he might do next.

Negron swung around. "What are you saying?"

"Loan me some money."

"Why didn't you say it—" He interrupted himself. "What's with the knock—you losing confidence? You want me to chop off my finger to prove something? This ain't a dream, Joe. I'm working here. It's real and it's planning, and I know that you know I can make a plan."

"Isn't," Whiten said.

"What?"

"This *isn't* a dream. So, where's the plan?"

"You can't see it, it's in my head. And it doesn't include you, not this time. You've got to be patient. Trust me. You can do that, can't you? I'll give you some money, and we'll call it a loan if you want to call it a loan, but keep off my back until I tell you that what I've got planned is done—it isn't going to happen overnight."

"I'll call it a loan."

"How much?"

"Three large."

In his excitement Negron knocked the straight chair over accidentally and it skidded across the floor toward the sofa and Whiten, who raised his legs to avoid it. The chair passed under his legs and came to a stop in front of the makeshift bar on wheels set up in a corner of the room.

"Three thousand? Are you out of your mind?"

Whiten sighed and smiled, and behind the sigh was empathy for Negron since Whiten himself didn't ever want to let go of anything he had in his hands, especially money, but he was flat broke, and the smile told Negron that Whiten knew he had it to give away.

"I'm clean out of cash, Vince. For Christ's sake, otherwise I wouldn't ask you for numbers like that."

Negron went over to the chair, picked it up and set it down gently and put himself on it with a look in his eyes that said he was adding up the idea of the loan and the amount of it, trying to decide if he'd give it to him, and it wasn't a question of whether or not he could afford it because the answer to that was a simple yes.

Negron turned his head and saw Whiten watching at him.

"I want to give it to you, Joe. I'm just figuring."

"Figuring what?"

"Maybe you don't really need it. Maybe you're testing me, and if I go ahead and give you three grand you aren't going to quit with three grand but go on asking until I'm forced to stop you—for good, permanently."

"For what good reason?"

"You mean how come you'd try to bleed me?"

"That's right."

"I don't know. I haven't got an answer. I'm just looking at the angles."

"There aren't any angles here, Vince. It's a loan."

Negron got up from the chair and headed for the door to the anteroom, and when he got to the door and reached for the door-knob, he turned around and said, "Ok, stay here."

Whiten sent his eyes toward the windows where the blinds were raised on the alleyway parallel to and between Seventeenth and Eighteenth that intersected Meyering Boulevard. He kept his eyes focused in front of him while his ears did a job listening to Negron in the other room. There was a scraping sound or a noise that reminded him of a sliding panel set a little too close to another fixed panel making it hard to move at first, but it must have been on rollers or a tongue-and-groove joint because it went smoothly on after the initial catch and he heard a click as the panel fell into place.

He didn't want to know where it was, he knew that Negron had a safe or storage place hidden in the next room. It wasn't important, he wasn't going to steal anything from Vince Negron. And he wasn't going to get himself in the middle of a fight for leftovers no matter how high the hidden sum was if Joslyn and Bielinski brought Negron down.

Five minutes later Negron came back into the room and handed Whiten a medium-sized envelope holding twenties and fifties but not many fifties, and when Whiten gave them a good hard look, pushing his index finger through the unruly stack, he figured it added up to three thousand dollars. Of the three thousand, he'd give Hargrove twelve hundred for the hotel and expenses.

70

BILLY GORMAN SAT IN a folding chair in the hallway outside
Frend's apartment in the townhouse situated on the Eastside
not far from downtown reading issue number fourteen of
Garage magazine. He'd started at the layout of tattooed girls in bathing suits at the back before moving on to an article about Buggs
Ochoa from Boyle Heights, who was a legendary painter of lowrid-
ers and a member of a car club called the Groupe. Frend gave him
a subscription to *Garage* as a present because Gorman couldn't live
without six issues a year and the pleasure it gave him to leaf through
it and look at the pictures and read and dream about what he'd always wanted which was a girl with a tattoo and a garage of his own.

Gorman was doing exactly what Frend had told him to do,
which was to sit out there at night to keep an eye on things since
Frend wasn't taking chances with Vince Negron or the twisted way
Negron was acting on his decision to rise in business by cutting in
on Frend. There hadn't been an incident in three days, but Frend
wasn't going to risk an all-out assault.

The windows of a Westside real-estate office in which Frend
was a silent partner had been smashed in the middle of the night
four days ago and anything of value was stolen by unknown assail-
ants that Frend knew were employed by Negron without having
had proof they worked for him. He didn't need proof. Negron was
one of the few people in town who knew he had a piece of that
real-estate business.

Gorman put the magazine down in his lap, thought about Frend
and how he had his share of trouble on his way up and there wasn't

any question Frend knew now that he hadn't known then what real trouble was because real trouble came when you had something to lose. Back then he'd had nothing to lose and nowhere to go but higher on the ladder he climbed, stepping on the hands and in the faces of a lot of guys who weren't around today to say anything about it. Frend made himself a legitimate success.

It was nine-thirty. Gorman picked up the magazine, turned the pages back toward the cover and stopped at a column on R. Crumb, promoting an exhibition on the West Coast. He didn't hear the elevator come up or Sender coming out of it and down the hall until Sender was right in front of him.

"Who let you in?" Gorman said.

He got up and put the magazine down, stuck his hand out. Sender shook it with genuine enthusiasm.

"Doorman—what kind of a hello is that, Billy?"

"Well, we're on medium alert here, Mr. Sender, you know that."

"So I've heard. No red alert? What about our respected friend?" He indicated Frend's door with a wave of his arm. "Does he have time for guests?"

"Not now. He's got a lot on his mind, and tonight it's Ms. Fleming."

"I've got something for him, Billy," he said without really listening to what Gorman said. "I'm expecting word any minute." He looked at the face of his watch. "Can I see him for just a few minutes?"

Gorman shook his head, no. "Can't say yes. I'm doing what he told me to do. You know how it is. Isn't anything we can do or say when he's got his mind made up and by the way Ms. Fleming looked when she came in tonight, I'd say his mind was made up for him." He winked at Sender.

"All right, then. It'll have to keep until tomorrow." Sender took hold of Gorman's hand, shook it. "See you later, Billy."

"Goodnight, Mr. Sender."

Frend listened at the door, heard Sender's voice but didn't open up for him because he was busy with Jean, and Gorman was taking care of it and sticking to the rules Frend laid out for him, whether or not it was one of Frend's friends that got as far as the front door of the apartment. The doorman made a judgment call with Sender based on experience and Gorman, who'd worked for him for so long he was practically a member of the family, kept anyone who got upstairs at arm's length until Frend told him otherwise.

"Lloyd honey, where are you?" Jean's voice came from the second floor and traveled down the staircase and hovered in the foyer at the entrance to the living room and bounced against the walls going backward to where Frend was standing in a silk robe with his back against the front door. Beneath the robe he wore a pair of emerald-green silk boxer shorts. Sender was gone.

"I'll be right there, baby," Frend shouted back.

When Frend worried about the signatures on a contract or felt uncomfortable with the way a vote at a board meeting went or it was the heart of winter or summer or he was just plain bored, he fucked Jean and played games with her and the idea was that the pleasure and smell of sex and sweat was a relief. And when it was really very cold, the wind chill factor put the temperature down below zero, he wanted it all the time. He wasn't going to stay holed up alone in the townhouse. In the present situation it was a distraction from the crucial matters of battle before victory, and a reward for figuring the next move in his campaign against Vince Negron.

So now he went into the kitchen fit out with every sort of modern appliance available on the market and switched on the warm-white fluorescents with a correlated color temperature of 2700K that were installed carefully so that they were all but invisible to the eye and glowed outward from where the walls met the ceiling and weren't dim and not too bright but bright enough to show off the quality of the grain in the handmade cabinets and countertops, the brushed metal refrigerator, the rugged-looking black and ironlike professional grill and polished stove and neat prep counter in the center of the room. He opened the refrigerator door and removed an ice-cold bottle of imported beer.

He opened the bottle, switched off the light, stood with the bottle in his hand while staring out the long rectangular window showing him the city skyline at night like a picture postcard, and the lights that winked at him from near and far away told him to wake up and quit dreaming it's for real and you earned it. He loved his kitchen. He put the bottle to his lips and drank, and the cold beer soothed his dry throat.

The beer refreshed him from the efforts he'd been making, they weren't anything like mild efforts, they were more on the order of a kind of strain that went on for a couple of hours, and it was the sort of overwork he really enjoyed because it was sex with Jean, which gave him a good erection, and if he didn't touch it himself the waiting would pay off and send him into the stars when at last she made him come. But those were the preliminaries, just warming up, and there were plenty of things left to do if she wanted to do them.

He finished the beer, set the bottle in a recycling bin under the kitchen counter. When he got to the main bedroom upstairs there was silence and then a groaning sound that came from the queen-sized bed and the groan was softened by the warm glow of the yellow light bulbs he left burning when he'd gone downstairs to listen to the voices on the other side of the front door.

Jean Fleming was lying on her stomach, tied to the bed, with a ball-gag in her mouth. She wore a four-garter standard weight translucent latex garter belt with a thickness of about 0.3 mm., and translucent latex stockings with a thickness of about 0.4 mm. that featured a rolled edge held up by black straps pressing into her very pale skin. He'd put a pillow under her stomach, and in that position her buttocks were exposed as a pair of inviting yellow hills in the yellow light with a shadow between them that was the crack of her ass. The hair on her head was more orange than red on account of the light.

Crouched next to the bed with his face near hers, he saw that her eyes were shut tight and her cheeks flushed deep red with beads of sweat on her forehead. She was shaking, trembling from head to toe, and the rope that tied her, spread-eagle, to the bed strained with the squirming movement of her legs. The large vibrating egg taped by a couple of pieces of wide flesh-colored gaffer's tape across, but not inside her pussy was inaudible, buried as it was in the twisted sheets with the full weight of her body pressing it against the mattress. It was the fifth time she'd come in the last half hour.

Frend wondered if she'd had enough. He waited for her to stop shaking. He took off his robe and stood there in his boxer shorts, looking at the woman he loved. He switched on a standing lamp with a yellow bulb and used the dimmer switch to keep the incandescent bulb down low. He loosened the straps of the ball-gag and saliva ran down her chin. He put four of his fingers in her mouth, stretching her lips, then stepped away, climbed onto the bed and got himself between her legs to put his face close to where the vibrating egg was humming.

He brought his face closer, saw a lot of fluid coming out of her, and the amount that had already come out of her when he was downstairs drinking beer had spread on the sheet covering the mattress and soaked it.

He took a deep breath and closed his eyes for a moment, breathed the smell of her and pulled it in deep so that it filled his lungs, said, "I love you," then put his hands flat on the insides of her thighs just above the latex stockings where his fingers pushed into her skin, opening the space between her legs even wider, and she let out a moan, maybe because it was uncomfortable or because it felt good, he couldn't tell and didn't care, so he stuck his face into the crack of her ass, licked the smooth skin and then licked around her anus before pushing his tongue inside her, the familiar bitter taste in his mouth.

For a minute he ignored the vibrating egg but when it got to where the vibration tickled him, he removed the flesh-colored tape he'd ordered from Japan, at first peeling it back little by little until there was no choice but to pull suddenly, quickly on the first strip, then the second, lying under the first, which was stuck to the skin, making Jean cry out. The wet vibrating egg fell to the mattress, the batteries were weak, he switched it off and brushed it aside.

He untied the knots he'd made in the ropes, loosening their hold on her wrists and ankles. She rolled over on her back and smiled at him as he climbed on top of her. Frend kissed her mouth. She wrapped her arms around his back, holding him there tightly. Her hands moved lower, caressed the silk fabric covering him.

He pried himself away from her without really wanting to move because for the first time in a long time he thought of having so-called normal sex with her, but he let go of the thought and kept the action heading where it was already going and got off the bed to re-move his boxer shorts. She turned onto her stomach, moved herself to a position across the width of the bed instead of the length of it.

"Cradle," she said, opening her mouth wide, wagging her tongue at him.

"Whose appetite is it?"

"Mine." She sent him another smile.

"Well, thank you."

With her arms behind her back and her legs bent, he tied the wrists to the ankles, and she rocked gently to and fro and forward on her belly so that her head was just over the edge of the bed. His cock was hard. She stuck out her tongue and curled it and he tapped it lightly with his cock, then put it into her mouth, sending it deep and down until he felt the head of it against the back of her throat. She started to gag, and he pulled slowly out of her mouth, then pushed his cock back in and went on fucking her throat for a couple of minutes, choking her until the sound she made and the spit and the drooling and her teeth scraping the skin of his cock made him pull out to come across her lips. A last powerful jerk sent a thread of come into her nose.

Sender hailed a cab and got in and told the driver to take him to an address on the Eastside. As he climbed out of the cab, he pulled his overcoat collar up and shoved his hands in his pockets. The air was cold and a biting wind came in off the lake and the cold got turned up a notch by the river not far away. He climbed two stairs and pulled the door open and went in.

It was a sort of nightclub but it was private and he could smoke a cigar without worrying about anybody objecting to cigar smoke, and the music that played from the speakers mounted on brackets in every corner of the bar took him far away from whatever worried him, and the bonded whisky for a change, instead of bourbon, tasted especially good. The bar and customers were bathed in the slow swinging rhythm of Benny Goodman and Lionel Hampton and Charlie Christian playing, "I'm confessin'." He sat in an real leather booth with a flickering candle standing in the center of it.

He held the glass of whisky in his hand, looked down at the paper coaster with the club's mark on it, listened to the music.

T-Bone Walker was singing, "Don't Give Me the Runaround," from 1946. He thought about what he hadn't said to Frend about López, that López was a wild card, running on his own and gone haywire on account of Jean Fleming. Even Coral told him she'd had a talk with López and figured he was pretty far gone on Jean, and while López wouldn't admit it to himself, he'd do just about anything to get her back even if it included playing one side against the other, putting himself in the middle and creating a big city version of a small-town nightmare on the order of a particular movie starring Toshiro Mifune.

The number of possibilities for violence were limitless. He didn't really want to get mixed up in it. Then he told himself he was already standing right in the middle, favors were favors and he'd exchanged them with all sorts of people in Lake City, big and small. He wished there was another way, but there wasn't. Just this one method, give and take. It wasn't his fault if López got something going tonight before he could warn Frend to keep his head down.

He raised his hand, waved the waitress over to the table, ordered another whisky.

He looked her up and down as she walked away, thought he'd really like to get her into bed, but didn't feel confident enough right now to make a move, he couldn't take it if she said no, and she didn't give him any sign that anything was on the menu. He yawned, took the band off a cigar and lit the cigar.

The ashtray was cobalt blue and it looked black in the candlelight. He sent clouds of cigar smoke toward the ceiling, they spun around before getting there on account of a slow-turning ceiling fan playing games with them. He set the cigar on the groove of the ashtray, took an envelope out of his jacket pocket, the envelope had a piece of paper in it, he unfolded the paper. The music was Louis Armstrong playing and singing, "Whatcha Say," with Dorothy Dandridge.

When he'd read the letter by candlelight he dropped it on the tabletop, then heard that the music was Hank Williams, and it was the sad, scratchy recording of "I'm So Tired Of It All," which he listened to while smoking as if it were playing just for him. When he added it up he knew he wasn't really down, just tired—unless he took the fresh news that his ex-wife was getting remarried as bad news in order to go on drinking, it made no difference to him, so he let himself relax, sat back, sent cigar smoke into the air and waited for his drink.

The waitress brought him another bonded whisky.

Jean rolled down the latex stockings, dusted the inside of them with talcum powder. The garter belt came off next, and it got the same talcum treatment. She went into the adjoining room, a spare bedroom, and put the outfit in a dresser drawer, then went back and got into the shower, which sent so much steam out, above and through the open frosted glass doors, that she couldn't see herself in the mirror.

Frend stood stark naked in the kitchen, finishing another bottle of imported beer. He switched off the overhead lights, went to the front door, put his ear against it. There wasn't a sound except the low rumbling of Billy Gorman snoring as he slept upright in a chair. He went back into the kitchen, found a large kitchen towel for drying dishes and held it front of him as he opened the front door a crack.

"Billy. Hey, Billy!"

Gorman snorted, his chin rose from his chest, his head snapped up, and he looked around as if he didn't know where he was, then said, "Who is it?" His eyes focused on Frend, standing there with a towel to keep him decent.

"What can I do for you, Mr. Frend?"

"Who was at the door about an hour ago?"

"Mr. Sender—said he had something to tell you. News, he said. Checked his watch more than once. He must've been waiting for a call. Didn't say anything more than that, Mr. Frend. You want me to get hold of him for you?"

"Not now, Billy. Keep your eyes open, that's all."

"Yes, Mr. Frend."

Frend shut the door, locked it, set the deadbolt and added the chain. He shut off all the lights downstairs, went up to the spare bedroom where Jean was stretched out under the clean sheets and tidy blankets with her red hair spilled out around her head, resting on two pillows.

"Let's sleep in here tonight," she said. "The other room's a mess."

He got into bed, put his arm around her shoulder, pulled her close to him, kissing her forehead and brushing her hair with his fingers and telling himself, She has the real quality.

He shut his eyes and fell asleep.

71

A ROCK-OLA PEACOCK JUKEBOX WITH six bubble tubes, rotating colors in the side column, and a kind of light polarization in which every feather in the peacock plumes changed color independently from the feather next to it—a machine with 900 watts of power, weighing 287 pounds—was delivered to the Seventeenth Street Social Club at ten-thirty on Tuesday morning when Vince Negron was straightening up after a planning session with Bielinski, Joslyn, Madley and Whiten.

Negron put a lot of time into research before buying the jukebox because he was spending big money, and he got the address of the original Rock-Ola facility, which used to be located at 800 North Kedzie Avenue. David Rockola got his start in the penny gumball business and founded Rock-Ola in 1927. Rockola's first jukebox success was in 1935, in competition with Wurlitzer, and Farny Wurlitzer filed a $1 million lawsuit claiming patent infringement on the Smythe 12-select jukebox mechanism reengineered for Rockola's machine. Rockola won the suit, but spent half a million dollars in legal fees doing it. The whole setup moved to another state long ago, bought by Glenn Streeter of Antique Apparatus Company.

I'm as tough as that Rockola guy, and as faithful to the history of things as Streeter, who's kept that business from fading away, he modernized it, just like I'm going to modernize El Manojo, Negron told himself.

And what Negron really liked about Rock-Ola was that during World War II they produced M-1 carbines—3,500 rifles and 100 boxes of ammunition a day. He could count on a machine made by a company that was directed by a man like that. But he didn't know how far he could count on Joslyn and Bielinski. Madley was dumb but loyal, and he trusted Whiten.

The conversation at the early morning meeting between the members of El Manojo began at eight-thirty and was accompanied by freshly brewed coffee and donuts from a nearby donut shop.

"What I'm going to say is important, Madley, so try and concentrate," Negron said. "Have another donut."

Joslyn pushed one of the waxed paper sacks toward Madley, who yawned, raised his cup of coffee to his lips and drank, then reached into the sack for a cruller.

"At three in the morning Joslyn and Bielinski are going to set fire to Frend's out-of-town cottage—his country house. Whiten's going to call Frend's townhouse at two forty-five to warn him." Negron paused to make sure they were all paying attention. "Frend will wake his driver, Billy Gorman, and get him to take him to the so-called country house, and while he's out of the way, Whiten and I are going to break into the townhouse with you, Madley, as lookout."

Madley finished the cruller, wiped his hands on a paper napkin, nodded in Negron's direction.

"You're going to keep an eye on things from a strategic spot on the street. Got it?"

"Got it, Vince." Madley got up to pour himself another cup of coffee.

"Where are you going?" Joslyn said.

"You can see where I'm going, Al. Need a map or something?"

"Is there any orange juice, Vince?" Bielinski said.

"Look in the fridge. I'm not a waitress, Jake—use your feet, get off your ass. If somebody bought orange juice and put it in the fridge and it isn't more than a month old you'll find it, and if it's more than a month old it'll find you."

"Ain't that the truth," Madley said.

"Isn't," Whiten said.

"What?"

"*Isn't* that the truth."

"That's right," Negron said. "Whiten's got it right."

"What've you been doing, taking lessons?" Whiten said.

"That's enough, Joe—if he don't know how to speak English it isn't his fault," Negron said. "Nobody taught him the correct way when he was a kid."

"Doesn't," Whiten said.

"Right," Negron said. "If he *doesn't* know how to speak English."

"Is this a regularly scheduled class or can anyone sit in?" Joslyn said.

"You sound like the TV, Al," Madley said, laughing.

"Shut up, Paul," Joslyn said.

Negron cleared his throat, said, "Okay. It'll take Frend around forty-five minutes to get from the townhouse in the city to the cottage out of town—"

"No juice." Bielinski interrupted him. He sat down at the two card tables pushed together so they'd have legroom for four.

"I'm so sorry," Joslyn said.

"Knock it off, Al. You can say what you want, but you've got to wait 'til I'm through here to say it. Now, where was I?"

"In the cottage out of town," Madley said.

"You *are* listening."

"Yes, I *am* listening."

"Okay. Then Frend's got to the cottage out of town. Are we straight on that?"

They answered in unison: "Yes, Vince."

"When he gets to the cottage out of town and Billy Gorman parks the Lincoln, he'll find most of the local fire department and its equipment in the street and the cottage turned to ashes." Negron looked straight at Whiten as he said, "Adding up the time it'll take Frend to travel in both directions—because he's going to come straight back to the city feeling pretty sick—you and I will have plenty of time to do what we're going to do in Frend's townhouse while nobody's home."

"And what's that, Vince?" Bielinski said.

"I'll worry about that, you take care of the fire."

Joslyn wasn't enthusiastic when he said: "I can smell smoke and see embers glowing already. You think that's enough to put the skids under Frend? You think he'll fall just 'cause we've burned down his out-of-town cottage? He's got a real genius for knowing when to fold and when to stay in or he wouldn't have got himself as far as he's gone."

"It's what I've got figured out, and we're going to do it whether or not you think it's going to make a difference one way or another, Al. There's more here than meets the eye."

"You're nearsighted, Vince. You can't see tomorrow."

"You're wrong, Al, that's just what he's looking at," Madley chimed in.

"Capital for tomorrow, that's my motto," Negron said.

"I'm with you, Vince," Bielinski said, nudging Joslyn under the table.

"Al, you're just going to have to take my word for it. It's too late for you or anyone else here to get out of the car now when it's moving along just fine and we're heading for home."

"If you say so, Vince."

"I'm saying so—you've got the nerves because you aren't taking those pills like you used to. That's a good thing. Trust me. Look what it's done to Madley. It'll work out all right. Just stay off the dope."

"You say something, Vince?" Madley said.

"Who said anything about pills?" Bielinski said.

"I don't take pills, Vince, you know that," Whiten said.

"I wasn't talking to you, Joe."

"Now, Jake and Al, you go shopping for the materials—I've got a few words for Whiten and Madley. When you get back with the stuff, I'll give you the last act to tonight's cookout, then we get some rest because we're going to need all the energy and wits we've got."

Negron left out a big part of the picture, the anonymous tip he was going to make to the police to put Al Joslyn and Jake Bielinski in a setup for a bust on an arson rap with proof for the cops beyond a reasonable doubt that they'd put the flames to the cottage because they'd be standing exactly where Negron told them to stand, with empty cans of gasoline, on orders to watch the blaze until Frend got there with his chauffeur sitting behind the wheel of the Lincoln. They wouldn't know what hit them until it was too late and they'd been fingered and cuffed and thrown into the backseat of the squad car and on their way downtown.

Bielinski and Joslyn got up from the card tables and washed their hands of the greasy donuts and headed for the anteroom to get their hats and coats. Madley started to say something but Negron put his finger to his lips, telling him to keep quiet. Negron leaned back in his chair, heard the door slam shut, reached for his coffee.

"We're going to have a conversation," Negron said, holding the cup with two hands.

"Any special reason?" Madley said.

Whiten didn't say anything, he sipped steaming coffee.

"I think you know what the reason is. I know I don't have to explain it to Whiten, and I'm wondering if I've got to explain it to you, Paul."

72

GRIFF EVANS ROLLED HIS chair back, swung it around to reach the office blinds and raise them. It was ten-forty and the winter sun shone through the windows, pouring sunlight across his desk and what was laid out on top of it that threatened to spill off every edge onto the floor; he'd left memos and scraps and full sheets of paper strewn there when he'd gone home to sleep at four o'clock that morning. Sender was due in twenty minutes.

He looked through the rectangular window to the room beyond that was busy with student interns and gofers and rewriters moving in every direction, while the majority of reporters were seated at their desks, one facing the other, with a couple of nearby television screens lit and the sound turned down. He stared at the movement and stillness which looked a lot like something on TV.

Evans wasn't paying attention to anything in particular when Sender opened the door without knocking. He turned his head at the sound of it.

Evans said, "You're early."

"Ten minutes only, Griff. Nothing to write home about." He sat down across from Evans.

"Relax, take a seat."

"Thanks, I *am* sitting. What's on your mind? You're drifting way out somewhere."

"Sleep, George. I haven't had a good night's sleep in a week."

"Who has a good night's sleep in this business?"

"Maybe the guys who sweep the place out at night."

"Anyway, you're the boss here. What're you doing staying awake all night? You've earned the occasional night's sleep, haven't you?"

"Have you' seen Johnnie To's movie, *Election*?"

"Yes, both of them. But what's that got to do—"

"What's happening with Frend and Negron in this city isn't any different than what the Triad Society did in Hong Kong before the handover—only on a smaller scale. The Society's principle is simply practical: money and power. Today, business means everything. The rivalry between Lok and Big D in the first part is a lot like what's going on with Negron and Frend. If somebody doesn't stop him, Frend's going to be running for office and he'll win because he's got the money to do it and that'll be a first-rate crime. And if the lid isn't put on Negron, we're going to have war. I don't even want to think about what it's going to be like if they start shooting it out. Then if Frend *does* get in office and starts playing with the big shots in Washington, we're going to have local corruption on a national scale—on a par with what's been going on in D.C. for the last seven years. Those guys like Cheney are just as obsessed with money and power as small-time crooks are here in town. I don't have confidence in Washington that they won't want to do local business with a player like Frend. This city isn't a kindergarten—it's major-league. We've graduated."

"And there's an election coming up."

"That's the point. You think it's going to make a difference? Politician and crook are spelled the same as far as I'm concerned."

"And you don't think we've got to play by the rules of who's got money and how much? A newspaper's a business like any other."

"You don't have to remind me. But you've got to admit some of us kept our integrity—virtue intact."

"You said we graduated, okay—but at the same time you make it sound like you want the newspaper business to be a fourteen-year-old virgin wearing glasses and white cotton underpants."

"You know I don't mean it that way, George. I'm just as realistic as the next guy. Everybody's got to grow up, and everyday I sit here looking at what goes on in this city and I'm getting calls from up-stairs from somebody who got the pressure put on them by whoever gave them a call, telling them to lean on me—well, it isn't good for the paper, but it's part of the job."

"That's right, Griff, and it isn't news. So what's the problem?"

"I'm getting fed up with it."

"You're just tired."

"That, too."

"And how do we fit in with this overall ugly picture?"

"That's what's keeping me awake nights."

"I'm thinking maybe I should talk to López again. Find out what he knows, or what he can find out. He's got something on his mind and it's personal and it's got everything to do with Frend. He's one impatient son of a bitch, that's the way I see it."

"Ok, if we can get a break, put it in the paper, maybe the whole thing will collapse and they'll all fall down and Negron will try his tricks in another town and we won't see the likes of Frend in local government—at least for a few years."

"We can dream, can't we?" Sender got up, leaned over the desk and reached out to shake Evan's hand. He took the band off a cigar, put the cigar in his mouth as he went to the door, opened it, turned around and said, "I'll see what I can do, Griff."

73

WHITEN MADE A POINT of waiting for Hargrove in a doorway near the appliance store, and when he saw him leave by the front door he stepped out into the sidewalk. It wasn't six o'clock, but it was already night. They shook hands, Whiten gave Hargrove's shoulder a bump with his own as they walked down to a nearby coffee shop, went in and straight to an empty booth.

Whiten passed an envelope across the table and Hargrove opened it after the waitress took their order, and when he saw it contained twelve hundred dollars, he said, "What's this?"

"Look at it as a little something to keep you and Coral out of the way for a few days until this blows over. How's the Gilbert?"

"A dive, but it's all right. Transient Rooms, Monthly Rates. Your friend Gracie's taking good care of us. Listen, I can't take this money from you, Joe."

"You can and you will. You've got to buy time, and it takes cash to do it."

"Everybody's giving me money," Hargrove said. "First a couple hundred loan from the appliance store, now this—I don't know what to think."

"You're a good investment."

"Well, thanks Joe. I was hoping you were going to tell me I didn't have to hide out anymore—it's been two nights and it feels like a week."

Whiten shook his head no.

"You think there's going to be a problem," Hargrove said, "but there isn't going to be a problem because I won't let it get to the point where there'll be a problem I can't handle, not with Joslyn. Besides, we're out of the picture."

"You aren't out of anything, yet."

"I'm out of it, Coral's never been in it. I haven't been to the club for two weeks. Maybe I'm exaggerating. Maybe it's a week or ten days." Then, his eyes narrowing. "I'm not worried, so you quit worrying."

Whiten wanted to say something reassuring, but he couldn't find the words until he heard himself saying, "If only I felt that way," and told himself, That wasn't encouraging.

"I'm telling you it's okay."

"Telling isn't enough. You can talk until you're blue in the face, and it isn't enough." There was worry in his eyes, his voice was heavy with doubt. "I just can't get rid of the feeling you're both in for a lot of grief. Why don't you get lost for a week? Leave town."

The waitress put two cups of coffee on the table. Whiten saw curdled milk in the pitcher, asked for fresh milk, and when she came back he poured a splash in his cup. Hargrove took it black.

They drank without saying anything. Hargrove put his cup down, looked out the window at the wintry street and the pale glow coming down from streetlamps lighting the sidewalk.

Whiten said, "Coral's not here so I can talk freely. Negron's wise to Joslyn and Bielinski, and I know what he's going to put in front of them—it'll be like hitting a brick wall—and the result's going to be worse than I thought, a bad dream for everybody, and anyway it won't keep Negron from going against Frend because Frend's in the picture on account of Joslyn's bright ideas—whether Negron knows it or not. The big picture's going to include you, and anyone who's had anything to do with El Manojo, and a lot of violence—and since you and Coral are joined at the hip, you're putting her on the spot."

"Okay, I get the picture, I'm sorry for all that, my curiosity and everything—it's my curiosity that put me in with El Manojo, and I wanted a little extra cash—but tell me something I don't know, like what's really going on?"

"I can't."

"You mean you can but you won't."

"I guess that's what I mean. I'm trying to give you the picture, without the details. The details aren't going to help you or anybody. As it goes, what you don't know won't hurt you."

"That's not how it goes for me. I'd rather see it coming if it's going to come my way."

"I'm trying to give you a couple of lengths."

"I know you're trying to help."

"Then do me a favor and forget it."

"It's heating up, and you want us out of the way."

"You don't know how right you are. If you don't do anything else, at least keep your heads down at the Gilbert. Take a couple of days off work. You don't want to get into some kind of fucked up thing with them, they'll rip you apart, then ruin Coral just for fun."

"I'm not brave enough—thing or no thing—and I'm no hero. I'd never take it that far."

"You wouldn't live long enough to know where to take it or who you are—any way you look at it it's a dumb move."

"I don't want anything to happen to Coral."

"Then listen to what I'm saying and stay out of it."

"Maybe I want to help you like you're helping me."

"I don't want your help, Walt."

"That doesn't convince me. You're going to need friends."

"Maybe yes, maybe no. But you're going to be dead if you get mixed up in it."

They picked up their coffee cups at the same time with the same gesture, raised them to their lips and each drank a mouthful like a couple of synchronized performers before putting them down in a single move. A handful of fingernails drummed on the windowpane from outside the coffee shop.

Jean Fleming, wearing a short fur jacket, blew into the coffee shop on Ramón López's arm, and he shoved her down next to Whiten, facing Hargrove, who held his cup of coffee in midair with his mouth open as López slid in beside him. Jean waved at the waitress, ordered a glass of beer and the waitress asked her if the place looked like a bar and she said, "More like a run-down joint to me. Bring me a coffee like the grown-ups."

"I guess it's time to meet Jean Fleming," López said to Hargrove and Whiten.

Hargrove got halfway up, leaned forward over the tabletop to shake Jean's hand and López pushed him back down into the booth before they could unclasp their hands and Hargrove's arm almost knocked over his cup.

Whiten looked at López and said, "Aren't you having anything?" when the waitress put a steaming coffee in front of Jean.

López shook his head. "No, this isn't a social visit."

"Now that we all know each other—what's the interruption?" Whiten said, frowning.

"I threatened to break her neck just to make her come along, give an excuse to Frend, get past Gorman in the palace downtown without him tailing after her into the street," López said, slowly. "That wasn't easy, nothing's easy, and why I did it isn't anybody's business, I do what I want, when I want to do it, and if I want to call it work I call it work even if I don't work for anyone but me since I retired from this city's sheriff's department—none of which is your business anyway."

Hargrove and Whiten looked at him and didn't get the meaning of it but kept quiet and listened. Jean stayed busy with her coffee.

"What she's got to say she's got to say now so I get her back before somebody knows she's gone out to meet me instead of going to the pharmacy, which is what she told me she told Frend, so we'd better hurry it up—start talking, Jean."

74

CORAL CURLED UP AGAINST Hargrove on the sofa in her apartment. He wasn't asleep but his eyes were closed and behind the lids there was a lot of action on the order of worry and the sort of pictures that went with it, pushing him far out of the apartment and away from Coral into a zone of violence and insecurity. The knee-length cotton robe she wore parted as she nestled against him, her bare knees made contact with his skin. Hargrove opened his eyes.

"Where were you?" she said.

"Drifting."

"I could see that."

He didn't want to say anything about what he'd learned from the conversation in the coffee shop, there wasn't any point scaring her more than she was scared already, and if keeping the truth from Coral made him feel better, it still didn't take away the threat of violence hanging over both of them. For tonight he was going to ignore the warning Whiten gave him because Carol wanted to stay in her own apartment on Cherry and not in the Gilbert, which she'd said gave her the creeps. The money in his pocket came to twelve hundred dollars minus fifteen for takeaway Chinese food.

There was going to be a massacre, and Hargrove knew it was going to happen just as he knew how much he loved Coral, though that knowledge wasn't anything like the same feeling since love was one thing and fear of bloodshed another. Then there was the ready formula: López was going to put himself between Frend and Fleming for the showdown; Negron, eliminating obstacles, was working the takeover from Frend, until one of them went down, despite the fact that Frend had more experience and an army of people in local politics and police behind him than Negron ever dreamed of having which put the weight of power with Frend at considerably more than a hundred percent.

Hargrove turned pale, put his arms around Coral, pulled her close to him and looked into eyes that drew him down until he was lost in a pool of liquid so thick the gears of time stopped shifting altogether. It was a very syrupy, very sweet tasting liquid, a lot like molasses. He enjoyed that feeling more than almost anything else. He kissed her, she opened her mouth wide, and her lips kissed back hard.

He went on kissing her and gradually it wasn't Coral he was thinking about even though the lips he kissed belonged to Coral, it was Jean Fleming, who came floating in on the liquid feeling and the jolt took him back to the coffee shop and straight to the words she'd said before López told them it was enough, they got the picture, didn't they? and there wasn't time for more because he'd risked plenty to bring her there. At which point he bundled her out of the place into the wintry street.

It wasn't until he felt the sting of Coral's open hand slapping his cheek that he realized he was daydreaming and not kissing or kissing while daydreaming and the expression on her face told him she was really upset, but the distress didn't last and pretty soon he saw the gentle radiance in her eyes.

"I'm sorry, Walt, but I didn't understand what it was and now I think I understand—so I'm really sorry."

"Coral, don't say you're sorry when you've got nothing to be sorry about. It's me, I'm the one who's sorry. Maybe we should go back to the Gilbert. I'm worried, and I guess I don't know how worried I am, or I would've stopped myself from going away from you like that. I love you."

"That takes it way beyond worry, Walt—for both of us."

"What does?"

"Love."

"But it doesn't make us bulletproof."

"You look knocked out. Why don't we go to bed?"

"All right, but I've got to tell you we're in a spot, more trouble than I figured at the beginning, and I didn't want to tell you, but we'd better hole up at the Gilbert until this thing blows over and there's nothing left to worry about."

She got up off the sofa and took his hand, led him out of the living room into the bedroom and shoved him gently back onto the bed. He watched her as she took off her robe and threw it over the back of an armchair. She stood in front of him in a pair of red panties.

75

Jean said, "I don't have to listen at doors. He trusts me."

"He's wrong," Whiten said. "The proof is you're here."

"No, he's right to trust me because the only reason I said anything to him"—she pointed at López—"and that I've said anything to you is that I'm afraid Vince Negron's going to kill him, and I'll do what I've got to do to keep that from happening, whether you believe it or not doesn't make a difference to me."

"I'm not trying to argue with you, Jean, I just want to understand why you're telling us what you're telling us," Whiten said.

"So what's any of this got to do with me?" Hargrove said.

"You've got a short memory, Walt," Whiten said.

"I'm not interested in any of it," López said. "Frend can climb into a wood chopping machine like in the movie, for all I care, but for Jean's sake I figured I couldn't handle the situation by myself and thought I'd make her put the facts to both of you, and maybe we'd come up with a plan."

"How generous of you," Jean said, looking at López.

"Shut up," he said.

"I can see this is going to get us everywhere," Hargrove said.

"You mean nowhere," Whiten corrected him.

"Everywhere and nowhere—that's what I mean," Hargrove said.

Whiten said, "I don't think we can afford to get involved."

López lowered his head, his face blushing. "I just want to help her," he said. "I can't help myself, maybe I can do something for Jean—make up with her for what a jerk I've been." He talked as if she wasn't sitting right across the table from him.

"Now, let's not get sentimental, Ramón," she said.

"Christ, can't I get anything right?"

The waitress came to the table, folded her arms across her ample chest. "Can I get you something else?"

López raised his head, saying, "A bottle of mescal."

"What's it look like here, a bar?"

"Don't start that again," Jean said.

"I'll start whatever I want to start."

Whiten said, "Just leave the check," and when she'd left the check on the table and walked away, he turned to the others, adding, "Let's adjourn to a nearby watering hole. What do you say?" He put a ten down on the table. "My treat."

"I'm going home," Hargrove said. "I've got to meet somebody."

"I've got to get Jean back before Frend gets wise. This so-called pharmacy trip's taking an awful lot of time."

"That's right," Jean said. "And I've got nothing to show for it."

"We'll pick something up on the way," López said.

"That's not what I'm talking about, you idiot—I mean you haven't done anything to help anybody. Sure as my name's Jean Fleming, that little spic with the long hair is going to kill Frend."

"A spic?" López said.

"He ain't a dago or Jew, I can tell you that much."

"Is that the way you get your kicks, insulting people?"

"No."

"Then keep your comments to yourself." López was burning up. "You're drunk, and I'm no Chinaman, you know."

"Right. Ramón López is López, as usual," she said. "And I'm not drunk, I just hate everybody today. We're all washed up in the same boat."

Whiten gave Hargrove a look, and his eyes were the eyes of a close friend, genuinely concerned.

"Let's get out of here," she said.

"We get out of here when I say we get out of here," López said. "Now, let's go."

They got out of the booth, adjusted their winter coats and

scarves, stood for a second in front of Hargrove and Whiten as López looked down at them with a frown on his face.

López said, "The picture's clear? You're minds are made up?"

"Clear as crystal," Whiten said. "I'm speaking for both of us when I say, no deal."

76

THE BIG PLASTIC CONTAINERS filled with gasoline were a lot heavier than Joslyn thought they'd be, and when he and Bielinski were finished loading a rented van with three of them, he opened the passenger door of the van and sat on the edge of the passenger seat to light a cigarette. Bielinski came around the van and stood in front of him wiping the perspiration off his forehead before it froze in the icy weather. A cold wind blew in off the lake.

A case of empty wine bottles with screw tops and a pile of rags and a jar of coal tar and a shopping bag with Styrofoam soft drink cups sat behind the passenger seat. Bielinski slid open the side door of the van and started counting wine bottles.

"Cocktails. There's enough here to keep an army away," he said.

"Leave 'em, Jake. We can't fill 'em up here—too many people."

"That's right, Al."

Joslyn finished his cigarette.

"Let's get back to the garage," he said, walking around to the driver's side and climbing in behind the wheel.

Bielinski took a Ziploc bag full of 100 mg. MS Contin tablets out of his coat pocket, dumped a few gray pills into the palm of his hand and tossed them into his mouth, swallowing them down with a mouthful of flat Fanta Orange.

"I don't know if I'm sweating from hauling those gas cans or if it's just I need more medicine," he said. "You want any?"

"Give me a couple."

"Purdue makes this stuff—and Senokot, too. We're faithful customers at both ends, going in *and* coming out." Bielinski laughed.

"I can't swallow these things without something to drink, Jake," Joslyn said.

Bielinski handed him the nearly empty can of Fanta. Joslyn finished what was left of it, making a face.

"How can you drink that?"

"You swallowed them, didn't you?"

They didn't talk as Joslyn took the van along one street, turned at another, keeping to the speed limit and watching traffic until they got to the garage on Fifth Street, rented in the name of the Seventeenth Street Social Club. It was located two and a half blocks away from their place on Meyering Boulevard. The van went down the ramp and started making its way to the second level where there was a lot of light and very few parked cars and ten individual, locked private stalls each with a metal door.

The gasoline cans were lined up along the concrete wall of the parking stall just behind the rear bumper of the van. The bare bulb in the ceiling lit their work. They filled a half-dozen wine bottles with gas and broken Styrofoam cups and a cubic centimeter of coal tar to create smoke, then screwed the tops shut to let the Styrofoam soak in the gas and tar. They put the six bottles back in the case and set the case in the back of the van.

Joslyn locked the van, Bielinski lowered the metal stall door, locked it, and they went to the staircase and climbed the stairs to get a late lunch, giving the contents of the explosive cocktails a couple of hours to get to know each other.

They found a place open serving food all day and ate with a lot of enthusiasm through the comforting warmth that coursed through them from the MS Contin. They washed down another couple of tablets with coffee at the end of their meal.

77

I T WAS SEVEN FORTY-FIVE pm. Sender was standing in front of the windows of his five-story apartment looking down at the heavy flow of evening traffic on Prospect Avenue when his phone rang. It was López calling him, and he answered it with his right hand. He rubbed his left hand up the back of his head against short bristly hair. The blue-black lake was almost invisible in the night, blending with the blue-black sky that ran down into it like a sheet of dull paper.

López talked using a fast stream of words that made Sender go directly to the nearby sofa and sit down with his legs stretched out in front of him. He listened. There wasn't any room between words for him to say anything. He leaned forward, took an apple from a bowl on the table, ate slowly, chewing thoroughly, savoring each mouthful. The noise he made taking bites out of the crisp apple didn't stop López from talking at him like the world was running out of time.

What López said settled a lot of questions in his mind that had clouded his brain since he'd promised Griff Evans he'd get something on the foreseeable war between Frend and Negron, and out of that information a story and words that would break the whole thing wide open and prevent more violence than Lake City was ready for or the local police could handle, maybe going as far as saving the lives of innocent people.

He dropped the apple core into the thick glass ashtray and took an unlit cigar out of it and stuck it in his mouth.

"All right, Ramón, all right, I get the picture," he said at last with the cigar still in his mouth. "What time exactly? Okay, I'll be there. No, I won't look for you, and if I see you I won't know you. You've got nothing to worry about. No, I don't want to know what you're going to do. That's right. Now hang up—I've got to make a call."

Sender hung up the phone, got up, went to his desk and picked up another phone to call Evans at home, and when his wife answered she told him Evans was still at the *Journal*.

The phone in Evans' office rang five times before Evans picked it up. Evans' voice was worn out from a long day that began before eight. Sender started slowly, built it into an important thing with the facts he figured Evans could grasp until Evans came down to earth and heard it, got interested and saw it really was the way Sender was putting it. It amounted to an opportunity they'd both been waiting for.

"I'll tell Gale Wicker to meet you, he's dragging himself around here with nothing to do, complaining about it, dying to take a picture. This'll make him happy, George—you've made two men happy tonight. Now I can go home and have dinner with my wife for a change, and you've made it all right for me to do it—no guilt, no worry, just happy to go home after a long day with nothing to show but complaints from upstairs and an empty twelve-ounce bottle of Pepto-Bismol—not a drop of scotch. Thank you, George."

"Tell him to meet me at Quail Street near the entrance to the expressway," he said. "There's a Chinese joint called The Blue Dragon. I'll be waiting in the parking lot."

"He's on his way. Let me know what you've got in the morning. Seven o'clock? If it's really big call me at home."

"At seven."

"Good-night, George."

"Good-night, Griff."

78

BIELINSKI STUFFED A RAG soaked in gas into each of the wine bottles leaving a rabbit's tail of damp cloth sticking out from the neck. The van was parked a half block from Frend's place on a dark, quiet road where the windows of houses were black and the houses themselves were just shadows in a winter sky without a moon. The yards in front of them were covered by a thin blanket of frozen snow.

Joslyn finished a cigarette keeping watch just outside the rear door of the van. He saw his breath mingle with the smoke that came out of his mouth, rubbed his hands together, then struck the rear doors of the van with the flat of his hand. One of the doors swung open and he saw Bielinski crouched inside with the overhead light on wiping his hands of gasoline with a dry rag. He moved his arm so the sleeve of his winter car coat wiped his running nose.

"I'm catching a cold," Bielinski said.

"You can't catch anything. I can't catch anything—I've tried. With as much dope as we've got in us, there isn't a germ in the world that'd survive. It's freezing, Jake. It's just the weather."

"You ready?" Bielinski pushed the wine case toward the rear door. "We aren't going to need a half-dozen bottles, Al. Not the way I figure it."

Joslyn reached for a couple of bottles, then stopped. "You think Negron can see what's going on behind his back with all the things we set up?" He put on a pair of gloves, picked up two bottles with a mixture of gas, Styrofoam and coal tar.

"I don't. Got an extra lighter?"

"Yeah. You don't think so?" He set the bottles down at his feet, gave Bielinski a black Bic with orange pumpkins on it.

"Halloween. No—not possible. He doesn't suspect a thing. This plan of his played right into our hands, it'll clinch the whole deal, and Frend will go after him like a rabid dog. The cards are stacked against him—the setup went our way. You can take my word for it, Al. It's a piece of cake from now on."

"Lock it up, Jake."

Bielinski got out of the back of the van, steadied two cocktails on the uneven icy street, shut the door, pointed the keys at the van and every door locked itself. "Great invention," he said.

Joslyn said, "Yeah, come on."

Bielinski caught up with him, Joslyn's long strides were careful on the slippery street, and they ducked their heads to avoid the leafless branches of trees that reached out above them as they climbed the slope of the yard that trailed downward from the front door and porch of Frend's house. They shivered as a gust of wind cut through them.

They crouched behind a row of shrubs, looked up through the spiky branches at Frend's house lit by a couple of lights that were switched on by a timer. They waited, listening to each other's labored breathing while they counted the minutes. There was no sign of life in the house. They had Negron's assurance that Frend was in Lake City.

"Looks like it's time to warm things up," Joslyn said, digging in a pocket for his Zippo.

"Right you are, Al."

Joslyn lit the rag stuffed in the mouth of one of the bottles.

The Halloween Bic was visible when Bielinski struck the wheel against the flint and got a flame, then the rabbit ears were lit and the rag was slowly burning and he jumped up from his crouching position with the bottle in his hand and his arm drawn back for a hard and fast pitch at the front porch of the house.

The yard lit up with spotlights trained on the house, yard and shrubbery that partially hid them, and the thin blanket of snow glowed like a waxy film of white phosphorus, and when Bielinski looked around he saw the sources of light and they were spots mounted on the side of squad cars that came out of nowhere and his arm went down slowly, and a voice on a loudspeaker was telling them to put the cocktails out, set them down, put their hands up in the air and come out from behind the raggedy shrubs in front of them.

It wasn't Bielinski's idea of what was supposed to happen so he ignored it and raised his arm again with the intention of setting Frend's house on fire to complete the job even if it was the last thing he did in his life, but before he could get the windup going and then the pitch, there was a burning pain that came right after a crack like a shot in the sharp air and a bullet tore through his arm near his shoulder. He dropped the bottle, which rolled into a heap of snow where the flame went out.

Joslyn wasn't standing up but when Bielinski spun and fell to the ground behind the shrubbery, cursing the world, he got to his feet, making an ugly face at the police he couldn't see but knew were standing somewhere behind the blinding array of spotlights, raised the bottle above his head, swung back his arm to throw the bottle at them when a rifle shot echoed in the night, and the bullet struck Joslyn in the forehead.

He felt a searing sensation in his brain that switched off the spotlights and everything else as he fell forward, turned, and his body dropped dead on top of Bielinski, who was writhing in pain, and their arms and legs entangled; the wine-bottle cocktail struck the sharp edge of a flagstone half-buried in the ground and burst into flames. They were burnt to a crisp by the clinging napalm-like effect of flaming gas mixed with bits of Styrofoam, the bodies hidden from view beneath a heavy cloud of coal-tar smoke.

When the fire trucks arrived the firemen hosed down the blackened bodies and extinguished the flaming shrubbery and smoldering dead earth beneath the melted snow and a melting plastic garbage can filled with recyclable glass that was caught in the creeping flames of gasoline.

What was left of Joslyn and Bielinski was gathered up and put in two bags and then into an ambulance that took them to the county morgue.

79

SENDER PULLED WICKER BY the sleeve of his coat toward the charred bodies and told him to take a lot of shots from every angle using the available light to exaggerate and give an atmosphere to the grotesque shape they made with their arms and legs twisted together like a couple of blackened scarecrows.

"Think of Weegee," Sender said.

Sender held a handkerchief over his nose, Wicker looked like he was going to throw up.

"Listen Gale," he said, "you can't get sick before you've got the pictures." He stuck a half-smoked cigar in Wicker's mouth and lit it. "That ought to do the trick."

The smoke went into Wicker's eyes and he couldn't focus through his tears and when he tasted the cigar he started to gag.

"Take this thing out of my mouth, I can't see anything," he said.

"You don't want to see what you're looking at—it's awful. Just shoot with your eyes closed."

"Give me a break, George. Just go away," Wicker said. "Why don't you ask the boys a few questions?" He indicated the handful of policemen standing around their captain, and a lonely sharpshooter with a blank expression on his face, his head bowed.

Wicker pinched his nose closed, took a deep breath through his mouth, held his Nikon in his right hand, let go of his nose and went to work, saying, "Christ almighty."

He got as close to the bodies as he could get. The strobe went off half a dozen times with the shutter; he crouched, took another half a dozen shots using only the crossed beams of light from the spotlights on the two squad cars that remained while the area was being taped off and photographed and the evidence recovery technicians were gathering and tagging evidence. One of them, a young woman, pushed him roughly out of the way.

Wicker walked up to Sender, standing in the middle of the street interviewing one of the patrolmen, and he listened without hearing what they were saying because the smell of cooked flesh, burnt grass and shrubbery and plastic filled his nose and went straight to his head, and again he thought he was going to be sick.

He ran to the other side of the shrubbery, vomited until his stomach was empty of the sandwich he ate and the coffee he drank during the early part of his nightshift at the *Journal,* and the burning in his throat didn't keep him from gagging while his head throbbed with the force of drawing up bile that stayed at the back of his throat; he had the sense to look down at the Nikon to make sure it wasn't covered with what had just come up.

He felt a hand resting on his shoulder, turned his head and looked up at Sender standing just behind him.

"You all right?"

Wicker straightened up, reached for the handkerchief in his pocket and wiped his mouth. "Yes, George. Okay. Did you call Evans?"

Sender nodded, then led Wicker away from the shrubbery to the street in front of Frend's house, then down the street to the corner, turned and walked a half block down that street until they got to where Wicker had parked his car.

"Give me the keys and get in—I'll drive," Sender said. "You're all shook up, Gale."

Negron paced the floor. There wasn't a lot of room to move in his apartment, but he had to keep moving, so he kept going from one end of it to the other, crossing over and starting again to make a sort of X out of the two paths he'd been taking for over an hour.

The phone rang. He was standing next to it, all he had to do was to reach out to lift the receiver, no effort involved, so he picked it up.

It was Madley with a report on the outcome of a case of arson north of the city that turned out to be a case of attempted arson in which the two perpetrators were killed. Negron couldn't stop himself from giggling quietly. He didn't bother acting surprised. Madley didn't find it funny.

Negron sighed, told Madley to relax, put the receiver down, went to the bed and sat on the edge of it with his feet planted on the floor. A *ranchera* sung by Raul Martínez and Juan González came up from the jukebox in El Perro Llorón two floors below. He wanted to dance, but didn't have the strength after all that pacing around.

His voice was dull and metallic as he told himself, "That leaves Frend."

Negron undressed, smoked a cigarette, got into bed, and went to sleep with the idea of getting up early and heading over to the social club.

80

THINGS WERE MOVING A lot faster than Lloyd Frend figured they'd move and he understood that Negron was trying to cover a lot of ground fast when he read Sender's account in the *Journal* of the attempt to burn down his house outside of the city.

The police had notified him right away, and privately, Sender had given him a lot of details, but it looked and felt different reading it in black and white. He knew who was responsible without having to look at the paper, even if Sender's article didn't put a finger on anybody and the police weren't ready to let go with what they knew or didn't know until they had something that would stick in court, Frend knew who'd done it.

He called Billy Gorman into the apartment from his place on a chair in the hallway outside the door. Gorman shuffled in while Frend held the door open for him. He led Gorman into the living room, indicated an armchair, and Gorman slumped down into the plush cushions with his head bowed.

"You look terrible," Frend said gently.

"I feel terrible. I haven't slept for days, my back's killing me from sitting in that fucking chair, and I haven't shut my eyes for three days, Mr. Frend."

"I know how you feel, Billy, and I'm sorry. Can I get you something?"

"An aspirin and some coffee would go a long way."

Five minutes later, Frend came back from the kitchen with a cup of coffee and a Tylenol, and put them in Gorman's outstretched hands. He pulled a chair up to face him, leaned forward in the chair.

Jean came into the room wearing a bathrobe and slippers and the bathrobe opened wide as she walked, showing a lot of leg; she stopped at the doorway surprised to find Gorman and Frend sitting opposite each other at this time of day.

Gorman looked up and saw Jean and knew she'd just woken up, there was sex written on her face and in her tousled hair, and the particular antics they got up to in bed were smeared all over her even if he couldn't see anything beneath the robe and it embarrassed him so he looked away from their inquisitive expressions.

"What are you staring at the carpet for? You haven't done anything wrong, Billy," Frend said in a friendly tone of voice.

"I'll just leave you to it, then," Jean said from the door, then headed toward the kitchen.

Gorman swallowed the Tylenol tablet with a mouthful of steaming coffee.

"You remember the boys who used to work for me that aren't working for me anymore but have jobs as muscle on the doors of nightclubs, union guys unloading trucks and working construction sites, and the rest of them who make up the security firm I bankroll?"

Gorman nodded, the coffee was so hot the tablet almost dissolved on his tongue, leaving a bitter taste.

"Of course you do. Well, I've got to get in touch with a few of them but I have to do it indirectly, if you catch my drift, and that's where you come in, Billy. You follow me?"

"Right behind you, Mr. Frend."

Gorman swallowed another mouthful of coffee that burned his throat. He was so tired the room began to spin and the caffeine joined with exhaustion and now he was more stimulated to go straight to bed and sleep than to sit there listening to Frend ask him a favor.

Frend leaned closer, with an air of confidentiality, and said, "You can call me Lloyd."

"Not now, I can't—not all of a sudden, not after all this time, Mr. Frend. It's going to be like it's been, and stay that way."

"Okay, Billy, that's fine. Where was I?"

"You want to get in touch with some men who used to work for you."

"That's right."

"Listen, I'm dead on my feet. I won't make it to the garage downstairs without falling down much less drive the car around town and not get pulled over or smash it up while I'm trying to catch up on old times with the boys, Mr. Frend. I'm wiped out."

"There's a bonus in it for you."

"You can keep your bonus, Mr. Frend. I've got to get some sleep."

Frend leaned back in his chair, Gorman nestled into the arm-chair. Gorman sipped his coffee, turned his head when he felt a pair of eyes on him and saw they belonged Jean.

She stood in the doorway again, leaning against the jamb with one ankle crossed over the other, one foot out of its slipper and the painted toenails on it poking at the runner behind her. She had a cup of coffee in her hand, looked at the two of them with her eyebrows raised, listening and pretending that she wasn't hearing anything.

At last she came into the room, sat down on the sofa, crossed her legs in such a way that Gorman couldn't help but notice them, then dangled a slipper off the end of one foot. Gorman blushed.

"Okay, I get the picture. You don't have to go if you don't want to go, but I'm sorry, Billy, I'm sorry you can't make it work out for me," Frend said, putting on an air of disappointment as he got up and rubbed his hands together.

"What's this all about?" Jean asked.

"Billy's going to go to bed."

"What's wrong with that, Lloyd? He's been awake long enough, hasn't he?"

"Yes, Jean. That's right."

Gorman stood up, finished his cup of coffee. "I'll just put this in the kitchen."

He weaved through the furniture and out the living-room doorway, turned left and went down the hall to the kitchen, then came straight back heading for the front door. He said good-night without turning around, opened the door and shut it softly behind him. It was nine-forty in the morning.

By ten-twenty Jean convinced Frend to call López and offer him the same deal he'd proposed to Gorman, but the deal included a lot more money, since López was a professional and Frend couldn't very well expect him to organize a thing like that at the same price he'd been willing to pay Gorman.

Now López would be on Frend's salary, and he'd be working for Jean, too.

She sat back on the sofa, opened the bathrobe, exposing her pussy, and she reached down, caressing herself and putting a finger inside, and the finger came out wet and she put it straight into her mouth.

Frend knelt in front of her open legs.

López wasn't surprised to hear Frend's voice on the other end of the phone, but what he didn't expect was the all-forgiving tone of it that sent waves of suspect sensitivity through the phone line into his head. It wasn't like Frend. The last time they'd seen each other Frend knocked him out and Frend's chauffeur Billy Gorman left him in his car by the side of the road, so he figured there was something more to it than a job and what it probably added up to was a setup that would put him out of business for who knows how long.

López remembered a couple of names and a few of the faces of the guys who used to work for Frend before he became a legitimate businessman and investor in Lake City. Frend told him to come to the townhouse and take a look in the scrapbook he kept of the days he was in the *Journal* under indictment before he'd become respectable, so he'd see the faces of the men he wanted for the job. López started to laugh, checked it, then told Frend he'd be there at one. It was almost noon. Frend didn't invite him for lunch.

Frend didn't take off his shirt right away, but his trousers were on the floor behind him as he moved his face close between her legs and breathed the smell of her into his lungs. He'd pulled the sleeves of her robe behind her and tied them loosely together and she was caught in the sleeves with the weight of her body pressed down on them, her head turned away from him, but she felt his breath against her, and she rolled her hips a little to the left and right, waiting for his fingers until the waiting that was anticipation built itself into impatience and she wriggled her arms out of the sleeves and they were free and she reached down and grabbed his head to make his tongue touch her pussy.

She had a feeling the living room was moving, and it was a very small room on wheels or the passenger car of a Ferris wheel going away from everything, falling off the edge of the world. His tongue licked her making her very wet while his wet thumb ran vertically over the lips of her pussy spreading them as he put the knuckle of his index finger against the opening without penetrating her. She lowered her head, her hands covered her face.

Then he was inside her.

They ignored the faint sounds of the humming kitchen appliances, the distant traffic rumbling on the streets below, and they didn't know whether or not they were living or dead because it was just skin burning and tingling and their brains traveling way out of the bones of their skull into another dimension, traveling very fast with so much pleasure as fuel and as if the singularity of that moment would hold them together forever.

But it didn't because it was like being asleep and dreaming and the dream as real and everlasting as life with nothing else in this world but the sequence of events, one following another, whether or not they made sense, until the dream ended with waking up, and it was another morning or after a siesta, and then Frend was putting on his trousers, Jean putting her arms in the sleeves of her robe, and Frend going slowly to the phone to dial López's number, just before noon, having a hard time on his feet, but thinking, If I don't get to that phone, I'm going to be in trouble, and then telling himself, Trouble, you don't know the meaning of the word.

It wasn't just that it was Saturday that Coral and Hargrove were lying in bed at two in the afternoon in the Gilbert with the sheets tangled around their legs and the bedcovers down at the end of the mattress, skin covered in sweat and their legs entwined while Hargrove shifted to the left and right trying to find a dry spot on the bed in the mess they'd made after fucking for more than an hour.

"Quit moving around," Coral said.

"I can't help it."

Her arm dropped across his chest and she put her head on his shoulder and looked down at his cock which was still wet with both his come and her own. She shut her eyes, smiled.

Hargrove thought she'd fallen asleep. He closed his eyes and on the lids he saw the Seventeenth Street Social Club, Negron and Whiten and Madley and Bielinski and Joslyn trailed by the ghost of Ray Graham, a progression of scenes that made him shiver without moving, and he wondered how he'd got himself into the spot he was in right now, and through a whirl of all the scenes coming together in a pool gone wild there was one he didn't regret, a particular moment, one that might come once in a man's lifetime, and he was really grateful for it, and that was the exception that was Coral Rasmussen, the best thing that had happened to him since he'd got to Lake City. And for all that was wrong in the world that rubbed up against him, there was so much right in it, because she was lying beside him.

Coral's voice snapped him out of it, saying, "When people decide they've got a good reason to get out of love even when they're in love, they believe their brains more than their hearts."

"Maybe that's true, maybe it isn't. It sounds right."

"And maybe Jean Fleming loved López then as much as he still

loves her now, and with some kind of misplaced expediency she
found an excuse to get out of it. And the excuse was money."

"Well?"

"Now look what's happened—we're staying in this crummy
hotel, a real dive, and there's trouble, and I wonder where it really
started—because she decided to follow the money?—and I wonder
if it isn't on account of Fleming and López that we're in this mess,
because I think either López or Fleming got us mixed up in this,
or both of them together, maybe not even knowing it, just so one
could get close to the other again."

"Somebody's pulling the strings, and it isn't López. I don't know
Jean Fleming. And you're forgetting that I got *myself* involved with
El Manojo—out of curiosity."

"I guess I just don't want to remember it."

"We ought to get out of here. Leave this place for good. I got
ideas myself."

"Right now, we're staying put, Walt. I'm scared."

"She's right, Walt. Both of you stay put," Whiten said. "Around
twelve o'clock today, I saw López give the doorman at Frend's a
nod and take the elevator cool as a cucumber on his way up to see
him. That means something—a nod. That means Frend asked for
him. That means Gorman isn't going to stop him when he gets upstairs. And it means Negron's going to be circling the drain before
he knows what's hit him."

"How come you know so much about it?"

"I've been living here forever, I was born here, and I've seen it
all, the rise and fall of every clown that thinks he's somebody—ever
since I was a kid."

Hargrove opened a cold bottle of beer from the six-pack
Whiten had brought to the room at the Gilbert, offered it to him,
then opened one for himself. It was about ten-fifteen. Coral had
gone out for Chinese take-out. A significant amount of lightweight

snowflakes tumbled past the windows to the street below, falling through the glow of sodium-vapor lamps lighting the sidewalks running parallel to the road.

"You think it's going to end soon?"

"I don't know what to think. It'll end, when I don't know, but there'll be a lot of bodies to account for before it does."

"Sad, isn't it?"

"What's sad?"

"The way we know something bad's going to happen and we talk about it like we're talking about the weather, and we've got no inclination to do anything about it. I call that sad."

"I can't argue that, Walt. In fact, it stinks."

"It's worse than a bad smell. It's being a coward without a conscience—we're all just looking out for ourselves. I haven't lived here long, but since I've lived here it's just about obvious to me and anybody else who comes here from outside the city to take a look at all there is to see—little men, big world—that nobody gives a rat's ass what somebody else does as long as he or she does it without getting in the way of whatever they've got planned for the rest of their lives. It isn't like that where I come from."

"It's no different in any city that's got a population this size, Walt. The world isn't that bad. You wouldn't have met Coral if you hadn't come down here *to take a look at all there is to see*, would you?"

"Now, it's my turn to say it."

"What?"

"I can't argue with that."

"Speaking of Coral—what's taking her so long with the food? The joint's not far from here. Maybe you ought to go out there and give her a hand."

"I really must be stupid if I need you to tell me that."

Hargrove pulled a sweater over his head, got into his boots and overcoat but kept looking around for something. He went for the door, saying, "I'll be right back." Before he got there he picked up his keys. "I'll call if there's a problem."

"Wear my hat, you'll stay warm and look like a Cossack."

Whiten tossed him his hat, he put it on and the hat was too big for his head, but right away he felt the lining warm his head. He turned the knob, went out, shut and locked the door. Whiten heard his footsteps in the corridor as they went along the creaky floor.

81

Dock Street, near the gym, without anything in the vicinity like a dock that functioned as a dock, was about as miserable a street in a heartless neighborhood as Hargrove could imagine from his limited experience in big cities, and he left the entrance of the Gilbert Hotel feeling down the minute he hit the street, heading away from the river, and started walking along the sidewalk.

He looked around at the bums in pairs in doorways with newspaper stuffed inside their worn-out clothes and boots, he saw the slumped shoulders and the lowered heads, the dim shapes huddled against dark walls, the stragglers looking at their feet as they walked aimlessly, searching for hoped-for coins and bills someone might have dropped in the snow, drifting women and men bundled up in warm coats against the cold winter night that might have been tourists in this part of town, looking for a bar or club that didn't have much in the way of rules about what did or didn't go on there.

He'd been an idiot to let Coral go to the Chinese take-out alone, and he regretted it and vowed he'd never do anything like it again, swearing that he'd go stark raving mad if anything happened to her. He didn't realize his coat was unbuttoned because his eyes and senses focused on the shapes in the dirty glow of yellow lamps, until the wind picked up more cold from the ice on the river and sent a chill through him on Dock Street. He started to button his coat and slipped on a patch of ice, grabbed at a lamppost, got hold of it, but fell down anyway.

Hargrove lay on his back with snowflakes drifting down into his open mouth. The light coming from the streetlight sparkled between snowflakes and gave everything a kind of starburst effect, or it was the blow to the back of his head, but the snowflakes accumulating on his face soon wiped out that effect and left him with blurred vision. He felt a throbbing pain, reached up to put his hand where the pain was and felt Whiten's Cossack hat that had miraculously stayed on his head.

A pair of hands and then the arms attached to them slipped under the bulky sleeves of his overcoat and tried to lift him, but the arms weren't strong enough, and when he got his eyes focused on the sleeves covering the arms, he saw they belonged to the coat that Coral put on when she left the Gilbert, so he made an extra effort to give her some help to get him up off the sidewalk.

They walked the half block back to the Gilbert Hotel, each holding one of the two medium-sized plastic bags with containers of Chinese food in their arms.

"Now that we've had something hot to eat," Whiten said, "I thought I'd tell you, I didn't come here just to say hello—there's a cloud around every silver lining."

Hargrove smoked a cigarette, Coral sat on the edge of the bed with her legs stretched out in front of her, Whiten got up to wash his hands in the porcelain sink in a corner of the room. Hargrove and Coral waited for Whiten to say something more, but he was too busy scrubbing his hands and drying them to go on with it for the moment.

"I didn't just watch López go into Frend's townhouse, I waited for him to come out, and when he came out I followed him and spent most of the day in a taxi following him about two car length's behind."

"Standard procedure. And what did you learn from this mind-numbing exercise?" Coral said.

She got up, stood behind Hargrove, put her hands on his shoulders, her fingers gripping them loosely at first as Whiten went on with his story.

"Not what I expected. And I don't know what I expected."

"We're listening." Hargrove looked over his shoulder at Coral, sent her a weak smile, then leaned toward Whiten, "All right, Joe, now tell me."

A dull tone crept into Whiten's voice, and he wanted to get rid of it but couldn't, as he said, "Today, and the early part of tonight, I followed him. López left in his own car. He got in touch with as many of Frend's ex-pals as he could find. He went to a gym—a boxing instructor, flattened nose and thick lips, he couldn't box his way out of a paper bag; a construction site—two guys, as much beef on 'em as pro athletes; in a mall—a security guard at a jewelry store; and tonight, half a dozen bouncers on the doors of three clubs, two downtown, one Midtown. Most of them weren't big, but they didn't look nice—a guy had a slice out of his face—and if they haven't done time, my name's 50 Cent—I'd make book on it."

"Who?"

"Doesn't matter."

"So, what's it mean?"

"Frend's assembling guys for a job that can't be traced back to him—unless you know his history. And that job amounts to wiping out everybody that's got something to do with Vince Negron. And when it gets that bad it gets to the point where nobody's tough anymore. That's what's staring us in the face."

"But why López? What's in it for him?"

"It'll put him closer to Jean, which is what he wants—and Frend knows it."

"I told you, Walt, on account of being in love and not being able to do anything about it—he doesn't know what he's doing," Coral said.

"That's the heartache department," Hargrove told her.

He looked at her again, her grip on his shoulders tightened, and he didn't know if the strength of it came from fear or love. She bent down, breathed in his ear, said she loved him, and the words went straight to his heart.

He looked back at Whiten, saying, "Where does that leave us, you and me?"

"Nowhere."

"That's too bad," Hargrove said. "Because then we'll both be nowhere."

"You're leaving Coral out."

"She *is* out."

"Nobody's out, Walt. We'll all be nowhere."

"So many angles I can't figure."

"There's nothing to figure."

"We can't just sit here and wait for it to come crashing down on us."

"That's what I want to talk to you about." Whiten got up and started pacing the small hotel room. "I went back to Frend's place, waited in the car. I'm sitting there about an hour when a couple of cabs pull up and some of the guys I saw López talking to get out and go straight in through the townhouse front door like it doesn't matter if anybody sees them."

"So?"

"So, Frend's not thinking straight, doesn't care who knows what he's doing. And that's not good." He sat on the edge of the bed. "Pretty soon another cab pulls up. It's two more guys, then a car—a beat-up van—and a tall, skinny guy gets out of it, goes in, and the setup's beginning to look like a town meeting. There's maybe six of them up there together."

"And López?"

"Not López. Then, a half hour later, most of them leave, go off in different directions, and the van comes back, pulls over and picks up the last guy—like clockwork, like it's arranged in advance, like the driver knew just how long he'd be up there. And now they all know why, and for what purpose Frend wanted them, and *we* don't know anything. And not knowing anything in a situation like this feels like choking on my own breath. Then it's Billy Gorman, all bundled up, behind the wheel of the Lincoln that's tearing out of the basement garage."

Joe Whiten shut the hotel room door behind him at a little before midnight, Hargrove locked it and put the chain on. Coral got undressed and under the covers. Hargrove, wearing the clothes he'd worn when he'd gone out to look for her, stood next to the bed. He made himself stand up straight.

"This is bad," he said.

"You mean that, really?"

He looked at her. He nodded slowly. "It's bad. It's definitely bad. If we take what Whiten said and add it up we get a ton of logical deduction that makes this a very bad situation."

82

THE MEETING WENT AS planned, Frend was happy with the result even though somewhere in the back of his mind he knew he shouldn't have let them come to the townhouse, but met them on neutral ground where he couldn't be traced to any of them. He didn't have a feeling of nostalgia, none at all, but the familiar though slightly older and more worn-out faces and the urgency of the situation gave him all the energy he needed to put the thing together with the sort of freshness he didn't think he had in him, since he'd figured legitimate business had knocked those legs out from under him.

Jean shouted from upstairs, he left the living room and climbed the stairs to the second bedroom where she was getting dressed in front of a full-length mirror.

"You look great," he said and sat on the edge of the bed looking her up and down. "I love you, baby."

"I know you do. Pink or white?"

"Pink or white what?"

"Panties."

"Black—those lacy, transparent things."

"No, I'm thinking innocence, underneath."

"I envy you your lack of introspection. For you it's a straight play for cock."

"What's that got to do with the color of my underwear?"

"You don't pay more attention to what's going on inside your head or your emotions than you do to how much money you spend. Just action and motion, that's you, and that's why I love you—a wildcat that'll scratch your eyes out, or a woman that gives the time of day and ten bucks to a bum. Quite a combination. But plans, you make plans all right, don't you."

"That isn't a question. Anyway, you're all the brains I want." She raised her skirt, wearing nothing underneath. "Pink or white, honey?"

"White, naturally. Now, come over here."

Even if they already knew each other, they didn't dare say their proper names, if they had anything to say, because names weren't important, it didn't matter if they used real ones or aliases, and it wasn't necessary to be on a first-name basis with anybody present at the meeting or grouped together after it, and nobody but Frend really knew who they were since they'd all worked for him at different times and stages of their careers. The final pick amounted to five of them, and Billy Gorman.

There was a tall and very skinny guy that got out of a van in front of the restaurant that was closed to the public but open to them by arrangement of Billy Gorman, and the tall and very skinny guy told the others right away out there on the sidewalk something on the order of maybe you know me, maybe you don't, but you call me Pete, understood? and they all knew it wasn't his name and that really his name was Nick Morales, but they'd happily call him Pete. He had to give them something because Frend asked him to be manager, and the rest of them could go by the letters of the alphabet for all he cared just as long as nobody gave out their real names.

Morales was Frend's right-hand man twenty years ago and it was impossible to pretend the others didn't know him since he had a reputation in Lake City that went way beyond the petty criminals and pros and traveled all the way up to certain members of the downtown detective bureau and more than one district police chief.

Gorman unlocked the front door of the restaurant called Riemen's and let them in, and Morales led the way into a room at the back with a long table reserved for parties of up to fifteen covered by a red-and-white checked oilcloth tablecloth. They all sat down at the table without sitting next to each other but leaving at least one empty chair between them. None of them had worked together before.

"It's simple," Morales said, sliding his chair up to the table. "This time tomorrow night Vince Negron will be permanently out of business and it's our job—each of you will get a very generous cut of what Frend's paying—to see that it's done well and without any trace of anything that might lead back to Frend."

"I got a question, Pete," said a man with a scar running down his face. "I know Negron, sure—it ain't that I got anything against popping a cap in him—but what kind of cut are you talking about?"

Morales reached for an ashtray, Gorman passed it to him, then Morales lit a cigarette, took a long haul on it but didn't let the smoke out right away as he said, "You're in it because Frend says you are, and if he says you're going to get a nice piece of change out of the business, well, you got to trust him and take it at that. This isn't a board meeting, there ain't no options. Now, close your head." He exhaled an impressive cloud of smoke.

"Okay, Pete," the guy with the scar said.

"Any more questions?"

Two guys said, "No, Pete, no questions," and the rest of them shook their heads no.

"Tools will be delivered here tomorrow at five," Morales said. "Be here at five-thirty—if you're late, you're out. Good-night."

They pushed their chairs away from the table, left the restaurant by the back door. Gorman locked it behind them, then went into the backroom, sat down next to Morales, who lit another cigarette, leaned forward, put his elbows on the table.

"'It ain't that I got anything against … '" Morales said, repeating the man's words. "They don't grow up no matter what they do—a bunch of sheep, they sound like bleating fucking sheep."

"They didn't go pro, like you, Nick."

"I'm strictly for hire. No permanent affiliations." He pulled at the cigarette and exhaled a mouthful of smoke. "Billy, you did all right for yourself."

"Yeah, steady. That's me."

"That makes two of us." He put out his cigarette, got up and moved away from the table, looked at the restaurant's main dining room. "What a joint."

Gorman got up, switched off the lights, yawned, and said, "Does just enough business to pay the rent. We close her up when we want her. Let's get out of here. How about going for a drink?"

"I can't make it tonight, but I'd like to take a rain check. I got to arrange the tools we're going to use, it's across town, and I'm already tapped out from a job I did last night."

"Broke?"

"No, tired."

They left Riemen's by the front door, Gorman locked up, and then they were in the parking lot and walking toward Frend's Lincoln. Gorman got behind the wheel, he was closing the door, the door was closed, a van pulled up out of nowhere, Morales walked toward it, he got into the van on the passenger side, sitting in the passenger seat, the two vehicles flashed their headlights at each other, they pulled out of the lot in opposite directions, the lot was quiet.

Sender got López on the line, it was on behalf of a request from Evans for an update, it was late and Sender was tired, but when López started talking he got him worked up right away as he told him what he'd been doing for Frend and his idea of what Frend was up to. They made arrangements to meet tomorrow night at eleven near El Puente High School at Sixth and Pierce not far from El Perro Llorón.

Sender was too excited to go to sleep. He went to his desk, found his address book in a drawer, and started leafing through it to find the name and phone number of the brunette who worked at the newsstand and cigar store in Midtown. It wasn't too late to take her out for a drink if she wasn't going to work the next morning. He lifted the receiver of the phone and dialed her number. He looked at his watch as he listened to the ringing, and it kept on ringing. It was only ten-thirty. The phone in his hand told him it had nothing to offer. She didn't answer.

He didn't mind that she wasn't home or didn't or couldn't pick up the phone because it didn't change anything, he felt the blood running very fast through his veins. He set the receiver back onto the cradle, picked the cigar out the ashtray on his desk, went to the sofa, sat down and lit the cigar.

He switched on the TV, smoked, and the smoke put him farther away from what was on the screen. Excitement rushed through him, and cotton was packed tightly in his throat. He was thirsty, but it was a healthy thirst and nothing to do with desperation. It made all the dull days of repetition worthwhile, but it was going to be a long night, he hoped he'd wear himself out watching the news at eleven.

Hargrove couldn't sleep. He got out of bed feeling clumsy, went to the bathroom, washed his face with hot water, dried it with a hand towel, then moved his face right up to the mirror above the sink and looked at himself in the glass. He couldn't remember when he'd looked so tired, it wasn't fatigue from working too hard or not sleeping enough, it was exhaustion from the weight of the battle he was fighting with mental and emotional stress that pressed down on him since they'd checked into the Gilbert Hotel.

He wanted to go out, take a walk, to breathe a little freezing night air that would shock him out of the nervous inactivity the fight put in him, but he didn't want to leave Coral alone and wasn't about to do it. He rubbed his hands into his eyes. His head was lowered and then he was shaking his head.

"Come on," he said. "Snap out of it."

And then he raised his head again, looked at the face looking back at him. The face was really tired, but the expression he'd given it looked strong. A sound that had nothing to do with where he was or what he was doing came rushing through his head, and it was an oncoming train, and it got louder as it got closer, but it wasn't a train, it can't be a train, he told himself. Whatever it was made considerable noise and the noise echoed within Hargrove's brain.

He told himself to go to the window, open it, stand there in his pajamas, take a deep breath of cold air, lean out and call for help. Then he laughed at himself and the laughter was attractive in a creepy sort of way so he laughed harder and then louder with the idea that someone might come from somewhere to help him until at last the laughing woke Coral and she was standing behind him with her arms reaching out to hold him. And he wanted that badly right now.

Ramón López paced his hotel room in Midtown and there wasn't far to go since he wasn't paying very much for the room and he got what he paid for. He couldn't eat or drink, and didn't want to smoke on account of the way his stomach felt when he ingested anything more than stale air. He was going to cause as much damage as he could, and the advantage in it for him lay in the overall hit Frend was going to take in his confrontation with Negron.

With that pacing came the repetition of words that made sense to him, but wouldn't make sense to somebody else if they heard them, any more than the babbling words of a crazy man made sense to anyone but a crazy man. The words were clear, just right, chosen for their proper effect, and he understood every one of them because they told him that if Negron finished off Frend he was going to have Jean Fleming for himself, and there was nothing he wanted more than that in this world. Conveniently, he had nothing to say of the possibility that Frend defeated Negron in a blaze of glory.

The words didn't mention anything about what Jean wanted or didn't want because that wasn't part of the equation, which was what made them the words of a man suffering at the very least from delusion.

Madley stood under a bright light in a corner of the backroom of the Seventeenth Street Social Club filing his fingernails. He had a key for the social club just like each of the others had a key but the others didn't amount to more than Joe Whiten and Vince Negron now that Graham and Bielinski and Joslyn were dead.

Whiten sat on the sofa drinking a glass of ginger ale. There was a lot of perspiration on Madley's face that didn't come from the effort he made filing his fingernails but from the number of 100 mg. MS Contin tablets he was taking, which recently kept him out of the bathroom for three whole days. Whiten watched him and debated whether or not he'd tell Madley there was going to be a big problem in the next twenty-four hours and that if he was going to keep out of it he'd better get out of town. At this point, he wasn't sure that Madley would even understand the danger he faced staying with El Manojo.

Lily Segura left a message on Hargrove's answering machine saying she'd just got back from downstate with her boyfriend, they'd left before the month was up because the lab lost its grant money due to the fact the organization that funded it went bankrupt and the lab couldn't cover the grant on its own, and then while she was packing her things down there and already disappointed her mother called telling her Hargrove might be in trouble, so she couldn't very well hang around feeling sorry for herself and her boyfriend, and then not doing something about whatever it was that was going on with Walt Hargrove, so they got the first bus out and heading north and now she was in Lake City.

"So okay I don't know what's going on, but how come my mother's thinking you're in a tight corner when maybe you just went someplace with Coral or you're working a lot and never home or staying with her on Cherry Street because I remember where you said Coral lives, or maybe you're both up against it, or best of all you've moved to a new address to live together, and if that's the case nobody's happier for you than I am—everybody's got to move on—but you'd better call me when you get this message mister or I'll come over to wherever it is you're living—don't worry, I'll find it—and camp on your doorstep until there's nothing for you to do but open up and talk because I've got a lot of things to say."

She put the phone down, went back into El Perro Llorón's kitchen to see her mother who was busy preparing something for her to eat. It was late, the restaurant was closed, Blanca the Skeleton was wiping down empty tables, putting chairs on table-tops, Chucho just finished straightening up behind the bar and was helping Blanca sweep out the place and mop the floor. Fat Jorge had already gone home.

83

THE FIRST THING MADLEY heard was a booming sound that might've come from a stormy, cloud-filled sky, but it was the heart of winter and the sky wasn't filled with those sorts of clouds, and then immediately there was a crash of shattered glass and splintered wood and smashed concrete as a garbage truck retrofitted with diesel engine emission reduction technology from a project initiated by the Department of Environment and the city's Department of Fleet Management, running from August 2004 through July 2005, rammed the Seventeenth Street Social Club while Madley was half asleep on the sofa, dreaming of nothing, in his MS Contin sleep at ten-forty at night.

He walked slowly dreamily toward the anteroom rubbing sleep from his eyes and saw the gathering concrete dust floating in the air and the gleaming splinters of glass on the floor and heard the groaning noise of a retreating engine just in time to see the blue garbage truck, with its white cab and white mechanical arm with a yellow claw used for gripping and lifting garbage containers, drag itself backwards out of the wrecked doorway and into dimly lit Meyering Boulevard opposite the Meyering Building.

The last thing Madley made out before he sat down in the worn leather chair behind the table with a task lamp on it was the specially made decal identifying the truck as a lower emissions vehicle.

He looked at what was left of the social club reduced to rubble and didn't know what to do, then got up out of the chair, got a coat out of the alcove and carefully made his way across the anteroom over pieces of broken concrete, crunching through a sea of shattered glass, and went out of the building through the nonexistent front door.

When he got to the sidewalk, he looked around at the deserted street, found nothing unusual, went to the pay phone, dialed Joe Whiten, who told him to get the hell out of there and meet him at El Perro Llorón.

84

NICK MORALES UNLOCKED THE back door of Riemen's restaurant shut for the night by arrangement of Billy Gorman on account of private business, and a short man about forty with a lot of muscles came in carrying a rectangular wooden crate in his arms. Morales pointed to the table in the back room, the man put the crate down, Morales handed him an envelope, the short man left the restaurant and Morales locked the door behind him.

At exactly five-thirty four guys arrived in two separate cars and parked in a parking lot behind Riemen's, deserted of other cars except for a rusted-out, decades-old orange Japanese heap of junk that Billy Gorman had towed there and was left as a signal to let them know it was all right.

While Morales checked and sorted the items he'd taken out of the crate and laid out in two rows on the checked oilcloth covering the tabletop, Gorman opened the back door letting the four men in and cracking a smile at their identical long green car coats that had been generously provided by Lloyd Frend.

The array of tools, as Morales called them, though none of them were new, was impressive, and the four men stood there looking at the neat rows of weapons and ammunition and nodded their heads at the visual power of seeing that much force and danger in one place, but not reaching out to touch anything until Morales gave them permission.

"Take off your coats, men," he said, "and take a chair."

They moved at the same time, made the same gestures as each one slipped out of his coat and selected a chair and put the coat over the back of it and sat down. Nobody said anything while Morales drew out his chair and sat down and folded his arms across his chest.

It was the guy with the scar on his face, a mean-looking scar that creased the skin from the corner of an eye to the corresponding corner of his mouth, who made a noise that started at the back of his throat, then said, "So, Pete, that's a fine set of tools you've got there. Who gets what?"

"Maybe you're one of those morons who thinks it's the trend to show off—it'll get you nowhere with me," Morales said. "This is business—you got to have a cool head."

"Okay, Pete," the scar face said, and the others nodded.

Gorman cleared his throat, sat down at the table, folded his hands in front of him on the oilcloth. He didn't say anything but he didn't have to on account of the way Morales gave him a sideways glance, and Gorman handed him a nod of the head that wasn't easy to discern because it wasn't meant to be seen, he was speaking without words for Lloyd Frend, which put him at the top in the gathering, and Morales was paid to respect it.

Morales edged his chair closer to the table, picked up a Smith & Wesson Model 22 N Frame, Thunder Ranch 45 ACP revolver with a Diamond Service Grip, 4-inch barrel, blue finish, 36.8-ounce steel, six shot, and more or less quoted Chuck Hawks, saying, "You can thumb cock a double action revolver before firing, just like a single action—a light press on the trigger fires the gun. And you can also use a long, strong pull on the trigger—the long trigger pull causes the cylinder to rotate as it simultaneously draws back the hammer. When the cylinder locks into firing position, the hammer's all the way back, and the last part of the trigger's rearward movement releases the hammer, firing the pistol. It's called 'trigger cocking,' and it's the second method of firing the pistol—double action, two ways to fire a pistol. Quick, fairly close-range shooting. DA revolvers are fast and easy to reload—the cylinder swings out of the frame, you eject all six empty brass cases with one push on the ejector rod. You can reload the empty cylinder very quickly using a 'speed loader,' a small device that drops new cartridges into all six chambers at the same time."

They listened intently, it was like attending a class in school, and they each concentrated on Morales's handling of the weapon in front of them. He set the Smith & Wesson down on the oilcloth, picked up another gun.

"Here's a single action revolver, safe to carry with all six chambers loaded—the 'New Action' (or 'two pin') Ruger SA Blackhawk revolver. It's a redesign of the old 'three screw' model, and it incorporates a modern transfer bar ignition system. The transfer bar doesn't let the hammer contact the cartridge until the hammer's fully cocked and the trigger pulled all the way to the rear."

He set the Ruger next to the Smith & Wesson, picked up the next weapon and held it in the palm of his hand like he was weighing it.

"The Colt 38 Special Diamondback double-action revolver, first introduced in 1966, has a 4-inch barrel—a six-shot revolver with a swing out cylinder and Positive Lock action. Used prices in 2006 were more than $600. She's got excellent sights, a good trigger, fine balance, safe action, and moderate size—a Diamondback makes an excellent training revolver for a new shooter. Here," he handed the Colt to the scar face, "this one's just right for you, handsome."

The scar face held it, then set it down gently on the table next to the other guns. Morales got up, went to the far end of the table and picked up a rifle.

"A hunting rifle, the BAR LongTrac, Mossy Oak Break-Up 7mm. It's got just the right power to knock the teeth out of a guy—and most of his head if you're a good shot, even though anything the 7mm can do, the .300 Win Mag does better. The 7mm doesn't kick as much, but it shoots lighter bullets than the .300, which allows for quicker bleed off of energy, and greater susceptibility to wind drift at longer ranges. But for our purposes we'll stay with the 7mm." He forced a smile as he put it down next to the handguns.

"I'm a good shot," the scar face chimed in.

"Shut up and listen," Gorman said.

"Another Smith & Wesson, but a whole different girl—a 410 40SW Crimson Trace Laser, stainless steel, with a ten round magazine, 4-inch barrel, traditional double action, semi-automatic," he said, just pointing at it. He reached across the table, unwrapped a big weapon from an Indian blanket. "And here's a beauty—an XM8 lightweight assault rifle in light machine gun configuration. Note the longer barrel and folded bipods under the forearm."

The scar face reached quickly for the assault rifle, Morales slapped his hand, the scar face jerked his arm back away from the rifle.

"Here's a Glock safe-action auto-loading pistol, model 31C, and it's a compensated full-size 357 SIG. We made a couple of changes—adding the Glock extended slide release, Meprolight tritium three dot sights, and some old pre-Brady Glock-22 FML magazines. This is for you." He gave it to Billy Gorman.

"Thanks, Pete," Gorman said, smiling.

"This one belongs to me," Morales said, reaching into the shoulder holster he wore under his jacket and drawing a Beretta Model 90-two featuring a removable polymer wraparound standard grip, rounded and snag-proof external surfaces, rounded trigger guard, integral accessory rail, increased magazine capacity, internal recoil buffer, captive recoil spring guide assembly, ambidextrous safety, reversible magazine release button, luminescent night sights, an automatic firing pin block safety that fired with the magazine removed.

"So, who gets what?" the scar face said and leaned back in his chair, folding his arms across his chest.

85

I T WAS A TYPICAL freezing mid-winter night in Lake City with wind blowing the fat, close snowflakes falling thick and fast from the blue-black sky to the corner of Sixth and Pierce near El Puente High School, where Sender stood stomping his feet in the cold. The dim circles of light from rows of streetlights revealed the oblique fall of snow. He looked around at the cars that passed, hoping to see a license plate that would tell him it was López, but it was useless, the fat flakes quickly blinded him when he tried to look up at an approaching car.

A car slowed down and the muffled sound of its tires gliding through the ruts of snow compressed by other cars made Sender lift his head and shield his eyes with his hand pressed close to his forehead. The snow stopped falling, then a sudden gust of wind blew the white flakes at virtually the same angle in the opposite direction, and Sender saw López waving at him from the driver's side of a car that had pulled up at the curb.

He got in on the passenger side, rubbed his hands together in front of the heat blowing out of the vent on the far right of the dashboard.

"Well?" López lit a cigarette.

"Give me a minute, I'm frozen."

"Take as long as you want." He hauled at the cigarette.

"You'd better park on Pierce near Fourth, we'll walk."

"I don't want to walk unless I have to, and it's so cold we're better off not going anywhere on foot."

"That's the way it's got to be, Ramón."

"That's the way it's got to be," López imitated Sender, mumbling to himself.

He swung the car around and drove to Fourth Street, pulled into an empty space, let the engine run to keep them warm.

"So what's with Frend?" Sender said, reaching into an inside coat pocket for a cigar.

"I told you. There's going to be a shootout."

"Christ—the Wild West."

"It is, and it isn't." López squeezed the cigarette, watched the burning end detach itself from unlit tobacco. He opened the window and tossed the cigarette into a considerably long and wide carpet of dirty snow spread across the street, then rolled up the window.

"Tell me how it isn't," Sender said.

"It's *isn't* because it's the only way Frend knows how to handle it—Negron's stirred things up, and now there's no backing down. It'll be the Wild West if the cops show, and when the shooting starts that's exactly what'll happen."

"Well, it isn't going to happen without me."

"It's a story you ought to miss."

"No, you know what's going on and where, and you're going to take me as close to it as you can without getting us shot up."

86

HARGROVE REACHED IN THE dark to switch on the bedside lamp, sat up and looked at Coral, who turned toward him and rubbed sleep from her eyes.

"What time is it?" she said.

He was already out of bed and putting his clothes on when he said, "Ten-fifteen. I've got to have something to read. I'm going to my place to get a book."

"Now? What are you up to? Don't go, you know what Whiten said."

"I've got to do something, I'm going nuts."

"Get back in bed."

"No. The only way to find out what's going on is to get out of this hotel, take a walk back to my place, and if I get there in one piece, I'll stay there, it'll be over, and you can join me and we won't have to hide anymore. Get the whole goddamn thing over with. Tonight, that's the way it's got to be."

"Why tonight?"

"What Whiten told us adds up to a move on Frend's part with immediate planted in the middle of it, and that means now."

"What makes you think it's tonight?"

"It's a feeling I've got—whatever's going to happen, it's going to happen tonight."

"Then I'll go with you."

"No, you won't."

"Yes, I will, and there's nothing you can say to stop me."

"Okay, get dressed, put on your coat and hat and let's get out of here and get it over with as quick as we can so we don't we freeze to death out there."

They went past the Gilbert's reception desk and out the door, Hargrove kept the room key in his coat pocket and fingered it as they walked into the freezing night air. Swirling fat snowflakes played in front of them as they marched along the sidewalk heading to a bus that would take them to Hargrove's apartment at Third and West Walker.

When they got off the bus it was eleven-fifteen, they walked for two minutes, turned left, passed under a streetlight, and climbed the first set of cement stairs to the front door of the house as icy gusts of wind threw snow in their face until the wind shifted and snow fell straight down at them from above.

87

L ILY SEGURA BUNDLED HERSELF up in a sweater and scarf, buttoned up a thick wool coat, pulled the hood over her head, left her mother asleep in front of the TV, shut the apartment door quietly behind her and went down the stairs to the street. She put her gloves on as she stepped onto the sidewalk. She looked at her watch, it said eleven-o-five.

Without hearing a word from Walt Hargrove, she'd decided to go directly to his apartment, ring the bell and find out whether or not he was there and it didn't matter if he wasn't alone and he was in bed with Coral Rasmussen. It was very cold, but it wasn't too cold for her to walk to West Walker and Third.

88

J EAN FLEMING SAT AT the opposite end of the leather sofa from
where Lloyd Frend was tucked under a cashmere blanket leaning against a couple of cushions with his hands folded behind
his head. They were looking at a map of the Midwest stretched the
width of the TV, listening to a weather bulletin; it was nine-thirty.
She held a glass of Médoc in her hand.

Frend threw the blanket off, slid across the sofa, moved right up
against her until their hips touched, put his arm across her shoulder,
got close enough to kiss her but didn't because she turned her head,
saying, "What? You want to sit here?"

He pushed himself back to where he'd been sitting, stuck his
bare feet under the blanket, his knees pulled up. He looked at the
empty glass of scotch with melting ice and told her to get him a
drink. He had so much money and power and influence in Lake
City that she did it without saying a word, but told herself she
wouldn't have had to get up for a guy like Ramón López. She intentionally bumped the low table as she went past him.

After some minutes he got up from the sofa, sat on a chair
near the windows and smoked cigarettes and toyed with the details
of the plan he'd put together to fix Negron once and for all and it
didn't play out so well in his imagination on account of the fact that
Negron was a shifty guy with a lot of brains, a good deal smarter
than he seemed to be. He told himself not to be too certain of anything. He didn't notice Jean come back with a fresh drink and put
the glass down on the tabletop. The third cigarette tasted bitter, he
crushed it out, ignored the glass of scotch.

When he added it up it came to just one answer which was that he had to be there, he had to see that Negron was finished, wiped out, and that he was going to be free to do whatever he wanted to do even if he retired in a couple of years, just as long as Negron wasn't there pestering him, scraping away at the shiny surface of the position he'd built for himself.

The idea that it was the right thing to do took hold, he was going to watch Negron go down, it was a crazy move but he had to go along with it, and now it was a healthy conviction, he liked the feel of it, and the soundless sound of believing it.

Jean was fast asleep at eleven-fifteen when he crept out of the bedroom, got dressed and went downstairs to the kitchen to drink a glass of water before leaving the townhouse. Frend had forty-five minutes to get to El Perro Llorón.

He put on a charcoal-gray cashmere overcoat, a silk scarf, a low, soft felt hat with a curled brim, the crown creased lengthwise, and leather gloves. Gorman was out with the rest of the men on a special nightshift. Frend took the elevator down to the garage and got into the Lincoln parked next to the black Audi TT coupé he'd bought for Jean.

89

AT ELEVEN-TWENTY, THE RETROFITTED garbage truck with a smashed front end was left on a deserted street behind a disused brewery waiting for remodeling into lofts and apartments, and the driver of the garbage truck hurried away moving through shadows, and in patches of dim light from streetlamps the scar tissue on his face was a long waxy ridge. He was in a hurry to join the others in front of El Perro Llorón, he took long strides, planting his feet carefully on the ground so as not to slip on the ice and frozen snow.

Snow had collected on the bench of the bus stop so he didn't sit down but stomped his feet to keep warm until the bus came that would take him to the heart of Pigsville, a block away from the corner of West Florida and Third Street.

90

JEAN FLEMING SAT UP in bed when she heard Frend leave the room because she'd been feigning sleep while Frend fidgeted nervously in bed. She got dressed as quickly as she could to find out what he was up to since she felt that something wasn't right, and she decided that if she didn't find him in the apartment, she'd get in the Audi and follow him if she wasn't too late to catch up with wherever he'd gone.

Gorman wasn't in the hallway when she went out, but the empty chair was there, and she impatiently rode the elevator down to the garage. The Lincoln wasn't in its space so she got into the Audi, left the garage, turned left, went one block to the first traffic light and saw the Lincoln stalled two blocks ahead of her. She took the car slowly up the street, pulled over to the side of the road until the light changed in front of Frend and he got the Lincoln going, then she pulled into light traffic and followed him, leaving two cars between them.

91

L UZ DEL ÁNGEL DE Segura switched off the TV when she heard Lily shut the apartment door and start down the stairs. She hadn't been asleep but waiting and the waiting proved fruitful because she'd heard her daughter getting ready to go out when it was so cold and snowy nobody should go out and it was after eleven o'clock, which tipped her off that her daughter was up to something out of her routine since she'd been back from downstate. It didn't smell right and she decided to go after her.

92

"NOW THAT WE GOT here, what are you going to do?"

"Nothing, I guess."

"That isn't what you were saying at the Gilbert."

"I found something to read—that's what I wanted after I wanted to know if we'd get here at all. Now we don't have to leave because here we are—and we can stay. I mean it."

"You said you want to know what's going on, and I know you won't be satisfied just sitting here thinking about it."

"It doesn't have to be that way, really, not anymore."

"We'd better get out and go for that walk if it's what you've got to do. I don't think it's a good idea, not from the start—it's a bad idea—but I know you want to do it, and so we're going out there together, like it or not, and probably both get ourselves killed."

"Okay. But you should stay. I'm telling you, you don't have to go with me. I don't want you to go."

"Get your coat on, Walt. And turn off the light."

From West Walker and Third, Walt Hargrove and Coral Rasmussen started the five blocks north on Third heading for El Perro Llorón. They didn't know it'd been shut early because there weren't enough customers on a very cold night.

93

WHITEN STOOD WITH MADLEY in the wide dark doorway of a four-story apartment building halfway down the block on the opposite side of the street from El Perro Llorón. The mercury-vapor light in a streetlamp flickered on and off and falling snow tumbled slowly through it to the street.

"Why don't we just go over there? It's freezing," Madley said.

"First, the restaurant's closed. Second, we're going to wait before we go up to see him."

"For what?"

"You still swallowing those pills?"

"Yes, but what's it to you?"

"Nothing. But Vince won't like it."

"He doesn't have to know."

"You hear your voice? Anybody who hears you talking will know you're high as a kite, Paul."

"We going in or aren't we?"

"You told him what happened at the club?"

"I told you, I called him after I talked to you."

"You sure?"

"I'm telling you, I told him. What I ought to do from now on is mind my own business. And fuck you, Joe."

"Just give it a rest, will you? The light's on in his window. He's still in there."

"Can't we just go over there?" Madley smashed his fist into the palm of his other hand but there wasn't any force behind it.

"Take it easy, Paul."

"Yeah, Paul, take it easy."

It wasn't Whiten's voice, so both of them turned around to see where it came from and whose face went with it.

"Jesus, Walt, what're you doing here?" Whiten reached out, put a hand on Hargrove's shoulder, pulled him into the shadow of the doorway, then saw Coral standing behind him. "Get in here," he told her, then to himself, "No, it can't be possible. Tell me it isn't possible."

"I see 'em, Joe, an' if I see 'em they're right there in front of us."

"You wouldn't know yourself in the mirror, you idiot. And keep your voice down."

Before Whiten got it out of him, Hargrove said, "I told Coral I wanted something at my place, but she knew I didn't want whatever it was I told her I wanted, what I really wanted was to find out if my guts were talking sense or I was getting onto the hysterical side, and now I'm sure my guts were telling me right or you wouldn't be standing here with Madley, freezing your balls off in a doorway almost in front of El Perro Llorón."

A beat-up van with curtains over the rear windows pulled to the curb under a streetlight half a block up, four guys got out, each wearing the same style winter car coat, and they stamped their feet and rubbed their hands together. The van drove off, leaving them standing at the edge of the snow-covered sidewalk in front of the base of the streetlight. A gust of wind blew the falling snowflakes almost horizontally, then sent them straight down.

Coral huddled against Hargrove, Whiten and Madley were pressed against each other. The four of them just fit in the wide doorway. Whiten tried to make out the men standing on the side-walk through the fat snowflakes.

A tall skinny guy was doing all the talking in a low voice with a cigarette dangling from his lips, they couldn't hear what he was saying, at the same time they knew he was the ringleader, but the faraway words were dampened by snowfall. Then the ringleader seemed to tell the others to hold on, he climbed the stairs to the abandoned building facing El Perro Llorón, came back a minute later. Whiten hadn't seen him before, but Madley said he thought the guy looked familiar.

"Some big shot," Madley whispered.

"Yeah, a tall guy," Whiten said.

But Madley didn't have time to come up with a name for the face that topped the skinny frame because all four men were fanning out in different directions, one was smoking a cigarette behind a parked car, two in doorways a couple of addresses apart, and the tall skinny one went straight to the other side of the street and put himself alongside El Perro Llorón, in a shadow between the sprays of light from two streetlamps. The sign in the restaurant was lit but there was nobody inside. Whiten thought he saw a glint of light strike metal in the hand of the tall man pressed against the wall of El Perro Llorón.

94

THE MAN WITH A waxy scar on his face walked up to the van parked two blocks from West Florida and Third Street with its back windows covered, and he rapped his frozen knuckles against the side of it. The side door slid open, an arm extended holding a hunting rifle in its hand, the scar face took hold of the BAR LongTrac, Mossy Oak Break-Up and raised and lowered his arms like he was weighing it. He frowned, the scar stretched downward, and he said to the man who'd given it to him, "I don't want this. I thought I was getting the Diamondback."

The man said, "You'll take it and like it. Pete changed his mind—said you told him you're a good shot. Well, here's your chance to prove it. Second floor front, window. Building facing El Perro Llorón, and the door's unlocked. Make sure you hit the target, pal. Now get going." The door slid shut in his face and the van drove away, its rear tires throwing dirty snow against his legs.

He ran down the street and was out of breath when he got to the building facing El Perro Llorón. The only sign he caught that the others were already there was an up-and-down waving motion of the stainless steel, 410 40SW Crimson Trace Laser in somebody's hand raised and signaling at him above the front end of a parked car.

He paused to light a cigarette, then looked up, climbed the stairs. The street door was propped open by a folded piece of cardboard, he went in and up to the second floor, opened the unlocked door of the front apartment and positioned himself at the half-open window, and because he was an amateur he stuck the barrel out the window, but he was careful not to get the sleeve of his coat caught on a nail or splinter.

95

MADLEY OPENED HIS MOUTH to speak and Whiten put his hand over it, then held his index finger up to tell Hargrove and Coral not to make a sound. He distinctly heard footsteps coming their way. They held their breath.

Billy Gorman, and then his shadow, went slowly past, but Gorman didn't turn his head to the left or right, didn't see anyone standing in the doorway, and Whiten spotted a model 31C Glock pistol in his hand. They waited until he was out of earshot to begin breathing again. Madley's mouth was still open, Whiten wiped the saliva off his hand.

"What's going on here?" Coral whispered.

"Gunfight at the O.K. Corral," Whiten said.

"Tombstone, Arizona. October 26, 1881. Lot 2, block 17, behind the corral. And in Fremont Street," Madley said.

Hargrove shook his head, saying, "I knew it."

"What are we going to do?" Madley said.

"We aren't going to do anything," Whiten said.

"It sounds all mixed up," Hargrove said.

"It's murder," Coral said.

"It's life," Whiten said.

"Why?" Madley said.

"I don't know," Whiten replied. "I can't hit an answer."

96

LÓPEZ AND SENDER WERE half a block away from West Florida and Third Street. They saw a van pull away after it left four guys on the street, who then stood huddled together on the sidewalk to listen to a tall man tell them what to do. They were sure of that, the tall guy was the boss. López hung back behind Sender, he didn't want them to see him because he knew they'd know him, he'd knocked at doors and called in debts to get this handful of guys to do the dirty work for Lloyd Frend, he wasn't proud of it, but just desperate enough to have done it to get closer to Jean Fleming.

George Sender didn't know any of the details but knew enough from what López told him to be certain he was going to see death in the street.

"Come on," Sender said, "let's get a ringside seat."

"I don't think it's a good idea. I don't think we ought to get any closer than we already are, George."

"Maybe you're right. Maybe we ought to go home, put our feet up, turn on the TV, wait for a broadcast—or open tomorrow's paper and see a front page item I didn't write about what happened here tonight. Or just maybe we ought to get a better look at what's going on so I can do my job."

"You can do it without me."

"Sure I can. But you're here, and you're part of it. Maybe you can keep me from getting shot."

"I'll do what I can, but I can't promise you anything."

"I didn't ask for a promise."

There was a Tudor-style wreck of a house on the other side
of the street with a ruined four-centered arch and the remains of
oriel windows, and they made their way toward it without passing
through any light cast down from streetlights onto the snowy sidewalk. The four identically dressed men suddenly scattered in the
freezing night, and they too used that instant to hurry across the
street and duck behind a chipped, crumbling and cracked wall at
the side of the Tudor-style house where the wide cracks made tiny
shelves covered by a thin layer of snow.

They crouched uncomfortably behind the wall while the four
men got in position. A man dressed like the others, carrying a rifle,
came out of the shadows for an instant, lit a cigarette, then climbed
the stairs of a building directly opposite El Perro Llorón.

Then a man approached from the other direction, kept close to
the buildings and avoided patches of light from streetlamps. López
recognized the man, but before he could whisper the name to
Sender, who'd taken a notebook out of his overcoat pocket, Sender
turned his head and said, "Gorman."

97

FREND WASN'T USED TO running, and the freezing air that filled his lungs was so cold it sent a bright ache shooting through them while the thoughts in his head spun around without making sense. He'd parked the Lincoln on Ferry Street near Seeboth where the icy wind off the river sent him quickly on his way south toward West Florida and Third, moving past First as fast as he could while paying attention to patches of frozen snow and ice that made him slow down to avoid falling down.

As he got closer to where he was headed he changed his pace to a fast walk and his mind slowed with his body and he started to think. What he came up with was a question, asking himself what he was doing here knowing it was where he shouldn't be. The answer came back and told him he had to see the job was done right, Negron had to be erased from the board, and it couldn't be traced back to him. But then the question about what he was doing here replaced the answer, and the possibility of being connected to the event grew at an exponential rate as he neared El Perro Llorón.

Then came another pair of footsteps sounding more like the cracking of thin ice covering a pond. Frend stopped at Second and West Pittsburgh, heading east. He listened, but the footsteps came to a halt and with it the cracking ice and crunching snow. He tiptoed over to a couple of dumpsters and stood behind them.

There wasn't any light where he stood but whoever was following him had to pass through the spray of a sodium-vapor streetlamp. He peered around the chipped corner of the steel dumpster. He had placed less than ten yards between himself and the approaching footsteps.

Frend didn't shout but let out a low grunt when he saw Jean Fleming wrapped in the fur coat he'd given her last year nearly stumble, waving her arms like a windmill after she'd slipped on a patch of ice. She was less than a couple of feet away, but didn't see him.

Frend stepped out from behind the dumpsters, reached for her arm, caught it but didn't pay attention to where he was walking, his right leg shot out in front of him the second his shoe hit a sheet of frozen snow, and they both went down together.

Jean didn't know what hit her. When she saw Frend on his back beside her she started a smile, worked at it, got it going, and he helped her out with it until it was one big laugh thrown back and forth between them.

"Couples in love are more vulnerable to accidents," Frend said.

98

GUNFIRE MADE LILY SEGURA turn her head at the moment her mother came up the steps to the entrance of Hargrove's building on West Walker. Luz del Ángel de Segura looked at her wristwatch. Without saying a word to each other, Lily showing no surprise at all, her mother acting as if they'd come there together, they ran to the corner of Third and walked quickly in the direction of the sound of weapons firing at midnight.

Madley ignored Whiten and pulled his arm away from him as Whiten tried to cling to the sleeve of his coat to keep him from leaving the doorway that was more or less a safe place to be under the circumstances. Bullets were whizzing through the cold night air in the direction of the apartment situated above El Perro Llorón, where Vince Negron lived.

Madley ran out into the middle of the street, drew a .38 Special and started firing, not knowing which way to turn as he felt a burning sensation on the upper part of his ear that came from a hole right through the cartilage. He put his hand there, felt warm blood running down the side of his face, looked across the street and up at the target he was going to defend. He worked a hundred percent for Vince Negron. The windows in Negron's room were shattered, the wrecked Venetian blinds rattled in gusts of wind as snow blew into the darkened room.

Vince Negron trawled sleep at midnight and in it dreamt of how he'd beat Frend down far enough to take over his business, he didn't have to kill him because he'd got him where he wanted him, Negron was a younger man, a lot smarter than Frend, who couldn't get his dick hard anymore, but then the dream told him he better let Frend stay on, that it was all right, he might need a guy like Frend so why not Frend himself, he'd have to sell the townhouse and keep himself out of the way, low profile, but an advisor maybe, and a contact, as Negron's empire took shape he'd want a middle-man, you sure couldn't let those years of experience go to waste, what was left of Frend ought to be good for something, then he saw the brick and glass townhouse with a bronze plaque at the entrance saying, Eduardo Negron Corporation, and a Mercedes and a woman who sucked his cock every morning—all this from what he'd got out of Frend's empire through strength of character and violence.

He was pulled up out of the dream by an agitated bottom tide starting upward in an arc that brought him sharply to the surface as his head came off the pillow, his eyes wide open, after a bullet from a BAR Mossy Oak Break-Up 7mm Remington Magnum ripped through one of the windows and must have ricocheted against something because cracked plaster fell out of the wall above his head, covering his face with dust.

Jean held onto Frend's arm in a dark doorway with a view of El Perro Llorón and a glow from behind the bar of an advertisement for beer with its electric waterfall flowing downward and the electric water feeding an electric river surrounded by an electric forest, and the battle that had begun a minute ago, just as they'd ducked into the doorway, flew into high gear. Jean gave him an elbow, Frend turned his head and saw a familiar figure moving erratically in the shadows between streetlights.

"What's Billy doing here?" Frend whispered.

Frend shook his head but decided to ignore it, figuring it was Gorman's dedication to his work, and anyway he was really pleased and gave himself an imaginary pat on the back since the attack was going as planned, bullets were flying, and the windows in the room occupied by Negron were broken into splinters gleaming in the light of a streetlamp in a wintry night. It was a blue-ribbon job.

"It's past my bedtime," Frend said to Jean, taking her by the arm, slinking out of the doorway, hurrying down the street and around the corner and out of sight of the action on West Florida and Third, heading north in the direction of where he'd parked the Lincoln on Ferry Street near Seeboth.

Lily and her mother got to West Florida and Third just as the gunfire was dying down, the first assault couldn't have lasted more than seven minutes, and there wasn't any smell but cigarettes hanging in the air over the sidewalk where they stood huddled against each other out of fear and freezing weather.

The second assault began immediately. It started with a couple of shots that were fired from Negron's darkened room, and the shots were followed by a grunt and a thud as someone on the street got hit, slumped and fell against a parked car before dropping to the sidewalk. A stainless steel 410 40SW Crimson Trace Laser skipped along a patch of ice and spun in circles just out of the dead man's reach.

It was as much as they could stand, there wasn't any reason but meaningful curiosity to stay where they were, and it just wasn't worth risking their lives to find out what was going on above the bar and restaurant, so they hurried back the way they came and found themselves in front of Hargrove's place again. From there they heard sirens accompanying the squad cars speeding toward West Florida and Third.

Coral shoved Hargrove as hard as she could with a few running steps to give her enough force to complete the gesture of saving his life after she'd seen a glint of light on the barrel of a rifle sticking out of a half-open window, second floor front, in the building opposite El Perro Llorón. The shot went off just as Hargrove reached for Madley—he wanted to do something to keep him from getting shot again—with Coral coming up right behind him, and she looked back at exactly the right moment, saw the danger, and then the 7mm Remington Magnum bounced on the cement where Hargrove had been standing a second before she'd pushed him, and he slid easily into a pile of snow heaped against the curb. Hargrove looked back at Madley as he started to fall, hit by a second bullet in the head.

Negron ran down the stairs with a SIG P245 police backup weapon in his hand, going past the yellowed walls with paint peeling off here and there and a bare bulb hanging from the ceiling, holding a handkerchief over a hole in his shoulder that bled but didn't hurt because there was a lot at stake, too much for pain, and he wasn't going to let some fucker's shot get in the way of surviving this fucked up situation he was in thanks to Lloyd fucking Frend. He wore a holster carrying a Glock 21C with the slide and barrel ported to reduce muzzle climb while firing.

For some special reason that summed up as a puzzle, he thought of Lilybourne, how he was going to have a fit when he saw what they'd done to his building, and that Zamora, who never showed his face in El Perro Llorón, would go to church and light candles, thanking God that the place wasn't completely ruined. Chucho and Luz never crossed his mind. Maybe that was because he'd got as far as he could go down the stairs and was concentrating on the silence coming through the door from the street and the building across the street and the night itself, and then police sirens filled the empty space of silence.

Negron slowly counted to five, knowing that when he got to five it would be over if he could just get himself out of the damn neighborhood before the police blocked it off because the boys Frend hired for the job who were still alive and posed a threat heard the same sirens and were already moving away from West Florida and blending into the shadows of night.

He opened the door a crack, peered around the edge of it, pushed the door open all the way and as it swung wide he was out in the street before it completed the motion; he stuck close to the building as he got to the corner, rounded it in a long stride and ran away.

99

O UT OF THE FIVE men that Frend hired, not including the driver and Billy Gorman, who didn't belong there in the first place, the tally came to two dead, one wounded, and three who'd escaped, including Gorman and Morales, and they didn't leave anything but casings behind with the weapons themselves because Morales had told them to wear gloves, cover the soles of their boots or wear galoshes so they didn't leave traceable footprints, drop the guns and get the fuck out if the police arrived. The guy with the scar on his face got out through the back door of the building opposite El Perro Llorón.

Madley lay perpendicular to the front of the restaurant and bar in the middle of West Florida with his opened head bleeding and bits of brain and bone sprayed from the exit wound at an angle 45° south vis-à-vis El Perro Llorón. There was a crumpled body stretched out on the sidewalk behind a parked car, another on his knees in a darkened doorway with his chin resting on his chest, and a third man sat on the curb squeezing his thigh to stem the bleeding from a wound just above the knee.

The only witnesses were a handful of neighbors who weren't really witnesses, they hadn't seen anything, but with the sounds they'd heard they imagined what they might have seen if they were looking when in fact they'd just had the courage to stick their heads out after the sound of gunshots was replaced by sirens when the police and ambulance arrived. They stood wearing winter coats over pajamas while officers took statements.

López and Sender stepped out from behind the cracked wall at
the side of the Tudor-style house and lingered with the rest of the
onlookers just outside the yellow tape going up around the crime
scene. Sender put a cigar in his mouth but didn't light it, spotted
a nearby pay phone and put in a call to Wicker, then dialed Griff
Evans.

Whiten, Hargrove and Coral Rasmussen walked slowly back to
Hargrove's apartment at West Walker and Third. "That was close,"
Hargrove said, worrying the thought for a minute, then inviting
Whiten to join them for a drink. Whiten accepted, climbed the
stairs behind them. "I'm going to talk to Frend," Whiten said.
Hargrove reached in his pocket for his keys, unlocked the apartment door. "I'm going to talk to Frend," Whiten repeated, "and I'm
going to work for him if he'll let me because there's nothing left to
say to Vince Negron if he isn't already dead."

Jean Fleming, driving her Audi, followed Frend in his Lincoln down
the ramp into the parking garage belonging to the townhouse. They
held each other before taking the elevator to the apartment, and
Frend kissed her neck, smelled her hair.

On their way up, Frend pressed himself against her, squeezed
the cheeks of her ass, and said, "I want to fuck you," and Jean un-
zipped his trousers, reached for his cock, got down on her knees and
started sucking it, and then there were words he barely understood,
he wanted to hear them again, he moaned, she nodded her head
and his cock moved with it, "Bullets get me horny," she said with
her mouth full.

Negron got out of the neighborhood without attracting attention
from the police, caught a late bus and headed for the Seventeenth
Street Social Club. Forty minutes later, when he got to the corner of

Meyering Boulevard and Seventeenth Street, he saw what was left of the building's façade, the broken concrete and shattered glass, and he didn't bother to go in or to cross the street to get a better look, he just sat down in a pile of plowed snow.

100

THE DRIVER KEPT THE engine running. Morales and Gorman got into the van out of breath, slid the side door shut, the driver pulled out, turned the corner and moved through traffic that was light on account of the weather, and they were quiet until the van came to the second stoplight. The driver didn't say a word.

Morales leaned forward, told him, "Head over to Federal and Nineteenth—make it fast," then settled comfortably into the back seat.

"If he got away, he went to the social club, Nick," Gorman said.

"He got away," Morales said, "or my name's Pete."

"There won't be much left of it, so he won't stay there long. We'd better get a move on."

"And when we get there?"

"We wait. We're ahead of him. For the first time tonight we're ahead of him. We've got the jump on him and we're going to make it work because Frend wants it to work and it's got to end and it's our job to end it. We've got to stop him while he doesn't know if he's coming or going—and he's on the run."

"He's going, whether or not he knows it—he's going," Morales said.

They were going to pick up the man with the scar on his face at the prearranged location, assuming he'd made it, at Nineteenth and Federal, and when he got into the van, the driver swung it around and sped away from the corner, heading for what was left of the Seventeenth Street Social Club.

They parked the van a half block from the Meyering Building and let the engine run to keep themselves warm while they waited for Negron to show up. Twenty minutes later a lone figure came cautiously out of the shadows, looked up and down the street, started toward the Meyering Building, staying close to the walls and out of the lights.

They waited until the dejected figure sat down in front of the Meyering Building, put ski masks over their heads, then silently slid the side door of the van open, the driver put the van into gear, moving ahead slowly until they were close enough to gun the engine without alerting Negron, who merely raised his head when he heard it. Morales and the guy with the scar on his face jumped out of the open door, grabbed Negron by the shoulders, raised him off the heap of plowed snow, took turns with their fists and knocked him out before Negron really knew what had hit him.

Negron was unconscious, blindfolded and tied up in the back of the van. Gorman called Frend from a public phone. He cupped his hand over the mouthpiece as he spoke quietly, "We've got him. That's right. I know I shouldn't be here, but I'm here doing what I'm supposed to be doing working for you. You trust me, don't you? You're welcome. Where? Okay. At nine in the a.m."

Morales gave the man with the scar on his face an envelope fat with cash and let him out at the corner of Third and Leavitt. Now it was just Gorman and Morales, and Vince Negron in the back of the van, rocking from side to side like a sack of potatoes, a dark-blue handkerchief tied around his head, covering his eyes. They were on their way to Riemen's, which hadn't been open for business for more than a week.

101

HARGROVE SAT DOWN NEXT to Coral on the sofa, Whiten sat in a chair facing them with a drink in his hand. There was a chill in the air because the heat went off at midnight. Whiten swallowed a mouthful of whisky. He looked at his watch, it was one-forty.

On the other side of the windowpane, Hargrove saw thousands of delicate little snowflakes fluttering in gusts of wind. The falling snow was a blinding onslaught of white specks coming down. It was comforting being indoors watching them. He put his arm around Coral, pulled her close to him.

"So, you're going to talk to Frend?" he said.

"That's right, Walt. I've got nothing to lose now that I've lost everything with Negron, and what I lost with him isn't worth counting on the fingers of one hand—it was over before it ended."

"Calm, cool, and collected."

"Maybe just realistic. What choice have I got? It doesn't pay Frend a nickel to kill me. And I've got to make a living—maybe I can make it on a legitimate angle, which means working for Frend. It's not like I can hand out my curriculum vitae along with a job application to a straight business."

"I almost got my head shot off, my nerves are crawling out of my skin, and you're already figuring your next move, Joe. If it wasn't for Coral—"

"Walt, please," she said.

"No, wait. You saved my life, Coral, and I want to thank you for it. I don't know what else to say. I haven't got the vocabulary, there just aren't words—"

"Tell me we'll get out of here, far away from Lake City, that we'll live anywhere else but here. We've got a reason to live—it's you and me, Walt."

"She's right, you've got to listen to her," Whiten said, finishing his drink. "Thanks for the whisky."

He got up as if to leave, but didn't go anywhere, he was waiting for something, and right now it was obvious to Hargrove that Whiten was waiting for him to say it, he was going to stand there until he said it, until he gave Whiten the adequate answer to the unspoken question, until the words came out of his mouth to let Whiten know they'd be out of danger once and for all and that Whiten could go on living his own life and stop trying to figure out their lives for them.

At last Hargrove let the words out slowly, as if they weighed a lot and wouldn't come out any faster even if he forced them, so they came out Indian file, one after the other, because they were words of a sentence that meant something: "Then let's go up north," he told Coral.

"New life up north, back home," Whiten said.

102

THEY WOKE NEGRON UP with a bucket of ice water in the face after they'd laid him out on the long table covered by a red-and-white checked oilcloth tablecloth in the room at the back of Riemen's. It was half-past two in the morning. They wiped the water and ice cubes off him, removed the blindfold and replaced it with a lightweight, breathable spandex hood with a built-in blindfold. They didn't say anything as they carried him to the toilet, sat him down on the toilet seat.

Negron felt a needle poke his arm, he knew the next thing was a plunger being drawn back to fill the syringe barrel with a tumbling cloud of blood as it registered a vein before what filled the barrel was shot into him. He drifted away, but remained conscious. His eyes shut, but he wasn't sleepy, and a wave of warmth traveled from his guts to the surface of his skin and flushed his face, then they raised the bottom of the hood and he was vomiting over a toilet, held upright by a couple of strong arms.

A half hour later they injected him with a dose of uncut amphetamines just to wake him up, then fifteen minutes after that they gave him another shot of dope to knock him down. It went on like that until daylight, with Negron merely trying to survive a horrible voyage from one side of a bad dream to the another.

Negron heard a voice he didn't recognize, the words weren't jumbled anymore, he understood the words, but they came out along with a very hoarse voice, and then he knew it was his own voice that sounded like a cat was scratching the inside of his throat, "Take me to Frend. I'm begging you. I've got to talk to Frend."

"Don't worry, Vince, you'll see him."

At nine o'clock, Gorman opened the back door of Riemen's, Lloyd Frend came in, Gorman shut and locked the door behind him, then shook his hand.

"Well?"

"This way, Mr. Frend. We warmed him up for you, and he's good and ready to talk if his brain cells aren't cooked."

"That's right, Billy. Let's have a little talk with Vince. Joe Whiten called this morning—bright and early. Wants to talk about a job." He took his overcoat off, draped it over a couple of crates. "I got a full view. I can see it from every angle. The Negron machine, it's smashed, it's off the rails and there's nobody to fix it—not just off the rails, it's permanently fucked."

"That's good news."

"You bet it is, Billy. Now, let's see the little chief, the big shot criminal."

He followed Gorman into the back room where Negron was sitting in a straight chair a couple of feet away from the rectangular table, wearing a hood over his head, his arms tied behind his back and his ankles tied to the legs of the chair. Frend walked a couple of circles around him eyeing the spots of blood that stained the loose shirtsleeves of both arms.

"Clean up this mess," Frend said, pointing at bindles of drugs, the syringes on the tabletop. "I don't want to see anything, or know anything."

Morales, who hadn't said a word, started straightening up, closing bindles, dropping them in a Ziploc bag, covering syringe points with the caps that went with them, wiping down the oilcloth with a damp sponge. Gorman moved a chair to a spot an arm's length away from Negron.

"That's better," Frend said, and he sat down.

"Lloyd—it's you?" Negron's voice came thickly through the fabric of the hood.

"Don't call me Lloyd, you prick. It's Mr. Frend—to you and everybody else who's got anything to say to me."

"What're you going to do?"

"I'm not going to kill you, if that's what's on your mind, Vince."

"I'm half-dead already."

Negron squirmed in the chair, he couldn't move more than a couple of inches. He told himself he was really dead, and as far as he was concerned his ambition was past history, the kind of history not worth remembering. And then the quiet calm in the room was acutely apparent to him, no voices, no sounds, just his own labored breathing, and the quiet had a certain pressure, a weight he felt pressing down on his chest.

"I'll do whatever you want me to do. Just don't hurt me," he said.

"That's pathetic, coming from you," Frend said.

"That really makes me want to cry," Morales said.

"Here's a handkerchief," Frend said, obligingly.

"Thanks, boss. I'll wash it before I give it back to you."

"Keep it. You've earned it."

Negron couldn't breathe under the hood, he choked, gasped for breath, a gurgling sound came from the back of his throat as he tried to speak but couldn't get enough air into his lungs, so he rocked back and forth in the chair, trying to pump himself like a bellows.

"I think he's trying to tell us something," Morales said.

"Why doesn't he just come out with it," Frend said. "Everything said here is confidential."

Gorman hadn't said anything, but now he walked over to Negron and slapped him with an open hand hard across his hooded face, saying, "Take it easy, will you. You're giving me anxiety."

"Don't be so rough," Morales said. "He isn't as strong as he was when he came in here."

"Rough? I don't think he's really convinced."

"He's been through plenty? What've you got in mind?"

"A nail gun that's sitting in the back of the van waiting for somebody to use it. Like a carpenter's version of kneecapping somebody—that'll convince him we mean business."

Negron stopped moving, caught his breath, but had nothing more to say than what he'd said already, "Tell me what to do and I'll do it. Just don't hurt me."

"Don't tell me something I already know," Frend said.

"He's repeating himself," Morales said. "We aren't going to hurt you, pal."

"He thinks we didn't hear him the first time," Gorman said.

"We don't need no goddamn nail gun," Morales said, then pulled a small caliber automatic from his waistband and put a bullet in Negron's kneecap. Negron screamed.

Frend put his hands behind his head, tilted the chair back. It was quiet again. They watched the fabric of the hood move where Negron's mouth sent out as much air as it could take in.

Frend said calmly, "You'll do what I want you to do until I tell you otherwise, you fucking has-been. Is that clear? You must be good for something besides food for fish at the bottom of the lake."

Negron nodded, saying, "Whatever you say, Mr. Frend."

Frend got up, waved at Gorman, then indicated the front of the restaurant and Gorman followed him.

"Listen, Billy, drive him over to the Congress Plaza, get him a doctor and a room for a week, and leave him fifty bucks. He'll live, but he'll limp."

"Yes, Mr. Frend."

"Pay off Morales, clean the place up. Neat and tidy like there's nobody but mice in here. Now, unlock the back door and let me out of this joint. Tell Riemen he's back in business."

103

CORAL RASMUSSEN CLOSED THE suitcase, set it on the floor next to another suitcase; it seemed she'd been packing for a month, and then she looked around at the bedroom of her apartment on West Cherry. The furniture that belonged to her went with the movers at ten o'clock, it was twelve-fifteen now, and she'd spent the last two days sweeping up the place, dusting it, room by room, without knocking herself out, but leaving it in pretty much the same shape she found it in when she'd rented it.

She looked at herself in the mirror above the dresser, she was a little tired from packing but her mouth was smiling, a happy woman with a bright future even if she knew she couldn't count on knowing what would and wouldn't happen in days and years to come. Leaving Lake City with Hargrove was good enough. A mattress and box spring stood in a corner of the room.

The buzzer sounded. She'd ordered a taxi for one o'clock, it was too early for the taxi. She went to the intercom, pushed the button, asked who it was, then held her breath. She was jangled nerves after what happened a few weeks ago. Sender's voice asked her to let him in.

She stood at the open door, waiting for him, and when he got to the top of the stairs she sent him a smile, he kissed her on the cheek, walked past her, didn't take off his overcoat, fidgeted with the top two buttons but couldn't get anywhere with them, paced the living room, looking at the only other occupants of it, a pair of empty straight chairs facing each other, a couple of phone books stacked one on top of the other, a disconnected telephone on top of the stack.

Sender didn't waste time because he knew he didn't have any to waste. "I came here to talk you out of it," he said. "I know I can't do that, it won't work, but I have to try or I wouldn't feel right about you going with him to live in some burg with too much grass and too many trees and not throwing you the pitch before you go that says it doesn't have to be that way."

She sat down in one of the straight chairs. He followed her over to the other chair, unbuttoned his coat, sat down and took a cigar out of an inside pocket, cut the cigar and put it in his mouth.

"There's plenty of it going around," he said, lighting it.

"Plenty of what?"

"People not being predictable, that's what. Not so long ago, I would've bet that Jean would leave Frend for López, but all that organizing didn't do Ramón any good, she's sticking it out with Frend, thick and thin, and with a lot of easy money. López went back up north to the technical college. He didn't waste any time."

"You can't dismiss him just like that."

"He dismissed himself by leaving town."

Coral didn't say anything more, she watched clouds of bluish smoke drift upward as Sender lit his cigar.

"And one of Frend's businesses is growing with Negron working for him—an interstate trucking enterprise that was just a write-off before he got started there. Negron working for Frend—I never thought I'd see the day."

Sender stopped talking when he saw a glint of light in her eyes that he hadn't been expecting so soon, and he knew from experience that when it got there he wouldn't have to go on with the pitch, it was over, there was nothing left for him to say, and she was going to give it to him straight.

"You haven't changed, George. You don't really want me, I know that, and I'd guess you know it too, but you don't want anybody else to have me, and you don't want me to go anywhere without you—when the whole thing isn't up to you, it's my choice, my life. That's something I figured out a long time ago."

"I guess I had to give it a try. You understand, don't you?"

"Sure, I understand. It had to happen, and I was beginning to wonder why it hadn't happened yet. Now it's done, out of your system, we can say good-bye."

Sender stood up, she stood up, they were facing each other, he reached for her, she leaned into him for a brief moment, then put the flat of her hand against the side of his face, kissed his other cheek.

"Okay, now get out of here," she said.

Hargrove watched Coral get out of the taxi in front of West Walker and Third and pay the driver. He ran down the steps to help the driver with the luggage she'd brought with her for their trip on the five-o-eight train heading north, carried the bags up to the foyer so she didn't have to do any kind of lifting because all his efforts were now synonymous with a renewed sense of energy and cleanliness, his moves were smooth and relaxed, as though there were no ice, no danger of slipping, his hands were wiped clean of the past because by definition the past was behind him, and that told him he'd gone back to zero and started again, and the start was a good start because Coral was part of it. The mess that was Negron and El Manojo was straightened out, there was only the memory of it. It was around one-forty in the afternoon.

His own luggage amounted to three bags standing next to the staircase in the foyer. He'd turned the apartment upstairs over to Lily and her boyfriend to rent from the landlord, who was happy to do it on Hargrove's recommendation. They were going to move in the following day.

Coral followed him up the cement stairs. They stood together next to the staircase in the foyer. The look on Hargrove's face told her the fear of danger that was as much a known quantity as a wrecking ball crashing into a building that was going to fall on them was gone, it left him a couple of weeks ago after the shootout on West Florida and Third. She'd had plenty of time to get used to it, it was a quiet expression. The equation that added up to the sum of their lives together was changed for good.

Hargrove put the bags down in the foyer next to his own suit-cases, took her in his arms and kissed her full on the mouth. It was a long kiss that said a lot without words.

104

THE MAIN OFFICE OF Frend's interstate trucking enterprise on West Lloyd at Fourth Street, which carried the name Trans-State Title Trucking, painted in medium-sized gold letters on the large windowpane, wasn't far from the appliance store on Walnut and Fifth, where Hargrove used to work, a quarter mile from downtown. The only light lit in the place was a desk lamp at the back in Vince Negron's private office. Negron was sitting at the same desk Lloyd Frend occupied when he'd started his first legitimate company with money he'd made running an illegal betting operation for major sports events across the Midwest.

For the third night in a row, Negron was working late, and the brain cells that had been thoroughly fried by amphetamines and dope and manipulated by a long convalescence from a shattered kneecap no longer kept him from concentrating, they were either recovered or had flaked away, replaced by other, healthier cells, so that he could work hard for Frend to build his credit with him in order to get a transfer to a better position in another business in the coming months.

Cold came into the office, settled itself on Negron. He lit a cigarette, got up from behind the desk, put his weight on the cane he used to get around, and stared past the raised blinds of his window at the front office with two empty desks occupied by two secretaries during working hours. He hobbled out there to look through the plate-glass window at the snowy street. He wanted to talk to somebody. He wanted to go out. He was tired. But there was enough work for him to do to keep him busy for another two hours, it was already late, and he didn't have the energy left in him for more than those two hours. It was nine-thirty. He went back to his office, put the cigarette out in the ashtray, leaned the cane against his desk, opened the ledger and started down the columns using a ruler to keep his eyes on the line.

At eleven-fifteen he shut the ledger, put the pages of notes he'd made in a manila file folder and set the ledger on top of it, put them both in the desk drawer, locked the drawer, switched off the desk lamp, got into his coat, put his hat on and went out the front door.

West Lloyd Street was cold, deserted. Negron locked up and put the keys in his pocket, rubbed his hands together, no gloves. His knee gave him a lot of problems on account of the weather. He wanted a drink but didn't know where to go because he didn't have the same position he'd had in the past, he was just another average workingman without the special privileges he was used to. He didn't want to go anywhere local for drinks if they didn't know him as somebody more important than just another one of Frend's employees.

He shook his head, remembered a place he went to a couple of times in the old days, and headed toward Reservoir Avenue and Fourth Street, to a tavern that used to be called Reinhardt's Tap, now called Turner's because an amateur ex-welterweight named Earl Turner bought it two years ago, a tavern where he knew they didn't know anything about him.

At ten-forty the next morning, Negron was at his desk at Trans-State Title Trucking with the phone cradled under his chin, listening to a driver reel off the standard reasons why he wasn't going to get the rig into Lake City on time when one good reason just for the record would've been enough because as far as Negron was concerned the driver was reliable.

He kept on listening just to be polite but his eyes were bored with the conversation so they stared out at the front office and his gaze went beyond the two secretaries at their desks and past the plate-glass window with gold lettering and they focused on Lloyd Frend's Lincoln as it pulled over to the curb. Billy Gorman switched off the engine, got out, opened the rear door for Frend, who climbed out slowly, almost theatrically, wearing a fur-collared overcoat and a wide-brimmed felt hat, and Jean Fleming came out with him, dressed like a high-class hooker.

He watched Frend sweep majestically into the front office before one of the secretaries was quick enough to get out from behind her desk to open the door for him. Negron felt the phone in his hand, decided to cut the conversation short, and told the rig driver to quit worrying the question of whether or not he'd get the shipment into Lake City on time since it didn't matter to him, he wished him luck, and hung up.

Frend opened Negron's office door, stood there looking at him. Negron's eyes were fixed on Jean, wearing a fur jacket, who was standing in the front office, talking to a secretary, leaning with the palm of her gloved hand flat on the woman's desk. Negron's eyes came back to focus on Frend, who closed the door behind him.

"How's it going, Vince? Working hard, or hardly working?" Frend said.

Negron lit a cigarette, leaned back in his chair. "All's well that ends well, Mr. Frend. Isn't that right?"

"You're doing fine, Vince. I know that."

Negron shut his eyes tightly for a second, begged himself not to say anything smart about it.

"You're a good man to hire. Gorman's been keeping an eye on you and says you're doing fine. Just don't get the wrong idea that you got this job out of the kindness of my heart. It's got to work both ways, you get a salary, I make profits. That's the way it goes. It isn't ever going to be like it used to be, not for you, and if you fuck up, you're out, and maybe you're all the way out and at the bottom of the lake. Like I said, Vince—Nutrifin Flake Food, keep it in mind. Now, let's see the books."

Negron unlocked the desk drawer, removed the ledger and file folder and handed them to Frend who sat down in an armchair opposite him. Frend checked every entry against the notes Negron put in the file, it took him fifteen minutes.

"That's right, everything checks." Frend got up, gave the ledger and folder back to Negron.

"I don't make those kinds of mistakes, if that's what you're looking for," Negron said. "Every shipment's accounted for and if there's some that aren't registered it's because you and Gorman told me not to keep records on them. The straight rigs are coming in and going out on schedule. You can count on it."

"What I'm counting on is just one thing—that you won't try and be too clever, Vince. It doesn't suit you."

Frend walked slowly back to Negron's office door.

"I do what I'm told, Mr. Frend." He knocked an ash into the ashtray, took a haul on the cigarette.

Frend turned around just as he'd reached for the doorknob but hadn't turned it, looked back at Negron, who sat at his desk looking up at him, and Frend eyed him for a minute, then raised the collar of his overcoat, turned up the brim of his hat, sighed, and said, "Every time you sit there and have a thought, just remember, I sat there and had it before you."

About the Author

Born in Milwaukee, Wisconsin, Mark Fishman has lived and worked in Paris since 1995. His novels, *The Magic Dogs of San Vicente*, *No. 22 Pleasure City*, and *Thirteen Heavens*, were published by Guernica in 2016, 2018, and 2020 respectively. His short stories have appeared in a number of literary reviews, such as the *Chicago Review*, the *Carolina Quarterly*, the *Mississippi Review*, the *Black Warrior Review*, and *The Literary Review*. A short story earned a first prize for fiction in *Glimmer Train*, issue 100.